Racing Hearts

By Sydney Lear

2025

Butterworth Books is a different breed of publishing house. It's a home for Indies, for independent authors who take great pride in their work and produce top quality books for readers who deserve the best. Professional editing, professional cover design, professional proof reading, professional book production—you get the idea. As Individual as the Indie authors we're proud to work with, we're Butterworths and we're *different*.

Authors currently publishing with us:

E.V. Bancroft
Valden Bush
Addison M Conley
Jo Fletcher
Helena Harte
Lee Haven
Karen Klyne
Sydney Lear
AJ Mason
Ally McGuire
James Merrick
JP Preston
Robyn Nyx (RJ Nyx)
Simon Smalley
Brey Willows

For more information visit www.butterworthbooks.co.uk

Cataloging information
ISBN: 978-1-915009-88-3
Credits
Editors: Victoria Villaseñor & Nicci Robinson
Cover Design: Nicci Robinson
Production Design: Global Wordsmiths

Acknowledgements

Jeannie, my love, you are my heart! Your unwavering love and support have been the foundation of this book. You've been there through it all, from getting sunburned with me at IndyCar races to vacationing with me in Spain for a writing retreat just so I could follow this wild dream. You've listened to me talk endlessly about these characters and the storyline, and when I doubted myself, you were there, supporting me every step of the way. I'm the luckiest woman alive to have you by my side.

I would like to express my gratitude to the sapphic authors who paved the way before me. Your well-crafted characters and stories have not only provided hours of escape but also inspired me to write my own.

This book has been in the making since 2009, and I'm pinching myself to believe it's finally being published. I could never have achieved this without the unwavering guidance, education, and support from Victoria and Nicci. It's like working with writing, editing, and cover art magicians. I feel incredibly fortunate to be part of the amazing Butterworth Books team! Your belief in me has truly made all the difference. Thank you!

A heartfelt thank you to The Hatchery for welcoming me with open arms from day one. Your support during the evolution of this book has meant more than words can express. I am excited about the journey ahead.

Mom, thank you for instilling in me the importance of reading. You were the first to show me the magic of books and the power of words. Thank you for always setting the bar high for what it means to be a strong woman, for standing up for what you believe in, and for showing me how to do the same. I love you deeply, and I'm forever grateful for you.

Dad, thank you for believing in me and supporting me unconditionally. All those trips to the tracks—whether dirt or asphalt—will always hold a special place in my heart. Thank you for sharing your love of racing with me. Your simple wisdom and storytelling is missed! You talk about a nice day!

Maureen, Bridget and Colleen, thank you for your endless support. Maureen, I'll always be grateful that you read the original version of this story in that spiral-bound notebook all those years ago and for encouraging me to finish it. You've all helped me grow into a better version of myself, and I love and appreciate you more than I can say.

Meg & Kara, thank you for always checking in and encouraging me in this crazy endeavor. Your support has meant more to me than you know. To all of my friends and family who've supported this dream—thank you. Your belief in me has been invaluable.

To the female racing community, thank you. You're all absolute rockstars. I hope you enjoy this book.

To the medical professionals in our communities, you are the silent heroes whose selflessness knows no bounds. Thank you!

Finally, to my new readers: thank you for taking a chance on this book. I hope you enjoy the story of Jordan and Quincy and the backdrop of LA that brings it all to life.

Dedication

To anyone struggling to live your truth and embrace your un-apologetic self, know that there's a community out there ready to welcome you. May your journey be filled with pride, joy, and the freedom to be exactly who you are.

Chapter One

QUINCY FITZGERALD STEPPED OUT of the Los Angeles Medical Center's Emergency Department conference room and closed the door gently behind her. She walked the short distance to the staff bathroom, entered, and locked the door before she picked up a roll of toilet paper from the stack by the door and threw it across the room with a grunt. It boomeranged back at her, and she swore as she walked to the sink and white-knuckled the edge, barely restraining the urge to put her fist through the mirror. Her reflection would show her disappointment, so she kept her gaze downward. *This was bullshit!* Ted Beatle was their choice for the Nurse Practitioner Supervisor role. He was terrible with patients, family, and staff. He was also an idiot who didn't have any idea what to do in a real emergency. She deserved that promotion, not him. Ten long years of double shifts and hard work, especially during the COVID pandemic, compared to his measly two, and he's the one to get the big break? *Q, just suck it up, stay in control, and finish your shift.* Tears pricked at her eyes, but she wouldn't let them fall.

A knock on the door signaled the end to her meltdown. "Quincy, you in there? It's Peter. The trauma is five minutes out," the ED charge nurse said through the door.

"I'll be right out." She picked up the toilet paper roll and slammed it into the trash. She finally looked at herself in the mirror and applied water to her eyes before blotting them dry with a paper towel. No need for anyone to see that she'd been rattled. She opened the door with the towel and then threw it in the garbage as she walked out.

Peter gave her a side hug. "Sorry, Q, we wanted it to be you. We all know Ted is awful. A little-known fact: he's the cousin of Margo, the Nurse Manager. Nepotism at its best here at Los Angeles Medical Center."

Quincy shook her head at the new information but remained silent since her voice would only betray her emotions. They marched together through the ER toward the helipad. As she walked out into the warm morning sunshine, she left her personal issues behind and focused on her job. She looked up at the incoming Life Flight helicopter as it slowly descended. Wind whipped at her hair, and she squinted against the torrent of air as the crew threw open the doors. She ducked and ran forward. Her pulse raced the way it always did when a trauma like this came in. Technically, her shift was over, but this patient needed someone now, not at shift change.

The flight medic jumped out of the chopper and pushed the gurney toward Quincy, shouting the details at her as they moved, "Hey, Q, we've got Julian Cortez, male, eighteen-year-old, helmeted, motorcycle versus car on the 10 Freeway, thrown about fifty feet. He was stable when we picked him up, but that changed as we landed. He's not following commands anymore."

Cool air and adrenaline focused Quincy as she gave orders to the nurses running alongside the gurney while she assessed Julian. "Head for trauma bay one. He isn't breathing, and he needs to be intubated. Let's start some rescue breaths, get me an intubation tray, and three more IV lines in him. Have the pre-ordered intubation medications ready as well."

Peter met the gurney at the ambulance bay doors and followed them into the trauma room.

"Call the CT scanner and have it ready for us in five minutes. Also, page trauma orthopedics about this arm, and give neurosurgery a heads-up. His pupils are unequal and non-reactive." Quincy took in the bruised and swollen left side of his face, the awkward set of the left arm, and the blood that oozed from under his leather motorcycle jacket. Her instructions covered everything immediately visible. "Okay, everyone, let's see if we can get him stable."

"Quincy, I paged all the teams and gave them an update on his status," Peter said. "The trauma team is finishing up in bay three, and then they'll be over."

Quincy acknowledged Peter as he left. "Okay, is everyone ready?" It was a rhetorical question as the skilled ER staff were always ready. Just as she started the intubation procedure, Dr. Edwards, the ER attending, strolled into the trauma bay.

"Hey, Quincy, how can I help?" He stood by the patient's bed with his hands in his white coat and watched her perform the procedure.

"Hey, Dr. E., how about confirmation of tube placement?" she asked when she was done.

Dr. Edwards pulled out the stethoscope curled in his right pocket and listened closely as breaths were given to the young man to provide an auditory confirmation of placement. He nodded and looked up at Quincy. "Tube's right where it should be. Good equal lung sounds on both sides, and the carbon dioxide color change was perfect. Great work as usual. Anything else?"

"His flank area needs an assessment. He had some bleeding coming from there when he rolled in, but I wanted to get his airway secured before I turned him to look at it."

"No problem. Let's see what we've got here." He quickly finished his evaluation of the area and pulled off his gloves. "He has a deep cut and some road rash that needs cleaning. I'll put a dressing on it for now. The exploration of the wound can wait until after his CT when the trauma team completes their full assessment."

"CT scanner is ready for him. Is he stable to head out?" Peter asked as he came back in.

"Yeah, the tube's verified and secured. His neurological and oxygenation status have improved, but I'm concerned about brain trauma, so let's get him packed up and off to scan, please. Thanks, everyone." Quincy stepped back from the head of the gurney, pulled off her protective equipment and gloves. She squeezed Dr. Edwards' shoulder as he moved away with her.

"Great work as usual," he said. "I've got some time right now, so I'll go with him to the scanner until trauma takes over his care." The nursing staff rolled the patient out to the CT scanner, and Dr. Edwards followed.

Quincy slumped against the wall, adrenaline from the trauma gone. She took a deep breath and rolled her shoulders, as the difficult shift began to overtake her. Ignoring the detritus of the trauma room she pulled the computer over to type in her clinical note. She looked up as her ex-lover and trauma attending, Dr. Rochelle Dixon, strode into the room followed by the chief resident, Dr. Jason Dye. *Could this day get any worse?*

Quincy groaned. *Of course Rochelle was the trauma chief today.* She was brilliant, confident, and beautiful with her strawberry blond hair pulled back in a ponytail, highlighting her green eyes. Rochelle strode into the room, and honestly, any situation, with grace and authority. She was the whole package and could easily be mistaken for a leading character in a TV medical drama. She approached Quincy and kept her back to Jason, blocking his view. Rochelle lightly traced her fingernail down Quincy's forearm, but she pulled away, irritated that Rochelle's touch still affected her.

Rochelle smiled knowingly. "Quincy, you did all our work for us as usual. Thanks for the help. Why don't you get us updated on the new trauma, so you can get out of here and on with your life." She looked up at the clock on the wall. Quincy began to leave, but Rochelle caught her wrist. "I'm sorry about the promotion; they were idiots."

Quincy shook her wrist free and gritted her teeth. She didn't want Rochelle's compassion—not today. Where was all that when she dumped Quincy for a new flavor of the month after six months of building their relationship? She took a deep breath and smiled, struggling to force away the thoughts of the hurt and loss. Quincy turned to Jason. "Julian Cortez is our eighteen-year-old trauma, and he just left for CT. If you're ready, let's get started," she said, making sure to keep her voice level and distant. Give Rochelle an inch, and she'd take a whole freeway. That was the last damn thing she needed today.

After Quincy had briefed the trauma team, orthopedics, neurosurgery, and the family, she felt like she could sleep for a month. Three back-to-back, twelve-hour night shifts as a nurse practitioner at one of the busiest ERs in LA wasn't for the faint of heart. She was barely fit to drive home, but nothing in the world sounded better than her bed. She loved the highs and lows that came with working in the ER, even when it left her drained. The complex patient care she provided to all walks of life, from the unhoused to A-list celebrities, was one of the best parts of her job, but that didn't mean it didn't utterly exhaust her. She walked into the parking garage and toward the refuge of her car, greeting the day-shift staff who trickled past her, but she didn't stop to chat. Had they heard about her being passed up for the promotion? If so, she didn't want any more platitudes or empathy.

Once settled in her car, she let out a deep sigh. She glanced in the rearview mirror and noticed the deep bags under her eyes and the way her hair was sticking up on one side but couldn't bring herself to care. Her patients certainly didn't while she was busy keeping them alive. She knew she didn't fit the stereotypical LA definition of beauty the way Rochelle did, and she rarely tried to fit that mold. There were times, though, when it would be nice to not look like she'd been dragged through a field behind a horse. *Maybe if I looked the part, that dumbass wouldn't have gotten my promotion.*

Quincy threw on her sunglasses and waved at a few other nurses as she drove out of the parking garage and onto the southbound 405. The early Friday morning traffic should be light, but anything could happen on the eighteen-mile-drive home to Redondo Beach. Thanks to the crazy shifts she worked, Quincy was notorious with her family for calling while on the freeway. She dialed her dad in Illinois.

"Katie's Kitchen, how can I help you?"

"Hey, Pops, how goes it?" Quincy ignored the tiny flicker of nostalgia at the sound of his chipper, baritone voice. She'd left that life behind, after all.

"Hi, honey, I'm doing well. We're just finishing the breakfast rush." He chuckled as she blasted the horn when someone cut in front of her. "Are you on your way home from work?"

"I guess I'm that predictable. You know my routine, at least for now." Quincy smiled at the driver she calmly flipped off.

"What's going on? You sound upset; is everything okay?"

Quincy leaned her head back against the headrest as the traffic slowed to a standstill. "I didn't get the NP supervisor promotion at work. It went to this idiot more junior than me. I'm just so angry and frustrated...but mostly, I'm disappointed in myself. I feel like a failure, and it's hard to look at my co-workers, knowing I didn't get it after all these years." She blinked away tears. "I'm not sure whether I should stay there. It might be time to consider a job change." Quincy blew out a loud breath. "Sorry, Pops, I know that's not what you wanted to hear, but that's where I'm at today. Let's talk about something else." Quincy wiped away her tears and then took a deep breath. "Let's talk about your upcoming birthday party instead."

"Oh, Quincy, I can hear you're hurting. I wish I could be there to hug you. I'm sorry about the position, sweetie. They're idiots. They wouldn't know a good thing if it kicked them in the shin. I'm always here if you want to vent."

The cash register chimed in the background, and Quincy chuckled. She loved how simple her father could be at times. "Thanks for your never-ending support, but it's still a little fresh to discuss. Now, your party; that, we can certainly discuss."

"Okay, I'll let the job go for now. As far as turning seventy, I'm not sure why you're making a fuss."

Quincy pulled into her driveway, shut off her car, and closed her eyes. "Because you're worth it, and we want to celebrate you. You're always giving yourself to the family and the community, it's the least we can do. You know as well as I do that you want this party like a seven-year-old wants one."

Her dad gave a knowing chuckle. "I do love a good party, but it's always different when you're the center of all that attention... It sounds like you might be home. I don't hear the traffic anymore. Should I let you go, baby?"

He called her that no matter how old she got, and these days, it sometimes felt like she was ancient. She laughed at their predictable behavior. "I've trained you well. You're right; I just got home. I'm going to head in now, but I'll call you later this week. I love you, Pops."

"I love you too, sweetie. Keep your chin up." He hung up, already talking to a customer.

Quincy pulled herself from the car and took stock of her house as she walked up the drive. It was built in the fifties and took most of her free time and money. She winced at the paint peeling on the black shutters; they'd have to be done next. The flowers she'd planted out front had started to droop, thanks to the lack of rain over the past month. If she didn't water them soon, they'd probably die. Through the glass panel on her front door, she saw Jada wagging her tail and running in circles. Jada had come to understand her schedule too, but that didn't stop Quincy's guilt at leaving her alone for long hours.

Quincy entered her house and knelt for Jada's morning kisses. "Good morning, girl. Are you ready to go check out the neighborhood?"

Jada grabbed her leash from the basket and brought it to Quincy, which earned her a scratch behind both ears. Quincy adored the peaceful morning walks before her neighbors powered up their leaf blowers and started their hammering. But the disappointment of the lost promotion was hitting hard, taking away her usual serenity. When they returned from their walk,

Quincy opened the front door and sighed at the familiar ache of loneliness. It wasn't that she necessarily wanted a partner. Dating life took time, and time was the one thing she didn't have a lot of. But it would be nice to come home to someone other than her dog who was happy to see her. Someone who wanted to know about her day. Someone who wanted to know about her dreams, desires, and fears. Someone to sympathize about those dreams crashing and burning. But seeing Rochelle earlier reminded her that she wasn't about to put herself through that again. She smiled when Jada jumped onto the bed and burrowed into the covers. For today, this would simply have to be enough. The future could wait until she'd had some sleep.

Chapter Two

JORDAN MARSH MIGHT ACTUALLY punch someone if they intruded on her hangover. Her dark sunglasses were wrapped around her eyes, and her noise-canceling headphones were in place. She leaned her head back against the headrest as the early morning first-class flight from New York City touched down in Los Angeles. The buzz she had from partying with Miss Universe, Lucy Chandler, and other A-listers at Club Patch last night had vanished and been replaced by a throbbing headache better dealt with in her bed with a hot woman, *not* on a commercial jet. Yeah, she'd managed to sleep through most of the flight, but the sandpaper lining her mouth and jackhammer in her head made her want to rip into someone. The jolt of the plane landing intensified her headache, but it was her manager's incessant talking and her text notifications that spiked her irritability.

Jordan leaned across the aisle rubbing her temples as the plane slowly taxied to its gate. "Tina, shut off your ringer and notifications. It's driving me fucking crazy. And remind me why in the hell we took this *commercial* flight? You told me the plane left at noon, not six a.m. Is this job security for you? Do you want me to look bad in the press? What happened to the team's jet? You know, flying commercial isn't a good look for my celebrity status. If anyone should know that, it would be you."

Tina held up her finger. "Casey, can you hold for a minute?" She muted the call, then stood in the aisle before the seatbelt sign was off and leaned over Jordan. "Jordie, the press is more interested in your antics at the club last night than the plane you flew on. The company jet was broken, and one first-class flight won't kill you.

And I hope you've sobered up. We're in LA, and there'll be plenty of opportunities for you to build your 'celebrity status.' LAX is a good place to start. If you want to let your fans and the city know you're here, there's no place better. You should consider that as you get off the plane. And really, could you be any more petulant? Just so you know, I've already fielded texts from Mama Vic. She doesn't like your attitude, nor this new publicity stunt you pulled last night. You can expect to be hearing from her." Tina shook her head and then walked to the airplane door, getting in the way of the flight crew. She gave Jordan a wave before she left the plane.

Petulant. Who wouldn't be if they had to deal with her? At least I'll get some peace for a few minutes with her gone. Jordan stretched across the seat to collect her backpack. As she stood up, she noticed someone hovering near her. *Here we go. Time to turn it on.*

Sara, the cute flight attendant who'd flirted with her throughout the flight, stood between Jordan and the door. "Ms. Marsh, I hate to bother you, but I'm a big fan of yours. May I have your autograph?"

Jordan would've loved to just push past and get off the plane, but her fans had to come first. "Of course, Sara. Not a problem." Jordan quickly scrawled her name on an inflight magazine. She removed her sunglasses and winced at the bright sunlight in the cabin. She gave Sara and the flight crew her best smile as they snapped pictures of her with her arm around Sara and the other crew members while the rest of the passengers deplaned.

"You're the hottest thing in IndyCar racing. Good luck at the LA Grand Prix." Sara batted her false eyelashes and pressed a folded piece of paper into Jordan's hand.

She squeezed Sara's hand and pushed the note into the back pocket of her jeans where she'd already collected two other women's numbers. "Thank you for your support." Jordan gave them the megawatt-smile she was known for and wandered off the plane and into the terminal. Fans were lined up at the gate, and she forced down the annoyance at being unable to simply leave the airport. She waved and stopped to shake hands and take photos, which slowed her progress to the waiting golf cart. She knew their supportive social media posts helped elevate her celebrity and racing status, more so than any paparazzi pics. She'd make the time, even if she was worried that she might vomit on some kid's shoes.

"Jordan, are you going to stay with IndyCar or join Formula One?" asked an older man wearing an Angel City jersey.

"IndyCar for now, but you never know what the future holds," Jordan said as she continued toward the waiting golf cart.

"Think you can win the Champions Cup this year?" a tall man in a polo shirt asked.

Jordan laughed and directed her fake smile at him as she shook his outstretched hand. "That's the plan."

A young girl of about twelve held up her phone. "Can I get a selfie?"

Jordan took the girl's phone and positioned them in front of the camera. "Cheese! Does it look okay?" The girl nodded as she turned away with a flushed face, looking genuinely awed. "Thanks for being a fan," Jordan said as the girl was lost in the crowd. The push of humanity around her brought with it the euphoria of being in the spotlight. Being sought after for pictures or autographs by fans was a drug she was addicted to, and her hangover was surpassed by the exhilaration of being idolized.

Tina sat on the golf cart, focused on her phone and not on Jordan. *Who the hell is supposed to be watching out for me?* Someone tapped her shoulder.

"Ms. Marsh, I'm Tony from LAX security. Let me help you get to the golf cart."

Jordan smiled and nodded, relieved to have some help. "Hi, Tony. Thanks, I could use it, otherwise I might be here all day."

He led the way, making a gentle path through the crowd, and they climbed on the golf cart and headed toward baggage claim.

Jordan turned to face Tina in the back seat. "I saw how concerned you were for me back there, thanks. You're my manager and run my public relations, yet you didn't manage that whole situation." She gestured back toward to the dissolving crowd. "What if there'd been an issue?"

Tina shrugged, not looking up from her phone. "What issue? You were fine. Security helped you."

"Right." Jordan turned back in her seat, her blood pressure rising. Damn it all, she hated being dismissed like some bratty kid. *Fucking Tina.* If it wasn't for Jordan's moment of weakness two years ago when she agreed to hire her just to appease her parents, she could have someone more effective on her payroll. *And* someone who didn't treat her like a dumb child. She should find someone new but going against her mother was something she had to avoid if she wanted to keep the peace. Jordan didn't care that Tina was a standout ex-student of her mother's at Georgetown. It was obvious Tina's loyalty was to Jordan's parents rather than to her, and yet, she couldn't bring herself to deal with the conflict firing her would bring. *Okay, Jordan, take a deep breath in. Hold for a four count. Now slowly release in an eight count, and let the toxicity go.* She heard her therapist's voice talk her through the breathing exercise. To be mentally focused for the upcoming Grand Prix, she needed distance from Tina, whose presence was feeling more and more like a fresh paper cut doused in hand sanitizer. She rolled her head side-to-side to release the tension from the morning flight. First things first, she needed to get out of LAX and into the oasis of her home. Her phone pinged with the tone she'd set up just for her mom, but she knew better than to check the messages. She didn't need that right now; she could wait for her judgment until later.

"I'll make sure they get all of our bags," Tina said, when the golf cart stopped at baggage claim near the VIP exit. She instantly harassed the porter gathering their bags and began a diatribe about how everything had gone missing on their previous flight.

"I'm going to the car." Jordan headed out the secure door to the waiting Cadillac Escalade parked at the curb and was assaulted with camera flashes and questions. *Shit!* Jordan put her sunglasses back on and pushed forward.

"Will you be the pole-sitter for the LA Grand Prix?" asked one photographer.

"Smile! Jordan, look over here."

A few more paparazzi yelled at her.

"Where's Miss Universe?" asked another. "Are you officially an item?"

She didn't mind adoring fans who wanted a picture, or an autograph, or to ask her a question, but the madness of the paparazzi mob was something altogether different. She'd known she'd be inundated by their questions and cameras, but that didn't make it any less irritating. She kept her expression neutral and waded into the press storm alone. Apparently, Tony's job had ended when the golf cart stopped, and Tina was nowhere to be found. A camera got too close, and she nearly knocked it to the ground.

Her recent domination on the track and first-place finish last month in Brazil, along with the racy nightclub photos with Lucy Chandler, had them hounding her more than usual. She wouldn't deny she liked the attention, but even she had her limits. The paparazzi horde was relentless as Jordan attempted to get to the waiting limo, and her heartbeat increased, as did the sweat on her palms. *Damn them all.* The push of the crowd and questions about her sponsor status, her lovers, and how long she'd be staying in LA kept her from reaching the car. Just as she was about to contemplate shoving her way through and screw the consequences, Tina, the porter, and airport security finally joined her. The officer pushed a path through the crowd in front of Jordan and pulled open the door of the SUV.

Jordan paused before getting in as her anxiety receded and looked at the officer's name badge. "Thanks for your help, Jim." She smiled, her heart rate slowing with his presence.

"You're welcome, Ms. Marsh. Good luck in the Grand Prix."

Jim puffed his chest up slightly and turned so a reporter had to back off.

Jordan jumped into the back of the SUV, and the door closed behind her. *Sanctuary*. The dark glass meant she could let the mask go and grimace at the hyenas outside. Their questions about racing were fine. She welcomed those, but the ones about her personal life irked her. They were about titillation, not out of any interest in her as a human being. The SUV headed south toward Jordan's beach home, so she could get a few days of much-needed rest before the racing festivities began.

Tina continued her nonstop chatter on the phone to sponsors, reporters, and whoever the hell else she dealt with on Jordan's behalf. Giving in, Jordan pulled out her phone and reviewed her mom's text messages. As usual, Mama Vic outlined her concerns about Jordan's brazen lesbian lifestyle and poor life choices. She excelled in the ability to wrap her disappointment in a blanket of love and support. Jordan snorted and shook her head at the final one.

Jordie, what's gotten into you? Why do you think so little of yourself that you'd have people take pictures of you in such a compromising way? That Lucy doesn't care about you. This behavior needs to stop.

She dropped her phone into her lap and stared, unseeing, out the car window. Maybe Lucy didn't care about her. But so what? Her mom wanted her to be someone else, and Tina wanted a meal ticket. As far as Jordan was concerned, she could behave any way she liked, since no one really cared about what she wanted or who she really was. She closed her eyes, hoping sleep might sweep away her increasing isolation.

Chapter Three

The driver pulled up outside Jordan's home and she breathed an audible sigh of relief as she blinked away the sleep, earning her a disgruntled look from Tina.

"I can't believe you slept on this short drive. If you hadn't partied until three a.m., you wouldn't need to sleep. You'd better be ready for this week. You're lined up for multiple new sponsors, and they'll be watching your every move. I don't want my efforts wasted."

"Whatever, Tina. I'll be fine." Jordan grabbed her backpack just as her car door was thrown open by her best friend, Dave, who greeted her with a warm hug. Just what she needed.

"Hey, girl! Welcome home. I've got a surprise for you. Let's go" He tugged at her arm and pulled her toward the house.

Jordan couldn't stop smiling. *Home.*

"I'll be back later this afternoon to go over your schedule for the week." Tina's shrill voice rang out from the SUV.

Jordan groaned as she crossed the threshold. "Fantastic."

Her custom-built home was on the Strand in Hermosa Beach with unobstructed floor-to-ceiling glass windows that highlighted the sweeping Pacific Ocean. Photos of her family, her racing life, and her travels made her smile as she passed them, bringing back that sense of belonging she missed when she was on the road. When Jordan was here, her soul settled, and after her recent travel schedule, she was glad to finally be back The briny ocean air, the sound of the surf breaking, and the gorgeous view allowed the tension to fall from her shoulders.

She looked at the display when her phone rang and placed it on Do Not Disturb. "Something smells good. I hope that's the surprise, because I'm starving." She had to stay healthy to race well, and she missed the not-so-healthy options Dave whipped up.

"I know that ringtone. What did you do that has Mama Vic calling you so soon after arriving home? Were you a bad Jordie?"

She laughed. "Let's just say I was a bit rowdy in NYC last night. I made *Page Six* and some other socials that didn't meet Mom's level of decorum." Jordan knew from the text and voicemail messages that her mom was furious. Mama Vic was the quintessential helicopter mom, doing all she could to control and direct Jordan's life. She'd been successful in that endeavor until Jordan turned sixteen and realized that her domination and approval was never love. The judgment and pressure her mom applied for Jordan to succeed was never for her benefit. It was simply a way to ensure that her parents remained in control, so she wouldn't embarrass them or bring them down in any way. When she came out as a lesbian and told her parents that she was going to race cars instead of going to law school, her mom's flawless face had finally cracked, and Jordan saw behind the mask. The onslaught of guilt and disappointment that was leveled at her never stopped, even when Jordan became a successful race car driver. She'd hoped her parents would love her for who she was, but even after attending events as their puppet and hiring Tina, they never changed.

"Hey, Jordie, are you okay? You look lost." Dave squeezed her shoulder.

Jordan shook her head and reached up to cover his hand. "Sorry, bud. Yeah, I just went down the Mama Vic rabbit hole. Thanks for pulling me back from the ledge. Hey, think we can we feed my socials before you feed me? Let's post a quick selfie together, then I'll change, and we can eat!" Jordan leaned into Dave and snapped a perfectly framed pic. She typed in *Home, sweet home* and posted it to her socials.

"I'll be back." Jordan dropped her phone on the island and ran upstairs to her master suite. She was so thankful to have Dave here. Someone who was truly on her side. Someone who allowed her to be herself and still loved her.

They'd known each other since their college days, and he knew firsthand that Jordan needed to decompress when she returned home. He'd been with her enough after her races to know her routine, and he was often the one who brought her back to reality. The racing world got left behind the moment she entered the house.

Breakfast allowed them to discuss the gossip in the neighborhood, from the new housing going up two blocks away to the approaching swell and surf report Racing and Jordan's celebrity status weren't talked about. Dave knew she could be a diva, and he never allowed it in their special space.

"Dave, you outdid yourself; that breakfast was amazing." Jordan sighed happily and leaned back, letting the stress fall from her shoulders like brake dust.

"Anything for you, my friend. Let's go get some fresh air," Dave said and headed out to the balcony. He threw on sunglasses and a hat to block the midday sun, and Jordan followed.

She sat on her balcony with a cup of coffee, relishing the peace. She inhaled deeply, coating her tongue with the salty air. She looked out at the surfers lined up in the water, and her happiness bubbled over. "Thank you for being here for me. That was just what I needed. What do you think, want to get wet?" She stood and slapped Dave's shoulder. "Go get your gear, and I'll meet you in the mudroom." The excitement of surfing pushed the hangover and travel fatigue away, and she propelled herself upstairs to change into a bikini. She left her clothes scattered across the room and ran back downstairs.

"Moving kind of slow today, Jordie?"

She flicked his ear as she walked through her mudroom that housed her surfboards and wetsuits. "Whatever." She put on her oldest ratty wetsuit over her bikini. Today was all about comfort and nothing about the way she looked. They grabbed towels, surf wax, and their boards and headed to the water's edge. The sand was warm under Jordan's feet, and she wiggled her toes, grounding herself in the moment. There were no cameras, no women to impress, no autographs to sign. Here, she was just Jordan. And right now, that's all she wanted to be.

Dave dropped his towel and surfboard next to her. "It's busy. Must be that southern swell that's coming in. Or maybe they knew super sexy Jordan Marsh would be here." He laughed, and she rolled her eyes.

"You're a funny guy." Jordan knelt by her board to wax the surface. "Come on, let's join them. Do you have enough wax to keep you on the board?"

"Oh, yeah, plenty." He stood up and stuck his board into the sand.

Once she'd finished waxing, Jordan zipped up her wetsuit and got ready to head into the water. "Do you need any help, old man?" She laughed as Dave struggled to get his zipper closed.

"Shut up, I can get it. And there's less than a year between us." He flipped her the bird.

Jordan laughed and shaded her eyes to look out onto the water and the lineup of surfers. "How about over there to the right? Not as much traffic. I only see one other person."

"I'll follow you."

They ran into the water together and paddled through the impact zone. "Oh, shit, this water is cold!" Jordan gasped as she tried not to hyperventilate.

Dave paddled next to her. "What do you expect? It's February in California; the Pacific is always freezing this time of year. Just be thankful the sun is out."

They paddled out past the wave break where they evaluated the next set of waves. "It feels so good to be out here with you. Thanks for today." It might have sounded a little corny, but she could always speak freely with him, and it was important that she remember to be grateful for the simple things too. The surfer they'd joined in the lineup charged the approaching wave and rode it into the white water, moving gracefully with skill that Jordan appreciated. "That was a nice ride. Do you think we should check that they're okay with us joining their lineup?"

"That'd probably be best," Dave said.

The surfer paddled parallel to them, and Jordan called out, "Hey, dude, do you mind if we join you in the lineup?" The surfer was facing away from them and didn't reply. Jordan shrugged, not sure if she was being ignored. "Hey, can we join you in the lineup?"

The surfer turned this time. *Damn. That's no dude.* Jordan couldn't stop her wide smile. She floated with the current toward Dave and Jordan. The confidence in the woman's expression made Jordan's mouth go dry. She had a sleek, muscular body that filled her wetsuit perfectly. Her blond, wavy hair was slicked back, she was lightly tanned, a ring of freckles dotted her nose, long, dark lashes framed beautiful indigo blue eyes, and she had deep dimples in her cheeks. Jordan's face flushed with heat, and it wasn't from the sun. "Hi. I'm Jordan, and this is my friend Dave." She didn't want any confusion about their relationship, just in case the stranger played for the rainbow team.

"Hey, there, I'm Quincy. I'm cool with sharing the spot." She smiled broadly, showcasing her pearly white teeth.

"Hi, Quincy. Nice to meet you, and thanks for letting us drop in on you," Dave said.

"You bet, but I call this wave." Quincy paddled into the wave and rode into shore.

Dave splashed Jordan with a stream of water. "Come on, Romeo, let's paddle a little further out so you don't drool on her." He nudged Jordan hard enough to almost knock her off her board.

"Thanks a lot, you dick." Jordan laughed and wiped the water out of her eyes.

Dave shook his head as he watched Quincy paddle out from the whitewater after her wipeout. "I know you, Jordie, and that poor girl doesn't stand a chance in hell, does she?"

Jordan only shrugged and looked at Dave as innocently as

she could manage. "I don't know what you mean." She waited until Quincy paddled back out toward them, ignoring a couple of sweet waves. "Great ride."

"Until the wipeout at the end." Quincy paddled alongside them in the lineup.

They spent the next hour discussing favorite boards, surf spots, and the state of the day's ocean. It was easy banal chatter that filled the lull between waves until Dave's watch alarm beeped.

"Need to feed your parking meter?" Quincy asked.

Dave gave her a big smile. "Nope, no meter. Just life on land. I guess this'll be my last wave for the day." He looked behind him at the next set.

Jordan paddled over to Dave. "Do you have a big sale today?" She turned to Quincy. "Dave is in real estate. He has the market covered in the beach cities. I don't suppose you're looking for something to buy or sell?"

"No, not today, but I'll keep you in mind if that changes."

Dave snapped his fingers with a playful grin. "Darn, I was hoping for a new client." He paddled his board closer to Jordan and gave her a big side hug. "I'm glad to have you back in town. I'll talk to you later." He sat back on his board and smiled at Quincy. "Nice to have met you, and I hope to see you again. Okay, here I go." Dave turned and paddled into a bomb wave.

A little flash of melancholy hit her as he rode away. He was her piece of stability, and she was bummed he wasn't sticking around. But then, it wasn't like she didn't have company.

Chapter Four

DAVE WAVED TO THEM from shore before he walked across the sand with his board under his arm and his towel around his neck. Quincy and Jordan straddled their boards and bobbed on the waves as they each waved back.

"And then there were two." Quincy was never one to shy away from a conversation, but she didn't want to look too interested. "So, old boyfriend?"

Jordan laughed and shook her head. "Strictly a friend. We met in college and have grown up together."

"Oh, I see." Quincy nodded and looked away to hide the smile of satisfaction at that news.

Jordan looked out to the horizon for an approaching wave and found one. She paddled her board into position, then looked back over her shoulder. "I don't have anyone special in my life right now. Do you?"

She caught the wave before Quincy could answer. She watched Jordan move in the water and appreciated her form on the board and in her wetsuit. There was something familiar about her and that wickedly naughty smile, but Quincy knew they'd never met. Jordan was way out of her league, but there was nothing wrong with enjoying the eye candy. *Come on, Q. You're here to surf, not hook up.* She lined up her board on the next wave and rode it to shore, where she met Jordan in the whitewater.

"Actually, I do have a special someone in my life. Her name is Jada." Quincy liked that Jordan seemed a little disappointed. "She's my five-year-old terrier mix," she said and paddled out into the ocean with a grin.

"Good to know," Jordan said, following her out to the break.

The day passed quicker than Quincy would've liked, but she enjoyed getting to know Jordan between rides. As they waited for the next set, Quincy noticed a fin approaching them to the left. "Do you see that?" She pointed to the oncoming pod of dolphins.

Jordan sat up on her board. "Wow, there're babies in the pod."

They sat in awe while approximately forty inquisitive dolphins surrounded them. Their sleek, glistening, gray bodies punched through the still blue Pacific water, which made for an amazing sight, and their intelligent clicking and squeals echoed around them as they sat motionless on their boards.

Quincy let out a deep sigh and laughed, as she realized she'd been holding her breath while the pod swam by. The magic of the moment lingered when she gazed into Jordan's eyes, and her breath caught once more at the beauty of Jordan's smile.

"That was simply amazing," Jordan said.

Quincy's heart raced. "It really was. What a wonderful day. It didn't seem like it was gonna be when I got off my shift this morning."

Jordan looked over. "What do you mean?"

Quincy thought of the lost promotion, ruining the peace she'd developed throughout the day. She ran her fingers back and forth through the water to help calm her fury. "I'm a nurse practitioner at the LAMC ER. I've worked there for over ten years, and I was up for a promotion for a supervisory role, but I found out this morning that I didn't get it. The rejection hit me harder than I expected. I imagine my exhaustion from working three back-to-back, twelve-hour night shifts hasn't helped my state of mind either. I was upset, but some pup time, a little sleep, and the ocean seems to have done the trick. Nothing helps me focus like the water, so here I am." What was she doing, sharing her story with a stranger? She looked at Jordan and then the departing pod of dolphins on the horizon. "I hate to be a buzzkill, but I'm going to have to head in. Final ride?"

Jordan grabbed her right hand as Quincy made a final pass

through the water. "Thank you for sharing that with me. They're idiots for not picking you."

Quincy's cheeks burned with the electric jolt from Jordan's touch. "You don't even know me. Maybe they made the right decision," she said, her voice quivering.

Jordan looked at her and squeezed Quincy's hand briefly. "I know enough. I'm a good judge of character. And you're definitely a character."

Quincy laughed and splashed her. "Nice. So much for sincerity."

Jordan wiped the water from her face. "Okay, buzzkill, you ready to head in before we become prunes? I've got this one," she said and rode an eight-foot face into the whitewater with power and grace.

Quincy enjoyed watching Jordan's powerful body. She followed her in on a ten-foot wave but lost her balance and was buried under its crushing power. She attempted to find the surface, but the waves battered her, and her leash had gotten tangled on kelp attached to the ocean floor. She wasn't able to surface for a breath before the next wave crashed over her. She tugged at the leash as tendrils of fear crept in, her lungs beginning to burn. She felt a sharp tug on her ankle, and she was free of the kelp. Strong arms grabbed her and brought her to the surface, where she sucked in a deep breath and then coughed out the salty water stinging her throat.

The strength and warmth remained wrapped around her until she could stand in shallower water. She bent over her board as she coughed and gulped in air. "That wasn't how I planned to end my day." Quincy wheezed slightly and gave Jordan a weak smile. Her panic was reflected in Jordan's eyes.

Jordan ran her hand through her hair. "Yeah, I can imagine. Let's get you out of the water." She helped Quincy out of the water and onto the beach. "Are you good?" she asked, removing some of the fiendish kelp stuck to Quincy's cheek.

Quincy took Jordan's warm hand and held it against her cheek.

"Thank you for saving my life," Quincy whispered and closed her eyes. How quickly someone could get into trouble out there. If it hadn't been for Jordan... She shivered, and Jordan wrapped her arm around her shoulders. Her radiant warmth spread throughout Quincy's body, almost eclipsing the near-death event. The worry in Jordan's sparkling eyes was replaced with another emotion that Quincy couldn't place. The opportunity to ask passed as Jordan broke contact and ran across the beach to retrieve her surfboard from where it had settled at the waterline. Quincy took a deep breath, ignoring the tremble still present in her legs and acting as though nothing had happened, but the fluttering in her stomach told her something different, something that had nothing to do with surfing.

"I live over there." Jordan pointed across the beach to a gorgeous multi-story modern glass home that overlooked the ocean. "Do you want to come up to the house so you can recover some more?"

Quincy noticed two people standing on Jordan's balcony. "Thank you so much for the offer, but it looks like you've got company. Maybe another time." She hoped that would be true.

Jordan stepped into Quincy's personal space and pushed a strand of her blond hair behind her ear. "I think you need to take a little longer; that was a big scare. Why don't you come over for a little bit?" She gently pried Quincy's surfboard from her hands and backed away, carrying both boards.

Quincy shook herself out of the fog that Jordan's touch put her in and quickly realized she had no choice but to follow. She needed to control her emotions and get her head on straight. All this floundering had to stop. She came out of her thoughts and had to hustle across the sand to catch up with Jordan's long stride. "I can carry my own board. I'm okay, honestly. Thanks to you."

They crossed the strand to the small mansion's gate. The house was much grander up close than it had been at the water's edge. Whatever Jordan did for a living, it certainly paid well. Quincy gave a low whistle. "This is a gorgeous house. I can only imagine what it's like on the inside. I bet your views are amazing."

"I know one room I'd like to show you... Are you fishing for a tour?" Jordan winked.

Quincy's mouth went as dry as the sand she was standing on, and heat ran up her neck. "No, I'm... Umm. I'm not fishing. For an invite. I'm just appreciating your beautiful home."

Jordan leaned the surfboards against the fence, entered a code for the gate, and held it open. "Uh-huh. Likely story." She grabbed the boards and secured them in a wall rack before she continued across her patio to a secluded outdoor shower. "Want to wash off?"

Quincy took in the private and secure manicured patio, gas fireplace, top of the line furnishings, and a full outdoor kitchen. "Yeah, thanks. It'll be nice to rinse off the salt and sand. I love how private this is, but the sound of the surf is on surround sound." She had a hard time focusing with Jordan so close to her. "Why don't you go first?"

Jordan turned the shower on full blast and stepped under the spray. Quincy watched what quickly started to feel like a lesbian's dirty dream as Jordan unzipped her wetsuit and pulled it down to her waist, exposing her muscular body, smooth skin, and a defined six-pack. *Magnificent.* Jordan stepped back under the water with only her bikini on and bent over while looking up at her. Quincy was no dummy; she knew a player when she saw one, and Jordan was most definitely a player. Her muscle flexing and bending over just so while looking over her shoulder to talk to Quincy was one amazing show, but she knew it was just that.

"Can you grab my towel, please?"

Quincy was brought out of her lustful haze by Jordan's voice. She held out the beach towel. "Is this what you want?"

Jordan grinned, looking Quincy up and down. "Yeah. It is."

Quincy tossed her the towel and stepped beyond her into the warm shower. She slicked back her hair and slowly peeled her wetsuit down. This was a game she could play too, and Jordan didn't look away for a second.

"Jordan, are you done playing with the surf girl? We've got things to do."

The woman's shrill voice startled Quincy from the heated moment. The serious-looking woman on the balcony above sported a full face of makeup, neatly coiffed blond hair, and designer clothes, and diamonds adorning her ears, neck, and fingers glittered in the sun. Quincy immediately didn't like her. The younger man standing alongside her wore dark sunglasses, a polo shirt, and jeans.

Jordan yelled up to the pair on the balcony. "Hey. We'll be up in a little bit. Just let us dry off."

Quincy could read a room easily enough, and it was evident she wouldn't be welcomed inside. She showered and stepped into the towel being held out for her by Jordan. "Thank you."

"Jordan, leave your beach trash down there and come up so we can do business as though you're a grown-up."

Now she *really* didn't like her.

Jordan grimaced as Quincy pulled away. "Tina, for fuck's sake." She raised her hands. "Don't listen to her; she works for me. The day doesn't have to end. You don't have to go." She rubbed her hands up and down Quincy's arms. "You know you want a tour of my house."

"Thanks, but even beach trash knows when it's time to go." Quincy stepped away. She wrapped her towel around her waist, grabbed her gear, and made her way out of the gate. She paused when she was on the other side of the wall. "It was nice surfing with you and Dave today. Thanks for your hospitality, and for saving my life." She looked up to Jordan's *people* on the balcony and shook her head before she started walking down the Strand toward the parking lot and her Honda. She looked back when she heard Jordan shout, and then she saw Jordan flip Tina off before she ran toward Quincy.

"I'm so sorry for her outburst. Tina's a bitch. Unfortunately, she's also my manager and publicist, so I have to keep her around. That doesn't mean she can say those things to you. Please stay. I want to spend more time with you."

Quincy loaded her board and opened her truck's door. "Honestly, Jordan, it was an amazing day. But I've learned to keep that kind of negativity far, far away from my life. Good luck with that." She leaned forward and kissed Jordan's cheek before she jumped into her truck and waved goodbye. She only looked away from the rearview mirror when she turned a corner, leaving Jordan behind.

Chapter Five

JORDAN FRANTICALLY WAVED HER arms as she chased Quincy's Honda down the center of the parking lot, trying to get her to stop. "Quincy, wait. Can I get your information? Or your cell? Email?" she yelled at the retreating truck while other beach goers watched. 1OCN4ALL. Jordan repeated the license plate number over and over in her head as she walked home. She met women all the time, but there was something about Quincy that she wanted to explore. "We'll see each other again. I can promise you that, Quincy." Jordan went back through the beach gate and ran up the stairs. The peaceful sanctuary she'd enjoyed earlier was gone, and her place was now packed with people. Any residual tranquility was sucked away. The PR and marketing teams had to plan her pre-race junkets and publicity events in the lead-up to the LAGP, but she hadn't signed off on all that happening *here*. *Oh, hell, no.* She looked across the crowded living space and saw Carl, Tina's lackey, standing at the kitchen bar.

She marched up to him. "Carl, what's everyone doing in my home? This is *not* okay. You need to move the staff and all future meetings to the comped hotel suites in Hollywood. Get all these people out of here. Now."

Carl looked around her kitchen but didn't make eye contact with her. "I'll have to run that by Tina," he said, his voice quivering.

Jordan was easily a foot taller than Tina's lapdog, so she used that to her advantage, stepping closer and towering over him. "No, Carl, you don't. *I'm* your boss. Get it done." She looked through the throng of people in her living room and then stared at Carl. She knew who she really wanted to unload on. "Fine. Where is she?"

"She's in your office."

Jordan headed to her office in search of the source of the madness. Her anger bubbled below the surface ready to spill over as she thought of the look in Quincy's eyes after Tina's crass comment. She found Tina behind her desk as she talked on the phone and barked orders at the other people in the room.

She looked up at Jordan and shook her head. "Don't even start. I know what you're going to say. We don't need you distracted right now. So, settle down. She wasn't even your type."

Jordan pulled the phone from Tina's grasp and threw it onto her desk. The room fell eerily quiet. "Are you listening to me now, Tina? Do I have your attention? Do that to *anyone* again, and there'll be consequences. You're replaceable, no matter what you and my parents think. I've told Carl to move all these people somewhere else. There's no reason to use my home. Get out." Jordan slapped the top of the desk and then headed to the stairs. The room remained quiet until the door closed behind her, and then Tina's irritated tone rang out once again.

Jordan climbed up the stairs to her exercise loft and started her CrossFit workout. She burned off some of her anger with sweat equity. When she'd finished, she headed out onto her deck to cool down. Car doors slammed, and her phone chimed with a notification that her front door alarm had been activated by Tina's code. *Thank God they're finally gone*. She leaned on the railing and watched the breaking ocean waves to center herself. Her thoughts turned to Quincy. How lucky to have met such a beautiful woman on the water, especially someone who didn't know her or fawn all over her. Jordan's mental images of Quincy surfing and showering made her pulse race. She shivered when she replayed the seconds that passed when Quincy wiped out and didn't resurface. Her heart lodged in her throat as she considered all the possible outcomes. Jordan had been lucky to find her on her second dive. The look of fear and panic in Quincy's eyes reflected her own feelings. She shook her head to clear the images from her mind. She'd watched

Quincy's eyes roam her body, which told her more than any words could. They had unfinished business.

She went to her bedroom to call Tito John, her uncle, confidant, and overall favorite relative, as well as a California Highway Patrol Commissioner. "Hey, Tito. It's your favorite niece. How are you?"

"Jordan? It's so good to hear from you. It's been a while. I'm hanging in there. How about you? Are you back in LA?"

Jordan couldn't help but smile. "I got back this morning, surfed a little with Dave, and now I'm getting settled for the lead-up to the race. I'm pretty sure I know the answer, but do you plan to attend the Grand Prix?"

Tito John chuckled. "You know I wouldn't miss seeing you race. I've been bragging about you all season. I think my coworkers want to throttle me. I don't want to wait until race day to see you. Your cousin Ate Theresa is having a party on Sunday evening, and you should come. You know the food will be delicious. We'll have pancit, lechon, lumpia, and probably all kinds of ube desserts. Everyone will want to see you, feed you, give you some love, and of course, give you advice on how to win. You know your Tito Jack will even tell you what odds you have for the race." He paused. "We've missed you, and we'd love to see more of you than what we see in the papers. Should I expect to see you there?"

Jordan thought of the years that had passed since she'd allowed herself to be part of any family celebration. It certainly wasn't her extended family's fault. They treated her with love and support, unlike her parents. The opportunity to hear their stories, eat their food, and just connect made her ache with longing. "You had me at pancit. I'd love to see the family and eat some homemade food. I've got some race meetings and a medical team training on Sunday, but I might be able to make it. Text me the details, and I'll let you know."

"We understand. I'm sending you the text with the menu and address on it. I won't tell the family. You know no one can keep a secret. It'd just be so good to see you." Tito John sighed.

She hadn't thought of family in years and what it truly meant, and she wasn't sure why she was today. "Just in case we don't see each other, I'll leave your tickets for my box plus garage passes for as many people as you want." She hesitated, but at the image of Quincy's smile, she jumped in. "Tito, I have another reason for calling. I need a favor."

"Ah ha, the real reason for your call. How many speeding tickets on the 405 this time?"

Jordan laughed. "That was a while ago and I learned my lesson. I try to keep my speed on the track now. I'm trying to find someone. I have her first name and a license plate." There was a long pause on the other end of the line. "Hello, Tito, are you still there?"

"That's a big request, Jordan. It may require more than just tickets to the race. How about a little race gear sent over to the station as well?"

Jordan heard the seriousness in his voice. "That's no problem. You let me know what you want, and I'll get it for you. But will my favor get you in trouble? I don't want anything to happen to you because of me." And yet, the thought of losing out on getting to see Quincy again made her hope.

"It'll be okay if it stays between us. Don't you dare mention this to Tina."

Jordan began to pace the room, slightly irritated that Tina's tentacles reached as far as Tito John. "No problem there. Let's not mention this to my parents either. I'll send over anything you want if you can help me. The plate is California 1OCN4ALL."

"Can you hold on a second?" John asked after another long pause.

Jordan stopped pacing when music came on. Was she in the wrong? Maybe she shouldn't–

"Are you still there?"

"I'm here." She grabbed her iPad to make a note.

"Okay, so California, *One Ocean for All*. Nice plate. It belongs to Ms. Quincy Fitzgerald, and she lives at seventy-two Opal Ave in

Redondo Beach. Her phone number is unlisted, so this is the best I can do." There was another pause. "Jordan, I don't need to tell you that this is questionable. You're not going to do anything stupid, right? My name is now electronically tied to her information, so if you do anything you shouldn't, everyone will know."

"Tito, I promise. She got in trouble surfing and nearly drowned today. I helped her out, and I just want to check on her. Promise." It wasn't a lie. She *did* want to check on her. But just showing up at her house would be too weird. Wouldn't it? Or did being a celebrity buy her some kind of leeway? "I hope to see you Sunday night, if not on race day. Text me the information or how many tickets you need and where to send the racing stuff. Thank you, Tito. Trust me, I'll be good. I love you."

"I love you too, Jordie. See you soon."

Jordan ended the call and looked down at the information in her notes app. Quincy Fitzgerald might be getting a surprise visit tomorrow. Once again, though, she wondered if that was out of line. *I'm Jordan Marsh, of course she'd want to see me.* Just because Quincy said she didn't want people like Tina in her zone didn't mean that included Jordan. She'd just keep them apart. The niggle at the back of her mind warning her off? She shoved that neatly into the box with all the other warnings she ignored over the years. What was one more, after all?

Chapter Six

QUINCY CHASTISED HERSELF FOR not giving Jordan her number but kept driving anyway. She was way out of Quincy's league and surrounded by toxic people anyway. *I've got to tell Lauren.*

Quincy sent a quick text and then phoned Lauren when she stopped at a red light but got voicemail. "Call me back. I've got something to tell you." Initially, she'd wanted to talk to Lauren about the promotion debacle. Now, she had a hot surfer to add to the mix. She looked down at her buzzing phone as she pulled into her driveway and slipped her earbuds in to talk. "Hey, Lar, do you have a few minutes?"

"Yep, Trish and I just got back from the grocery store and planned to chill the rest of the night. How're you holding up? We heard about the promotion. That's such bullshit."

Quincy unloaded her truck and hung her wetsuit in the sun to dry. "Honestly, I'm devastated I didn't get it, but maybe this means I should look for greener pastures, especially if I'm not going to be respected and rewarded for all I've done. I'm still processing it, but I'm keeping my options open." It felt good to acknowledge the potential change out loud to someone who would really understand.

"We'll support you in whatever you want to do. It's a massive loss for the department and for the patients. That guy is an idiot."

Quincy entered her house and Jada circled her feet, wagging her tail wildly. She gave her some love and closed the door. "Believe it or not, I didn't call you to wallow in the drama, although it's good to talk with you about it, but...I freaking met someone today when I went surfing."

"Wait, what? You met someone? What does that mean?"

"I went to the ocean to work through my anger, and I met a woman named Jordan out in the water. She was *gorgeous*. Short dark hair and hazel eyes that alternated between gold and green. An amazingly perfect smile and a super-cute, crooked nose. She was tall, athletic, funny, and very rich if her house was anything to go by. She also saved me from drowning, so I probably have a hero complex going on."

"Whoa, slow the fuck down, Quincy. That's a lot to process. What do you mean by drowning? Are you okay?"

Quincy shuddered as she retold the story of the waves crashing over her head, the way she couldn't figure out which way was up, and Jordan's rescue.

"Damn, Quincy, I told you that you shouldn't surf alone. You could've died."

"I know, *Mom*, but luckily, I didn't."

"She sounds like something from a movie. Are you going to see her again?"

Quincy flopped down in the den and Jada sat next to her. "You know better than anyone that I won't. We didn't exchange numbers. She wanted to, but...you know."

"This again!" Lauren huffed loudly. "Quincy, you're a sweet, kind, and wonderful person. I don't understand why you can't drop that iron curtain around your heart. Open yourself up to the unexpected opportunities life throws at you. Like hot surfer women. I know trust is hard for you after Rochelle shattered your heart. Along with the unfounded guilt you carry regarding your mom's death, you've got a lot of bruises on that gentle soul of— Did you just turn on the TV while I'm making a very important point about your heart?"

"I want to see the news, but I'm focused on our conversation, don't worry. I know all of what you're saying on some level. But seriously, I was out of this woman's league. Her publicist called me 'beach trash,' and while Jordan said she's just part of her life and that's how it is, I felt so out of control around her, and you know how I like control."

"Yeah, trust me, I know. But you know where Jordan lives, right? You could go back there, introduce yourself properly, and at least see what the sex is like. You'll never know unless you try. And it's not like you have to sleep with the publicist too."

"Lauren, oh my God," Quincy said as she realized what she was watching on the TV.

"Well, I thought it was a good idea, but I didn't think you'd be that impressed with it," Lauren said.

"Lar, you aren't going to believe who Jordan is. She's an IndyCar driver. I've seen her photo in the training I've been doing for the medical team. I *knew* she looked familiar. She's the gorgeous driver of the number twenty-two Pink Triangle Racing car. The same driver who has a woman in every town and a new one on her arm for every event. How many times has she been on the cover of magazines? Can you hold on? I want to hear what they're saying."

"Turn it up so I can hear," Lauren said.

The slick-looking announcer stood in front of LAX. "Two years ago, if you didn't follow IndyCar racing, you wouldn't know who Jordan Marsh was. Now everyone knows her name. Jordan's status as a fierce and successful female driver in this male-dominated field has been cemented into history. She's an out and proud lesbian, and fans from around the world, especially within the Filipino and LGBTQ+ community, show up to support her at each race and at her celebrity events. Here's footage from LAX earlier today when the IndyCar sensation arrived to a mob of fans, press and paparazzi. As you may recall, Jordan was last year's Open-Wheel Driver of the Year. This season, she's captured two pole positions and four first-place finishes with the win in Brazil a month ago. The heat is on for Jordan and the Pink Triangle Racing team with only two races left in the season, the LA Grand Prix and the Indianapolis 500. She's positioned as the top contender for the 2025 IndyCar championship *and* the $15 million purse. We'll see if she can keep her standings in the race to the championship with a win next weekend in the LA Grand Prix."

Quincy watched footage of Jordan and her publicist making their way through a sea of people to a parked Cadillac, and she couldn't stop the excitement of seeing a close-up image of Jordan on the screen.

The reporter came back into the frame. "As you can see, Jordan didn't provide an interview or any answers to the multiple questions we all have, though she did take the time to talk to fans. She and Lucy Chandler, the current Miss Universe, were captured last night in some racy pics at Club Patch in New York City. Ms. Chandler didn't travel with Jordan to LA this morning and has declined to comment on their relationship. We'll stay tuned to see what comes next from Jordan Marsh on and off the track in her quest to win the LA Grand Prix."

A pang of jealousy struck her at the thought of Jordan with another woman.

"I just googled her, and she's *fine*. I can see why you're drooling over her. She and Lucy Chandler were certainly 'racy' at the club if those pictures are anything to go by. *So steamy.*"

"Look, Lar, she saved my life. What celebrity does that? I mean, she could've just walked away. She did put off a total player vibe, so it isn't surprising about the pics or the women. I mean, if she's flirting with me after a night with *Miss Universe*, then clearly, I made the right choice not giving her my number. At least I've got a new celebrity crush." So why was she disappointed? They'd spent all of a few hours together. Hardly soulmate material.

"Who wouldn't crush on her? She's sexy as hell. Lucky you, getting to spend unfettered time with her today. Maybe you'll see more of her since you're volunteering on the Medical Safety Crew for the Grand Prix. Aren't you going to be up there for the big race?"

"Yeah, I started the virtual training a month ago. The hands-on training with the car will be Sunday. I'm excited for the opportunity."

Even more so, now that she'd get to watch Jordan in action. "Did you know that IndyCar only selects ten local providers to supplement their own Medical Travel team?"

"No, race nerd, I didn't. Of course you got chosen. You're a rockstar in the ER, and so calm in any emergency, you might as well be watching it on TV. I imagine your family's annual childhood trips to the Indianapolis 500 probably didn't hurt your application. It makes sense that you'd be involved in this"

Lauren had given her plenty of grief about watching the races on TV during their two months together and knew full well how much Quincy enjoyed it.

"Thanks, Lar. That means a lot. I did say I had IndyCar spectator experience in my application, but who knows if that had anything to do with my selection? The moonlighting I've been doing as an NP with the Fire Department to make money for my South Pacific trip probably helped more than anything since it was all about emergencies out in the field. The extra income will be a nice buffer for the trip. I mean, the trip was the main reason I even applied." And now the reason seemed extra justified. Would Jordan even give her the time of day if they met up there?

"Oh, right. I forgot you're leaving us all behind to go rough it 'n the South Pacific. How long will you be gone?"

Quincy felt almost giddy just thinking about it. "Three weeks total, and I cannot wait! Two of the weeks I'll spend volunteering on a newly found shipwreck with Dr. David Lamoille's team of underwater archaeologists. And one week of downtime that's just for me. I can't wait to get some space from work, especially after today." Some of the giddiness receded. "On a different note, I wanted to remind you about my monthly BBQ on Wednesday. Are you coming?"

"I'll be there, but we'll need to let you know closer to the day if Trish will make it. You know how crazy work is for her right now."

"No problem, I understand. I just wanted to get a headcount. Plan to bring your usual salad and a dessert."

"Okay, will do. I need to go; I'm getting 'the look' from my wifey," Lauren whispered.

Quincy laughed. "Give Trish my love. We'll talk soon. Bye, Lar."

She shut off the TV, leashed Jada, and headed out on her nightly walk around the neighborhood. She thought about Jordan and their non-stop conversation. She was surprised she hadn't recognized her as the superstar driver, but that wasn't who she saw. She saw a beautiful, funny, and kind woman. Quincy finished the walk and as she opened her door, the intense sense of longing and loneliness washed over her again, and she headed to bed. *Let it go, Quincy. You'll probably never see her again that close, and she's way out of your league.*

Quincy woke Saturday morning to a sunny, warm spring day. The excited chirps from the house sparrows in her backyard beckoned her outside. She loved to grow plants for her own consumption but also for hummingbirds, bees, and butterflies. Yesterday's emotional roller coaster had left her feeling unbalanced, but the balm she needed could be found right here. She'd neglected her hummingbird garden in the front yard due to her busy work schedule, but today was the day it came off life support. She gathered the tools she needed, slipped on her well-worn gloves, and began the necessary pruning. After a couple of hours, the bite of the sun's rays tingled on her shoulders, dandelion leaves prickled against her skin, and the overall Zen-like feeling she'd hoped for wrapped around her like a favorite blanket. She looked at her work proudly as she stood and stretched. Just as she planned to head inside for a shower, her neighbor Nick stopped on the sidewalk by her fence.

"Hey, Q, how've you been?"

"Hi, neighbor, I'm good. How're you and the family?"

"We're busy, as usual. I'm just trying to get back into running." He pulled his leg behind him to stretch, using her fence as support.

"I can only imagine. Any big plans today?"

Nick bent over to stretch, but he looked awkward as he seemed to peer between his legs. "We'll probably go to the farmer's market later. Do you need anything?"

"Thanks for the offer, but I'm good."

Nick looked up and tilted his head toward a dark-colored SUV that was slowly making its way toward them. "I think that person is lost. I saw them driving down the street the other way during my run. Seems weird. Anyway, have a great weekend. Watch out for stranger danger."

"Thanks. You too." Quincy watched the SUV approach. The navy-blue Range Rover pulled a U-Haul car carrier with a silver sports car attached. The truck stopped at the curb in front of Quincy's home, but the tint was too dark for her to determine who was behind the wheel. There was a pink triangle on the door, and people she knew didn't ride around with cars like that attached to other expensive cars. Her heart pounded in her chest as Jordan climbed out of the SUV. She wore a tight, navy cap-sleeved T-shirt with the Pink Triangle Racing logo, a snug pair of faded jeans, and black leather boots. Black sunglasses blocked Quincy's ability to track her gaze. Dirt fell from her hands as she quickly brushed them off. Sweat stuck her hair to her face, and she groaned inwardly. How the hell had Jordan found her? And why, *why*, did she have to find her looking like this?

Chapter Seven

Jordan smiled as she jumped out of the car. Her unscheduled visit to see Quincy had seemed like a good idea yesterday. Quincy's home was less than a mile from her own, although it was quite a bit smaller and in a different type of neighborhood. The manicured front yard edged by a modern white vinyl fence was quaint, and the cutout of glass in the center of the door was painted a warm, inviting red; she hoped that'd be the reception Quincy gave her now. The flower gardens wrapped around the front porch provided a burst of color that seemed to match Quincy's personality.

Jordan waved as she left the safety of her car. "Hi, stranger. Nice home." She walked up the driveway to the gate. The little dog at Quincy's side barked and ran toward Jordan. The pup sniffed her through the gate and then jumped up and licked her hand. Jordan pushed her sunglasses up onto her head. She smiled and made eye contact with Quincy. "This one's a regular Cujo. Can I come in?"

"What're you doing here?" Quincy asked, then winced. "I'm sorry for being blunt, but I'm surprised to see you." She grabbed Jada's collar to keep her in the yard. "Come on in."

She looked as uncomfortable as Jordan felt. Her arms were folded across her chest, her feet were planted on the grass, and her head was cocked to one side as though she was trying to figure out the situation.

Jordan stayed focused on the pup at her feet and not Quincy's glare. Damn. Maybe she'd overstepped after all. "This must be Jada, the someone special in your life. I can see why. She's a cutie."

Quincy looked down to Jada, and her expression softened.

"Yes, she loves the ladies, and she's a great dog." She looked up, and the steel came back into her gaze. "Well, Jordan Marsh, you either have some mad detective skills, or you've got the kind of resources few people do to find my name and home address within twenty-four hours of meeting me. While I'm flattered, you aren't the only one in the know. Hello, Ms. IndyCar Driver, Open-Wheel Driver of the Year, and lesbian heartthrob. It's nice to formally meet you."

"I guess you've done your homework too." Jordan tucked her hands into her back pockets and rocked on her feet. Why was it disappointing that Quincy knew who she was? It wasn't like she was keeping it a secret. But still, it'd been nice to feel anonymous and liked for who she was, just for a minute.

Quincy shook her head. "Hey now, I've been an IndyCar fan since I was a kid. Unfortunately, with the focus on the promotion I've been chasing, I stopped paying attention to the races. I wouldn't say I've dug into your backstory; I simply watched the local news and saw some video footage of your arrival at LAX yesterday. They provided a nice summary of your biography, including your professional and personal history. All within a five-minute segment."

"Yeah, well, maybe five minutes is all it takes to sum me up." Jordan removed the sunglasses from her head and looked down at them to cover her embarrassment. She knew the sensational stories that were reported about her on local and national news. Of course she did. Sponsors liked that she was someone to talk about. But for some reason, that wasn't what she wanted Quincy to hear about her. "I mean, maybe there's more than five minutes to my story…if someone really wanted to know." She held out her hand. "It's lovely to formally meet you too." She noted the streak of dirt on Quincy's cheek and fought her desire to gently rub it away.

Quincy followed Jordan's gaze and rubbed at her cheek. "So, to what do I owe the pleasure of two audiences with the IndyCar vixen, and at my home, no less?"

"I'm sorry. I know this probably comes across as a bit weird. I promise I'm not a stalker or anything." She wanted to explain to Quincy what brought her here uninvited, but she wasn't even sure. She was acting like a nervous teenager as she regarded Quincy in the afternoon sun. She looked just as beautiful with her dirt-streaked cheeks as she did yesterday in her tight wetsuit. Her dark-blond bob was tied up in a mini ponytail that showed off her graceful neck, natural beauty, and her questioning eyes. The AC/DC tank top and the cut-off jean shorts outlined her toned, tanned arms and legs. She was barefoot with her gardening clogs off to the side and her Barbie-pink pedicure stood out in the green grass. The look Quincy directed at her confirmed her awareness of Jordan's ogling.

"Okay, here's the thing," Jordan said. "I enjoyed our time together yesterday. I haven't felt so at ease with someone in a long time. I wanted to ask if you'd like to go out with me this evening?" She had to keep going, or she'd never get it all out. "I'm going to drop off my car at a friend's business, and then go to an outing for work, all between here and Long Beach." Where the hell had her usual smooth words gone? "It won't be anything fancy, but I'd hoped you'd join me." She held her breath for Quincy's answer.

Quincy smiled, but there was a sadness to her eyes. "I won't lie; I enjoyed our time together surfing, and I'd hoped to meet you again. I'm flattered that you found me, but just so we're clear, I don't appreciate the resources you used to find me, nor do I appreciate you ambushing me. It's creepy, and if you weren't a global superstar with a known background, I'd send you packing. I prefer to have control over my life and home, including who I invite into them."

"I'm sorry for encroaching, I just thought you'd be happy to see me. Most women are." Jordan realized how egotistical she sounded and sighed deeply. She couldn't seem to get out of her own way. She hadn't expected that to be Quincy's response and started to slowly back away. Why didn't she ever listen to that little voice that told her the difference between right and wrong? She stopped when Quincy held up the dirty trowel.

"I am, but this is a lot for anyone to take in. Just give me a minute."

She waved her hand to encompass Jordan and her car. She looked at the SUV parked on the street and then at Jordan, and it was obvious she was weighing her options. "While it's probably not a good idea, I'd love to spend some more time with you. Tonight sounds like an adventure, but if it includes people who are fueled by negativity, then I'm out."

Quincy wrung her hands together while she spoke, not looking nearly as confident as she sounded, which told Jordan that she *had* overstepped. She regretted the method but was ecstatic Quincy agreed to go out with her. "I probably understand better than you know about people digging into your personal life without your blessing. I should've contacted you in a better way, and I'm sorry. Honestly, I skipped the line because I really wanted to see you again, and I couldn't bear leaving it to chance. I'll do better, I promise. I'm excited to have you join me tonight, and I'll keep the negative Nellies away from you," she said and smirked.

Quincy nodded and then swept her gaze over Jordan slowly. Very slowly, like she was undressing her with her eyes. At least that's how it felt.

Quincy cleared her throat. "Would jeans work for tonight?"

Jordan's thoughts were anything but appropriate. "Casual will be fine; whatever you're comfortable wearing." At Quincy's motion, she followed her around the side of the house and into her landscaped backyard. It was an oasis; lush dark green shrubs towered ten feet above them, with purple and yellow flowers scattered throughout. The ground under the shrubs had lavender and gardenia bushes alternating in purple and white along the U-shaped yard. The delicate smell of gardenias transported Jordan to her childhood home in Maryland and with it, back to the unreachable expectations of her parents. She shook off that memory as Quincy walked ahead to the gardening shed and dropped the bucket full of shears and tools inside. "Your yard is gorgeous. You obviously have a green thumb."

Quincy turned to face her. "Thanks. I had help with the original planting, but the day-to-day maintenance is all mine. I'm happy with how it turned out. This yard was my respite during the early days of COVID. Nature has always been my touchstone, be it my simple yard, the ocean, or the mountains. I maintain this to keep that connection." She shrugged. "But you probably don't want to hear about that, so let's head inside, and I'll get ready."

Jordan followed her through French doors and into a den. "This is a great house, so light and bright. How long have you lived here?" She looked around the home and appreciated the simple, clean coastal design. The use of light wood and shades of blue infused a stylish warmth throughout, making it feel quite different from her own glass and steel house. There were only a few personal touches, like a collection of antique, blue glass medicine bottles. She picked up the only framed photo; Quincy stood in the center, flanked by a woman and a man. The family resemblance was unmistakable, so she guessed that it was her sister and possibly her father. Jordan put the photo down and then sat on the couch next to Jada and began petting her.

Quincy straightened the photo. "I bought my home ten years ago, and it's still a work in progress. Do you want anything to drink while you wait?"

Jordan couldn't smother her curiosity about Quincy's life; she wanted to know everything about her. "No, I'm fine. Who's that in the photo with you?"

"It's my sister, Katie, who's two years younger than me, and my dad, Brian. It was taken three years ago in Illinois where I grew up. Okay. I shouldn't be too long. Are you good?"

Quincy's words were perfunctory, as though it was a practiced answer. Jordan nodded. She understood complicated family relationships and knew better than to pry any further. That told her all she needed to know about Quincy's family connections, or at least, all Quincy wanted to share. She realized she hadn't replied. "Sorry, yeah, I'm all good. I'll be out here with Jada awaiting your return." She gave Quincy a wide smile

"Oh, let me text my dog walker to check on Jada tonight." She paused and bit her lip. "It's weird leaving you out here alone, but I'll be quick." Quincy turned and walked down the hall.

Jordan looked at Jada, who continued to follow her owner's progress. "What do you think, Jada girl? Do I pass the pup test?"

Jada nudged her head into Jordan's hand, and she resumed petting her while she waited. It was interesting that Quincy felt weird leaving a stranger in her living room. Their lives were so different. How often did Jordan have a ton of people she didn't know in her hotel room or at parties? The peace in this house was undeniable though. Was that the reason? Too many deep thoughts could ruin the night, so she pushed them away. "I should let Eric know we're headed his way," Jordan said to Jada as she picked up her cell to text him.

Less than thirty minutes later, Jordan looked up as Quincy appeared in the doorway. *Breathe, idiot.* Quincy looked beautiful wearing only just enough makeup to enhance her natural beauty. The pink lip gloss drew Jordan's attention to Quincy's full lips, and she wanted to kiss the shine off them. Her hair was styled in a messy bob, and she wore a tight white T-shirt, dark jeans, and leather loafers.

"I'm just about ready to go, but there's one condition," Quincy said.

"Okay, whatever you want," Jordan said and meant it. The jasmine-infused air around Quincy made her lightheaded, and her twinkling eyes boring into Jordan made it difficult to distance herself.

"I need to know we won't be around Terrible Tina tonight. I'd rather not see that woman ever again, and I certainly don't want to see her tonight."

"I meant to apologize again for that. I'm sorry for her callous behavior yesterday. I promise you won't see her tonight." She took Quincy's hands. "You look gorgeous." She took a step closer and tucked Quincy's silky hair behind her ear. She was drawn in by

Quincy's simple beauty, but she needed to show some restraint and get some distance or else they may not make it out of Quincy's living room. Jordan's heart jackhammered in her chest as she dropped her hands and stepped back. She was used to moving fast and getting what she wanted, but with Quincy, that felt wrong. She wanted to take the time to get to know more about her. She shook her head and pulled away.

"Ready to go?" Jordan opened the front door.

"Sure, let me close the back and grab my jacket. Jada, be good." Quincy grabbed a brown leather jacket and headed out the door to Jordan's car. As they reached the street, Quincy gestured to the carrier. "Don't most lesbians wait for the second date before bringing their U-Haul?"

Jordan laughed a deep knowing chuckle, which pushed away the awkwardness from earlier. "What can I say? I do things fast." She held the passenger door open for Quincy, who walked past with a roll of her eyes before climbing into the seat. Jordan's heart lifted at the tension easing between them. The spark of hope for a second date ignited, as did the promise of the evening that stretched out ahead.

Chapter Eight

THE HUM OF THE tires as Jordan maneuvered the SUV through local traffic helped take away Quincy's confusion from the near kiss. At least, she thought it was going to be a kiss, but then Jordan backed away and the moment was lost. Jordan left her unsettled and out of control; neither were welcome feelings for her. Her joke lightened the mood, but her anxiety over what the night held remained.

"Quincy, are you with me?" Jordan asked.

Quincy noticed they were stopped at a light. "I'm sorry, I was enjoying my first ride in a Range Rover."

"Just to be clear, I hadn't intended to pull up to your home with a U-Haul trailer tonight, but the drop-off window to Eric's shop was very narrow. I was given this Aston Martin One-77, and before I drove it, I wanted the P-Three team to perform their magic."

Quincy looked back at the gleaming silver car. "You were *given* that car? Wow, that must be nice. What magic could they possibly need to do? It looks pristine." Quincy wasn't familiar with Aston Martin, other than she knew James Bond drove them, but she was pretty sure it was a six-figure car.

Jordan chuckled as she looked into the rearview mirror. "That's the goal: to keep it pristine. Eric developed a polymer film that goes over the paint to protect it. His business has made a killing, and he has an amazing following in the high-end automotive world. Only the most influential people get to use his service. I'm very lucky he decided to be one of my sponsors, so if I can give him business, it's a win-win."

"What if you aren't an influential person? Don't they cover a regular person's car too, or do you have to be ultra-rich?" The have, have-not issues of the world irritated her, as always.

"That's the way the world works. People with more money can get better services. It isn't news, is it?" Jordan frowned at Quincy as she pulled up in front of a nondescript brick building and jumped out of the truck.

"Okay, I guess the big Jordan Marsh doesn't like a little pushback," Quincy said to herself as she climbed out of the cab. Maybe this impromptu joyride had been a mistake after all. She joined Jordan at the back of the car carrier and a tall Hispanic man wearing a black T-shirt with the P-Three logo came out from the open garage door.

"Jordie, how's it going?" Eric hugged her.

"Hey, Eric, I'm doing well. How're you?"

"All good here. Who'd you bring with you tonight?" Eric smiled broadly.

"Eric, this is my new friend, Quincy. Quincy, this is Eric."

"Hi, Quincy. It's nice to meet any friend of Jordan's." Eric offered his hand.

Quincy quashed her simmering anger toward Jordan for her elitist and dismissive behavior; she didn't know this guy, and there was no reason to be an ass to him. "It's nice to meet you." Quincy shook his hand. "Jordan mentioned that you were one of her sponsors."

"We've proudly sponsored the number twenty-two car for the past two years. The publicity we've gotten drove our business well beyond where we would've been on our own. We owe a lot to our relationship with Jordan and the Pink Triangle team." He patted Jordan's shoulder, then gestured to his team to remove the car carrier. "Well, Jordie, are you ready for the Grand Prix?"

"Yeah, I can't wait to run the new circuit in the car. I've visually and virtually driven the track, but once I'm in the car and get the G-force, I'll feel much better about the race. Thanks again for your ongoing support of the team; it means a lot to all of us. Oh, did you receive the tickets and passes your team needed?"

"We're all set, thank you. Good luck, go win it all, and don't worry about your Aston Martin. We'll take care of her."

"I know you will. We'd better get going. We've got a few more stops tonight." Jordan turned and walked around to the driver's side.

Quincy hung back, curious about the painting protection and not wanting to be seen as just another of Jordan's groupies. "Jordan explained what you do for fancy cars like hers, but do you provide services for Hondas or Fords? For regular people?"

Eric nodded. "Hell, yeah, that's how we got here. Here's my card. Just call this number or use this QR code and make an appointment. We offer a ten-percent discount if you mention Pink Triangle Racing when you call or add it in as a promo code."

"Cool, thanks, Eric, I'll look for your logo on her car come race day." Quincy waved and headed back to Jordan's car. She couldn't help but feel a little deflated. She'd been ready for a fight about only providing good things to wealthy people, but he hadn't blinked. Now her righteous anger had nowhere to go.

Jordan looked straight ahead with both hands on the steering wheel. "Are you good?" Jordan asked. "We okay to go ahead with the night?"

Quincy noticed the way Jordan's hands gripped the steering wheel and how her jaw clenched a little. It appeared she wanted an answer before she'd pull out onto the busy street. Quincy decided an educational tactic was better than confrontation. "Yep, I'm good. Eric said that they'll do any type of car and not just for affluent clients. They also offer a discount if you use Pink Triangle Racing. Isn't that cool?" Quincy watched Jordan's expression. She was adept at reading body language, and Jordan's told her that she didn't like to be challenged. *Well, now she'll see that I don't back down.*

"That's good to hear, and it's something I didn't know," Jordan said after a moment of quiet. "Are you sure you still want to hang with me tonight?" She thrummed her fingers on the steering wheel.

Quincy imagined Jordan had plenty of women she could spend the evening with, and none would be as challenging as she could be. But she was following life's open door, or whatever nonsense Lauren talked about. "I'm still game, if you are."

Jordan blew out a breath and gave her a hesitant smile. "Okay, our next outing is in Long Beach, so we've got a bit of a drive ahead."

The radiant glow of the setting sun provided a soft halo of light around Jordan's face, making her even sexier. This night might be her only one with Jordan, so she may as well make the most of it. "Sounds good." Quincy leaned back into the leather seat and thought of how surreal this situation was.

"So, you said you were from Illinois. What brought you to LA?" Jordan pulled onto the street.

Quincy smiled. "Ah, the ultimate LA icebreaker since so few people who live in LA are from here. I grew up in Pioneer. It was a small town surrounded by corn and bean fields, and it had a population of about eight hundred. I left as soon as I could." She knew her tone revealed the turbulent emotions she still had about leaving home. "I attended Notre Dame for my bachelor's degree in nursing. Then I headed to Chicago to work in the Cook County ED for a few years, before I completed my master's degree at Northwestern and became an ER nurse practitioner. As luck would have it, I was offered an NP job at LAMC ten years ago, and I've been here ever since. I fell in love with the vibe of LA, as well as the oceans, mountains, and desert. It was so vastly different from Illinois, but I felt so at home."

At a stoplight, Jordan glanced at Quincy and smiled. "That's so brave. It must've been a huge change to leave such a small hometown to come out here. Do you have family in the area?"

Quincy's stomach flipped at the tender look Jordan gave her. "No, my immediate family all lives in Illinois. My dad, my sister, her husband, Colin, and my three-year-old niece, Becca, all live in the same town. I've got extended family around the US, but no one out here... Just me."

"Do you plan to work at LAMC forever?" Jordan asked as she maneuvered the car through traffic.

Quincy rubbed her hands up and down her thighs as she tried to work out the frustration about her job. "That's a good question; one I'm still working out. Since I didn't get the promotion, I've been thinking about looking elsewhere. I love the job, but the politics are difficult to handle." She looked out the window at the world passing her by. Did she really want to let that happen with her job too?

Jordan grabbed her hand and squeezed lightly. "I'm sorry that didn't work out for you."

Quincy sighed at Jordan's warm touch, surprised at how it calmed her. "Thank you. I'm frustrated because it went to a nepo baby: the nurse manager's cousin. He's only worked two years in the ED, and he hides any time a trauma comes in. I got outplayed, and it hurts. I think it might be time to look outside the hospital walls for something new." Saying it out loud and to a practical stranger was another step closer to her believing t herself.

"We're here," Jordan said as she pulled up outside the Long Beach LGBTQ+ Center and parked in a reserved spot.

Quincy looked out the windshield at the gathered crowd. Most were race fans who wore Jordan's car number and Pink Triangle gear. And there were plenty holding rainbow-colored signs saying, "I love you, Jordan" and "Good Luck." The fans were all ages, races, genders, sexual orientations, and abilities. "I guess *outing* was the perfect choice of words for tonight."

Jordan smiled. "I guess it was. Ready to go?" She slipped from the truck before Quincy could reply.

"Ready for what?" She watched behind the dark tinted windows as Jordan, assisted by security, moved seamlessly through the crowd. Jordan took the time to meet, greet, and sign her way to the door of the center. Quincy decided to hang back until the sizzle that surrounded Jordan passed. The realization that tonight's pictures would link them romantically gave Quincy pause. She decided not to put that on Jordan or herself. She waited until the fans had their backs turned to her before she slid out of the truck. Just as Quincy left the confines of the car, strong arms enveloped her from behind. She turned to see Brett, a nursing friend, who gave her a big bear hug.

"You scared the shit out of me." Quincy slapped him on the arm and returned his hug.

"Sorry, sugar. I was just surprised to see you." Brett gave her a wicked grin and wiggled his eyebrows. "Nice ride. I saw who this car belongs to."

Quincy shook her head. "We just met yesterday."

"Uh-huh. Well then, you work fast, don't you? Or is it Jordan who works fast? I've heard that about her."

This was exactly what she'd been worried people would think. Just as she was about to explain, she was approached by an older woman with a center volunteer badge.

"Are you Quincy?"

"Yes."

"I'm Betty, and I was asked by Ms. Marsh to help you into the center. She said you were separated, and that she needed help to locate you. Will you please come with me, and I can take you to her?"

Separated is one *word for being abandoned. I bet she doesn't even realize she does it.* Quincy realized she hadn't replied to Betty when Brett nudged her.

"You bet, Betty. Lead the way," Brett said and gently pushed Quincy forward toward the building.

The crowd thickened near the entrance, so Brett pushed his large frame through the crowd and through the front doors. Quincy saw Jordan as they entered the lobby, and her mouth went dry.

"Damn," Quincy mumbled, tugging at her shirt to let some heat out.

"Uh-huh, girl. I knew you had it bad." Brett touched Quincy's cheeks and draped his arm over her shoulder.

"You're such an ass. Even you have to agree she's hot. It doesn't mean there's anything more to it than that." Quincy wriggled under his heavy arm as he laughed at her. It was clear that Jordan was in her element: surrounded by a security team and a horde of her fans where she signed autographs, posed for pictures, and laughed with all those in attendance.

"She's hot and she's a queer icon in mainstream media, and that's what matters to so many of us. Quincy, I just love to ruffle your feathers. For the eight years I've known you, you've always been so controlled. It's nice to see you a little unglued. Who knew it would only take Jordan Marsh?" Brett squeezed her shoulder.

What *was* she doing here, so out of control? Jordan and this public event were far from her comfort zone. Maybe she should just walk away right now. Although she couldn't deny the physical attraction, she also couldn't deny the potential pitfalls. Quincy chose to flee the madness and turned to head back outside.

Betty grabbed her arm and stopped her retreat as they approached the security perimeter. She flashed her badge to the guard, and Quincy and Brett were escorted inside the secure perimeter, which was just a set of red ropes next to Jordan. Quincy felt like a bug under a microscope as Jordan turned away from her fans and locked eyes with her. A look of relief passed over Jordan's features before her megawatt-smile covered anything real. Quincy caught that look though, and she couldn't help but wonder who the real Jordan Marsh was. "I guess we got separated."

"I guess we did. I was worried that you freaked out because of the crowds and press and abandoned me. I'm so glad you're okay," she said softly and gave Quincy a genuine smile, one just for her.

Flustered, Quincy glanced away and attempted to get her emotions in check. Her fight or flight response had been activated, and she was ready to flee from this crazy scene and leave Jordan behind. The crowds and the attention were overwhelming, but Jordan's warm smile grounded her and calmed her desire to run.

Her heart rate slowed as she looked into Jordan's questioning eyes. "Thanks, I'm fine," she said, though she doubted that could ever be true.

Chapter Nine

Most women stuck to Jordan's side for the publicity and media spotlight they gained from her celebrity status, desperate to be part of her media circus. It'd never occurred to her that Quincy wasn't one of those women. Her natural beauty, unshakable confidence, and deep-rooted authenticity made her like no one else Jordan had ever met. She half-smiled then stopped her train of thought. *I can't have distractions.* She told herself to focus for the umpteenth time. There was no denying though, there was something about Quincy's presence that made it feel like someone was there for her. Not for her public persona, but just for *her.*

Quincy made the introductions to her large friend.

"Nice to meet you, Brett," Jordan said as his large mitt enveloped her hand and pumped her arm up and down enthusiastically.

"I'm a big fan of your work," he said then pulled Jordan forward slightly. "Just so you know, Q is a peach who never lets anyone down. So you do right by her." He dropped Jordan's hand and winked before he hugged Quincy. "Okay, sweetie, it was great seeing you tonight. I'll catch you later. Jordan, good luck."

Jordan watched the giant leave and become engulfed in the crowd. Was he wishing her good luck with the race or with Quincy? "He seems like a nice guy. Too bad he had to leave." She took Quincy's hand and intertwined their fingers. "I've met my fan quota for tonight. What do you say we find someplace a bit more private?"

Quincy looked around at the wall of fans with their cell phones raised, videoing their interaction. She nodded but gently pulled her hand away and shoved it in her pocket. "That sounds like a good idea to me."

Not like other women. Jordan motioned to security that they were on the move before she turned and led them behind a rainbow curtain and into a private room at the edge of the stage. "The center set this up as my green room for tonight. Make yourself comfortable. There should be water, energy drinks, and some of my favorite snacks." Jordan paced the room, not sure how Quincy was feeling.

"I'll just take a water," Quincy said and sank onto a green velvet couch.

Jordan pulled out a bottle from the fridge. "I'm sorry for losing you. That doesn't usually happen. Most women who come with me to my public events like the publicity it generates. By the way you looked out there, I'm guessing that you don't."

Quincy took the water, leaned back on the couch, and crossed her arms and legs. "I thought you figured out I wasn't like most of 'your' women on my lawn earlier."

Jordan sat on the far end of the couch facing Quincy. "I did, but you intrigued me. I had this event scheduled, and I thought you'd be impressed by my fans and the crowds." It sounded absurd when she said it out loud.

"It's been something, that's for sure," Quincy looked around the green room and then at Jordan.

Jordan edged closer to her on the couch and took her hands. "Hey, I never meant to leave you in that sea of humanity. I've learned when security moves me, I move. Like I said, most of the women I'm with are right by my side. I never expected you to not be there." Jordan rubbed her thumb across Quincy's palm.

"Yeah, I'm not going to lie; it was overwhelming. I was glad Brett was there for support. While I can certainly take care of myself, a heads-up next time would be nice."

Next time... Yes! "Okay, next time I'll be more aware, and I won't leave you, I promise." Most women were happy to throw themselves at her whenever the opportunity arose. Maybe she was losing her appeal. She couldn't explain the anxiety that filled her, thinking Quincy didn't want her.

Quincy got up to check out the snacks on the table. Jordan needed validation. She needed to know she hadn't lost her touch. She needed an answer to put this feeling to bed. She jumped up and caught Quincy in a light hug from behind. "What looks good, besides me?"

Quincy's silken hair gently grazed her cheek, and she leaned back into Jordan's embrace. It felt right to hold her, but this feeling with someone she'd just met was weird. Before she could narrow down what was going on, there was a rapid-fire knock at the door, and Quincy bolted from her arms.

"Ms. Marsh, five minutes."

"Okay." She looked at Quincy, who'd acted like a startled teenager after being busted by her parents. "You okay?"

"Yeah, I'm just a bit jumpy, I guess. This celebrity stuff is all new to me."

Jordan squeezed Quincy's shoulders. "Don't worry, babe, you'll get used to it. Everyone does. Just give me a sec, okay? I need to check everything's perfect before I go out there. "Do I look okay?" Jordan turned to the mirror to check her appearance, and before Quincy could reply, there was another knock and the door was thrown open.

Bert Downey, the center's firecracker of a CEO walked in. She wore faded jeans and a *Love is Love* T-shirt under a navy blazer. She walked with the confidence of a woman comfortable in her own skin as she made a beeline to Jordan and hugged her briefly.

"Jordie, it's been too long. How've you been? You haven't been staying out of trouble if the New York pictures are anything to go by. Well, we can't expect a leopard to change her spots, now, can we? Thanks for coming tonight, it means a lot for the community and the Center," Bert said.

"Of course, I'm always happy to support the center and the work you do. But you're hardly one to give me a hard time about changing spots. We can discuss that later," she said, uncomfortable with the trajectory of the conversation with Quincy present. What a strange feeling to care what she thought. She certainly didn't need Bert to start in on their shared club stories and embarrass her anymore. "Bert, this is my friend Quincy." Jordan indicated to where Quincy stood behind her, then she turned to finish finger-styling her hair. In the reflection, she saw Quincy give Bert a hesitant smile. Jordan's stomach dropped at the warmth in her gaze and instantly felt jealous, wanting that look directed at her.

"Hi, Bert. Thanks for all you do for the community. I've been a supporter for years. I even attended your black and white ball last year. It was amazing."

"I'm always glad to hear that. Thanks for your ongoing support; it means so much." She met Jordan's eyes in the mirror. "Are you ready to go, hot rod?" Bert asked.

Jordan stuck her tongue out. "Yeah, I'm ready to give the fans what they want." She did a final check of her reflection and saw Quincy roll her eyes as she followed Bert to the door, causing Jordan an uncomfortable moment of insecurity. She hurried to catch Quincy, but as they came through the doors, they were swarmed by security. The guards walked them to the side of the stage and made a perimeter around them. Quincy wrapped her arms around herself, and her eyes darted around the room as the fans screamed when Jordan came into view. Jordan caught Quincy's pinky finger and gave it a small squeeze to help settle her. "Q, trust me, you'll be okay. Just stick with Bert, and you'll be taken care of, I promise. I just need to get the crowd ramped up for the race, make sure we're trending on the socials, and then we can go." She pushed Quincy's silken hair behind her ear. Her fingers tingled at the contact, and Quincy seemed to tremble at her touch. She'd give anything to explore that more, but she was brought back to the moment by the tap on her shoulder.

"Ms. Marsh, Bert's introducing you now," the staff member said and then directed her up to the stage.

Quincy gave Jordan a sweet smile and then leaned in to kiss her cheek. "I'll be fine. Good luck."

Jordan's heart rate doubled, and it wasn't from the fans or the fear of speaking in front of everyone. She wanted more contact, more kisses, but it wasn't the right time. When would it be? She climbed the stairs onto the stage to become *Jordan Fucking Marsh*: every lesbian's wet dream. She took a deep breath and looked out over the packed crowd. The butterflies in her stomach never seemed to lessen, no matter how many times she did this kind of thing. But all that mattered was that no one saw how she really felt. As long as they bought into the persona, she was doing her job.

"Hello, Long Beach. Thank you for being here tonight. I'm Bert Downey, the CEO for the Long Beach LGBTQ+ Center. Tonight, we're excited to have Ms. Jordan Marsh here. She's a true champion on the track but, more importantly, she's a champion of our community. In case you weren't aware, the Pink Triangle Racing team donates annually to our center. The publicity we've garnered by having a free sponsorship sticker on Ms. Marsh's car has brought in donations from around the world, and they've allowed us to advance our community outreach right here in Southern California. Please join me in giving a warm welcome to Ms. Jordan Marsh."

The crowd erupted as Bert passed the microphone to Jordan. She smiled and waved at the packed crowd. "Hello, LBC!" The crowd chanted her name, which filled Jordan with an intense jolt of energy that thrummed through her. Adoration like this never got old. "Thanks for coming out tonight to support the Long Beach LGBTQ+ Center, the Pink Triangle Racing team, and me. It's so amazing to feel your love, and I'm sending it right back to you." Jordan raised her arms, and the room erupted again.

"Jordan, Jordan, Jordan," the chant continued from the crowd.

Jordan was energized by the outpouring of support. So what if they didn't know her or care about her personally? They were still behind her, chanting her name, and she loved the attention. She made a heart sign with her hands. "Community is priceless. We each walk our own path in life to find our personal truth. At times we may need a guide or support along the way, and that's why our queer community is so important. When we stand up and show our true selves in a world that wants to keep us hidden, the impact is transformative. My journey hasn't been easy—hell, I'm still on it, but I know the value of owning my story, the worth of embracing my true self. I'm honored to represent the LGBTQ+ community in IndyCar racing and on the worldwide stage. I'll continue to do all I can to remove the stigma around our community and work to normalize attitudes toward queer people. Let's all do what we can for our neighbors no matter who they are, how they identify, where they're from, or who they love. Remember, it's not about how well you blend in but how boldly you stand out." She smiled at the roar of approval that met her words. Her own family might not approve of her, but her community damn well did.

"You've been an amazing crowd, Long Beach! None of this could've happened without Bert's leadership and your fantastic center. I'm a proud Filipina American, lesbian driver of the number twenty-two Pink Triangle IndyCar. I'm honored to have your support and partnership. I hope you'll join me at the track next Sunday for the LA Grand Prix, but if you can't make it, I hope you have a fabulous watch party at home. Share your experiences with us at #PinkTriangle. No matter what, I'll make you proud on race day. I'm gonna take that checkered flag and turn it into a rainbow one!" Jordan yelled and smiled broadly as she clapped along with the crowd.

The crowd started chanting her name again.

She waved and yelled, "Thank you," as she was directed by the center's staff off the other side of the stage. The swarm of waiting fans engulfed her, and her adrenaline spiked. Her vision tunneled when the beautiful faces of her fans surrounded her.

Bert met her at the base of the stairs. "Fabulous speech, as always. Come with me, Jordie. We've got some special fans who'd like to meet you."

Jordan followed Bert through the crowd, stopping to take photos with fans. She also autographed posters, checkered flags, and even breasts. The noise was deafening as people screamed for her attention. Bert pulled her behind a red velvet roped-off area where multiple people waited. She recognized a few of the celebrities from prior center events. She looked out to a line of female fans looking at her as though they were starving, and she was the feast. They looked her up and down, and she could tell they liked what they saw. She sent them her cockiest smile. *It's on.*

An hour passed in a flurry of fans, supporters, and press before Bert led her back to the green room. The energy from the crowd flowed through her like an electric current that she never wanted to disconnect from. Jordan let out a sigh as she plopped onto the sofa and put her feet up on the coffee table. "That was amazing, Bert. Thanks for setting all this up. The positive press for the team, the LAGP, and me will be awesome."

"Oh, shit, what happened to your friend? I lost track of her after your speech. I just assumed she came back here to wait for you like they all do."

Jordan rubbed her hands over her face. "Quincy. Damn, I forgot about her. All those women and fans. It just slipped my mind she was here." She dropped her hands from her face and looked at Bert. "You're right. Most women would wait, but she's not like most women. Man, I fucked this up. Do you think you can take a quick look around to see if she's here?" Jordan pushed up from the sofa and anxiously paced the room.

"Sure, let me go look." Bert gave Jordan a curious look before she left.

Jordan's excitement from the speech and the energy from the fans' love evaporated and was replaced with a dull ache in her gut as she paced the room. *I knew she was different. Why'd I think she'd be waiting around?*

Bert knocked and walked back into the room shaking her head. "No go. She's gone. The security watching your truck knew she was with you, so they let her leave a note on your windshield about an hour ago."

Jordan rubbed her temples, then sighed and shrugged. "Great. Well, nothing I can do now. Do you have someone to escort me out?" Jordan asked sharply. The dull ache intensified with the knowledge that she'd failed to keep her promise to Quincy.

"Let's go." Bert opened the door, and security flanked them on each side. The center had emptied of the fans, and only staff remained.

Jordan had to maintain her celebrity veneer, so she smiled and waved on her way out, but her stomach dropped like she was on a roller coaster when the cool night air hit her face. The white paper under her wiper blade was a physical reminder of her failure. *Nice speech. You looked busy, so I met up with some friends. Good luck at the Grand Prix! - Q.* Jordan turned to Bert. "What's that look for?" She didn't want Bert's judgment right now.

"Nothing, chica. I'm just surprised you care about this one, that's all."

"I don't care. I just feel bad that I fucked it up. But, I mean, what did she expect? Did she expect to latch onto me all night?" The lie tasted bitter on her tongue. She opened the car, screwed up the note, and tossed it inside. "On to the next, right, Bert? Thanks for tonight. I'll see you soon." Jordan hugged Bert briefly before she got in and drove off.

She was a few blocks away before she pulled off to the side. She picked the note up from the floor and smoothed the crumpled paper on the steering wheel, then read the message again. The gnawing feeling of shame ate at her for breaking her promise. She couldn't really blame Quincy for not sticking around. It wasn't like she needed to be shown off to anyone or pose for photos. *She was just there for you, dummy.* But Jordan was so used to going it alone that she wasn't ready to believe that could actually be true.

Chapter Ten

QUINCY WOKE UP TO a dry cotton mouth, a searing headache, and confusion as to where she was. She squinted and remembered leaving the note on Jordan's SUV outside the center. Her anger for letting her guard down rushed back too. She'd fallen for Jordan's emotional push-pull and made an idiot out of herself. As she lay on the couch rubbing her temples, the memories filtered in of the bar where Brett and his friends listened to her bitch incessantly about Jordan the player and the elitist world she lived in. "Tequila," she mumbled. She sat up on the couch, and the room swam around her. Brett came out of his bedroom, dressed and ready for the day. "Good morning," she said softly.

"Morning, sunshine. You don't look too good. Let me get you some juice and water," he said as he walked into the kitchen and returned moments later. "Drink this." Brett handed her the water and then sat next to her on the couch with his arm around her. "Feeling rough?"

"Like sandpaper. But the water is helping my cotton mouth." She rolled her eyes, then kept them closed to keep the room from spinning. She leaned into him for support. "Thanks for everything last night, especially for taking my drunk ass in."

"You bet, sweetie. We've all been there, and you know it." He squeezed her shoulder. "Q, you're an amazing woman, and you've got a lot to offer some very lucky woman. I know that Jordan pushed those buttons in you that you don't like. The ones that make you feel, the ones that make you open yourself up to all that stuff you shove down."

Quincy tried to disentangle from Brett's grasp. "That's not true.

She's a literal stranger. I don't know what you're talking about."

"Girl, please. I could tell when you walked into the bar that you were spiraling. To listen as you told us how Jordan made you feel discarded and dismissed hurt my heart." Brett pulled Quincy back into his embrace and turned her to face him. "It reminded me of how you looked after your relationship ended with Rochelle. Look, I know that Jordan is a force of nature that knocked you on your ass last night, but you'll get back up and be better for it." He lifted her chin and looked at her seriously. "You know I'll always be here for you. Don't give her your energy. You're Quincy Fitzgerald, dammit."

She sipped the water to keep from crying. He seemed to know she couldn't find her voice and waited until she was under control before he stood.

"Unfortunately, I need to go meet a special someone for brunch, but this discussion will be continued. I'll put coffee on to brew, and you can stay as long as you like. There's a travel mug by the pot for the ride home." He leaned down and hugged her.

"You're an angel. Now go have a fabulous brunch date," Quincy said.

An hour later, Quincy leaned back in the rideshare and sipped the hot black coffee in the travel mug. Traffic on the 405 was light this early on a Sunday, so she'd be home soon. The headache had eased, but being discarded by Jordan last night still stung. She'd known when Jordan came off stage and disappeared into the sea of adoring women that she'd forgotten about Quincy. She was a player, plain and simple. Just move on, she thought, as she passed billboards along the freeway emblazoned with reminders of the upcoming LAGP.

"Thank you," Quincy said to the rideshare driver before getting out. At her front door, Jada jumped up and down behind the glass. Quincy opened the front door, and Jada ran out to greet her, circling her legs. She rubbed Jada's ears. "Are you happy to see me, sweet girl? I bet you'll be happier to have your breakfast."

She completed Jada's morning routine, accompanied by lots of belly rubs to make up for being gone overnight. She slipped into a hot shower and tried to wash off last night's events. She couldn't stop the images of Jordan in her bikini or her strong persona as she held the audience in awe last night. *Damn that woman.* Why couldn't she keep the image of Jordan walking away into the horde of women out of her mind?

Quincy dressed and returned to her den to relax and check her messages. The only text notification came from Lauren.

Hi, Q, hope you're having a better day! I wanted to let you know Trish won't be able to make the BBQ, but I'll be there. Did you start your packing for the Cook Islands yet? At work, so response may be sketchy.

Quincy was bummed Trish wouldn't be there, since it'd been over a month since they'd last seen each other. But at least she had one good friend coming. *Thanks for the heads-up. Sorry to miss seeing your better half. Give her my love. Maybe we can chat later? I've got an update on the Jordan front, and no, I haven't started packing!* Quincy grimaced after she sent the text, not sure she wanted to relive last night. Right now, she wanted to decompress with the morning talk shows and Jada. The thirty-minute LA local news lineup included missing children, crime, and a forecasted heatwave. The sports section was full of updates on the forthcoming race as the sportscaster stood beside an IndyCar.

"The LA Grand Prix course opens today to all teams and drivers. Each driver will be allowed two warm-up and two full-speed laps to familiarize themselves with the course changes this year. The field remains open as to who'll lead the pack of twenty-two drivers in the pole position. Will it be Kent Carver, Jordan Marsh, or a rookie? Whoever that lucky driver is, they'll win a million-dollar payday, provided by Paramount Studios, for capturing the pole. Our team coverage continues of the LA Grand Prix as we hear from Diamond Phoenix, our celebrity correspondent. This has been Lenny Fremont reporting from Paramount Studios."

Quincy groaned at the photos of the drivers as they flashed past. Why did Jordan have to be such an entitled ass? Why couldn't she be that hot and be...well, just a nice person?

"Thank you, Lenny. I'm Diamond Phoenix reporting from the IndyCar Racing Expo at the Loews Hollywood Hotel. The Expo was kicked off this morning by LA Mayor, Sharon Glass. She said that the city of LA was excited to host the LA Grand Prix once again. The IndyCar Racing Expo, which you can see behind me, allows fans to meet their favorite drivers, learn more about IndyCar racing, and buy all kinds of gear. We can't forget it's LA, and the large celebrity-infused parties planned all week will rival Oscar week. The city is roaring with life as the annual LA Grand Prix hits town, and we'll be covering it all. Check our socials for updates and invites to events and parties. I'm Diamond Phoenix reporting from the IndyCar Racing Expo."

Quincy clicked off the TV. "I'm glad I won't have to deal with all of that celebrity nonsense." Her phone pinged with an email. She read the message from the LAGP medical team, asking for her to confirm her contact information for tonight's meeting. It shouldn't have surprised her that they'd sent an update, given that the race prep was underway. She looked down at Jada, keeping a wary side-eye on her.

"This is going to be so cool." Quincy felt like a kid at Christmas as she read the details. They'd cover the driver's restraint system, removal of an injured driver from the car, helmet removal, IndyCar protocols, and race day team locations. She hugged her phone to her and a buzz of excitement she hadn't had in a long time zipped through her.

"Screw that promotion. What do you think? Should I look for a job that gets me this excited?" Quincy asked Jada, who looked up briefly before heading outside. Her mind slipped back into thoughts about Jordan. "Dammit, Quincy, let it go." *But what if I see her?* Could Jordan get her fired or make the job complicated because of last night? Quincy headed into her office. It was unlikely, but a small kernel of hope remained that she'd see her. *You need to focus.* Quincy decided to take advantage of the late meeting time and did her research on previous medical emergencies at other races. The videos were sobering, and she made notes about what she saw and what she might have questions on.

She spent the rest of the day relaxing and doing her best not to think about Jordan. She reviewed her trip plans she'd started on an Excel sheet and lost hours researching the various places she might want to go. Lunch was an enormous salad delivered from her favorite local place, accompanied by a National Geographic program on deep-sea diving. If it hadn't been for sneaky thoughts of Jordan intruding, it would have been an idyllic day.

Chapter Eleven

Jordan had nonstop positive notifications on her socials from fans, plus texts and emails from friends and family praising her words and representation from the LGBTQ+ Center event last night. Pumped by the outpouring of support and that fact that her followers had increased by over one hundred thousand since yesterday, she took to her socials to reciprocate. *TY for the love & support! Join the team at #PinkTriangle.* She did all she could to ignore her parents' disparaging comments, which also flooded her inbox.

Jordan, you really need to stop using such profane language when you speak in public, it makes you appear uneducated. I'm sure Tina wrote a wonderful speech before you tarnished it with your language. We've discussed this with you, and you know that every time you bring up your lesbian status in public, it reflects poorly on your dad and me. Our club friends feel uncomfortable with your sexuality, so stop flaunting it. And what made you say you're Filipina American? Was that your Tito John's doing? You are American, plain and simple. Don't let him into your head. At least you were dressed better than you were in the club photos from last week. Who's the blond woman with you in the pictures? She didn't look your type. Is she new security? Your Dad and I don't think we will make the race Sunday.

She knew it was wishful thinking that being true to herself about her culture, sexual identity, and the way she lived her life would ever be accepted by the people who should love her unconditionally. She usually didn't allow it to bother her, but sometimes it cut deeper than it should. Today was one of those days. She'd been busy with multiple sponsor events and was now running late for her race team's meeting. The text unsettled her and reinforced that she really was alone. She blew out a breath and headed into her RV for a brief reprieve from her responsibilities. She had to focus on racing and the team's needs but to do that, she had to put her mom's comments out of her mind. She rolled her shoulders to stretch out the tension in her neck and looked at herself in the mirror.

"When are you going to be the one in control? When will you live your truth, like you told the crowd last night, instead of hiding behind a persona?" She was unable to meet her own eyes. "Well, fine, it's not going to be today. Get focused, Jordie." As she stepped out of her RV and into the bright California sun, her phone pinged. She looked down at it with a scowl, expecting another virtual punch from her mom.

Jordie, just reminding you about the family party tonight at Ate Theresa's. Get there when you can. Food will be on around seven. We all hope to see you. Love you.

She let out a deep breath, relieved it was Tito John and not her mom. *Shit.* She'd completely forgotten about the family dinner. The pull of her mom's voice that warned her to stay away from her extended family played through her mind. She decided to think for herself and join the party tonight. Fuck anyone telling her what to do anymore. *Hi, Tito John. Busy day here, but I'm hopeful I'll make the party after I've done the race prep. Hope to see you later. I love you too!* She hustled down the paddock, walking between the different race teams, waving and saying hi as she went.

"Jordan, wait up." Tina grabbed her arm and directed her away from foot traffic. "Why'd you take that beach trash to the center's party? I told you she wasn't good for your image. I've got plenty of women ready to be on your arm who *will* help your celebrity status. Don't contact her again, or there may be consequences."

If I won't take that from my parents, I'm certainly not taking that from you. Jordan towered over Tina, her anger redlining. "You don't get to threaten me. Quincy isn't beach trash, and I'll do whatever I want." Her pulse throbbed in her temple. "You don't get to tell me who to date or any fucking thing about my personal life, frankly."

Tina crossed her arms. "This's hardly me threatening you, Jordan. We both know what happens when you do what you want. We've seen what happens when no one guides you the way I do. And really, you're off the rails if you think a normal person would last a day in your world. Think about how it will affect her. And don't expect me to clean it up when she goes to the press crying about her broken heart and what a womanizer you are."

"Fuck you, Tina. I don't need this today." Jordan pulled her arm away from Tina's grasp and jogged the remaining distance to her team's RV, its headquarters on the road. Joe Driscoll, her lead mechanic, held the door open for her and tapped his watch. "I know, Joe. Tina held me up." Jordan climbed into the RV. "Hi, team, I'm sorry I'm late. We should get started, so we don't miss our track time today," she said and sat at the table.

The team packed the RV as Joe, her lead engineer, Nate Franklin, and her spotter, Randy, ran the meeting. They outlined the IndyCar updates, which included new protective measures for crew and spectators, as well as the emergency evacuation plans along the course, and Sunday's race schedule of activities. Once the general race information was covered, most of the team left. Jordan met each team member at the door and gave them each a high five.

Jordan stayed for the strategy planning with Nick and Joe. "I hear the car's running well, but a few laps around the course today will tell the full story. Let's talk strategy before I take her out this afternoon."

Two hours later, Jordan's adrenaline spiked as she floored her car on the second warm-up lap. The joy she had behind the wheel compared to nothing else in her life. "Joe, the car feels solid, the steering was responsive, and the suspension needs only minor adjustments," she said into her helmet microphone, ready to get up to racing speed for the final two laps. "Let's see what she can do." She hit the throttle on her first timed lap and completed it at 1:11, and then the second lap at 1:10.

"Good driving, Jordie. Bring her back in," Joe instructed from the pits.

"The car feels like a winner. Great work, team. There're only minor adjustments needed." Jordan maneuvered the car back into the pit and waited for her crew to help her out. A 1:10 was a respectable speed, but it was only the third fastest speed of the day.

"Well, your run was good enough to keep you in the fast crowd. We just need to improve on it." Joe took Jordan's helmet as she climbed from the car.

"I agree. The suspension on the left front was loose around the turns, and you know the streets of LA; they can be rough."

"We'll work on the car. Third place for the first day of practice runs isn't bad."

"It's not bad, but it's not the top position. You know I want pole or at least the front row come Sunday." Jordan knew the car could get her there. She'd just need to put in the work to improve her track times. That started with reviewing today's data.

An hour later after everyone but Joe had left the garage, Jordan felt they had a working plan. "Okay, Joe. After analyzing everything, we agree that pole position is the plan?" Her phone pinged for the thousandth time, and Joe growled.

"Jesus, Jordie, is that thing ever going to stop buzzing?"

"Sorry." She pulled the phone out of the leg pocket of her race suit to stop the alarm from blaring and then looked at the notification and swore softly.

"Yeah, Jordie, pole position is the plan. You have somewhere to be?" Joe looked up from the computer screen while she checked her hair in the chrome of his RV.

"Yeah, we'll have to discuss this later. I need to get going. I'm late for the Medical Safety Support class Tina volunteered me for. Let me borrow one of your spare hats. I've got helmet head," she said, running her hand through her hair.

He dug into his bag on his golf cart and handed one over.

"Thanks, Chief. We'll get into it first thing tomorrow." Jordan grinned and headed off. She thought about the car, and her excitement grew. If everything went to plan, they'd be able to make her the first woman pole-sitter and possible winner of the LAGP. Whatever mess the rest of her life was in, she was good at this part.

Chapter Twelve

Quincy was impressed with how much Paramount Studios embraced IndyCar on their lot. There were race-themed decorations everywhere that only elevated her excitement. She walked through the racing paddock and the race teams' garages on her way to the Top Gun conference room. The smell of hot rubber, gasoline, exhaust fumes, and oil permeated the air and took her back to the track from her youth. The laughter and clanking of tools provided a percussive soundtrack, before it was interrupted by the whine of an IndyCar being started. She had to get to her meeting, but she wanted more than anything to explore the racing paddock. Her watch alarm pinged, indicating she had to hustle. She'd need some time to allow her heart and mind to settle from the joy she was experiencing from being here.

She entered the conference room and spotted the sign-in desk. "Hello, my name is Quincy Fitzgerald, NP."

"Hi, Ms. Fitzgerald. Please sign in, grab your packet, and sit wherever you like. We'll get started shortly," said the woman staffing the table.

Quincy did as she was told, then headed into the room filled with local paramedics, physicians, and nurse practitioners ready to support the traveling IndyCar Medical Care team for the racing weekend. Although some of the medical professionals were strangers, she knew many of those present. She introduced herself to the different attendees and took a seat. She watched as a middle-aged woman with flowing black hair and kind eyes stepped in front of the group.

"Ladies and gentlemen, please take a seat, and we'll get started.

My name is Nancy Alvarez, and I'm the Director of the LA Grand Prix Health and Safety team. We, and IndyCar, want to thank you all for your time and clinical support of the LAGP. We'll start with an introduction by our drivers, followed by hands-on training. During the evening, you will have multiple opportunities to ask questions. I'll now turn it over to one of our IndyCar drivers, Mr. Kent Carver."

A short man with slicked back hair and a lopsided cocky smile exposing blindingly white teeth stood in front of the gathered medical team. "Hi, you likely know me as the best IndyCar driver of all time, and I know it's an honor for you to be here with me. I'll be available for autographs later tonight."

Quincy realized he was completely serious. *Boy, this is gonna be a long night.*

"Let's be clear; my role tonight is to make sure you don't kill us on race day, so I expect for you to pay attention. Of course, Nancy and IndyCar had me take time away from my busy schedule to perform this training, because there's no one better than me to make sure you're ready." He placed his hands on his hips and puffed out his chest. He locked eyes with Quincy and gave her a wink along with a creepy smile.

Ugh. She looked away and surveyed the room. It was clear that the rest of the medical team was pissed at his dismissive attitude toward a room of seasoned staff. She knew of Kent Carver, and while he *was* one of the top drivers, he was also reported to be a misogynistic and homophobic ass. If this current behavior was anything to go by, the rumors were certainly on point. She listened as he droned on about driving as though he had divine intervention.

Quincy jumped when the back door of the conference room slammed closed. Another driver in a baseball cap and racing suit emblazoned with sponsors' names joined Kent at the front. Quincy didn't recognize Jordan until she saw those dazzling eyes shielded under the hat. She took the opportunity to check her out. It looked like Jordan had been racing all day, and she looked smoking hot, all sweaty and dirty and still with helmet lines marking her face.

Quincy's fingers tingled at the prospect of following the lines that tracked from her eyes down to her full lips.

Quincy recognized that she'd just gotten what she'd secretly wanted all day. Despite everything that happened last night, she couldn't stop the attraction and the swarm of butterflies in her stomach. But she needed to stop her infatuation and walk away. Jordan only saw Quincy as arm candy and not relationship material. She'd had enough of that already and had to protect her heart from any further damage. Quincy tried to control her expression as Jordan scanned the audience with a neutral look, but when she spotted Quincy, she raised her eyebrows and gave her a small smile and the lesbian nod. Quincy's heartbeat thumped in her ears so loud that she didn't notice Kent had stopped speaking and Nancy had taken over.

"Thank you, Kent, for sharing your experience. Ladies and gentlemen, if you'll excuse my interruption, another driver, Jordan Marsh, has arrived to help us with the demonstrations and safety overview. Kent and Jordan will each take half of the class to the race cars parked in back, and they'll go over the safety apparatus and how to get the drivers out in case of an emergency. It's imperative that each group practice on one of the drivers before they leave today."

Quincy kept her eyes on Nancy, but she felt her skin crawl as Kent stared at her. She knew that her blond hair attracted all kinds, but she wasn't interested. Jordan seemed to follow his gaze before she stepped forward.

"I apologize for being late. I'll take this half of the room to perform the safety demos." Jordan's tone brooked no argument as she gestured to Quincy's side of the room.

Quincy stood and walked with her team behind Jordan toward the door. Just as Jordan passed Kent, he grabbed her left arm.

"You're such a bitch, always in the way. Mark my words, Marsh, I'll make sure you're out of racing for good," he said then pushed Jordan away from him.

Jordan stumbled forward then regained her balance. "Whatever, Carver. Keep dreaming. You know I'll beat you on Sunday like I have the last few races. You'll be second to a woman, again. Checkered flag for me, nothing for you, as usual." She smiled and walked away.

The venom in Kent's voice riled Quincy. Entitled bullies simply pissed her off. "You aren't too bright, Kent. Everyone just heard you threaten Jordan, and if anything questionable happens, you'll be the first person they look at."

Kent sneered. "Who're you to talk to me? Mind your own damn business. My side of the room, outside now," he shouted and stormed away.

Quincy knew she should have stayed out of it, but her heart instinctively defended Jordan and her honor, regardless of what her head told her.

Chapter Thirteen

Carver is such an asshole. He may be the current IndyCar points leader, but he was also Jordan's nemesis on and off the track. He believed women were best at home, barefoot and pregnant, doing exactly as their man told them to. Everyone on and off the track knew his thoughts and opinions on women because he made his feelings known every chance he got. Why they asked him to be part of tonight's training, she'd never know, but saving Quincy from his greasy paws was the least she could do to make up for last night.

She stepped out of the conference room into what seemed like high noon. The parking lot where the two drivers and their respective demonstration race cars sat was illuminated like they were the stars of a movie. Jordan didn't want to overthink it, but it felt...good to have Quincy there in her world. Her silky hair blew in the evening breeze and revealed her graceful neck that Jordan wanted to taste. She radiated a calm confidence that drew Jordan to her like a bee to honey. She was quite simply breathtaking.

Jordan took a deep breath and turned away from Quincy to collect her thoughts before she began the important safety training. "We've got a lot to cover, so let's get started. God willing, I'll be your pole-sitter come race day. To my left, we have Mr. Felix Harper, an IndyCar representative, and Mr Terry Burnett, who's a paramedic and part of the traveling IndyCar Safety team. These gentlemen are here to ensure we train you properly and answer any questions you may have during this hands-on session. Mr. Harper, I believe you wanted to say something?"

"Thank you all for being here," Felix said. "You were selected for your medical knowledge and skills. The local support provided to our traveling safety team is paramount to a successful and safe race. While this was covered in your online training, I need to state again that only IndyCar's Safety team will extract drivers from the cars, should that become necessary. The reason we provide the hands-on training tonight is to be prepared for the "what if" situation. What if a driver is in harm's way due to fire, and there's a delay to the safety team getting there? What would you do? Well, we'll go over that. Let me be clear that the medical teams must be ready to provide care as soon as the driver is extracted from the car, no matter who does the extraction. We know the drivers will be in your capable hands. Terry, did you want to add anything else?"

Terry nodded. "I know from the selection process that each of you has trauma or emergency response experience, and that's a good foundation. The speed of these high-tech cars will make this much different than your usual freeway crash. The cockpit is complicated, and while we'll touch on this tonight, we're hoping you won't have to see it in action. If the safety teams do perform an extraction, we'll then need your team to board and collar the driver and take them to the trauma center. Please feel free to ask any questions you have, but let's get the demonstration underway. Jordan, take it away."

Jordan stood in front of the parked IndyCar and smiled. She enjoyed working with these teams, but an unusual anxiety fluttered through her when she saw Quincy watching her intently. She raised her arms to herd the group closer to her and the IndyCar. "Okay, everyone, please come a little closer. Contrary to what you may have read in the tabloids, I won't bite." Jordan winked at Quincy, who gave her a small smirk in return. The rest of the crowd laughed and moved forward. "This is the moment you've all waited for, the Jordan Marsh striptease." Jordan unzipped her dark blue racing suit down to her waist. Now that she had everyone's attention, she could begin.

"I know you received prior online training on our race gear, and while each driver wears something a little different, it's all mostly the same. I want you to all have a good look at the pieces of safety gear that are in place, so you've got a baseline." Jordan pulled open her racing suit like Superman and pointed to her light gray undergarment embroidered with her sponsors logos. "This is my breathable Nomex layer all the way down to my socks, which are heat and flame resistant. On the outside, we've got our fire-retardant Nomex racing suit, gloves, and boots, which allow layers of driver safety from road rash as well as fire. We've got a fire-retardant hood that's secured into our racing suit, and then we add our carbon fiber helmet and the all-important neck support, or HANS device. We're driving the ultimate convertible with our open cockpit, so it's imperative to have a secure helmet and neck support." Jordan grabbed the steering wheel from the car and handed it to Felix. "Terry's going to assist and secure me in the car, and then we'll begin our hands-on demonstrations."

The class remained engaged as Jordan completed the verbal instructions on the layers of racing safety. Each medical team included two paramedics and one provider, and they were all given education on the clothing, helmet, race car, and the six-point seat belt release mechanism needed to remove a driver. The paramedic teams were instructed on release and extraction of Jordan from the race car in case of an emergency. Terry provided standby assistance and ensured each team met the necessary standards. The final element after each extraction was to complete the safe removal of the helmet and the head restraint system. The training took over an hour, and Jordan watched as Quincy stood back during the extraction and only came forward to assist with the helmet removal. Her expression was so serious that Jordan couldn't help but wink at her once they removed her helmet for the last time, and she enjoyed the deep flush of Quincy's cheeks.

Jordan sat up from the gurney and clapped. "You've all done amazing work. We're almost done, but I wanted to offer to teach the providers how to remove the six-point restraint if you're interested. Are you?"

They replied with a collective yes.

"Okay, I think we'll start with you." Jordan pointed at Quincy and grinned. She wasn't a distraction if she was involved in the safety aspects, right?

Chapter Fourteen

THE SMIRK ON JORDAN'S gorgeous face put Quincy on edge. This was serious, but Jordan didn't seem to be taking it as such. Quincy was prepared for her team's turn at extraction, board, and collar, but as she watched a lifeless-appearing Jordan removed from the car over and over, the reality of the situation took hold. The idea of Jordan being injured or worse on Sunday turned Quincy's stomach. She looked up and met Jordan's eyes before she could hide the fear.

Jordan frowned slightly before turning to the group. "Okay, so this time the MD/NPs will be focused on the restraint release only. No extraction. This is for educational purposes only." Jordan climbed back into the car, and Terry reapplied half of the restraint system. "Quincy, you're first. Are you okay?" Jordan motioned Quincy over to the car, while her paramedic team hung back, talking amongst themselves.

"Yes, I'm, fine. Where do you want me?" Quincy leaned over the car and looked down into the snug cockpit to begin her lesson. Her heart hammered in her chest at the scent of Jordan's cologne mixed with the engine oil.

"As you can see, there's a right and left shoulder belt which makes up part of the six-point restraint system," Jordan said, verbally directing Quincy to the shoulder restraint release strap as she'd done with all the other teams. She looked around and then took Quincy's hands and placed them on the strap, right over her breasts.

"Oh. That's the strap," Quincy said, breathless as she felt the hard nipples underneath Jordan's racing suit.

Jordan kept hold of Quincy's hands but gave her a smug look. "This is the release for the shoulder strap. As you can see, they meet the lap belt and the anti-sub strap at the black circular piece, which is the rotary buckle. Why don't you go ahead and snap all the belts into the rotary buckle? I can help you if you like." Jordan moved Quincy's hands slowly down her torso and to the rotary six-point quick release. She continued past the buckle and pressed Quincy's right hand between her thighs while she squeezed her legs closed, trapping her hand.

"I think I might need some help," Quincy whispered. The searing heat burned through her right up to her cheeks, and her breathing stuttered.

"Great work on finding the restraint system. Now that it's locked, let's unlock it by turning the rotary buckle ninety degrees to give me my release," Jordan said.

Quincy decided to play along. "Like this, Jordan?" Quincy pulled the rotary release away from Jordan's body, tightening the belts so they pulled hard between her legs.

Jordan exhaled loudly before Quincy turned the rotary buckle which released her from the restraints.

"You've got it. Great job. Extraction wouldn't be expected from the providers, but it's never bad to have as much safety knowledge as possible on the track." Jordan smiled warmly as some of the others moved closer.

Quincy stepped back from the car and sucked in the cool night air to slow her racing heart. She crossed her arms to cover her nervous energy. She glanced around the group and waited for a comment about her fondling Jordan, but it didn't come. She was relieved that no one noticed their cockpit escapade, but she couldn't erase the memory of Jordan's firm body under her hands.

"Okay, who's next?" Jordan asked, and the other NP stepped up for training.

She better not get the intimate hand-holding that I did. Quincy shook her head at the way her palms still tingled.

The two groups reconvened in the conference room to complete the training. The logistics of how and when they'd respond to an accident were explained, and Quincy's team was provided their trackside station location for race day. The directive from race control made it clear that any medical transport would go to LAMC for medical care. Quincy enjoyed working with Tim and Paul, her paramedic team. They were very professional, and she knew they'd work well together on race day.

"Okay, everyone. When I call your name, come up and get your packet. It'll have your race suits, credentials, and instructions on where to meet for Sunday's race," Nancy said, then she read off the names, and her staff handed out the IndyCar duffels. The race suit was royal blue and had yellow trim. It had the LA Grand Prix logo across the chest and *Medical Team* emblazoned in red on the back, with NP on her left arm in white. Quincy's youthful excitement for racing came through when she stepped up next to the IndyCar. She took a selfie with the suit and texted it to her family with *#INDYdreams #lifegoals* and a picture she'd taken earlier of Jordan standing next to the car. She knew her family would love the pictures, and they'd be shown around town in no time. Her phone beeped almost immediately with a reply from both her dad and sister. Her dad just gave her a thumbs up while her sister Katie replied, *Get those #INDYdreams girl, so proud of you, let's talk soon! xo.*

Quincy texted back a quick reply, then looked up from her phone to see Jordan standing in front of her with her hands on her hips.

"Fancy seeing you here. I guess you didn't feel like mentioning this last night?" Jordan raised her eyebrows so high they were buried in her hat.

Quincy mirrored her stance and scoffed. "Right, because you were so interested in what I had to say that you stuck around to chat last night... Oh, that's right, you didn't. You left to dive into a harem of women, leaving me standing there like an idiot. So no,

I didn't feel like mentioning that I'm actually a huge racing fan, and I was really excited about doing this until last night. But I'm determined not to let anything ruin it." Quincy's blood pressure rose once more, and she wasn't about to back down.

"Jordan, can you come over here for a minute?" Nancy asked from across the room.

"I'll be right there," she said.

Quincy deflated as Jordan walked away. "Yeah, you go, as usual," she said under her breath. She decided to take the opportunity to leave and grabbed her new gear. She should've known Jordan was just teasing her in the car. She was an idiot for thinking it meant anything. She just wanted a quick good time, and Quincy had let her have it. She headed out with a few of the others.

"You've got my number if you need anything," Quincy said to Tim and Paul before they each headed toward their vehicles in the parking lot. She leaned into the back to dump her bag and as she closed the door, she met some resistance.

"Hi, again." Jordan gave Quincy a hesitant smile.

"Oh, you startled me. Did you need something?" She noticed the looks sent their way from the others, and her unease began to build. "What do you want from me, Jordan? We both know I don't fit into your celebrity lifestyle or your income bracket, and I don't ignore people and leave them to their own devices after parading them around at events. So what exactly is it that I can do for you?"

"What're your plans for the rest of the night?" Jordan asked.

"Did you not hear me? I'm not giving you the opportunity to make a fool of me again."

Jordan breathed out slowly. "You're not making this easy." She took Quincy's left hand and slowly caressed the top of it with her thumb. "I didn't get a chance earlier to tell you that I'm sorry for being a pompous ass last night. I'm sorry I broke my promise that you'd be taken care of. I dissolve into the public persona, the person the cameras and fans want to see, and I forget there are still some people who could like me for *me*. I'm sorry I hurt you.

I'm not surprised you left. But honestly, I was worried about you, and I'm so glad you're okay." She sighed deeply and bit her bottom lip. "Since you're here, would you like a tour of our garage? And maybe consider joining me for some of the best Filipino food around? No pressure. After everything, I'd understand if you're not interested."

Quincy couldn't think straight when Jordan touched her. The sincerity was clear in Jordan's expression, and Quincy melted like ice at the beach. "Dammit, you drive me nuts. I told myself to walk away and not engage, but *you're* the one not making this easy." She pulled her hand away and closed her door. "You don't know this about me, but I've been a big fan of IndyCar since I was a kid. A chance to see your garage up close is hard to pass up. I'm not so sure about dinner. We'll need to take one thing at a time."

"Okay, I understand. But that's a yes to seeing the garage?"

"It's a yes." Quincy shook her head and internally chastised herself for folding so easily. *I'm in so much trouble.* "Should I leave my car here?"

Jordan smiled. "No, we'll move your car over into my parking spot until we get back." She walked around the car and sat in the passenger seat. "Okay, let's open her up and see what you've got under that hood," she said and smiled broadly.

Focus. Being so close to Jordan made her heart pound like she was about to code. She wondered if Jordan could hear it in the quiet car, so she let out a deep breath and followed Jordan's directions. They made their way around the building where the class had been held and into a night of unknowns. As Quincy drove across the studio lot and further into the racing paddock, she couldn't help but feel like she was in a dream. Her Honda was flanked by the different racing teams' garages, which were set up next to their transport carriers emblazoned with the different racing team logos. Each area had organized carts filled with tool chests, car parts, and stacks of Firestone tires. Even at this hour, the clanking of tools and the high-pitched buzz of a wheel gun accompanied their drive-by. The area was alive with people roaming around in colorful racing suits and street clothes. No one paid them much attention until Quincy maneuvered her car into Jordan's visitor parking spot.

"Lady, you can't park here. That's a reserved spot." A tall white-haired man dressed in a Pink Triangle polo shirt and pants came toward them. He stood with his hands on his hips in the beam of her headlights.

Jordan jumped out of the car, and he gave her a big smile.

"Oh, it's you. I didn't recognize the car. Sorry about that, Jordan," he said.

"No problem, Joe. Thanks for protecting my real estate." She gave him a side hug. "I want you to meet Quincy Fitzgerald. Quincy, this is Joe Driscoll, my crew chief. Quincy is a big IndyCar racing fan. *And* she's going to be a medical provider on the Medical Support teams for Sunday's race."

"Hi, Quincy. Sorry about the parking misunderstanding; it's just that people park anywhere. I have to protect our spots; I hope you understand. Wow...the medical team. You'll certainly have one important job on Sunday."

"It's a pleasure meeting you, Joe," Quincy said. "You're right about that, but I'm hoping I'll just get to watch, totally uninterrupted by any emergencies at all. I imagine you're busy. I'm sorry to have pulled you away from what you're doing."

"No bother at all. Would you like me to show you around?" Joe elbowed Jordan in the ribs. "You could get the tour by Jordie, but this is my domain, and I can guarantee it'll be worth it."

Quincy liked Joe immediately. She smiled widely and nodded, feeling like a kid in a candy store as he led her into the garage. "If you don't mind?" Quincy looked over at Jordan, who seemed totally relaxed.

"No, of course I don't mind. I agree that Joe gives the best tours, usually with a souvenir at the end if you're lucky." Jordan pointed to an RV parked to the right of the garage. "I'm going to take a quick shower, and I'll meet you in the garage in about fifteen minutes."

Joe took Quincy's arm and patted it as he waved at Jordan. "Don't you worry. I'll keep Quincy entertained."

Jordan disappeared into her RV, and Quincy swallowed hard, imagining her naked body in the shower. She shook her head and turned to Joe. "I'm all yours. Give me the two-dollar tour."

"For you, the million-dollar one."

Joe gave her an enthusiastic tour of the garage, then he followed that with the team's specialized transport trucks that hauled equipment, race cars, and people from one city to the next. He had stories for each section of the tour that left Quincy in tears with laughter. He ended his tour at Jordan's rainbow-wrapped navy blue, pink, and white race car. Quincy gawped at it in awe. "This car is a mechanical marvel. I've got goosebumps standing next to her." Quincy ran her hands up and down her arms.

"I can tell this isn't your first race. How do you know so much about racing?"

Quincy lightly ran her fingers over Jordan's name painted near the cockpit. "My dad. I grew up in a small town in Illinois, and he took my sister and me to just about any race running when I was a kid It could be motorcycle or stock car, it didn't really matter. It was the speed, noise, and mechanics of it all that he loved. The one race we attended religiously was the Indianapolis 500. The Granddaddy of all races if you ask him. He'd always try to get us into Gasoline Alley, closer to the cars and drivers. It never happened, but it was magical." Quincy looked up at Joe with a warm smile from the memory. Talking about it made her think about the vibration in her chest as the cars sped by, the smell of rubber and popcorn, and the feel of the first warm sun of summer that left her cheeks pink.

"Is he still alive?" Joe asked with kind eyes.

She startled at that question, lost in her own thoughts. "Yes, he's just older now and more likely to watch the race from an armchair than the grandstands. Thanks so much for taking the time to give me the tour. You've checked off some of the things I've had on my bucket list since I was a kid. It means a lot."

"You're welcome. It was fun to share our world with someone who really loves it." Joe looked over Quincy's shoulder. "Well, don't you clean up nice?"

Quincy turned as Jordan walked up to them, unable to take her eyes from her. Her hair was styled as a tousled quiff over her left eye, and tortoiseshell glasses covered her gorgeous eyes. She wore a purple button-down tucked into her dark jeans and soft black leather boots. Her unique scent, which was a clean juniper blend, filled the air around them. "I agree with Joe. You do indeed clean up well." Quincy's own engine purred as she checked Jordan out from head to toe. Now she really couldn't wait to see what the night had in store for them.

Chapter Fifteen

J ORDAN SMILED AT J OE , who'd seen her listening to Quincy's story as she leaned against the door. Quincy didn't seem to talk about personal things very often, and it was nice to hear them coming out so unfiltered. *Beauty, brains, and racing.* Could there be a more perfect woman? "Do you want to sit in the car? We can use your cell to take some pics to send to your dad?"

Quincy hesitated only for an instant. She looked between Joe and Jordan. "If you're sure I won't hurt anything, that would be amazing. Thank you." She smiled broadly at Jordan and handed her phone over.

Jordan helped Quincy into her seat. She loved the feel of Quincy's tight body in her arms. "Say cheese." Jordan backed up and got a great shot of Quincy sitting in the cockpit with a wide grin on her face. Then she took out her own phone and took another. That would be just for her.

"Let me get a picture of the two of you together." Joe held out his hand for Quincy's phone, then snapped a few shots. "Okay, I've got the serious ones, now how about something silly?" He directed the pair as Jordan leaned against the car. "Hold on, let me get the Polaroid. It's a tradition to take a Polaroid of anyone who sits in there." Joe came back and shot the picture with Quincy looking out at Jordan from inside the car.

Tradition? Jordan shook her head. There was no such thing. He'd use that picture to remind her of Quincy repeatedly. Not that she needed one. Jordan lifted Quincy out of the car and held her body snugly against her. Quincy slowly slid down her front until her feet were on the ground, and they were a breath apart. She couldn't shake the feeling that they fit together seamlessly.

"Thank you." Quincy gently kissed Jordan on the cheek before she broke the embrace and stepped back, an inscrutable look on her face. "Let's see your work," Quincy said to Joe as she took her phone back and thumbed through the pictures. "These are fantastic. This has been such a wonderful experience. I can't wait to share them with my family. Thank you both!" She held out her hand after Joe had shaken the Polaroid picture.

He was quite the photographer: he'd snapped not only the one of Quincy in the car, but also the two of them in their intimate embrace.

Joe pointed to the Polaroid of Jordan and Quincy together but slid the one of Quincy alone out of her hand and tucked it in his pocket. "A souvenir for the lady. I've got to get these old bones to bed, but please don't be a stranger," Joe said as he headed out of the garage.

"I won't. Goodnight," Quincy said but didn't look up from the photo.

"Goodnight, Joe," Jordan said. "We look good together." *Crap*. She shouldn't have said that out loud.

"Yes, we do," Quincy said softly as she wrapped her arms around herself like armor, the photo tucked against her side.

Jordan's phone pinged with a text message, and she checked it. Tito John was asking if she was going to make the party. Taking a chance, she said, "Do you still feel like some Filipino food?"

"I'm starving, but maybe you should give me a bit more information on where we're going. Will there be press around? I'm open to going, but let's not make too much out of it other than getting food."

"There won't be any paparazzi or fans. It's a low-key place, and you'll get to meet my tito, my Uncle John."

"Okay."

They headed to Jordan's car, and she drove toward her Ate Theresa's house, her mind working overtime with all the things she wanted to say. Another apology should probably be first. "I'm sorry again about last night. I totally get why you left and why you don't trust me."

"I accept your apology, but just so you know, I won't be dismissed like that again. I thought it best to leave instead of getting into a fight with you. I'm not arm candy, and I'm not interested in the limelight. If you don't have time for me, that's fine. But I'd rather not go to something with you at all than feel like some kind of hanger-on."

Jordan felt terrible about the whole night, and no amount of sorry would take back her actions. "You're right; I was disrespectful. Again, I'm sorry for my behavior. I'm still surprised you didn't mention your role in the LAGP when we were talking last night."

"Honestly, Jordan, I didn't think we'd ever see each other again, and it really wasn't like we had a ton of time to chat. I've got personal reasons for being part of the LAGP. I told Joe earlier about my dad taking my sister and me to races, but the best race was always the Indy 500. It was a tradition we shared and enjoyed then and now. When I saw a flyer at work about volunteering for the race on the medical crew, it seemed like an amazing experience to be behind the curtain. To gain access and be trackside for a race in my own backyard. I applied with no expectation of being chosen, so I was floored that they picked me. I'm living my childhood dream." Her cheeks turned a cute shade of pink, and she looked out the window. "I think I've overshared."

Jordan looked at her side profile in the glow from the dash and was again struck by her simple beauty. "I liked it, thank you." How long had it been since she'd dated someone so real?

"Joe seems very nice," Quincy said.

"Oh, he is. He's my surrogate father, mentor, and confidant when we're on the road. We've been friends for years. He's from New Mexico, and his family lives there year-round. He joins them there in the off-season. When I can't handle being around my own family, I hang out with his."

"How about you? Where did you grow up? I know what it says

in the biography provided by IndyCar, but I want the real Jordan Marsh story, from the source," Quincy said as a blush colored her cheeks.

Jordan shifted in her seat; the switch into personal territory was unsettling for her too. But if she wanted something real... She squeezed the wheel and then relaxed a little, hoping to release some of her anxiety. "What, you didn't read my Wiki page or my *Vanity Fair* article? I feel so common. Woe is me." She flung her hand against her forehead.

"Dramatic much?" Quincy asked, clearly working to hide a laugh.

"Okay, here we go. My name is Jordan Cavite Marsh. I'm twenty-seven, a Gemini, and I love long walks on the beach."

"Okay, so now sarcasm. I guess I'll grab a copy of *Vanity Fair*."

Jordan let out breath. She was about to blow it, yet again. "Okay, here are the ugly deets. I'm twenty-seven, a Gemini, and I *do* love long walks on the beach. I'm also the only child of a strict but checked-out Filipino dad and an American helicopter mom. I was born and raised in Maryland, outside the Beltway but within white privilege. My parents were very busy when I was growing up. They both worked in Washington, my dad for the Philippine consulate, and my mom for a clean energy think tank. They're now semi-retired, and they both teach at Georgetown. They still live in the house where I was raised." She swallowed hard, ready to let the next bit flow out. "I've never really fit the mold my parents created for me. While most kids I grew up with rode horses in fancy threads, I preferred a dirt track and torn jeans. I was heavy into go-karts and mini-bikes, and I fell in love with speed. It just so happened that I was also very good at racing, much to my parents' chagrin. I would've been fine going into professional racing earlier in life, but they forced me to go to college. It was a condition of their financial support, even if they never really backed my racing career. So I went to UCLA, my dad's alma mater, and completed a degree in mechanical engineering, which has served me well.

I haven't married, as I'm sure you know, and my 'lesbian lifestyle' remains a touchy subject for my parents."

She took a deep breath but plunged forward; it was too late to slam on the brakes now. "Today, I got a tersely worded text telling me to not flaunt my gayness. My mom can be relentless in her dictates for love, and my dad has written me off. We don't really speak any more unless we're forced to. The road has become my home over these past four years of racing. The different cities, time zones, and tracks along with the nonstop pressure to be the best has helped me keep from focusing on feeling like I let them down. I'll never be what they'd hoped for." Jordan gripped the steering wheel harder than ever.

Quincy was quiet for a moment. "Wow, that's a lot. It sounds like you and your parents have a challenging relationship. I can't believe they're still so judgmental after all your success. It's too bad they can't see beyond their own issues to know you. I mean, not that I know you all that well. It's just I feel very blessed to have my dad and sister as strong supporters of my life and my choices. It'd be hard for me to not have that." Quincy touched Jordan's arm briefly.

"Thanks for saying that. It's been that way for a long time. Nothing I can do about it. How about a topic change?" The vulnerability of pouring out her past, along with Quincy's support left her feeling raw.

"Okay, so, how many races are left for the season?"

Jordan couldn't believe she'd just shared all that information with Quincy without a non-disclosure agreement. What was she thinking? "There are two races left for points, but closer to ten if you include celebrity races or other events."

"How much longer do you plan to race?"

Jordan looked over at Quincy, surprised by the question. "I don't know. There have been job offers as a sports anchor for *Sports Now* and *Racer's Life*. I've also mulled over the idea of running my own team. It's only my fourth year in IndyCar, so I'd like to have a few more years before I leave the track. I'm aware it could all be over tomorrow, even though I'm still young, so it's tough to say. I love it, and I've never had a reason to stop nor a good enough offer to make me want to stop racing." Jordan shook her head, willing her mouth to stop running. "I'm not sure what truth potion you gave me, but please don't share any of this with anyone." Jordan glanced at Quincy.

"Of course, I won't." She looked a little baffled, and then her expression softened. "I'm sorry you even have to think that way."

The streetlights highlighted Quincy's hair, making her appear angelic. What would a normal life with someone like her look like? What the hell was she thinking? She was Jordan Marsh, racing superstar, a woman on each arm all the time. She had no business thinking about a "normal life" when she'd only known her for three days. She let her thoughts drift away as she pulled into the circular drive of her family's home.

"No restaurant then?" Quincy eyed the different cars parked along the drive.

"No, this is my Ate Theresa's house. Ate means big sister in Tagalog. She's an older cousin, and she's having a family party. We won't be here long. I just wanted to come see them and thank them for their support through the years. And well, it *is* the best Filipino food around. Are you ready to head in?"

Quincy bit her lip. "Sure. Why wouldn't I be ready to meet your family?"

Jordan closed her eyes. "I'm sorry. What was I thinking? I mean, I know what I was thinking. I wanted to hang out with you and them and have everything be great. We can leave—"

"It looks like the welcome wagon is here for you." Quincy pointed to some of her family members walking toward the SUV.

"I guess that means we're staying." Jordan waited until Quincy gave her a smile and a little shrug. "I'm going to say hi." She jumped out of the car. "Hey, everyone. We made it. Better late than never, right?" Jordan hugged and kissed each of her family members.

Tito John held her in a side hug. "Jordie, we're so glad you made it."

Ate Theresa looked her over. "You're too thin. You need to eat. Come inside."

Jordan fought back tears as their overwhelming love enveloped her.

"It's so good to see you. Who's this?" Tito Jack asked as they all looked at Quincy, who stood awkwardly beside the truck.

Quincy waved. "Hello, I'm Quincy, a friend."

Ate Theresa left the group and gave Quincy a hug. "Welcome to my home. My name's Theresa."

"Thanks for having me," she said. "Jordan told me you have the best Filipino food around, so I'm excited to be here."

Tito Jack motioned toward the front door. "Let's head inside. I'm sure the rest of the family will want to say hello,"

"Sounds good." Jordan held out her hand and was glad when Quincy took it. Again amazed at Quincy's ability to adapt to any situation, she squeezed her hand as they walked. "Thanks for joining me for family dinner."

"Jordie!" the family screamed from inside the front door as she came into the house. Every one of the nearly thirty party attendees crowded forward to give her a hug.

Jordan blinked away tears, the unwavering love and support overpowering, and cleared her throat. "I'm sorry I haven't seen you all in so long." She lifted one of the kids and swung her around, making her giggle.

"Don't you worry. I keep them up to date on your life off the track," Tito John said, and everyone nodded, their collective gazes moving toward Quincy.

Theresa pulled Quincy forward. "Everyone, this is Quincy. She's a friend of Jordan's and will be joining us tonight."

Everyone shouted out their greetings.

"Kamusta kayo," Quincy said, and the room erupted in laughter.

"Hey, we have an honorary Filipina!" one of the cousins said as the rest of the family looked pleasantly surprised.

Tito John chuckled. "I guess we do."

Quincy looked over at Jordan and Theresa. "I...I hope I said that right."

"Yes, amazingly you did. You'll have to share with us where you learned Tagalog. Now, let's get you in the front of the food line. Enjoy!" Theresa walked them to a buffet of food in chafing dishes was arranged on the table.

"Thanks, Ate," Jordan said as she let Quincy go ahead of her in line. "Let me know if you need any help with the food options."

"Thanks, but I'm familiar with Filipino food. Remember where I work? We have some of the best Filipino nurses around, and they always make sure I eat. Pancit, lechon, adobo, sisig, sinigang, turon, halo halo; you name it, I'll eat it. Except balut and bagoong. Those, not so much." Quincy scrunched up her nose and piled her plate full of the delicious delicacies on offer.

She's so damn perfect. She'd already overshared on the way there, so she decided to continue her truth-telling. "It sounds like you know these foods better than I do. I've had really limited exposure to my extended family, and you could count the family parties I've attended on one hand. I guess I always linked them to my parents, but they're nothing like them." A little weight fell from her soul, but it was emotional stuff she'd have to sort through later. "You continue to surprise me, and I really like that." Jordan grinned widely but she was uncertain how Quincy would take her oversharing, so she redirected the conversation back to the food. "I'm starving, and this all looks so good."

"It really does. I bet it tastes good too. I love to travel and try new dishes wherever I go. It's the best way to learn about a culture. I haven't traveled to the Philippines yet, but I've learned so much about the food from my work wives. They're always trying to feed me." Quincy smiled. "I'm hungry too. Let's eat."

The family's chatter continued until late in the evening. Jordan loved listening to the exploits of the kids, the aspirations of the people around her age, and the way the older relatives commented on all of it. And Quincy...she was relaxed and intelligent, and the family seemed to like her as much as Jordan did. At nearly midnight, Ate Theresa and Tito John escorted Jordan and Quincy outside, loaded down with Tupperware filled with leftovers.

"Salamut. Thanks for having me," Quincy said.

"It was wonderful having you and Jordie," Theresa said. "Don't be a stranger. If you ever need anything or want to swing by, you're always welcome. But we'll have to work on your mahjong game. Thankfully, your racing skills are much better." She hugged Jordan tightly. "And that one there," she whispered loudly, "she's a keeper. Better than those girls we see pictures of you with. Hang on tight."

Jordan's stomach flipped at both the acceptance and the idea that Theresa was right. "I'll do my best. Tonight was so special. I can't really explain what it meant to be here. I'll keep in touch." She hugged Theresa and John before getting behind the wheel. "Where to now?" she asked when they got to the bottom of the driveway, not wanting the night to end.

"My car, I think." Quincy hid a yawn behind her hand.

"Sounds good. It's late. Did you have a good time?"

Quincy rested against the soft leather headrest. "I had a wonderful time. Your family is so gracious and kind, and wow, that food was amazing."

"Yes, and yes." Jordan thought of the stories that were told, her memories that flooded back, and the simple joy of being a part of a real family. Sure, Tito Jack wanted to get inside information to bet on the race, and some of the cousins took nonstop selfies with her and posted on their socials, but it had still been a wonderful night. A lot of that had to do with Quincy being so grounded and real. Jordan's anxieties were nonexistent when she was around. What did that mean? And how the hell was she going to deal with it without screwing it up?

The ride back was quiet, and Quincy drifted to sleep. Jordan pulled through the outer gate at Paramount and reluctantly woke

Quincy by softly stroking her cheek.

"Wow, traffic was light. We're already here," Quincy said with a yawn as she rubbed her eyes. "You know, Jordan, you certainly do things in an interesting order. Our outing last night included a U-Haul, and tonight's included your family. I guess you're speedy in places other than the track. Good night." Quincy slipped out and headed to her car without waiting for a response.

Jordan followed Quincy out of her truck as the humor of the situation struck her. "Quincy, wait up. You make a good point." She hurried over to Quincy. "What should our third outing entail?"

"Outing three, huh? Well, it's already a new day, so we could just call this the third one."

"No, I think we can do better than that. Maybe moving in together?" Jordan failed to keep a straight face.

Quincy snickered. "Now, that *would* be speedy."

"Can I text you tomorrow once I see what my day is like?"

"Sure," Quincy said. "Do you have my number?"

Jordan handed her phone to Quincy. She entered her information and then called herself, so she had Jordan's number too.

"You're something else, do you know that?" Jordan gently tucked Quincy's hair behind her ear. "I'm not sure I can wait until then to taste you." She grazed Quincy's cheek with her lips, overcome with the faint smell of jasmine on her skin.

"Then don't," Quincy said breathlessly.

Jordan didn't waste any more time and as their lips met, time paused. Their kiss was soft and hesitant at first, a gentle exploration that spoke of longing and promise. It was a moment suspended in bliss, where the world around them faded away, and all that mattered was the closeness, the shared breath, and the undeniable magic of that perfect kiss. A kiss that weakened Jordan's knees with the rightness of it. And a response she'd never experienced with any woman before. She didn't want to break the embrace, but she slowly pulled back, knowing this was something she wanted to cherish and not rush. Quincy's dazed look told her she wasn't alone in the bliss.

Quincy's eyes refocused, and her control returned. "Um, I'm sorry, but I have to go," she said softly. Her hands shook when she directed the key fob at her car and unlocked it.

"Are you okay?" Jordan asked, concerned that she may have overstepped. She shoved her hands in her pockets to keep from pulling Quincy into her arms and devouring her luscious lips.

"I'm good...more than good." Quincy traced her fingers over Jordan's lips. "Thank you for a wonderful night."

"Thanks for coming to the family party. I like how this night is ending," Jordan said softly. "Will you please text me when you get home? I'm staying here tonight." She indicated the RV behind them.

"I will. Goodnight, Jordan." Quincy closed the car door and gave a final wave before she drove away.

Thirty minutes later, Jordan was still revved up with the lingering images of Quincy and their kiss when her phone chimed. She picked it up, excited to see the text like she was a teenager with her first crush.

Home safe. Sleep well.

She wanted to say so much, but she decided a simple message would do. *Sweet dreams.* Jordan undressed and got into bed. The fine cotton sheets caressed her naked body, and she thought back to Quincy's hands on her breasts in the cockpit. The reminder of Quincy's lips, her intoxicating scent, and the feel of her firm, slender body under Jordan's hands made her groan. Quincy Fitzgerald was becoming a distraction, whether Jordan liked it or not.

Chapter Sixteen

Quincy was distracted, and there was absolutely nothing she could do about it. The kiss was on playback in her mind, along with their conversations. She couldn't believe she'd kissed Jordan Marsh, and her lips burned with the memory. She stared at her lips in the bathroom mirror as though they'd changed.

She was startled by Jada's bark. "Okay, Jada girl, I know, I know. Let's go for a walk. How about the long walk today?" she asked the pup, whose tail started wagging. "I guess that's a yes." She leashed Jada, and they left the house. While her neighbor took good care of Jada when she was away, after her disappearing act with Jordan the last few nights, she owed it to her pup to show her some love. After the walk, they played fetch in the backyard until Jada gave up the toy to lay in the sun. Quincy headed into the kitchen for breakfast. She stared out at her garden with thoughts of Jordan until her phone pinged. She was a little disappointed that it was Lauren.

Where you been? I texted you yesterday. Up for yoga today?

Quincy winced. She'd been neglecting her best friend too. *Morning, Lar. Sorry, I was at the LAGP training last night. Hike and coffee instead?*

Sure, that sounds good. Jada joining? Either way, I'll pick you up in thirty.

Quincy looked down at her pup, who sat at her feet and looked at her with her soulful brown eyes. *Jada refuses to be left behind. See you in thirty.* She checked for other messages. Nothing. She changed into hiking clothes and gathered Jada's supplies, doing her best to put Jordan out of her mind. The hike wasn't all that strenuous along the Palos Verdes coast, but she'd seen enough cases of dehydration and injuries to know what happened when you weren't prepared. She prepped her backpack and placed it by the front door before she leashed Jada. She scoffed at the bulging bag, which looked more like she was doing a week hike in the Grand Canyon than a local day hike. It was overkill, but she was ready for any eventuality. She heard Lauren's car in the drive and was out the door before Lauren could honk.

"Let's go get some coffee. Where're we headed?" Quincy looked over at Lauren. She appeared tired, with dark smudges under her eyes and her normal effervescent energy notably less this morning. "You okay? You look exhausted. Why don't you come inside, and we can chat instead?"

"I'm okay. I worked a tough double shift yesterday that stayed with me when I left the hospital. We had a twenty-two-year-old involved in a high-speed rollover car accident, and while he wasn't my patient, we were all in his room to help. He coded multiple times and then died." She shrugged, but the sadness was clear in her eyes. "It's just one of those non-Teflon times; all the bad's sticking to me this week. Hopefully some ocean air and a strong cup of coffee will help." Lauren gave her a hopeful smile.

Quincy gave Lauren a strong hug. "So sorry you had a rough week. I get it, and I'm here for you. Forget the hike, we can get coffee and donuts and watch the waves."

"Let's start with coffee." Lauren backed her car out of the drive and headed toward the coastal route up to Palos Verdes.

An hour later, they'd completed their vertical hike up to the top of a hill that had a 180-degree view of the Pacific. After a brief catch-up over coffee, they'd had little breath to talk during the hike itself, meaning Quincy had too much time to think about Jordan, about work, about life. When they finally made it to the top, she was glad to force the thoughts away as she took in the horizon.

"This's exactly what I needed." Lauren puffed out her breath and took in the vista. "Look, Q, whales! You can see their blows from here." She pointed to spray that was suspended in the air above the ocean, and a few seconds later a pair of flukes appeared. "Aww, that looked like a mama and baby gray whale."

The beauty of nature held Quincy in awe as they sat on the rock and watched the whales migrate past. "So amazing that this is in our backyard."

"Speaking of 'in our backyard,' how'd the race training go last night? You said you had a Jordan update the other day, but you haven't told me anything. What's up with race girl?" Lauren bumped Quincy's shoulder.

Quincy couldn't hide her smile or the joy that filled her at the mention of Jordan's name.

"OMG. What the hell have you been up to? I haven't seen you smile like that in a long time. Spill."

Quincy picked up a stick and started idly drawing in the dirt. "It's been an intense couple of days." She filled Lauren in, starting with her concerns about Jordan's celebrity attitude and how that clashed with what seemed to be a good heart, and ending with their kiss. "We might get together today, which is why I've been watching my phone like I was on call." She threw the stick and dusted off her hands. "Lauren, she's silly, smart, gorgeous, and has a kind heart, but she's far from perfect. She's used to getting what she wants, and I'm not her normal woman in any way. I mean, she even said that to me. Even though her home is here, she's on the road most of the year. We'd never see each other even if it did work out. Honestly, I think I'm just a sice project she's interested in for a while." The reality of the statement weighed on her heart.

Lauren smacked Quincy's shoulder. "What the hell, Q? You kissed Jordan Marsh. Why can't you let yourself just be present in the now? You and your never-ending attempt to control every situation. No one knows what the future holds, so why can't you just enjoy the journey? You don't know what she's thinking. You might be the right kind of different for her. Did you ever think of that? You're exasperating with your fatalistic approach to love."

Lauren sighed dramatically.

Quincy thought about the kid Lauren had just told her about and shuddered. Life could be so fleeting. "If, and it's a big if, we worked out, I'm not sure I could cope with knowing Jordan's life would be at risk every time she raced. Last night it was so hard to watch her being removed from her race car over and over like she was unconscious. I don't know why, but my heart broke every time." Quincy hugged herself. "What if I had to see it for real when I'd actually fallen for her? I think that would break me."

Lauren squeezed Quincy's hand. "Love and loss are part of life's journey. None of us have a crystal ball to read the future. You need to make the most of your time with Jordan, and you should leave your heart open to love. It's certainly too early to put on the brakes." Lauren burst into laughter. "God, I'm good. Just for you, I'm going to work on my racing puns. Let's go, so you can be ready when hot stuff calls."

Quincy hugged her and then grabbed Jada's leash. "You're crazy. Thanks for always being there for me. I channeled you the other night when Jordan showed up at my house. I was like, what would Lauren do? I think I might need to get a bracelet that says that." Quincy headed back to the car, feeling a little lighter, but having no better answers as to what to do about Jordan.

"Get a bracelet that says this." Lauren flipped her off.

"Hey, I'm being serious. I'll think about what you said." She laughed as Lauren threw a dandelion at her. "You wound me."

"Good thing you're an NP; you can mend your own wound. Oh, I forgot. I heard the ED management is throwing a party to celebrate newly minted NP Supervisor Ted on Thursday. I know you're on a month-long vacation and a work thing is the last place you want to go, but I thought you should know."

Quincy's stomach dropped. "That didn't take long. I guess they knew all along who they were going to pick. That's another area of my life I need to figure out. You know how much I love my job, and it's been the focus of my energy, my identity for so many years...but it doesn't feel that way anymore. I'm not sure what's next for my career, but I do know there's no way in hell I'm going to that party. I'm pretty sure I've got a root canal without Novocain scheduled for that night."

"But how do you really feel?" Lauren laughed as she pulled into Quincy's driveway. "You know that Trish and I support whatever comes next for you in love and life."

Quincy looked over. "How is Trish? I'm sorry I won't see her at the BBQ on Wednesday." She couldn't help but feel guilty that their whole conversation had been around her messy life.

"We're good. Enjoying being ridiculously happy and all about each other. We'll need to get together when you're done with the LAGP and South Pacific thing and all your busyness. We'll be here."

"Sounds good. Give her my love. I'll see you on Wednesday." Quincy unloaded Jada from the back, and her phone pinged.

"Ooh, maybe that's race girl. You better check it while I'm here." Lauren leaned out of the window and read the text with her.

Good morning - sorry I didn't text earlier. It's been a bit cray around here. R U busy tonight? & Joe says hi.

Lauren cleared her throat. "Love ya, girl. I'll leave you to chat with race girl. Q, you know you're interested. You should invite her to Wednesday's BBQ. What do you have to lose?"

"It's a hard maybe on inviting Jordan. We may not want that kind of celebrity vibe. Take care of yourself, Lar." She waved as Lauren backed out of the drive and then led Jada into the house. She grabbed some water and got comfortable on the couch, butterflies fluttering in her stomach as she started typing. *Hey there, tell Joe hi for me. Just got back from a hike with Jada and my friend Lauren. Tonight's wide open. What're you thinking? Ya know you do have a big race on Sunday—not surprised you're busy.* She waited, giddy as a teenager, as the reply dots blinked. When was the last time she'd felt this way about someone?

A big race, you say?? LOL! Dave and his partner, Elliot, are cooking at my place at 6:30 p.m. I'd love to have you and Jada join us. You know you want a tour inside my house! I'll need to head to a sponsor party after, but it won't be until later.

Quincy was beyond excited to see Jordan again, not to mention she'd now get to see her inner sanctum. Taking Lauren's advice, she ruthlessly pushed aside her doubts and worries. *Sounds great. What can I bring?*

An appetite, Dave's a great cook, and he makes a lot. Maybe a dessert?

Dessert – check, see you then.

CU L8R

Quincy leaned back and closed her eyes. The spinning of her thoughts sounded like a whirling slot machine in the quiet of her home. Yes, she was immensely attracted to Jordan, and their kiss had left her hungry for more. She couldn't stop the giddiness that welled up in her as she thought of seeing her tonight. *Get a grip.* She's still an entitled celebrity, Quincy had seen that firsthand, and that was not going away. Could she be second fiddle to Jordan's career and fans like she was at the center? Could she give up some control and see where this might go, like Lauren suggested? Sure, Lauren made a good point about the excitement of a potential relationship with Jordan, but her Jekyll and Hyde persona was difficult. Did she really want to put herself through it? Quincy opened her eyes and stood up from the couch, disgusted with herself.

"Enough. It's just dinner. You've got a million things to do before the trip. Focus on that, not Jordan." Quincy headed off to the bedroom, wondering if she still had the family pie crust recipe and if Jordan liked blueberry pie.

***

Quincy gathered Jada and her homemade pie into her Honda for the short jaunt to Jordan's place. She parked in front of the two-car garage behind Jordan's Range Rover and took a deep breath. She pushed aside that ever-present feeling of being not enough and headed to the front door. It opened, and Quincy's breath caught in her chest. Jordan's hair was perfectly styled in a messy quaff, and her eyes glittered in the hall light. The sleeves on her white Oxford were pushed up her strong forearms, and it was untucked from her faded and torn jeans that covered her strong legs like a second skin. Was this what it felt like to swoon?

"Hey, there, great timing. We just opened some wine. Come on in." Jordan held out her hands. "What can I take to help you? The pie or Jada?"

"The pie," she said and passed it over to Jordan. "This way, I can acclimate Jada, so she doesn't go crazy in here."

"How about I acclimate Jada?" Jordan closed the door and unleashed the dog. Jada looked between them as though waiting for instructions. "See, she'll be fine. There isn't anything she can hurt. Dave and Elliott have dogs, so they're prepared for whatever she does. Let's head upstairs."

Quincy took a deep breath as she looked around the foyer of the gorgeous home and then headed up the stairs to where she could see the orange and pink sky from tonight's sunset through the glass walls. "Does everything always go your way?"

"Not everything, but in my home, I prefer to have control. Unless of course, I submit to you," Jordan said with a wink. "Who knows? I might prefer that. We'd have to see."

Quincy passed Jordan on the stairs, grazing her forearm with her fingertips. "Oh, I think you would," she said with a knowing smile. She stopped as she came into an open concept room that had a two-story glass wall with breathtaking views of the Pacific. The home had clean lines that blended with the sand and ocean just outside the windows. "Jordan, your home is gorgeous."

Jordan leaned into her from behind as Quincy took in the view. "Thanks, I knew you'd love it. Come in and make yourself comfortable, and I'll give you a tour later. Dave, I'm sure you remember Quincy?" Jordan asked as he came around the kitchen island.

He wiped his hands on a towel and hugged Quincy. "Of course! It's so good to see you again."

"You too," she said and meant it. Her nerves from flirting with Jordan a few minutes ago were enough to set her on edge but seeing Dave helped her settle.

Dave turned to the blond-haired, blue-eyed man who was chopping something on the kitchen island. "This is my partner, Elliott. Elliott, this is Quincy. She was our fellow Friday surfer."

Elliott hugged her. "I've heard *everything* about you," he said with a quick grin before turning back to his chopping.

"You have?"

"What can I get you to drink?" Jordan threw a warning look at Elliot and opened her refrigerator. "I've got wine, water, hard liquor, or juice?"

"A glass of wine would be perfect, thanks." Quincy surveyed Jordan's home. The sleek modern lines of glass and metal gave way to the warm stone and subtle green walls. She wanted to know Jordan better, and her gorgeously decorated home seemed to reflect the woman. The strong firm lines of the glass and metal beams matched her racing persona, and the warm colors and natural elements reflected the woman she was getting to know.

Dave lifted the pot lid and released a mouthwatering smell into the air. "I hope you came hungry. Dinner will be steamed shellfish and chorizo in a garlic wine broth with crusty bread. It should be ready soon."

Quincy leaned against the island. "That smells divine. Anything I can help with?"

"No, just relax. Dave and Elliott know their way around my kitchen and home better than I do. They're a well-oiled machine. Trust me, we'd just be in the way." Jordan took a drink of ice water. "I'll go turn on the heaters and make sure the table is ready on the balcony. Care to join me?"

"Of course." Jada was settled on the plush rug by the fireplace and didn't move as Jordan pushed the glass door to the balcony into the wall. A flick of a switch, and the floor and overhead heaters turned on to warm the space. The table was already set and ready for the feast. "Glad I could help," Quincy said, feeling out of place as she simply stood there.

Jordan stood with her back against the railing and faced Quincy. "I just wanted you to myself," she said and gave her a shy smile. "How was your day? Did you have a good hike?"

Quincy felt the warmth of Jordan's admission to her core. She smiled and walked over to stand beside her. "It was good to catch up with Lauren and talk about some of the stuff going on in my life. We also saw whales." She stared at Jordan's lips, plump and pouty, glistening in the balcony lights. She was drawn to her with a desire to taste her kiss. She stepped closer just as Dave and Elliott came onto the balcony.

"Dinner is ready." He set the steaming bowl of seafood in the center of the table while Elliott placed the basket of crusty sourdough beside it.

Jordan kissed her cheek when she passed by. "To be continued," she murmured, her eyes holding a promise for later. "Thanks, guys. This smells fabulous. Let me grab another bottle of wine and some water."

Quincy shivered at Jordan's scent and touch. She took a deep calming breath and turned with a smile to the chefs. "It smells delicious." She sat in the chair Dave held out for her. "Thanks, Dave."

Dinner was oddly normal. She expected the conversation to be about Jordan and her celebrity status, about influencer things and sponsors, about racing statistics and projections. But none of that stuff was mentioned. The only exception was when Jordan said she'd need to leave to attend a sponsor's party later. But mostly, they shared stories about their teenage years, the people who taught them to surf, and home ownership. Quincy felt utterly at ease in a way she rarely did around people she didn't know.

Dave and Jordan's depth of conversation and teasing proved how close they were. The food was fabulous, and they devoured the pie, which pleased Quincy. Elliott made her promise to share the crust recipe. Quincy was so comfortable that she invited everyone to her BBQ. Dave and Elliott had a work trip to Santa Barbara, so they begged off. Jordan didn't reply, and Quincy's insecurities took hold. Why would Jordan come to her simple backyard BBQ when she lived this kind of life?

The night slowly came to an end as Dave and Elliott made quick work of the kitchen clean-up and then they headed to the door for hugs and kisses. Quincy was disappointed their night was ending. She'd enjoyed the conversation and camaraderie with the trio, and now the butterflies were taking flight at the prospect of being alone with Jordan. She quickly leashed Jada and followed them to the door.

At the front door, nerves got the better of her, and she floundered for something to say. "Your home reflects you, warm and beautiful. Thank you for inviting me tonight."

Jordan reached out and pulled Quincy to her, pressing her body close. "No stroll on the beach? Jada said she wanted to take her nightly walk here."

Quincy grinned, her body on fire. "You don't fight fair. Since she was a good girl tonight, I guess we'll do what Jada wants and stay here."

"Yay!" Jordan grabbed her race team leather jacket, and they headed to the sand.

They walked together in companionable silence, while Jada sniffed and took care of her nightly needs. When Jordan reached for Quincy's hand, she let her take it and felt like a high school kid walking with her first crush.

"I've been thinking about what you said about your family's love of racing. The IndyCar Racing Expo is open, and I have a scheduled appearance there tomorrow. I thought maybe you'd like to go. You could get some loot for your dad or even yourself.

I'm pretty sure I know someone who can get you passes, if you're interested."

Quincy took a deep breath, enjoying the salty air, the mist on her face, and the way Jordan's warm hand felt in hers. She was overjoyed that Jordan didn't want her to leave and that she'd used Jada as a reason for them to spend more time together. She could get used to this feeling, but she shouldn't. "That sounds like fun, but I've got a class tomorrow. I won't be available until early evening. Does the expo go into the evening?"

"It does. We could go there first and then go to dinner. We could meet at my garage like we did last time." She grimaced. "*If* you're interested."

Attending the Expo with Jordan had implications beyond a normal date. The press pressure on her would be intense. Did she want to go through that again? Could she cope with Jordan's persona, with the woman who was so different from the one she was walking with now? They finished their walk and stood outside her SUV. She couldn't seem to make herself say no. She loaded Jada in and stood at the driver's door.

"I'm interested, but I'd understand if you change your mind. Why don't you text me with details tomorrow? Thanks for tonight and the invitation. I appreciate you thinking of me."

Jordan traced her fingers over Quincy's lips. "Oh, I think of you." Jordan lightly kissed her cheek then stepped back from the truck. "Goodnight, Quincy."

Quincy's heart jackhammered in her chest. "Those damn lips." She grabbed Jordan's jacket and pulled her in. Their lips met in a slow rekindling that quickly turned into an inferno. Quincy was lost in the kiss, her control slipping, when a loud ping interrupted them.

"Damn, I'm sorry about this." Jordan pulled away, breathless, and yanked her phone from her jacket.

"Me too." Heat flared in Quincy's cheeks.

"Bad timing. I need to head up to the party. I guess the sponsor's looking for me. We'll come back to this, you can guarantee that."

She stepped closer and gently kissed Quincy again. "I'll see you tomorrow?"

"Um, yes, tomorrow." Her thoughts had been obliterated by that kiss. She slipped into her truck and watched Jordan head into her home. Quincy drove home with all of her senses on overdrive. Everything felt amplified, from the tingling of her lips to the brightness of the streetlights, and even her truck tires sounded different on the road. She couldn't wrap her head around it, but Jordan's kiss awakened a part of her she'd never known existed.

Chapter Seventeen

"Come on, Jordan, you need to focus. Let's take a break, everyone. I'm going for a walk. Let's meet back in thirty minutes." Nate closed his laptop and left her with the other Pink Triangle racing engineers and strategists. They all filed out of the RV after him and left her alone.

Fuck. Jordan was distracted by thoughts of Quincy; there wasn't any other way to say it. She thought about how their kiss had short-circuited her brain last night and even today. She smiled at how Quincy had blended in with her extended family and now with her chosen family too. Dave had texted this morning to rave about her, and Jordan couldn't argue. But she needed to focus on racing and not on the new woman in her life. *What is she doing right now? What did she think about my house? Was the dinner okay? Did she like my friends?*

"Get a grip, Jordie. Focus on the win." She stared at herself in the mirror. Women never got under her skin this way. She could enjoy a woman for a night and barely remember her the next day. That was the lifestyle, and no one had complained about it before. But Quincy had her thinking about what it would mean to settle down, to be with one person. She snorted and shook her head. That led to distraction, and distraction meant consequences on the track.

Her phone pinged, and she left the bathroom, hopeful it would be Quincy. "Yeah, you've really got a grip."

Jordie, what's this about you going to family parties? You know how I feel about your father's extended family. They'll just bring your image down. Tina told us that blond girl was trouble too.

None of those people are good enough for you. Stay focused on what Tina has planned for you, and you'll go far. Think about your image and what's important, because it doesn't sound like you're doing that right now.

Jordan paced the RV and tried to shake off the bad energy her mom always provoked. "Forget her. She doesn't control your life, and she certainly doesn't know what's best for you." She shook her arms and tried to picture the track, tried to feel the steering wheel under her fingers. Instead, she saw the way Quincy had looked at her right before kissing her senseless. She picked up her phone. *Hi. Will I see you tonight? 6 at the garage? I hope so!*

Hey there. Sounds good, I'll see you then!

Good, because last night's kiss left me on fire.

LOL, I know. I keep doodling your lips. See u at 6!

Jordan smiled. The brief chat calmed and focused her for the first time all day and helped wipe away her mom's negativity. She tackled the afternoon sessions and each meeting with the strategists, engineers, and mechanics. When she stepped into her car for the afternoon practice run, both she and it were in sync.

Joe leaned into the cockpit. "You ready to take her out?"

"I'm ready. Let's see how we do." Jordan gripped the wheel and released some nerves before she pulled down the visor on her helmet. She revved her engine and pulled out of the pit lane, and the feeling of rightness settled in her soul. Everything else disappeared. The responsiveness of the finely tuned, turbo-charged engine improved as she increased her speed. The sense of calmness that came over her increased with each lap until she was in the zone. The white flag caught her attention; she had one lap left to complete her practice run. She pulled into the pits, sure that the changes the team had made had shaved seconds off her previous run, making her a true contender for the pole position. She jumped down from the car and was inundated with back slaps from the pit crew and mechanics as they positioned the car into their garage. Everyone clapped and cheered, and she felt the momentum shift in their favor.

"The car was awesome! Great work, everybody. Our car's going to win the pole and then the LA Grand Prix." Jordan looked up, and her throat constricted when she saw Quincy outside the garage. Jordan motioned that she'd be a minute, then she headed into the garage to find Joe. "Hey, Joe, I don't have any feedback for you on the car. It drove perfectly. There isn't a thing I feel we need to change. Is there anything else you need from me, or am I free to go?"

"Yeah, I saw why you want to go. You can go with Ms. Quincy, but that's the only reason I'm letting you leave." Joe gave a stern look.

A pang of guilt hit her, but when he smiled, she let it go. She probably should stick around, but she deserved some play time too. "I'll be at the Racing Expo if you need me. I'll see you later."

"Tell Quincy I said hey."

"Will do," Jordan said over her shoulder as she grabbed her keys and a Pink Triangle hat before she headed over to Quincy. She was embarrassed by the sweat and oil that covered her racing suit when she saw Quincy looking gorgeous in a soft black leather jacket and an emerald cashmere V-neck sweater that enhanced her eyes. The sweater was tucked into black jeans, and the look was completed with chunky black motorcycle boots that got Jordan's heart racing. She denied the temptation to engulf her in a hug and gave her a warm smile instead. "Hey, there. Thanks for waiting."

"You bet. I haven't been here long, but it seemed like you had a good run. Everyone was excited when you came into the garage," Quincy said as she looked Jordan over.

Quincy's gaze burned like a laser beam. "I think we're set for Thursday's qualifying run." She led Quincy to her SUV and drove out of the studio. "Joe says hey, and just so you know, he said I could only leave because I was going with you."

Quincy laughed. "He's such a sweetie. Where are we going? I

was in a class all day and didn't get a chance to look up where the IndyCar Racing Expo was being held. They mentioned it on the news, but I couldn't remember the location."

"It's at the Loews Hollywood Hotel. A section of rooms and suites are set aside for our team. I'm going to go up and shower, if you don't mind joining me. I mean, in the suite. Not the shower." Jordan rolled her eyes and sighed. Damn, she used to be way smoother than this.

"Sure, I'll join you." Quincy's lips quirked in a grin.

"After the center, I feel like maybe I should prepare you," Jordan said, hoping this kind of honesty wouldn't backfire. "There'll be a lot of fans, phones, and press. More than any other outing. You might want to decide if you want to go through with this." She watched Quincy, who seemed to be watching the Hollywood streets as they came alive the closer they got to the hotel.

Quincy finally sighed softly and looked at her. "Jordan, I'm sure there'll be some kind of repercussion for going through with tonight's date. Maybe it'll be with IndyCar, the press, or Tina. Somewhere, somehow, there will probably be an issue, but I've thought about it, and I just want to be with you."

Jordan pulled the car to the curb and breathed a sigh of relief. She smiled and intertwined their fingers. "I want that too. I can't promise there won't be issues with jumping into my crazy world, but I'll do my best to protect you. Let's have fun tonight and see where this takes us. Sound good?"

"Sounds good." There was no mistaking the hint of doubt in her eyes, but she squeezed Jordan's hand.

Jordan pulled back out into traffic and turned into the Loews Hollywood Hotel valet, where a crowd of racing fans waited.

"Here we go." Quincy gave Jordan a fleeting glance then stepped out into the onslaught of the press, racing fans, and hotel guests.

"Ms. Marsh, please follow us," hotel security said as Jordan slid out of the car and was immediately flanked by them.

She went around the car to Quincy to see her smiling at the crowd, her head held high. The security team slowly ushered them through the front doors. Jordan stopped herself from holding Quincy's hand, but her right hand ghosted Quincy's back as they were led across the lobby. The press and fans shouted questions at them as the progressed.

"Who're you with tonight, Jordan?"

"Where's Miss Universe? Is this her replacement?"

"Are you going to win the Grand Prix? Kent Carver said you were on your way out. Is that true?"

"Jordan, we love you!"

They were interrupted multiple times while Jordan stopped for pictures and autographs with her adoring fans. Quincy graciously gave the fans room and even offered to take pictures of them.

The security detail moved through the lobby and an older man in a suit joined them in the struggle. "Ms. Marsh, welcome to the Loews Hollywood Hotel. I'm Frank Jenkins, the hotel manager. Please let me accompany you to your suite."

They entered a private elevator with the security detail along with Mr. Jenkins. He swiped the room card and pressed the button for the top floor, then handed her a room key.

"Ms. Marsh, you'll be in the Lana Turner Suite." Mr. Jenkins stepped off the elevator and indicated the left outer door of the two on the floor. "I hope it'll be to your satisfaction. If there's anything we can do, please don't hesitate to ask. Would you like me to give you a tour of the suite?"

"No, thank you, Mr. Jenkins. I've stayed here before and know my way around." Jordan shook his hand, knowing full well the importance of a good relationship with all the staff who put up with the chaos around her race team.

The plushness of their surroundings blocked out any noise from the hall or even outside. The suite's floor-to-ceiling windows provided a commanding view of the Hollywood sign and the Griffith Observatory in the distance. Jordan stood beside Quincy at the window, and she found it difficult to keep her hands to herself. "You were amazing down there. It was crazy, even for me. How were you able to keep your composure?"

Quincy tore her eyes off the view and faced Jordan. She smiled sweetly. "I'm an ER nurse in one of the busiest hospitals in LA, and I'm used to having people get crazy all around me. Your fans and press line downstairs were like a busy Friday night at work," she said and smirked. "I simply reframed the situation in my mind, so it didn't feel so out of my control."

Jordan couldn't help the rumble of laughter that popped out. "That's hilarious and unexpected. I guess it shouldn't be though. You've told me you like control." Jordan cupped Quincy's jaw and rubbed her thumb over her left cheek. The self-talk about distancing herself was over. She wanted to feel, touch, and taste Quincy.

A knock at the door interrupted them.

"Yes, who is it?"

"Room service, Ms. Marsh. Compliments of Mr. Jenkins."

"Not sure about their timing, but that's very thoughtful." Jordan opened the door, and a sharply dressed attendant pushed a cart full of champagne, fruits, chocolates, and small sandwiches into the suite.

"Welcome to the Loews Hollywood Hotel. We're proud to have you stay with us. Please accept this with our compliments, and if you need anything at all, please don't hesitate to ask." He quickly backed out of the suite and closed the door.

"So can I interest you in some champagne or a bite to eat?"

"I can't pass that up," Quincy said as Jordan popped the champagne and poured two glasses. "May your troubles be less, and your blessings be more, and nothing but happiness come in through your door." She smiled, and they clinked their glasses.

Jordan took a sip. "You had that loaded and ready."

Quincy blushed and sat down. "It was an old Irish proverb that was on the kitchen wall when I was growing up. It's stuck with me."

She shrugged. "What time is the IndyFan event?"

Jordan checked her phone. "It starts in thirty minutes. I guess I should get cleaned up."

"I'm sure many of the fans would love to meet you in your racing suit, for the authenticity of it." Quincy took another sip of her champagne.

Jordan shook her head and smiled. Her die-hard racing fans *would* love to have any connection to the track. "That may be, but not tonight. I need a shower."

"What're you wearing? I didn't see you bring any clothes with you."

"My sponsorship and PR team set me up. I'm sure there'll be something from Kirrin Finch and Tights, the leather shop in West Hollywood. Do you want to come into the bedroom and look?" *Please say yes.*

"Thanks, but no, that's okay. I'll...I'll wait out here until you're ready. You need to be somewhere, and if we both go in there..." She gave Jordan a look over the edge of the champagne glass as she took a sip.

Jordan's knees went weak, and she let out a sigh. "Damn, woman, that look makes me want to cancel everything." She pinched the bridge of her nose, pulling on all the reserve she could find. "I'll be out after a *very* cold shower." Jordan closed the door to the bedroom, wishing like hell Quincy would join her. *I'll see if I can change her mind about going home with me tonight.*

She stepped from the shower, checked out her body in the mirror, and then wrapped one of the luxurious towels around her middle. "She won't be able to resist this," Jordan mumbled and smiled at her reflected image before she styled her hair and went back into the living room. Quincy was lying on her side like a movie star, her arm draped over the end of the chaise lounge as she looked out on the city lights far below.

Jordan approached, but Quincy didn't look up or react. She chuckled softly when she saw that Quincy was sound asleep, and

Jordan couldn't bear to wake her up, even if doing so by dropping her towel was tempting. She sucked in a breath and quietly watched as Quincy's long eyelashes fluttered with dreams not shared. She returned to the bedroom, pulled on a white cotton shirt with the Pink Triangle racing logo in dark pink embroidery on the cuffs and collar, dark jeans, black leather low-heeled boots, and a navy-blue leather jacket with the team logo on the chest and her top five sponsors on the left arm organized with repeating embroidered triangles down her arm. A light dusting of facial powder and lip gloss finished her look, and she then put on her custom Breitling Marsh racing watch.

She checked her look and closed her eyes briefly. She'd never been worried about whether or not a woman would find her attractive. But everything about Quincy was different. Quincy's image burned itself into her mind and heart, making her lean against the wall to steady herself.

She walked across the suite, the sound of her footsteps quieted by the plush carpet, and left a note with an all-access pass. *You're gorgeous when you sleep, and I didn't want to wake you. Come meet me downstairs in the Expo when you're ready. Use this pass to get in. Not sure I'll hear my phone if you text. I'll be at the IndyFan table. Come find me. I hope you had sweet dreams. xo.*

Jordan closed the door behind her softly just as Tina came off the elevator.

"What, no race girl on your arm tonight? I would've thought that trollop from the beach you came into the hotel with would be hanging off you." Tina looked over Jordan once they entered the empty elevator. "Nice hotel entrance. While the sponsors will love that you came in your racing gear, you could've given me a heads-up." Tina threw her arms up, appearing exasperated.

Jordan's patience with Tina waned, but she hadn't responded before Tina exploded out of the elevator when the doors opened to the lobby. She snapped her fingers at the security guards standing nearby, and they flanked them as they entered the conference hall.

Each driver had Expo time, and tonight was Jordan's. Her fans would get to meet her, get her autograph, and buy items from her sponsors. Jordan took in her family of supporters as they hoisted their rainbow and Pink Triangle Racing flags prominently in the air. It was almost like an indoor Pride parade with all the rainbow colors on display. The noise was deafening, but she was pumped by the buzz of the crowd. She thought of Quincy and wished she was beside her to enjoy the moment and feel the energy. But she had to get her head focused on tonight's events and not on the woman upstairs.

"Ms. Marsh, are you ready?" the event security team asked before they led her to the main stage, where she was introduced to the animated crowd.

Jordan waved as she stepped up to the podium. "Hello, Los Angeles! Hello, race fans! I'm excited to be back home in LA. We love you, LA!" She paused as the crowd went nuts, clapping and screaming their support. "Thank you, I'm feeling your love tonight." She made a heart sign with her hands. "The Pink Triangle Racing team appreciates your support. You've shown up at every race, and we wouldn't be here without all of you. Who's ready for me to make history and win the LA Grand Prix?" The crowd erupted, chanting her name and waving their flags in the air. "Me too! Come over and meet me at our booth, and we hope to see you all trackside at the race. Thanks for your support, LA." Jordan jumped down into the crowd like it was a mosh pit.

She signed skin, hats, shirts, pictures of her, and anything they put in front of her. With security's help, she made her way over to their booth. Above her hung her official IndyCar racing photo on a banner, and next to it was the team's Incy NXT series driver, Lex Ortega.

"Nice speech!" Lex stood up from the table as Jordan approached and gave her a hug. "What's up, superstar?"

"Not much, player," Jordan said.

Lex's easy smile made her a fan favorite. She could make

anyone feel comfortable until they met her on the track. The Indy NXT was a steppingstone for drivers before racing in IndyCar. Lex drove for their team, had racked up wins, and made a name for herself over the past few years. It was only a matter of time before she took the next step into IndyCar.

Jordan looked around the Expo, internalizing the energy around them. "This night's going to be crazy. Check out that line of fans going around the bend." She sat down at the table.

Lex looked out over the sea of people. "Let's get it on." She cracked her knuckles and picked up a sharpie.

Jordan picked up her pen, rolled her shoulders, and smiled. Then she nodded to Tina, who was holding the first fan back from the table. For a moment, she looked beyond the line of fans toward the elevator. There wouldn't be anything she could do while Jordan was at the booth but just knowing Quincy was in the room would be nice. Jordan pasted on a smile as the first fan came forward. Quincy wasn't some race girl who'd want to just hang around to make Jordan look good. So why did Jordan want her there so bad?

Chapter Eighteen

Quincy woke in the suite alone, but Jordan's sweet note made her smile. She thought about the fire in Jordan's eyes, and it stoked the embers of Quincy's passion. She stepped into Jordan's room, and her lingering scent ignited Quincy's arousal. She fixed her hair and rubbed at the subtle lines on her face from the couch pillow. She didn't want to waste any more time, so she grabbed the pass and headed downstairs.

The large hall was eerily quiet, except for the low-level chatter from a huge line of fans waiting to see Jordan. She was obviously going to be busy for a while, so Quincy decided to check out the Expo. She went from booth to booth, picking up swag as she went. She headed over to the IndyCar Medical team's booth and listened to their presentation on driver safety and treatment, nearly word-for-word what she'd been taught over the last couple of days.

"Please let us know if you have any questions," the woman at the booth said. Fans dispersed toward the booths promising more fun.

Quincy bit her lip. Was this a sign from the universe? "Hi, I'm Quincy. I work in the ED at LAMC, and I'm one of the local NP's who'll be working with the medical support staff for Sunday's race. I was curious about any positions that might be available with your team." She got it out in a rush, afraid she'd lose her nerve if she didn't.

"Nice to meet you. I'm Dr. Constance Mackey, the medical director for the IndyCar Medical Travel team as well as the Infield Care Center at the Indianapolis Motor Speedway. You must be really good to have been chosen for the race. It's a very selective process."

"That's good to hear." Quincy's nerves settled. She was simply talking to a doctor, nothing more. "I've read about the changes you've made to improve the safety of the IndyCar drivers."

She looked surprised. "It's good the information is getting out into the world. As far as hiring is concerned, I can tell you it's a lengthy process. I'm just one of the many decision-makers. I do know there's going to be a staff opening in the next few months. Why don't you take my business card and email me your CV for review? I'll have my assistant, Stephanie, let you know when the job opens so you can apply."

Goosebumps ran up Quincy's arms, and she rubbed them away, her excitement for this potential career change overtaking any fear. She shook her head to clear her thoughts. What was she thinking? Did her interest revolve around her desire to stay in Jordan's orbit? She didn't want to think about that. Could she even leave the roots she had here in LA? Dr. Mackey cleared her throat and stared at Quincy. "Sorry, Dr. Mackey. It's such a great opportunity that I was a little lost in thought. It'd be a challenging new step in my career, and it's gotten my mind spinning. Thanks for the information. I'm sure there'll be a ton of applicants, but I'm definitely interested. It must be kismet, because I attended a professional development class today and just finished my CV. Can I send it over now?" Quincy was trying not to be too eager but was having a difficult time reining it in. She pulled out her phone, drafted an email to Dr. Mackey, and attached her CV.

Dr. Mackey looked Quincy over and nodded to herself, almost as if she'd come to a decision on something. "Well, aren't you prepared? I'll take a look in the next couple of days. Have a good time tonight, and hopefully we won't need your expertise during the race this weekend."

A large group of fans descended on the booth.

"So nice to meet you. Have a great weekend in LA." Quincy left the booth, optimistic about a lead for a future career change. *Don't get ahead of yourself. You'll have to share this opportunity with*

Jordan and see what she thinks. Was it a real career choice option, or was she getting carried away with being part of Jordan's world?

She watched a fan walk by with a plate of nachos and her stomach grumbled, but they were supposed to be going out for dinner. She looked over to check Jordan's progress and caught her eye. Her heart rate doubled with just that look. Maybe she should turn up the heat. She held their eye contact with a half-smile and licked her lips. Jordan's eyes widened, so Quincy motioned toward the food area and gave Jordan a big smile.

Jordan laughed out loud, clearly startling the fan in front of her. She shook her head and returned a sly smile, which was all the invitation Quincy needed. She made her way over to Jordan's table. As she approached, Tina stepped in front of her, arms crossed, blocking her way, so she joined the autograph line instead. *Bitch.* Jordan looked up and then called Tina over and whispered something in her ear.

"Thank you, IndyCar racing fans who came out tonight to support the Pink Triangle Racing team of Lex Ortega and Jordan Marsh," Tina said in a voice only dogs should hear. "On behalf of the team and our sponsors, we hope you enjoy the IndyCar Racing Expo and the LA Grand Prix. We have time for five more autographs."

Quincy counted the fans before her and grinned. She approached Lex Ortega for an autograph as Jordan took a selfie with a fan.

"Hi, what name should I put with my autograph?" Lex signed her image and looked up at Quincy with a flirty smile. "Would you like my number as well?"

"Quincy, and no, she doesn't want the number you change every week." Jordan punched Lex on the arm.

Quincy smiled inside, enjoying Jordan's jealous display.

"Damn, Jordie. Not my signing arm." Lex rubbed her arm and laughed. She looked between Quincy and Jordan and nodded. "If you tire of this old woman, let me know." She smirked at Jordan. "I'll see you in the morning for press day. Wear something pretty." Lex picked up her jacket and headed over toward Tina.

"Good nap?" Jordan reached out but stopped just shy of taking Quincy's hand.

"I guess all these late nights with the soon-to-be LAGP pole sitter must have tuckered me out," Quincy said and laughed as Jordan signed a picture for her. "Aw, you shouldn't have. I'll cherish it always," she said, mimicking more than one fan's high-pitched voice.

Jordan grabbed Quincy's hand. "I hope you do. Let's get out of here and go have dinner."

Quincy nodded toward the crowd, who were hooting and hollering at them. "Looks like they're getting restless. I think we should go before some crazy fan bumps me off so she can take my place."

Jordan motioned at Tina, and the Expo security materialized at the booth.

"Ms. Marsh, are you ready to leave?" a giant guy asked.

"Yes, we are."

"The valet stand is swarmed with press and fans, so we had your car brought around to the side alley."

"Thanks, we'll follow you." Jordan held Quincy's hand and led her through the throng.

The open sky in the alley allowed her to breathe again, and she nearly giggled when Jordan opened the car door for her. The hotel became a blur in their rearview window, and Quincy realized she had no idea where they were heading. She looked at her phone as notifications pinged from all her social media accounts as well as her text messages. She saw her name popping up as someone mentioned on other people's platforms. Perfect strangers were talking about her. "I guess the word is out that we're together." She fiddled with her phone and then shook her head. "I'm not going to look at what the trolls are saying. I think I'll just put this on silent so we can enjoy the evening."

"Great idea. Who cares what people think? I'm glad you're with me, and that's all I care about. I don't know about you, but I'm starving. I almost took a bite of a fan's hot dog while they were waiting in line. What sounds good? I can get us in anywhere you want to go."

That was something she'd only ever heard on TV. "I'm hungry too. How about chicken and waffles at Roscoe's? I'm not sure you'll want that if press day is tomorrow, but it sounds good to me." The restaurant had experience with celebrity diners but kept the atmosphere relaxed. The likelihood of being bothered by hordes of fans there was low.

"Perfect. I haven't had that in years." Jordan plugged the address into her GPS, and they headed to the LA staple a short distance away.

They were seated quickly in a high back booth near the back of the restaurant. Jordan faced away from the other patrons to keep her anonymity. They ordered and sat back to enjoy the atmosphere, but Jordan seemed distracted. "You okay?'

Jordan began folding her napkin into triangles. "I was just thinking that you can google me, and you'd probably get a mix of truths and lies. If you do, I'm hoping you don't find out a bunch of stuff you don't like. Plus, I don't know much about you, and I'm interested. Will you tell me more? Maybe start with the conversation you had tonight with Dr. Mackey." Jordan winked.

"Good to know you were watching me instead of giving all your attention to your fans." She grinned when Jordan shrugged, apparently unapologetic. "It was an honor to meet her. I mean, being the first female Medical Director for IndyCar is a big deal, and she's working to revolutionize the way trauma care is provided. While it affects you as an IndyCar driver firsthand, it also gets applied to anyone in a car accident. I asked her about any open positions within her team. She mentioned there might be one in the coming months, so I sent her my CV, and I'll apply if there's an opening." She waited for Jordan's reaction. Never had she needed anyone else's approval. Why did it matter so much that Jordan thought it was a good idea?

"IndyCar would be lucky to have you on their team. I saw how focused and in control you were in the training the other night." Jordan covered Quincy's hand with her own. "You're obviously good at what you do."

"Thank you. I'm a bit of a control freak." Quincy laughed uncomfortably, but when she looked into Jordan's kind eyes, she felt heard and supported in a way she'd never experienced before. "I've been this way since I was young. My sister, Katie, is two years younger than me, and we grew up as latchkey kids. When I was ten, she fell down the stairs, knocked herself unconscious, and broke her arm. I couldn't wake her up, and I couldn't reach my parents, so I called 911 for help. This wonderful ambulance crew came to the house and took us to the hospital. They praised me for keeping a level head and staying in control of the situation. The hospital staff talked to me at my level, so I could understand why Katie's sleeping was a concern because of her concussion. Their encouragement stuck with me when I was considering careers. I wanted to be that for others, to make a difference."

"I'm sure you have," Jordan said as she caressed Quincy's hand.

Quincy gave her an uncertain smile. "That positive energy from the medical staff changed when my mom arrived at the hospital. She yelled at me. Told me I was worthless and a disappointment. Even though my sister made a full recovery and had no lasting impact from her fall, that didn't change anything. In her defense, she was being questioned about child abandonment and abuse. Anyway, her opinion of me never changed from that day forward. She verbally abused me throughout my childhood. I'd keep the house clean, get straight As, play sports, even date boys, and nothing changed her opinion. I tried to be the best version of me, but I finally realized the one thing I couldn't control was...well, her." She blinked away the tears she'd thought had long dried up. "I received a scholarship to Notre Dame's College of Nursing.

During my first year, my mom was diagnosed with pancreatic cancer. She refused to allow me to come home and help with her care. She went for her first chemotherapy session and had an allergic reaction to something and died. We never got a chance to mend fences. The lessons I learned early on about controlling my environment have stuck with me. If I can control everything in my orbit, then maybe it won't fall apart." It was the first time she'd told anyone other than Lauren that story, and she couldn't fathom what had possessed her to share something so personal. "Well, that's my depressing story. How about your relationship with your mom?" Quincy took a deep breath and squeezed Jordan's hand.

The server came to the table. "Who had the Carol C and the Scoe's quarter chicken?" the waitress asked.

"I had the Carol C," Quincy said.

"Okay, here you go. Hot sauce is on the table. Let me know if you need anything else," she said after she set Jordan's food down too.

They dug into their meals and fell silent. Quincy was glad for the interruption, because she didn't want to think about her family.

"I forgot how good this is. Thanks for thinking of it," Jordan said and grinned widely.

"If you don't like your press event pictures tomorrow, don't blame me."

"I won't. There'll be all kinds of pictures and videos taken, so it's a given something won't look flattering. And I'm wearing my racing suit all day; I never look good in that."

Quincy choked on her water. "I think you look hot in your racing suit."

Jordan smiled and met Quincy's eyes. "You do, do you? I'll keep that in mind." Her expression turned serious. "Given what you've just said about control... The press is going to ask about you tomorrow. What would you like me to say?"

"I'm sure Tina or your PR folks will direct you on what to say. I'd prefer you not bring me into the conversation if possible. Let's just go with we're friends."

"Sure. Friends." She looked into Quincy's eyes, her expression inscrutable.

"So, you were going to tell me about your family?"

Jordan shook her head. "I really wasn't. They aren't that interesting."

"I beg to differ if Victoria Valentine-Marsh is your mom," Quincy said.

Jordan rolled her eyes and stabbed at her chicken. "Okay, fine. Yes, she's my mom. The only child of the Newport Beach Valentine real estate empire. She went to USC and double-majored in environmental studies and biology. She did a year in the Peace Corps and saw how plastic was affecting the most remote beaches of the world, then she developed a sand vacuum that revolutionized the ocean's health. She sold that for a lot of money and then worked at the State Department where she met my dad. They worked on clean energy in the Indo-Pacific region for years before they married. I was an oops baby—not in their plan at all. Now she's a part-time professor at Georgetown." Jordan popped a piece of waffle in her mouth, and they were quiet for a minute. "For all the good and bad, she was responsible for my drive. From the time I could walk until I turned sixteen, she helicopter-parented the hell out of me. She pushed me to be the best in all things. It took me a while to realize that she considered me a reflection of herself. Her love and support were always dependent on what I achieved. It was never about how I felt, or how it affected me. When I found racing at sixteen, the outlook on my future transformed, and I changed my path. But just like your issues with control have stayed with you, anxiety and self-doubt that was ingrained in me early on has stuck to me like glue. Is what I'm doing good enough for Mama Vic? Am I good enough? Nope. Never." Jordan blew out a breath. "Shit, I've never shared that with anyone, ever." She leaned back and appeared to emotionally distance herself.

Quincy gave Jordan a sympathetic smile. "Thank you for

trusting me with your story. It means a lot. I've only told my ex and close friend Lauren about my control issues and where they stem from. People see that as part of my personality, but no one knows the source of it. Hell, I'd love to find someone who could help me carry the load, so I wouldn't have to feel so in control." She shook her head at her honesty once again.

"I hear you. I'd love to find someone I could trust to *help* with my baggage instead of *adding* to it. Now I just assume everyone is out for something. People use me to get on TMZ or to blow up their social media accounts. Sometimes it feels like my mom all over again, because she uses me like a puppet. My control over my own celebrity is limited." Jordan sighed. "I mean, it has its good parts, believe me. I know I can be an entitled jerk, and I really do try to rein it in. I think..." Jordan wadded up her napkin and threw it on her plate. "I think I've got to find some balance."

"Well, we're a bunch of sad sacks," Quincy said and laughed. "I guess having awareness is a good place to start. I'm sorry if I gave you more information than you were expecting."

Jordan squeezed her hand. "I loved hearing about your life and how you became so wonderful. I hope this is just the beginning of sharing stories about our lives." She gave Quincy a warm smile. "Shall we go?" She got up and held out her hand to help Quincy out of the booth.

The electric spark that ran up Quincy's hand when they touched didn't stop buzzing even as they walked out of Roscoe's holding hands. A rush of liberation raced through her from sharing her past with Jordan. Each confession stripped away layers of guilt, leaving her raw yet exhilarated. The vulnerability deepened their connection, and for the first time, she glimpsed a future filled with possibilities. As the night wrapped around them, she wished she could freeze time, not wanting to lose this fragile moment that felt like the start of something extraordinary.

Chapter Nineteen

Jordan didn't want to break the warm rush that their combined hands elicited. Tonight was unexpected, but that seemed to be the norm when she was with Quincy. Jordan was surprised how well she fit into her life, how she handled the fans, the press, Lex, and the Expo experience. Dinner was fun and a nice change from the high-end places her dates usually requested. She had zero intention of sharing her past and the ongoing anxiety she carried, but with Quincy, it seemed like everything was up for grabs. Now, she couldn't stop the train of thoughts running through her mind.

When had she stopped living for herself? When did she allow other people to control her life again? Her truths unsettled her, but she felt seen in an unfamiliar way, and that was a balm to her anxiety. She drove through the busy night traffic to the Paramount Studios lot to retrieve Quincy's car, trying to come up with a reason not to drop her off. But with the upcoming race, she couldn't justify another late night.

"When will I see you again?" Jordan asked, praying this wouldn't be their last night together. "I'm likely free the next two nights after my runs on the track. Can we get together?"

"I'd love that, but I'm hosting my dinner party tomorrow night. Will you join me? I've invited Lauren, some coworkers, and neighbors. It'll be low-key with steak, wine, good conversation. Nothing as upscale as you're used to." Quincy ran her fingers over Jordan's hand on the gear shift.

Jordan intertwined their fingers and turned in her seat so she could fully take in Quincy's beautiful face. "I'll be there when I finish my afternoon practice runs," she said, overly excited at the opportunity. Maybe she wouldn't have to leave when everyone else did. Maybe...

Quincy kissed Jordan's cheek and lingered briefly before she opened the door, the dome light setting her face aglow. "Tonight was special. I'll see you tomorrow."

You can't let her go. She looked around and didn't see anyone other than the security guard, and they were over a hundred yards away. She jumped out of her truck and ran around it to pull Quincy against her tightly.

"You smell like syrup," Quincy murmured, her eyes half-lidded.

They melted into one another as the kiss crackled with fire that set off a desire hotter than Jordan had ever felt. Jordan cupped Quincy's face and deepened the kiss. She peppered kisses down her jaw and along her soft, smooth neck. Quincy scratched her nails along Jordan's shoulders as Jordan nibbled her earlobe. She pinned Quincy against the back of her truck, her knee pressed tightly against Quincy's hot center. She reveled in the feel of her curves, her breasts, and her responses as she came alive under Jordan's touch. The taste of coffee and syrup on their tongues blended as their passion ignited, and their kiss took on a frenzied pace. Jordan ran her hands over Quincy's hips, cupping her ass and pulling her closer. She grazed Quincy's taut nipples and wished she could taste Quincy's jasmine-scented skin beneath the thin sweater.

Quincy let out a deep moan and ground herself against Jordan's leg. They broke their kiss briefly to catch their breath, blowing steam into the cool night air. Jordan's next exploration was more playful as she nibbled at Quincy's neck, cupping her breasts and keeping Quincy pressed intimately against her thigh. "I want you so bad."

Quincy moaned. "Same." Quincy bit Jordan's bottom lip before pulling away. "I don't want to go, but it might not be the best for you to have the just-fucked look for media day. I promise to make up for it tomorrow." She pulled herself off Jordan with one last sweet kiss. "You should plan to stay and play tomorrow night."

Jordan pulled Quincy back to her. "I don't want to let you go tonight," Jordan said, trying to restrain herself. Intoxicated by Quincy's scent and taste, she didn't think she could wait until tomorrow. One taste, and she was addicted. She didn't want to break the embrace as they slowly walked to Quincy's Honda. Before she could open the door, Jordan wrapped her arms around Quincy's waist from behind. Quincy melted into Jordan as she kissed the back of her neck, her earlobes, and then finally turned Quincy around to place one last hot kiss on her lips.

"I'll be there tomorrow night, and I want to kiss all of you," Jordan whispered, wondering if she would actually explode from lust.

Quincy met her steady gaze. "I'll hold you to that." She got in the car and blew out a deep breath. "You've got my engine purring."

Jordan leaned in for a final kiss. "Text me when you get home. Thanks for a wonderful night." She watched Quincy's taillights clear the Paramount Studio gate and breathed in the cold night air as she tried to get her bearings. *What are you doing to me?* She knew damn well and liked it too much to stop. Her attraction to Quincy just kept building, and after what she'd learned tonight, she admired her even more. *Damn, I can't wait for tomorrow night to finish what we started.* She'd just settled into the soft leather seat when she noticed movement in the garage area. Jordan hit her headlights and illuminated Joe. She got out of her truck and walked over to him.

"I'm sorry. I was headed back to the RV, but I didn't want to interrupt you ladies, and I got stuck." Joe looked down and kicked his boot on the concrete.

Jordan shook her head, knowing him well enough to know that was true. "You couldn't drop a tool or something and announce you were there? What're you doing out here so late anyway? Isn't it past your bedtime?"

Joe was known for his early starts and earlier nights. "Well, I was settled in for the night when I thought I heard someone out near the race car, so I went out to check on things, and then you two showed up."

The news made her uneasy. Millions of dollars were sitting in the garage in the form of tools, tires, and the race car itself. The steering wheel alone was $30,000. "Did you find anyone out here?" Jordan scanned the darkness around them as though she'd see someone.

"Nope, nothing." Joe yawned. "Probably just a raccoon or something."

"Okay, but we should review the cameras and tell security so they can increase patrols. We haven't even started qualifying rounds. Sabotage is always possible."

"I'll call security now, and we'll review the video in the morning. I'm going to get back to the trailer and hit the sack." He began to walk away with his hands in his jacket. "She sure is a nice one, that girl. Different from the others you've had around." He motioned toward the exit gate. "Here you go." He turned and handed Jordan a Polaroid. "I thought you might like a souvenir too."

Jordan put the picture up to her car's headlights to see it was of Quincy sitting in her race car.

"That one's priceless. Night, Jordan," Joe said and walked away.

"Night, chief." Jordan drove back to the hotel through light traffic, humming a few bars of the familiar song on the radio and feeling lighter than she had in years. As she pulled up to the valet, she was glad to see all the fanfare had diminished. Only a few racing fans remained out front. She headed through the lobby to her room, and one paparazzi captured her photograph and peppered her with questions.

"Jordan, you going to bed all alone? What happened to the blond from earlier?" He trained his camera on her, hoping to get a response.

Jordan said nothing. She walked across the lobby and entered the elevator, and pure joy filled her at seeing Quincy's name on her phone.

Home safe. Thanks for an amazing night! Sweet dreams.

Glad you're safe! They'll be sweet cuz I'll dream of you, see you tomorrow. Jordan settled into her bed and closed her eyes, relieved Quincy was safely at home. *Wait, what the hell?* She sat up straight in bed and shook her head. She *never* checked in to make sure the woman she was with made it home safely. Why Quincy? And what possessed her to share her origin story *and* the lingering anxiety and self-doubt she carried? *What did Joe mean about Quincy being different? Was that a jab at me? Am I not good enough? Was it a warning to tread lightly with her? Or is it that she's trouble, and I should stay away?* Jordan plopped back onto the pillow and sighed deeply. She didn't have the answers, but she knew what she felt, and she liked it, more than she'd admit to anyone else.

***

Jordan woke revitalized for the busy day ahead. She checked her phone for the schedule of events Tina had sent over and saw it was full of practice and press. She packed an overnight bag and answered the door as Jessica, her trainer, arrived for the morning's workout.

She lost focus near the end of the first hour, and Jessica ended the plank exercise. "Your mind is someplace else. I don't want you injured. We're done for today." She wiped sweat from her forehead and placed the towel around her neck.

Jordan dropped down onto the mat and looked up at Jessica. "I'm sorry. You're right, but don't call it. I promise I'll give you thirty more minutes."

Jessica grinned. "Just remember you asked for it. Give me fifty burpees."

Jordan complied and remained focused for the rest of the workout. When she had nothing left, Jessica left the suite and Jordan got ready for the day, her muscles pleasantly sore and all the tension worked away. As she turned to go into the bedroom, the pink, orange, and purple of the morning sky bled into the suite like a piece of stained-glass artwork. She walked over to the window where Quincy had stood last night and admired the view. She smiled at the memory of Quincy's beautiful face highlighted in the glow of the city lights. She'd been thinking of their kiss and the promise of more tonight during her workout, but she couldn't tell Jessica that. She grabbed her phone and texted her favorite florist to arrange an order, then she took a picture of the Hollywood sign with the gorgeous morning sky behind it and sent it to Quincy. It was early, and she didn't expect a reply, but just that contact was enough to feel connected.

Jordan arrived at their garage and saw Joe standing near the car, surrounded by other team members. He looked exhausted and worried.

"Jordie, have you got a minute?"

"What's up? You're looking rough this morning." She placed a hand on his shoulder to look at him more closely.

He took a deep breath. "I couldn't sleep last night, so I reviewed the video footage we talked about. I was right; there was someone in the garage last night. They showed up around ten thirty, right before you and Quincy. They were dressed in a black hoodie and mask, so there's no way to tell who it was. They were only on camera for a few seconds, so they probably knew where they were."

A blanket of unease shrouded Jordan. "That has to be someone with garage clearance." It might be someone she trusted. "Did they do any damage, or steal anything?" she asked, walking around the car.

Joe pointed to the area of the car where the intruder had been. "They punctured small holes in all our hydraulic hoses. We wouldn't have known until you had the car up to speed on the track. We'll do an inch-by-inch check of the rest before you get in it."

"Jesus Christ." Jordan ran her hands through her hair and blew out a breath. She picked up the punctured hose, and a chill passed over her as she ran her fingers over the holes. Then she threw down the hose and worked to maintain her cool as she realized that kind of leak could've killed her. "What did security say? What's being done?"

"They said they'll increase their patrols. I've told some of the other crew chiefs, so they can keep an eye on their garages too. Jordie, you know you've got a big bullseye on your back—that's not new—but we've never had someone get this close. You need to be careful." Joe's dark eyes were even darker with worry.

Jordan crossed her arms and widened her stance. "Joe, I'm not going to be less than I am, which is a kick-ass race car driver. Someone obviously feels threatened by us to do something like this. I'll take my chances, but I certainly don't want anyone on the team to get hurt. We need to come up with a plan to make sure everyone is safe. Any thoughts?"

Joe met Jordan's eyes. "I reached out to Ms. Kincaid, and she's going to hire extra security for the garage until race day."

Jordan clenched her jaw. "You talked to Florence Kincaid before me? I mean I know she owns the team and writes our checks, but we should've discussed it first." The last thing she wanted was for Florence to think she needed a babysitter.

"I'm sorry, Jordan. She called this morning to check on things and it just slipped out. She said she'll be here Friday for qualifying and through to the race Sunday. She was happy to hear that the car and you are doing well on the track."

Florence Kincaid, the no-nonsense lesbian billionaire who started the team had chosen Jordan as their principal driver over four years ago. "I haven't seen her since Brazil, so it'll be nice to catch up." She looked over at Joe, who looked ready to drop from exhaustion. "Joe, great detective work. You saved my ass, yet again, but, buddy, you should get some rest. We'll figure this out, so everyone stays safe. Right now, I need to head over for media day, but I'll see you later." Jordan squeezed his shoulder and headed to her RV.

Fucking sabotage. When she reached the inner sanctum, she paced the kitchen area, trying to work out who could be doing this and why. She'd be lying if she said it didn't scare her, but it pissed her off just as much. She was glad Joe had given her a heads-up about Florence's visit too. They could tackle the team's security, and she could prepare a proposal about bringing Lex up from Indy NXT as their second driver. Her phone pinged with a text.

Top Gun conference room, ten minutes. Look presentable. You'll start with Racer.com. Check the email I sent.

What a pain. Her phone pinged again, and she wanted to ignore it as it was likely Tina.

Good morning, early riser. Gorgeous picture from a gorgeous woman. Have a great day being beautiful and fast! x Q

Jordan swelled with happiness. *Fast & beautiful, I like it! U have a great day too. See you tonight. I'll text when I'm on my way. Can I bring anything? x*

Jordan walked into the conference room and thought of being with Quincy tonight. She looked up at the cameras and lights set up for her interview. *You need to focus. Get your racing mindset on, Jordie.* A production assistant placed her microphone on her racing suit as she sat in the chair as directed.

Max Franklin from Racer.com was already waiting. "Good to see you, Jordie. How've you been?"

"Hey, Max. Hanging in there. How're Maggie and the kids?"

Max laughed and shook his head. "I can't believe you remembered her name. Maggie's good. We're empty-nesters now, so it's taken some adjustment. Want to get started?"

Jordan nodded and felt her racing persona slide into place. The team's logo was projected behind her on one television screen and the IndyCar logo on the other.

"I'm Max Franklin from Racer.com, and today I'm here in Los Angeles covering the LA Grand Prix. I have with me Jordan Marsh, driver of car number twenty-two for the Pink Triangle Racing team. Jordan, thanks for joining our fans today as we discuss the upcoming qualifier and Sunday's race."

Jordan turned on her megawatt-smile at Max and, more importantly, the camera that was over his shoulder. "Thanks for having me, Max. Let's get into it."

The morning was a Groundhog Day of interviews. She answered questions from racing reporters as well as the mainstream media. The news of the team's sabotage spread like wildfire, and every interviewer asked about it. She didn't have much to say, so they turned their questions to her personal life and asked her about the new blond she'd been seen with last night. She went with the "friend" category, although every time she said it, she felt like she was being untruthful. Would there be a point when she could call her something else? Hope was fragile but definitely there.

She rubbed her jaw as she walked back to the garage, her face hurt from holding her big smile for so long. While that was all part of the job, she was happier getting to focus on driving for the rest of the day. She received a confirmation notification of Quincy's flower delivery. It might have been cheesy giving her a rose for every day they'd known each other, but she hoped Quincy would appreciate the gesture. Fifteen minutes later, she got a text.

The roses and Jada's biscuit are so thoughtful. Thanks for thinking of us when you're so busy x

Jordan smiled broadly. *YW – cul8r, going to go drive fast now!! xo* She drove her final practice lap for the day, needing all her concentration for the course. It shouldn't have been a difficult run, but the fear of more sabotage kept her from fully focusing on the car's setup and the track. What if her team missed something, and she plowed into the palm tree on turn three? Those thoughts made her cautious when she needed to be aggressive, and it pissed her off. *This is just what that asshole wanted. Screw them.* It didn't help that the alternate tires weren't gripping. "Joe, it feels like I'm on ice skates out here. Our times won't look good today," she said and smacked the steering wheel.

Joe and the rest of the crew watched the car's telemetry on the computers in their pit lane stand. Those numbers, along with Jordan's helmet camera, would give him inside knowledge of what was happening on the track. "Just get in safely, and we'll check it out and make adjustments."

"Roger that. On the last turn. Heading in now." Jordan pulled the car into her assigned pit box and was met by Joe and her crew, who helped her out. She walked to the rear of the car and squatted down to visually inspect the tires. "We should look at these. It felt like they were unravelling." She stood up when the crew began to roll the car back to the garage.

Joe squeezed her arm. "Those tires weren't the only thing unravelling out there. I've been with you a long time, and I know you, Jordie. You were driving scared, and that's not going to win this race or keep you safe."

Jordan shook her head, angry that she'd let the situation affect her driving. "I know. Trust me, I know, but I just couldn't shake the feeling that the team could've missed something, and I was going to crash and burn. I'm always comfortable in that cockpit but today, I wasn't. I want to punch someone for putting me in this position." She kicked a rock, and it skidded across the ground before smacking into a metal sign and making a satisfactory clang.

"Jordie, you're like a daughter to me, and I won't let anything happen to you. I promise that you're safe, and that the car is safe."

Jordan's guilt at not trusting her team ate away at her. "I know, Joe. I think it was all the talk about it during the interviews today. It was just front and center in my mind. I'll shake it off and be ready for tomorrow."

"You better be. We've got the car and the garage covered. Nothing's going to happen there."

Jordan blew out a deep breath. "Thanks, Joe. I've been freaked out since I saw that video. I wish we knew who it was."

They walked into their paddock, and Joe pulled out his laptop. "Well, we don't know, but you need to get out of your head if we're going to win this. Let's look at your telemetry and work on the changes needed for the car's setup."

Jordan leaned back in her chair and rolled her shoulders. "We're slated for a one p.m. qualifying run tomorrow, right?"

Joe nodded. "Yeah, but we should meet around ten to discuss any changes we made and confirm our strategy for the laps. Will you be around tonight?" he asked as he checked his phone for messages.

"Nope. I'm gonna shower in the RV and head down to Quincy's for a BBQ with some of her friends."

Joe snickered. "Good. You need to get your mind on something other than sabotage, and Quincy's the perfect distraction. You've been tight-lipped about her all day. Don't think I didn't notice how freaked out you got when I mentioned her name this morning."

"Dude, I've been busy. The press asked about her today. I mean, everyone saw us together at the Racing Expo last night. I hope it won't be an issue for IndyCar. I'd hate for her to be blacklisted from the Medical Safety Support Crew because we're friends." She looked at the time on her phone. "I've got to go. Text me if anything changes about tomorrow. Thanks for listening, Joe." She headed over to her RV for a shower.

"Jordan. Jordan, wait," Tina yelled from across the garage.

"What now?" Jordan mumbled. "What's up, Tina? I'm in a hurry." She slung the bag over her shoulder and tapped her foot.

"Jordie, you did a nice job with the press, but you should've told me about the sabotage. You know I need to handle these things. We also need to handle the whole beach babe thing. I need to get into this, so we don't have any surprises. Don't forget we want to sell your edgy image to draw in the fans and sponsors. You having some kind of wholesome girlfriend isn't going to help with that."

Jordan gritted her teeth. "Her *name* is Quincy Fitzgerald. She's a nurse practitioner in the ER at LAMC, and she's part of the Medical Safety Support Crew for this race. We're friends, and she's not interested in being part of the press packet."

Tina tsked and put her hands on her hips. "You're more than friends. I saw the way you were together last night. That isn't how friends act. You told the press today that you were just friends, but what's the play here? I mean, less than a week ago you were with Lucy Chandler at Club Patch and before that, you were with Juliette Meadows in Brazil. Those women will keep you relevant and in the news. Let's be clear, they're more your league than this nurse." Tina tapped her iPad again as though to drive home her point.

Jordan turned her back on her and headed toward her RV. "Tina, I'm late for a date with Quincy. I suggest you slow your roll on insulting her. Maybe you could focus on promoting me to my sponsors and the press with regard to my driving instead of who I'm dating. I'll see you tomorrow." Jordan shut the RV door in Tina's face and headed to the shower. Maybe she should've told Tina about the sabotage. At least that would've given her some news to spread among the vultures and take the focus off Quincy. But then they'd use it against her saying she was making excuses for her performance before she even hit the track. *Never can win.*

Jordan pulled up to Quincy's thirty minutes later with butterflies in her stomach. She'd dressed casual in her favorite jeans and a hunter green long-sleeve shirt that brought out the green in her eyes. Quincy had liked her scent, so she covered her entire body with it, hoping that Quincy would get to discover all of her tonight. The duffel bag in her trunk had all the gear she needed for tomorrow if tonight truly was a stay and play. She certainly hoped it was. Soft music and women's laughter floated out to her as she opened the front screen door and walked into Quincy's living room after knocking but not getting an answer.

Quincy looked gorgeous in a blue dress that enhanced her curves. Jordan watched as a woman stepped back from what looked like an intimate embrace. She felt like she'd been punched in the gut and began to back out of the door until she met Quincy's gaze. The look in her eyes told her everything she needed to know.

Jordan hadn't realized it, but she needed to see that to be sure Quincy felt the same way about her. That look unleashed Jordan's desire. She walked into the kitchen and any reason left her mind as she pulled Quincy into her arms and claimed her tongue. She craved her like an addict and took her fill of her favorite drug as she kissed Quincy. As Quincy slowly pulled away, Jordan became aware that the kitchen was filled with Quincy's friends. How the hell were they ever going to find the time to be together?

Chapter Twenty

Still in Jordan's arms, Quincy introduced Jordan to her friends. Clearly she had to put Jordan's mind at ease if her expression after Lauren's hug was anything to go by. "Jordan, this is my good friend Lauren. Unfortunately her wife, Trish, couldn't make it tonight. These are my coworkers Renata and Paula. They're ER nurses. These lovely ladies are Sally and Jessica, my neighbors." Quincy inwardly sighed with relief when no one immediately recognized Jordan except Lauren.

Quincy had anxiously awaited Jordan's arrival. She felt starved in a way she never had before, and it had nothing to do with food. She'd welcomed her friends into her home for a monthly BBQ, but this was the first one of the year, and there was plenty to catch up on. Conversation was fast, and Jordan seemed content to sit and listen. The party picked up steam, a lot of steam after that kiss, and she couldn't wait to be alone with Jordan. Surprisingly, they flowed well together in the kitchen, moving past and around each other with ease as Jordan helped with the food. Her small, simple touches set Quincy on fire; they either needed to be alone or she needed a cold shower. "Thank you for your help with dinner. I didn't invite you to make you work," Quincy said as she headed into her kitchen with Jordan on her heels.

"I enjoyed it. I don't often get the opportunity to grill, and we make a good team." Jordan leaned in, and they shared another scorching kiss.

She grazed Quincy's jaw, cheek, and earlobe with her teeth, quietly whispering how much she wanted her. Her words stoked the heat that had engulfed Quincy with Jordan's first kiss, and it grew as Jordan continued to whisper dirty things in her ear. While she agreed with Jordan that she'd love nothing more than to head back to her bedroom and get a release, she shook her head slowly. "I want you too, but I still have hungry guests." She indicated the plate of steaks and vegetables they'd just grilled. "It would be bad form to head to the bedroom and start screaming your name while they're still here."

"Ya know, we don't have to go to the bedroom. Here works." Jordan trapped Quincy against the counter, and she shook her head again. "Okay, I'll be good, for now." She gave her a quick peck on the cheek, picked up the food, and headed out into the backyard.

An hour later, she opened another bottle of wine, but just as the cork popped, so did Renata.

"Oh, my God," she said, looking up from her phone.

"What is it?" Lauren asked.

Renata stared at Jordan. "You're Jordan Marsh, the famous lesbian race car driver. What're you doing *here*?" She looked between Jordan and Quincy.

Jordan gave her a small smile. "We're friends, and she invited me."

"We can see you're some kind of *friend*." Lauren laughed and tapped Quincy's leg, then everyone buried Jordan in questions about her racing career, her love life, and travels.

Quincy grimaced as that overtook normal conversation. "Okay, everyone, that's enough. Leave Jordan alone." They ignored her. It was too much like the other events where she felt left out, so she got up to get the coffee and dessert. Quincy had plans for her own special dessert later tonight, but that meant clearing the house of her friends, and the quickest way to do that was to finish feeding them.

Lauren came into the kitchen, plates in hand.

"Thanks for your help," Quincy said but only got silence in response. She turned to see Lauren looking serious. "What's wrong?"

"There's nothing wrong. I know you're into her, and I can see why. She's so dynamic and gorgeous. I know I pushed you down this road, but I don't want you to get hurt by this fast and furious woman." Lauren shrugged and leaned on the counter.

"Don't worry. I'm a big girl, and I'll be okay. Thank you for caring." Quincy didn't want to talk about the questions that still bothered her and the way Jordan's notoriety continued to make her a little uncomfortable.

"You know I love you, and I only want the best for you." She gave Quincy a quick hug and headed outside with the coffee.

While Quincy plated her famous peanut butter chocolate pie, she thought about how her chosen family made her feel supported. She grabbed the dessert and plates then headed back outside. The food coma that came after dessert slowed the tide of questions aimed at Jordan, and for that, Quincy was relieved. She grabbed Jordan's hand and gave it a small squeeze. Just the touch of Jordan's skin lit the fire in Quincy, and she knew it was time for them to be alone. She stood to clear the plates as Paula took a call from her sitter and had to leave. Sally and Jessica left soon after saying they were driving to Palm Springs in the morning. Everyone hugged Jordan and wished her well in the race on Sunday.

"I'm pretty tired. I'm going to head out," Renata said to the group in the kitchen.

"I think I'll head out too, Trish should be home soon," Lauren said. "You all good? Do you need any help cleaning up?"

"No, we can clean up what's left, thanks. Please give my best to your wifey and tell her I hope she can come next month," Quincy said as she hugged Lauren.

Lauren headed to the door with Renata then stopped. "Jordan, it was a pleasure to finally meet you. Quincy has been telling me only good things, and it's good to see she hasn't been lying. Good luck Sunday, give 'em hell. Go Pink Triangle Racing team! Lesbians rule," she shouted as she closed the door behind her.

Jordan slid her arms around Quincy's waist. "I like that you've been talking to your friends about me. I wasn't too sure about Lauren because she has this whole lioness protector thing going on, but she's great. The rest of the ladies were lovely, though that might have more to do with the tickets I offered them for Sunday's race," she said and laughed.

"You didn't mind all of Renata's questions? Some of them were really personal. What was that question she asked about sabotage in your garage?" Quincy slowly stroked Jordan's forearms.

Jordan gave her a smile that held a mixture of warmth and mischief. "Okay, you got me there, but they were less than what I fielded today by the media, especially about the sabotage. Someone broke into our garage and sliced holes in the hydraulic hoses. We've increased security, and there haven't been any new issues. It's no biggie. Let's talk about you. You, Ms. Fitzgerald, throw a fun BBQ, even if you do put your celebrity guest to work." She kissed down the side of Quincy's neck and along her jaw. "We're finally alone," she whispered into her ear.

She pressed Quincy against the countertop and kissed her. The slow burn exploded into an inferno and engulfed them both. Jordan pressed her hot body against Quincy. The intensity overwhelmed her, and she pulled away to catch her breath. The raw need had her vibrating from the inside out. She explored Jordan with her fingertips and tongue. She followed the slope of Jordan's jaw, to her lips, chin, and neck and caressed her arms. She kissed Jordan, deep and warm, then she pushed away from the countertop and held out her hand. She sucked in her breath, uncertain of what would come next, until Jordan grabbed it and followed her into her bedroom.

"I've wanted more of you since last night. Your lips are so soft, and your taste is addictive."

Jordan explored Quincy with butterfly kisses and light nips along her neck, down her collarbone and across the simple buttons of the dress that was pulled tight over her breasts. Jordan's nimble fingers worked to open the few buttons and exposed her bare pale breasts and taut nipples.

"You're so beautiful," Jordan whispered.

She ran her tongue over Quincy's left breast and caressed the nipple of her other one until it was fully erect.

Quincy moaned, her body alight and needing more of everything. Jordan pulled away and removed Quincy's dress, leaving her in just her silk panties, then she drew her hand across Quincy's belly.

"I want to see your hot, hard body." Quincy pulled Jordan's shirt out of her jeans. She unbuttoned the top buttons, and Jordan pulled it off and flung it across the room. "I love that you aren't wearing a bra. It made me crazy when I felt your nipples against my back tonight." She took Jordan's breasts into her mouth one at a time and teased her with her tongue, lips, and teeth until Jordan was moaning and grinding against her. The quick removal of Jordan's jeans and boyshorts was next, which was almost Quincy's undoing. Jordan was a goddess come to life, and Quincy couldn't stop herself from touching the chiseled planes of her body. She was like a carved sculpture, and Quincy needed to feel every inch of her body. "You're so gorgeous. I've been wet since last night," Quincy said, breathless as she worked her hand over Jordan's toned abs. Her pulse hammered in her chest, and her control continued to slip away.

"So have I." Jordan pushed Quincy back onto the soft mattress.

She continued her exploration of Quincy's body, delicately kissing every inch as her skillful fingers and tongue worked Quincy's breasts to hard peaks. She slid her hand over Quincy's stomach. She cupped Quincy's hot wet mound through her panties, and she moaned.

"Oh, fuck." Quincy arched into Jordan's touch. She wanted Jordan's hands, tongue, and fingers on her and in her now. She slid her panties down and flung them off. The fire burning in Jordan's eyes made her weak as she straddled Quincy, locking her in place with her strong thighs.

"You're mine tonight," Jordan whispered before she deepened the kiss and teased Quincy until she began to whimper.

"God, you feel so good. I need to touch you." Quincy slid her hands up Jordan's powerful arms and strong sculpted shoulders around to her firm breasts. Quincy could see Jordan needed release as bad as she did. She continued mapping Jordan's body with her fingers and tongue, reveling in the taste of her skin and the ways her muscles twitched.

Jordan slid down Quincy's body, peppering her skin with kisses and nibbles until her hot breath caressed Quincy's swollen clit and wet core. She ran her hands through Jordan's hair, trying to direct her own pleasure. "Now...please. I want you in me now."

"I've wanted to taste you since I watched you straddle that surfboard." Jordan placed a light kiss to Quincy's swollen lips. "Oh my God, you taste so sweet." She moaned as she licked and flicked Quincy's clit with her tongue.

The sensation drove Quincy crazy. "I'm so close," she whispered as Jordan licked her length, then curled her tongue and drove it into her wet core. "Oh, yes. Oh, fuck, yes!"

Jordan pulled out and flicked Quincy's clit with her tongue, sending Quincy bucking against her face, then she filled Quincy with two fingers, bending them just right to hit her most sensitive spot. Jordan moved up Quincy's body and planted a deep kiss on Quincy's waiting mouth. Her long slender fingers found their home as Quincy arched in rhythm to Jordan's beat until she erupted in waves of pleasure.

"You're amazing. Simply amazing." She exhaled deeply as she came down from her release.

Jordan lightly traced Quincy's freckles as she recovered and smiled. "We're just getting started."

"Yes, and now it's my turn." Quincy ran her hands along Jordan's strong back. "I need more of you. I want to explore." Quincy pushed Jordan onto her back and straddled her. Heat radiated from Jordan's core, and Quincy wanted to turn up the flames. She leaned back to run her fingers up Jordan's thighs, increasing the pressure between their bodies.

"Oh, fuck, yes," Jordan groaned.

She grabbed Quincy's hips and ground against her as they increased their rhythm. Their intimate movement continued until Jordan began to quake. She repositioned herself over Jordan's clit and gave it her full attention. She kissed and sucked her clit with increasing speed.

"Damn, that feels good," Jordan yelled, grinding her hips into Quincy.

Quincy ran light touches against Jordan's swollen lips, feeling the electric hum of Jordan's body as she got closer and closer to the edge. With one last deep kiss, Quincy's fingers replaced her tongue without missing a beat. She straddled Jordan and thrust her fingers deeper into Jordan's wetness.

"Oh, baby. Oh, Q, baby." Jordan thrashed until Quincy finally short-circuited her system, and she released.

Panting, they lay intertwined, and Quincy enjoyed the feeling of their naked bodies together.

"Thanks for coming to dinner," Quincy said, slightly breathless.

"I liked what was on the menu, and I plan on having a few more courses before the night's over," Jordan said with a devilish gleam in her eye.

"I think I'll join you," Quincy said and kissed her, savoring the bliss of the moment, the letting go. Jordan had melted her mind, leaving her with the desire to live in the now—at least for tonight.

Chapter Twenty-One

THE DISTANT BUZZ OF a lawnmower woke Jordan from a dream with disturbing flashes of masked people creating chaos during a race. She'd fallen asleep with Quincy in her arms, and now she watched as her dark lashes fluttered in her dream world. Jordan relished making Quincy crazy, and her cheeks flushed with the memory of their night together. She was baffled by how much Quincy had come to mean to her in such a short period of time. Yeah, it was an intense physical attraction, but she couldn't deny the desire to talk things over with her or get her opinions on the simplest and most important decisions she needed to make.

Quincy opened her eyes and caught her staring. "A penny for your thoughts?"

"No penny needed. I was thinking of how wonderful last night was, and how much I don't want to leave for the track this morning."

Quincy gave Jordan a light kiss then rolled out of bed. "Not a problem. I know you've got to prepare for the big race. I'll go make us some coffee while you get showered and dressed. Come on, Jada, let's go make some high-octane caffeine for our race girl." She grabbed her robe and left the bedroom.

Jordan slapped the pillow that Quincy just vacated. "Dammit." She knew when Quincy got out of bed that the special moment would be shattered. Why did she talk about leaving before Quincy had even properly woken up? *Get a grip, Jordie, you do need to leave. You haven't talked about what this is or isn't. There's no expectations.* She slipped into the shower and brushed her teeth quickly while both admonishing herself and wishing Quincy was in there with her.

"Why does this feel different from just a good time? It doesn't matter. You need to focus on racing, not on whatever this feeling is," she said to her reflection. She finished in the bedroom and followed the scent of coffee as she checked her phone and saw multiple missed calls and texts from Tina. She had to get going.

She walked into the kitchen, and her heart revved at the sight of Quincy at the table, her robe slightly open to expose shadows Jordan wished she had more time to explore. She leaned down for a sensual kiss and tasted Quincy's coffee. "That coffee tastes good mixed with your sweetness, but I really have to leave."

Quincy backed away and eased herself off the chair. Jordan was certain it was due to her insensitive comments. Why'd she always have to be an ass.

"I figured you'd want a to-go cup. Black, like you like it," Quincy said and handed over the travel mug.

"Thanks." Jordan read the name on it. "Neptune's Underwater Archaeology. Is this the diving operation in the South Pacific that you're joining?"

Quincy leaned against the counter. "Yep, they're a great group led by Dr. David Lamoille; he's a maritime archaeologist. Most of us are volunteers, and this year, we're hoping to work on a recently discovered, unnamed ship from around 1730. So far, they've found some coins, nails, and ballast stones."

Quincy's enthusiasm for her diving adventures lit up her eyes. Jordan's gaze drifted from Quincy's tousled hair to her swollen pink lips. She'd done that; she'd made Quincy lose control, and the thought of doing it again thrilled her, though she knew it was crazy. She didn't do relationships. She never stayed with anyone because in time, they always used her. Quincy would likely be no different. Jordan needed to control her attraction for both their sakes. Racing was the only commitment she should be focusing on right now.

"How long will you be gone?" Jordan asked, surprised by her conflict at the idea of being apart.

"Three weeks. I leave on Wednesday. The first two, I'll work with Neptune, and the final week will be mine alone in paradise. I honestly can't wait." Quincy busied herself by wiping down the already clean countertop.

Jordan heard the excitement in Quincy's voice, along with something else that she couldn't place. *Did she not want to go?* She didn't want to encourage her leaving, but what could she say? What could she do? She was leaving LA after the Grand Prix to get ready for the Indy 500 anyway. *What the hell, Jordie? Do you just not want to be left or is it something else?* But now wasn't the time for those deep thoughts. She needed some distance from Quincy and her pull. "That sounds amazing. I'm glad you'll get some time away. Well, I better get going; I don't want Tina knocking down your door looking for me."

Quincy shuddered. "No. I've seen enough of that woman for a lifetime. Thanks for coming to dinner and staying for breakfast. I had an amazing time." She gave Jordan a wicked smile.

Her pulse raced under Quincy's intense gaze. "In case it wasn't obvious, so did I." She pulled Quincy into her arms, kissing her, soft at first, then with a fiery passion that stirred emotions she couldn't ignore. She craved more, but time wasn't on her side. Her career and her personal goal to be the best IndyCar driver consumed her. No one would cut her slack because she was a woman, and that left no space for a relationship. She wasn't even relationship material—past experiences made that clear. So she would leave, like she always did, before she ended up hurting Quincy.

"Bye, Jordan," Quincy said softly as she opened the door.

"I'll try to text you later." She waved and headed to her SUV. "Damn, that woman is one deadly drug." She took a sip of the silky-smooth hot coffee, and all she could think about was Quincy's silkiness. *Dammit. Focus.* She started the car and pulled away.

An hour later, Jordan pulled into the gate at Paramount and showed her badge to the guard. "Hey there, Frank, why's it so busy today?"

"Today's the first practice for the celebrity race, and the garages are open to the ticketed public."

"Oh, right, I forgot about that. Guess you'll have a busy day." She hated that there'd be a ton of people around, people who couldn't be watched as they roamed around, possibly free to mess with the cars.

"It's looking like it. Good luck on Sunday. My husband and I will be rooting for you to win," Frank said.

"Thanks." Jordan drove toward her garage and couldn't help but scan the area, as though she'd see someone behaving strangely. She pulled into her parking spot and checked her calendar for the day's activities. Luckily, it was light on public relations events and heavy on driving and tackling problems with the car. She had her one p.m. qualifying, and that was the priority of the day. She headed toward her RV to store her bag and change into her racing suit. Joe would've fixed most of the hiccups from yesterday, but she wanted to focus on any issues early. When she got to the garage, the tension was intense. "What's going on? What happened?"

"Tina's on the warpath," Joe said as he placed his hands on his hips. "She's been through here being her nasty self. I guess she's been trying to find you since last night. She mentioned Juliette was in town. We're staying out of it, but I thought you should know. Just keep her out of here. She doesn't belong in the garage, and she knows it."

"Thanks for having my back. I'll keep her out of the garage. Sorry you had to deal with her." *Oh, yay, Juliette is back. I'm sure Tina had nothing to do with that.* Jordan headed into her RV. Juliette Meadows was one of the many women who'd used Jordan's platform to either launch or re-launch their careers. She was an A-list star featured in a few blockbuster movies, but her career had stalled. For six months, she used Jordan's edgy, race girl, lesbian status to support her image and redevelop her name in Hollywood. The paparazzi ate her up, and about the time she became attractive to Hollywood again, she became less so to Jordan. It'd always been about what she could gain by being seen with Jordan instead of the relationship itself. She'd been no different from any of the other women she'd been with through the years. But now there was Quincy, who wanted to be with Jordan the woman, not Jordan the race car driver or celebrity. A taste of that kind of attention made her want more. But she wasn't ready to settle down, was she?

Jordan groaned and thumped her head on the doorframe. This wasn't the time for relationship woes. She sent a terse text to Tina, telling her to back off until she was done prepping for the day and didn't wait for a reply. Nothing mattered now but the car, the track, and getting ready to win.

***

"This car is fucking magic," Jordan said into her helmet microphone. She couldn't believe how tight and responsive it felt compared to the day before. It took turns and gripped the corners without losing speed, catapulting Jordan down the straightaway at almost 208 mph with a lap speed of 1:073. When the green flag came out for the ten-minute qualifying time trials, the car only improved. Joe remained on the radio in her ear, but Jordan didn't have much to say. Lap after lap, her speed improved until her final lap was clocked at 1:062. There were only two more drivers scheduled to run today, Kent Carver and a rookie named Scooter. Her fastest lap time assured she'd advance to tomorrow's qualifying as one of the six fastest drivers who would battle for the pole position. As Jordan drove to her pit spot, she exhaled, letting go of the fear of sabotage she carried during her run. The new security team in the paddock gave her hope there'd be no more issues. She was so relieved that Joe was right: it would be okay. Her team greeted her in the pits, excited by the run and their progress.

Joe leaned over the car and gave Jordan a high-five. "Fantastic run, Jordie!"

"The car is perfect. Don't change a thing, and we'll win everything coming our way," she said and climbed out of the cockpit.

"You bet." Joe high-fived the rest of the pit crew, and the team readied the car to return to the garage.

Carver sneered at Jordan and her team as he passed by on his way to his car for his qualifying lap. "Don't celebrate yet. You'll be behind me where you belong when I'm done today."

"Good luck with that. My 1:062 is the time to beat." She pointed to the recorded time on the jumbotron overhead.

She left her team in the garage to ready the car for tomorrow's final qualifying and headed into her RV with Joe to watch Carver's time trial. She could talk a big game, but she was nervous about his run. She wasn't worried about besting him during a race, but in qualifying, she didn't get to use her skills, so all she could do was watch.

"Carver's car is running fast too, but I don't think he can beat us," Joe said and turned on the TV.

Carver ran his ten-minute qualifying laps while Jordan fidgeted in the small space. Jordan jumped up when he finished his final lap with a top speed of 206 mph and a best lap time of 1:072. She high-fived Joe. "Yes, I still have the advantage. Let's see what Scooter does." She pulled a couple of waters from the fridge and handed one to Joe.

She didn't think Scooter, aka Jimmie Fong, could beat her, but sometimes rookies got lucky. She fidgeted with her water bottle as they watched him head out to the track for his qualifying run. He made a good effort, but his fastest lap was only 1:084 and his top speed topped out at 189 mph. Tomorrow they'd have the six fastest drivers' shoot-out to decide who would win the coveted pole position and take the $1million prize. "Talk to me. What do we need to do differently tomorrow? Any changes planned with the car? Should we review the telemetry for the track? Are there turns where we can improve?" Jordan wanted to plan for every eventuality. Carver's smug face made her even more determined to get the top position.

Joe shook his head. "I think we have a good setup. We'll put on some fresh tires and run the course tomorrow. We'll have the last slot to run since we've got the best time. It'll be warmer, and the tires will stick better," Joe said as he reviewed the data from the earlier run.

Jordan's phone pinged, and she groaned after reading the message from Tina. "So much for an early night. I've got a mandatory sponsors dinner with Margaret Reacher of Ophelia Travel and Amanda Sosa from SapphicSpark."

"Speaking of dinner, how was your BBQ at Quincy's last night? Did you have a good time?" Joe chuckled.

"You've been waiting to ask me that all day, haven't you? Yes, I had a good time. A very good time. Nice dinner, nice friends, and Quincy was the ultimate hostess." The fire on her cheeks spread. "I need to text her actually, so this conversation is over." Jordan grinned.

"Uh-huh, I knew you looked all loved up this morning." Joe laughed and leaned back, looking smug.

"Yeah, yeah." Jordan grabbed her phone and sent a quick text. *Hey there, hope you had a great day. Mine's been awesome so far. I started in your arms and then we made the fastest lap time. Been thinking of you. Heading out to a sponsors' dinner. See you tmrw?*

"I'll be around tonight if you need to talk after the chaos. Good luck with the sponsors. Keep the money flowing in, so we can keep that car pretty," Joe said and got up to leave. "Night, Jordie."

"Night, Joe." She set her phone down and got ready for the dinner. It was common for sponsors to want to wine and dine their drivers, but she didn't know why Tina hadn't told her about the meeting before now. But then, it wasn't like she was easy to reach, since she ducked Tina's calls and texts as often as possible these days. Joe was right; it was essential to keep the sponsors happy to keep the team financed and running. A driver and team's sponsorship were big business, and it was the difference between racing and sitting in the grandstands. The placement cost of a business's logo on her helmet or car ran from three hundred thousand dollars up to five million dollars per season. There'd been a time not so long ago when she really enjoyed it all, the wining and dining and nearly sycophantic attention. It made her feel on top of the world, like she could do no wrong. Lately though, she felt like a show pony at a carnival. Or was it just since she'd met Quincy and tasted a little of the world outside her bubble? If that was the case, then being with Quincy could be extra dangerous, and she should tread carefully. She had professional goals still to achieve, and if she lost her interest in playing the part, she might never get those opportunities. She needed to rein in her thoughts and be ready for tonight's meeting. She pulled out the Pink Triangle outfit Tina had placed in her closet for tonight and stripped down before she turned on the shower. *Would Quincy want to go to dinner?* She looked at herself in the mirror. *Jordie, focus on your work and stop obsessing about her.*

She left her RV, disappointed that she hadn't gotten a reply from Quincy but thinking it might be for the best. Jordan pulled up to the STK valet, where Tina was waiting, and waved to the few race fans gathered nearby. Someone, most likely Tina, had notified the paparazzi of her presence. They were across the street, taking pictures and yelling questions.

"Why wasn't this dinner on today's calendar?" she asked quietly as they entered the restaurant.

Tina shrugged. "It was a last-minute request. These are your biggest sponsors, and the team needs their money, so play ball, Jordan." She gave Jordan an unnatural smile and walked ahead of her into the private back room.

"Jordan, it's so good to see you." Margaret Reacher, CEO of Ophelia Travel, stood and hugged her briefly. Margaret had helmed many Fortune 500 companies in her career and at sixty-five, remained one of the fiercest women in business. She and her wife Janice had built Ophelia as a business that became their passion project as they moved on to bigger things.

"Hi, Margaret. It's lovely to see you again. You look well. How's Janice?" Jordan smiled.

"Great job capturing the fastest lap time today. What're our chances tomorrow for the pole?" Amanda Sosa asked as she stuck out her hand to shake Jordan's.

As graceful and professional as Margaret was, Amanda was sharp-edged with street smarts. She was a self-taught coding and engineering expert who'd built a lesbian dating algorithm well before anyone else. Her ability to capture the market and develop the SapphicSpark business ahead of all others made her financially flush and a businesswoman to watch. If Jordan wanted to emulate anyone outside the racing world, it would be these two women. "We're going to win the pole and the race on Sunday."

Amanda gave a sharp laugh. "That's what I wanted to hear."

"Amanda and I have a lot to discuss with you, so we should get started," Margaret said. "Did you want anything to drink? I thought we could eat after our discussion."

"Just some sparkling water, please." Jordan indicated to the waitstaff and sat down on the leather banquette across from Amanda and Margaret. He brought her drink and left the room. Tina sat near the door, focused on her phone, but still clearly listening in.

"I know it may seem strange to discuss business with us together," Margaret said, "but since you're on each of our NDAs, we can share with you that the Ophelia Corporation will be buying the SapphicSpark algorithm and app in the next quarter, and our companies will merge next year."

What would that mean for the investment in the team? "Congratulations."

"Jordan, we've been proud of what you've accomplished in the past four years," Amanda said. "With your pole positions, laps led, wins, and media attention, it's been an amazing year on and off the track, and that's reflected onto us as your sponsors. Both companies have had a lucrative fiscal year largely due to your influence on our clients. We'd like to re-invest in the Pink Triangle Racing team *and* in you with some of those dividends. We've heard the rumblings about bringing up another driver and our sponsorship money could support that if Florence agrees." She paused and looked at Margaret, who smiled. "We're going to double our sponsorship. We want to give the team $20 million next season."

Jordan's world tipped sideways for a second before it righted as she thought of the numbers. "Wow, that's quite a generous investment. Thank you. I'm honored by your continued support of me and the team. This is so exciting. We could think about expanding with that level of investment. I was planning on talking to Florence this weekend about bringing up another driver. Does she know of your plans?" Jordan thought about her ideas of bringing Lex up to the big leagues and expanding the team with other successful drivers. This could be everything she wanted to push her career to the next level.

Margaret held up her hand. "Florence knows we'll be investing again, but we hadn't gotten into the details. We'd expect an overhaul of the car, helmet, and gear before the start of next season to reflect the merger. We also have some personal modifications that we'd need you to agree to before we'd finalize the deal." She hesitated. "Our data shows that both of our companies do best when you remain in the spotlight. You're tied to us and vice versa. The revenue generated when Ophelia had destination events with you headlining or speaking were immense. The public loves you, and the lesbian public *really* love you. We'd need for you to remain the edgy, single lesbian icon you've been for the past few years. Your failed attempts to find a partner and have it play out in the news push up the enrollment for the dating app. Lesbians travel to your races and events because they know you're single, and you might be available. We need that to continue."

Jordan's stomach dropped as Margaret outlined the strings attached to the money. Of course there were strings. The opportunity for Lex and the rest of her hard-working team was too great to pass up though, wasn't it? So what if she had to live her lonely life in the public eye for another year? Another year of playing the puppet. Did it even matter when so many others would benefit? But what about Quincy? She mattered.

"We've watched you with that blond woman. What's her name?" Amanda asked.

"Quincy Fitzgerald," Tina hissed, still not looking up from her phone.

"Jordan, let's be clear, that relationship needs to end, or at the very least, you need to keep it in the shadows," Margaret said. "You need to be in the public's eye and not at some BBQ like every other lesbian. No one gets excited about a celebrity who seems like an everyday woman. You need to live the image, Jordan. That's what we're paying for, and while we're aware that it's a morally gray area, we're prepared to put it in the contract. You decide what you want, but we think this is too amazing of an offer to pass up. There are other necessary items as well, like posting on social media, winning races, etcetera, but those have some room for negotiation."

"Okay, ladies, I see the proposal in my inbox. I'll review and discuss it with Jordan, and we'll get back to you before Sunday. Shall we order some food?" Tina walked over to the table and sat next to Jordan, making it clear that the business portion of the meeting was over.

Jordan made it through the meal in a state of shock, though just the smell of the food turned her stomach. The increased sponsorship offer was amazing, but her own personal investment left her dazed. Two weeks ago, the requirement that she keep up the single life wouldn't have fazed her. Now, though... She wanted to drive to Quincy's house and talk this over with her, but that was the last thing she could do. How did you tell a woman you were into that you had to choose between dating her and $20 million? It seemed so seedy, so shitty. Jordan made her exit with the excuse of needing rest for tomorrow's qualifying race, which was true, but what she really needed was space to work through their proposal. She headed across the restaurant to the valet. Her stomach dropped when *that voice* called her name.

"Jordan, darling, how are you?"

Juliette looked even thinner than before, which Jordan hadn't thought possible. When she kissed Jordan's cheek, Jordan felt absolutely nothing but annoyance. "Nice to see you. I'm on my way out." She gestured toward her car pulling up.

"Oh, wonderful, can you give me a ride? I'm just down the block at the Waldorf Astoria." Juliette took Jordan's hand and led them outside.

"Sure, I can drop you off." Her reply was drowned out by the media frenzy outside the door. Camera flashes exploded in their faces. Questions were lobbed at her like grenades. *What the actual fuck is it about this night?*

"Jordan, you're back with Juliette? What about Quincy?"

"Did you have a nice dinner?"

"Are you going to win the pole tomorrow?"

"Jordan, having some pre-race fun tonight?"

Jordan couldn't get through the crowd quickly enough. She let the valet open Juliette's door and ran around to the driver's seat before he could get there.

She pulled out of the parking lot too quickly, making the tires screech. "Did Tina set this up tonight? How'd you know I'd be here?"

"Jordan, it was fate. I just happened to be leaving as you were." Juliette shrugged.

"I don't think so. Luckily, I don't have to play this game with you. Goodbye, Juliette." Jordan pulled up to the front of the hotel.

"You don't want to come up? Talk a little? Play a little?" Juliette ran her hand up Jordan's thigh.

She pushed Juliette's hand away. "No, I have a race tomorrow, and tonight has been stressful enough. Please get out," she said through clenched teeth.

"Ouch, you're a crab tonight. Okay, fine. Good luck tomorrow. I'll be right at the front, rooting for you," she said and got out of the car.

Jordan drove back to her hotel to rest for tomorrow's big day, beyond frustrated by tonight's turn of events. She entered her suite already knowing sleep would be elusive. *If only I could share this with Quincy.* But now, it looked like she'd have to keep Quincy at arm's length. She wasn't the kind of woman who'd accept being kept a secret, and Jordan sure as hell wouldn't want to treat her like one. Was it only this morning she'd woken with Quincy in her arms? It already felt like ages ago, and it wasn't like she'd left Quincy's with a promise of forever. Jordan fell onto her bed and tears welled in her eyes. She'd always been willing to sacrifice everything for her dreams. Now that sacrifice meant losing a woman who made Jordan feel like life could hold more than what others wanted from her. But what choice did she have?

Chapter Twenty-Two

QUINCY FINALIZED HER FLIGHTS and lodging for her South Pacific trip. Now she just needed to start on packing. She was distracted all day as her thoughts were peppered with images of Jordan in her home, in her bed, and against her body. She remained in a state of arousal for most of the day, but she hadn't jumped to respond to Jordan's text. There was too much uncertainty, too much unsaid between them, and she needed time to process. Jordan's career was demanding and required that she spend a lot of time in the spotlight. Could Quincy deal with that in the long run? It meant giving up a measure of control to the press, who could say and do damn near anything and get away with it. Not to mention the kind of women Jordan was surrounded by. Wasn't there a princess recently? How the hell could she compete with that? In the time Quincy was going to be gone, the likelihood was that Jordan would find another woman or five to replace her. It would be ludicrous to fall for someone like that. And yet... Quincy sighed, picturing Jordan's sweet smile and the way she looked as she gave herself over to an orgasm.

Her phone rang, and she breathed a sigh of relief at the intrusion to her thoughts. It was someone from work, asking if she could cover the last four hours of Ted's shift since he'd fallen ill and was going home.

"Of course he is. Wasn't his promotion party today? I can't believe that wuss couldn't finish his shift. What an ass." Just when she needed to figure out what swimsuits to bring and which sandals would best go with everything, so she didn't overpack. She agreed to be there at seven and finished the few chores around the house.

Her phone pinging disturbed her again.

I had a good time last night. Probably not as good as you! It was great meeting Jordan. She seemed very into you. I hope you didn't get any sleep!

Quincy shook her head. *It was a fun night and nope, didn't get much sleep!! Heading into work at seven to cover Beatle's shift.*

Is the sexiest woman alive good in bed? Inquiring minds want to know!

Quincy laughed and shook her head. *Like you have to ask.*

That good, huh? Okay, fine.

Quincy loved the lift she got from talking or texting with Lauren. She always knew how to look at life with a broader lens. She walked Jada and then left for the hospital.

Quincy walked into the shared locker room, stashed her work bag and tucked all her equipment into the cargo pockets of her scrubs. She sat on the bench and took a deep breath to steady herself. She'd worked the ER for over ten years but tonight was different. Tonight, she'd face the pitying glances of her coworkers and the jerk who'd taken her promotion. *You can do this, Quincy. It's just one shift, then three weeks off. Hell, it may even be one of your last shifts here if you land a new job.* With that thought, she left the locker room and headed for the nursing station, the pulse of the ER awaiting her. She walked up to the main ED nursing station to find Ted but found the ER's two biggest gossips, Maxine and Ruby, leaning close together, their expressions suggesting they were engaging in their favorite pastime.

"Hey there, Ruby. Where's Ted? I need to get a sign-out on his patients before he leaves," Quincy said, twirling her pen in frustration. The motion did little to calm her. Instead, she kept visualizing burying the pen in his ear when she saw him.

Ruby smiled. "I think he already left. Maxine, is Ted still here?"

"He left thirty minutes ago. He said his patients were 'stable,'" Maxine said.

"I doubt that. The weasel just doesn't even have the balls to face me," Quincy said and gave them both a big smile.

Maxine and Ruby laughed. "You said it, girl. Forget him. Tell us how it feels to be a celebrity?" Maxine asked.

Quincy's stomach dropped. "Jordan and I are just friends. We've just been seen in public together, that's it." She studied the patient board like it held all the answers. This was exactly what she'd been worried about when it came to dating someone so high-profile.

Ruby shook her finger. "Quincy, you can't lie to us. Look at these photos of you together. You even have a celebrity couple name! "Hashtag JorQuin." She pointed to a website on her computer screen with pictures of Jordan and Quincy. "Tell us what it's like. Is she fast at everything? Those eyes... They just look through you. Oh, what I wouldn't give," she said and fanned herself with a chart.

"What the hell? You've been married for thirty years."

"Girl, a woman can dream. She's one of my freebies, and my hubby knows it," she said then turned around to answer the phone.

"Okay, then. Good to know. That's a terrible celebrity name," Quincy said as she looked over Ruby's shoulder at the images of them at the Racing Expo. Heat climbed up her neck and into her face. It was time to go see some patients and calm down. "I'll go check on Ted's patient in eleven; it looks like they're supposed to be discharged." Quincy indicated the patient board as she started down the hall. She could hear Ruby's laughter as she walked away. She knocked on the door and walked into the room to find the patient was being assisted into a wheelchair by a staff member. "Hi, Mr. Jameson. My name's Quincy. I wanted to be sure you were stable before you went home."

"Hi, Doc. Yeah, I'm good. Already beer cleared. See you next time," he said with a quick wave as he was wheeled out the door.

So much for that assessment. Quincy shrugged and turned away.

"Tier one trauma. Tier one trauma. Tier one trauma," the automated notification rang out in the ED.

Quincy hurried back to the nurse's station. "Which trauma bay and who's receiving the patient?" Quincy asked.

"Trauma two, and Rochelle is receiving. It's a driver from the LAGP celebrity race. I don't have the details, but I guess they hit a wall during their practice run," Ruby said, all earlier levity gone as she typed details into the computer.

"Okay, I'll go over and see if they need help. Page me back if we have any patients I need to see from triage." Quincy headed over to trauma two. Jordan wasn't on the celebrity team, was she? She hadn't mentioned it. Still, Quincy's breath caught in her chest until she saw the person in the bed. The patient's helmet remained on their head, and the racing suit was being cut off by the staff. She was instantly struck by the image of Jordan's body being extricated from her car and the agonizing feelings that image evoked. She had to take a deep calming breath before she stepped into the room. The staff held the driver down on the table as they thrashed in pain. The paramedics were giving details to the ED staff.

"Kennedy Marks, twenty-five-year-old female, lost control of her race car at ninety mph on the LAGP celebrity circuit. She ran into the SAFER barrier head-on. Positive loss of consciousness at the scene and then agitated when awake upon extraction from vehicle. Only oriented to self now. Failure of helmet removal system at scene. She needs cervical spinal traction for removal, concern for spinal injury. Her right ankle is misaligned with noted abrasions to hands bilaterally. Vitals have been stable, IV started, and 500 milliliters of fluids given. She has no known allergies and no medical conditions. Her wife, Peyton, is following in a private vehicle. She should be here shortly. We'll be here for a while if you've got questions, and the IndyCar race officials are also enroute." The paramedic lowered his clipboard.

Rochelle took over the care of the celebrity driver and directed her treatment. The team performed an initial assessment and then provided pain medication to help keep her calm. Quincy stood at the door to the room and made eye contact with Rochelle.

"Q, did your LAGP training cover helmet removal?" she asked.

Quincy nodded. "Yeah, I can help." She stepped to the top of the gurney, and Rochelle stepped aside. She looked at the lead nurse and pushed aside all personal feelings. "Sally, now that she's calmer, apply cervical traction while I attempt to inflate the helmet removal airbag. If this doesn't work, we'll have to manually remove the helmet." She attached a sixty-milliliter syringe to the port and pushed the air into the balloon, meeting some resistance. The helmet lifted away from Kennedy's skull, and Quincy was able to remove it without further manipulation.

But when she saw Jordan's face, not Kennedy's, she trembled and stumbled away from the gurney with the bulky helmet in her hands. She placed it on a nearby table, wrapped her arms around herself, and watched the team care for the patient. Her help was no longer needed, and she wanted some space.

Rochelle grabbed Quincy's arm as she passed by on her way out. "Great work, Quincy," she said and smiled. "Okay, everyone, let's get a new cervical collar on her before she goes to imaging."

"I'm stepping away. Call if you need me." Quincy's voice trembled as she walked from the room and out into the staff kitchen. She sat at the table with her head in her hands and jumped when Rochelle sat down across from her at the table.

"What's going on?" Rochelle asked gently, pulling Quincy's hands away from her face.

Quincy shrugged. "What do you mean? Kennedy Marks is an action star. It's just tough to see someone so vibrant lying on the gurney."

Rochelle squeezed her hand. "I'm not buying that. We see this every day, so why is this different? Is it Jordan? Have you fallen for her? I saw the pictures of you at the Race Expo, and you both looked smitten." She smiled kindly.

Quincy glared at her. "Don't act like you care. I was just a notch on your bedpost and as soon as I find someone new, be it Lauren or Jordan, your green-eyed monster comes out, and you get interested again."

Rochelle took a deep breath and released it along with Quincy's hand. She met Quincy's fiery gaze and nodded. "You're right. My apology is well overdue. I wanted you and once I had you, I really didn't know how to keep you. I did what I always do and moved on, and I hurt you in the process. Quincy, I respect you, and I'd like for us to be friends again. I recently met someone who's changed my perspective on what it means to love. So if Jordan is someone you love, I'm here for you."

Quincy's mouth dropped open. She never expected to hear that from her, and in truth, she really needed someone to talk to. "Thank you for apologizing. I don't know about being in love with Jordan, but yes, she means a lot to me. I'm attracted to her body, mind, and soul. When I saw Kennedy on the table with the helmet and racing suit, all I could think was, what if this was Jordan? I don't have any control with this relationship. I can't keep her from getting hurt. I can't keep the press out of my life. I can't know if she's going to find someone new by the time I finish washing my hair." She shivered and hugged herself.

Rochelle gently placed her hands over Quincy's. "You live in the real world. You know you can't control other people's lives. You can't prevent injury or bad things from happening to them. All we can do is be there to love and support them and then help to pick up the pieces when things fall apart. You have friends here who respect and love you. You can always lean on us too."

Quincy took a deep breath and fought off the tears. She swiped her eyes and looked at Rochelle. "Where did the old cocky Rochelle go?"

Rochelle laughed. "She's still here, trust me. I just want you to be happy, to lead with your heart. And if that means Jordan Marsh, then lucky her. Don't let fear win. You know life's too short." Rochelle's pager beeped. "I need to head in, but let's meet up outside work sometime, and I'll introduce you to the woman who's changed me for the better."

"She must be someone special. I'll look forward to that. Thanks,

Rochelle, for your apology and support. It means a lot." She stayed to think about Rochelle's revelation and apology, both of which had healed a hole in her she didn't even know existed. What would it be like to have a real relationship with Jordan? Was Rochelle right? Was it nothing more than fear holding her back? Maybe, like Rochelle, Jordan could settle down and be with just one woman, if it was the right one. She wasn't sure that was what Jordan wanted, but she'd have to ask her and find out. She finished her shift and headed to her car, where she debated on driving home or to Jordan's garage.

She opened her phone to check her texts. Notifications swarmed the lock screen, and she immediately saw images of Jordan and Juliette Meadows in an embrace. She read the caption on TMZ: *It appears Jordan Marsh and Juliette Meadows are still an item as they're seen tonight leaving STK together before heading to the Waldorf Astoria.*

Her stomach dropped, and the excitement woven around her earlier unraveled. *What the hell? She was in my bed this morning and ended the night with her? I'm sure there's a good reason...* But it certainly made the decision on where to go next easier. Quincy headed home and gripped the steering wheel as she thought about how stupid she was for thinking they could have a future. *Zebras don't change their stripes.* She'd always thought Jordan was out of her league, and it wasn't like they had some kind of commitment. Jordan could date whomever she wanted. So why did Quincy feel like she'd been dropped into a frozen tundra to freeze all alone? Her phone pinged with an incoming text, and she was flooded with anxiety at the thought of it being Jordan.

Saw TMZ article - I'm sure it wasn't anything. Here if you want to talk. Xo

Quincy debated if she should respond to Lauren. She certainly didn't feel like talking about it. *Just got off shift and saw it too. I need to decompress. Talk tomorrow.* The only thing she wanted to do was shower and sleep. She was tired from their all-night lovemaking and the emotional turmoil at work. She couldn't make any rational decisions now, and she didn't want to make any rash ones. But that cold feeling in her heart and soul persisted. Jordan lived a life of danger and freedom, with women throwing themselves at her left and right. Quincy was just...Quincy. How could she compete with everything Jordan's life already offered?

Chapter Twenty-Three

Focus was impossible. She wanted that pole position and honestly, she deserved it. But as much as she needed to listen to her team and focus on the race, her thoughts returned to the sponsorship offer from last night, what it could mean for her team, and what it would be like to bring up another driver. She was excited at the prospect but unsettled at the idea of cutting Quincy from her life. She'd developed real feelings for her. Quincy challenged her, made her think about her actions, think about the real world that existed outside her bubble. She wasn't sure she could walk away, but she didn't see how she had a choice. She sat in the kitchenette and nursed her protein shake as she ran through her options. She was startled by a knock on her RV door.

"Jordie, you in there?" Joe asked.

"Yeah, Joe. Come on in."

"What're you doing? Why aren't you out in the garage? The IndyCar media staff were there a few minutes ago looking for you. Are you feeling okay? Nerves got a hold of you?" He sat down on the other side of the table and looked her over.

Jordan stared at the drink in her hand, unable to make eye contact with him. She was afraid he'd judge her for what she was going to do to Quincy. "No, not driving nerves," she said softly.

"What happened at the dinner last night? Are they cutting their sponsorship money? Are we losing the ride?" he asked quietly.

Jordan had to talk to someone, and there wasn't anyone more invested than Joe. "Not exactly. On the business end, things will be changing with our two biggest sponsors, but the one thing that isn't changing is the money they're sending our way. They want to support the team with a $20 million investment for next year."

"Hot damn, that's amazing! We could run a second team with that kind of money."

Jordan slowly nodded. "Yes. Yes, we could."

Joe frowned, settled back in the seat, and folded his hands over his stomach. "What aren't you telling me?"

Jordan got up and paced the length of the RV. "There are conditions. For one, I would need to stay an edgy, *single* lesbian icon. I'd have to keep living my personal life in public and be '*Jordan Marsh*.'" She made air quotes and shook her head. "According to them, being edgy doesn't include Quincy. I'd have to stop seeing her or tuck her into a closet so no one would know."

Joe's face flushed beet red. "What the hell? They're making a business decision that revolves around your personal life. That's crazy and wrong."

Jordan shrugged. "Is it? I mean, I'm the brand. I'm the face of Pink Triangle Racing, and they think if other women know I'm available, it helps sell their products. I'm the product that sells the rest of their shit."

"In all my years." Joe slapped his hand against the table. "They don't ask that of the guys, do they? They let them be boring married men or playboys, but they don't have money used as a lever for their actions. This is bullshit. I can tell you really like Quincy. You're more of your true self when she's around. What are you going to do?"

Jordan sat back down at the table. "That's why I'm in here instead of out there doing what I'm supposed to be doing. I don't know what to do. Tina has pushed Juliette back into my orbit, and now the press thinks we're together again. The media storm is insane, and I've already had texts from the sponsors telling me that's exactly what they want. It's all a mess, and I honestly don't know what to tell Quincy. It's unfair to her, no matter what. I stay with her, and we lose our biggest sponsors, and the media fallout from that will paint her as a villain. Plus, we won't be able to bring up a second team. Is my personal life worth the cost to everyone around me?" She sighed and pinched the bridge of her nose. "I'll get it together and be out shortly. Let's keep this conversation between us for now. I want to talk with Florence before I accept anything."

Joe got up and headed for the door. "You know I've got your back, whatever you decide. Come out when you're ready to race. Let's get this pole position today, so they can talk about your skill behind the wheel and not just in front of a camera."

"Thanks, Joe. I'll be out soon." Once the door closed, she did what she'd been dreading all morning and called Quincy. She just wanted to hear Quincy's voice, talk to her about the time trials, the car, and pole position. She could text, but she just wanted to hear her sweet voice. She got Quincy's voicemail. *I hope she's all right.* "Hi, Quincy, it's Jordan. Um... We need to talk. It'll be a busy day here, but maybe you can come by the garage? Or I might be able to stop by your house. Let me know if you'll be up for that. Hope to talk soon. Bye." It was stilted and awkward, just like the situation she was in.

She began her pre-race visualization and meditation to center herself. But the pit in her stomach wasn't going away. Jordan left her RV focused on winning the pole position for the LA Grand Prix. She focused on the fans and VIPs that were brought around by IndyCar to keep her mind off Quincy. The closer it got to track time, the more she focused on what the crew was doing. Because of the earlier sabotage, they'd gone over every inch of the car to make sure it was perfect. The car was towed out to her pit lane, and she remained there until she was given the authorization to get in by the officials. Jordan climbed into her cockpit and was assisted with the safety gear. The routine of it settled her, and then there was nothing but her and the car. Her engine was started, and she gave Joe a thumbs up that all systems were go. She had ten minutes to run the fastest laps possible around the circuit. All other drivers had gone before her, and the time to beat was 1:062 for her to win the coveted pole position. She drove the car around the circuit twice and then radioed into Joe. "A little oversteer. Tires are gripping better today."

"Telemetry is green, all systems look good here," Joe's voice crackled through her headset.

Nate announced in her ear, "Green flag, Jordie, green flag."

"Okay, grab your balls. Let's see how she does." Jordan brought the car up to speed through the straightaways and maneuvered through the turns. Her first lap was 1:061, and her times got quicker and quicker. "Car feels good, Joe. Let's finish out this qualifying." Jordan finished the final two laps with the fastest time of 1:041. The car was part of her, and the strange combination of peace and adrenaline was all she needed to make her dreams come true.

The crew erupted into cheers in her headset. She'd won the pole position and the million-dollar prize. She pulled the car back into the pit lane and got out as quickly as she could. The team picked her up and carried her to the wall of the pit lane. IndyCar media reporter Clark Rasmussen had his microphone and camera focused on her as she celebrated with her team.

"Congratulations on your LA Grand Prix pole position and your big bonus, provided by Paramount Pictures. You had amazing times. What came together for you today?" he asked.

"My team had a fantastic setup all week. We've been communicating and working through the problems together, and this is what happens when you have the kind of team I do. I wouldn't be here today without all the Pink Triangle Racing team members. They each played a part. Thanks so much to my sponsors, Ophelia Travel, SapphicSpark, and P3," Jordan called out as she was swept away from Clark and into the crowd.

The fans and team members surrounded Jordan as they walked back to their garage. The other racing teams came out to congratulate them as they passed. All but Carver's team, who turned their backs when they walked by. When she reached her garage, she pumped her arm and then hugged Joe. "Let's celebrate."

IndyCar staff wheeled over bottles of champagne in a cooler. One of the mechanics popped a bottle and sprayed everyone, but no one minded.

Jordan leaned against one of the workbenches as she took it all in. Her team would start first in the field of twenty-two cars. They would have the number one pit position too, which would make the pit stops more accessible. Each member of her team was awarded with a Craftsman tool chest filled with tools, so everyone had something to celebrate.

Jordan caught sight of the photo of her and Quincy on the wall, and the buzz faded. It would've been amazing to come out of the car and jump into Quincy's arms as part of the celebration. She missed their talks and the joy she saw in Quincy's face whenever she spoke about anything she was passionate about. How could she let her go? Why did she have to choose between love and her career?

"Earth to Jordan. Hello, you with us? You aren't drunk, are you? The press room is ready in the Top Gun conference room. Maybe you should clean up a bit before we walk over." Tina flicked her manicured nails in Jordan's direction.

"Sure. Let me run to my RV for a minute. Joe, I'm heading over to the press event," she said as she passed him on her way.

"Okay, sounds good, Jordie. Go give 'em hell," he said and laughed.

"I'll wait for you out here, and we can walk over together," Tina said, engrossed in her phone.

Jordan nodded. She didn't want Tina's company, but she was too tired, too excited, and too distracted to bother arguing with her.

A few minutes later, Jordan emerged from the RV. "This will have to do. I'm wearing all my sponsors, there are no more champagne bubbles on my face, and my helmet hair is covered. Let's go." Her phone was blowing up with text and voicemail messages from friends and family, but she hadn't seen anything from Quincy. She silenced the notifications and focused on the walk that took them near the parking lot where Quincy had parked that first night. Fans filled the area and cheered Jordan on as she walked by. She waved to the crowd and looked back as she thought she caught sight of Quincy but blamed it on her imagination when she scanned the crowd and didn't see her. IndyCar arranged Jordan's press briefing to include multiple large and small networks to discuss her pole position and Sunday's race. It was an amazing opportunity to showcase her team. But all she really wanted to do was take her phone into a quiet area and call Quincy.

She took a deep breath and forced herself to smile and focus on the achievement of the moment. Her love life would have to wait.

That would have worked better had Juliette not appeared, waving and smiling like any supportive girlfriend might. She stood just close enough for the cameras to occasionally catch her as they panned the area, and Jordan gritted her teeth. So it wasn't so much that they didn't want her to be seen with someone. They were happy for her to be seen with a celebrity, just not an everyday person. *Bastards.*

Soon after the questions ended and Jordan stood up to leave, Juliette looped her arm around Jordan's waist and planted a deep kiss on her lips. The flurry of flashes was dizzying. *I'm sure that'll be on the first page of the sports section tomorrow and probably every social media outlet within the hour. Just what everyone wants.* Jordan smiled for the cameras, trying to hide her irritation at the façade.

"Jordan, are you and Juliette back together?" a reporter asked.

"No—" Jordan tried to pull out of Juliette's embrace.

"Aren't they the cutest couple?" Tina asked, speaking over Jordan.

Stacy Madison, a local reporter, yelled out, "What about Quincy Fitzgerald, the woman you were with at the Loews Hollywood

Hotel and the Racing Expo? I thought you were together?"

"Wasn't she also the one you were with at the Long Beach LGBTQ+ Center?" another reporter asked.

"You move on quick, Jordan," said a reporter from the back of the room, and everyone laughed.

"Don't forget, fast is her business," Tina said. "She's a race car driver, the pole position holder for the LA Grand Prix and poised to win it all on Sunday. That woman you're discussing was a nobody, a stand-in, and we won't answer any more questions about her. Okay, that's it for tonight. Thank you, everyone. No more questions." She smiled sweetly and led Jordan and Juliette from the room.

Fury, hot and nearly overwhelming, filled her. Her jaw ached as she bit back the words until they returned to the privacy of the RV. "Tina, get inside now." Once the door was shut, Jordan unloaded. "Quincy isn't *a nobody*. If there's a nobody here, it's Juliette! Juliette and I are over, do you get that? You've got to stop talking shit about my personal life, or you'll find yourself unemployed. Do you understand? I'm not playing."

Tina crossed her arms. "Jordan, what would you do without me? Do you really want to find out? What about the sponsorship offer? You heard them yesterday. Do you really want to pass that up for someone you don't even know? You'd put your team in jeopardy for Quincy Fitzgerald?" She stared hard at Jordan. "This thing with Juliette will change soon enough when you both move on, and you'll hook up with another A-lister that suits your celebrity standing."

Jordan took in Tina's crossed arms and pinched lips, but she didn't care; she wouldn't give in. She stared back at her, biding her time, not wanting to say anything she couldn't take back.

"Okay, Jordan. Fine, whatever you say." Tina sighed dramatically and raised her hands. "Juliette needs the publicity this faux-relationship can give her, and it can also help you with the sponsors. Let me give her track and pit passes so she can stay around the media, but you don't have to interact with her. It doesn't have to mean anything."

Jordan felt her blood pressure rising. "I'm done with the games." She stormed out of her RV to the garage. Who the hell was in control of her life? She'd just won the LA Grand Prix pole position and a hell of a lot of money, and she should be on top of the world. Instead, she was arguing with her agent and being handled by sponsors. The one person she wanted next to her was the one person she couldn't have.

Joe looked up when she entered the garage. "Jordie, are you okay? You look mad as a snake caught in a cage."

Jordan blew out a deep breath and shook out her arms. "Tina's games."

Joe nodded. "Ah, well, let that go, and let's analyze the data from your last two laps, so we can replicate it on Sunday and walk away with a win."

Jordan smiled and pulled up the stool next to him. Everything else might be out of her control, but the driving? That was all hers. "Let's get started."

Chapter Twenty-Four

QUINCY JOLTED AWAKE WHEN Jada nudged her hand with her wet nose. She wasn't sure what time it was or where she was. Her eyes felt like gravel when she blinked them open, and only then did she notice the pattern of her couch as the memories from last night returned. The bright sunlight pierced her skull, and she buried her face in the couch pillow to block it out. She'd stayed up late last night looking at the photos of Jordan and Juliette at STK. The images alone stung, but the articles about their past relationship hurt like a thousand cuts. *This is what happens when I let down my guard.* She hadn't listened to her sensible side, her reason. She'd let herself hope. She'd let her control slip, and now she looked like a fool. What a fucking week: dumped on at work and dumped out of Jordan's life. *I'm such an idiot.* The two glasses of wine she'd drunk on an empty stomach swirled in her system, and she rolled over, wishing she could escape into sleep. But Jada wasn't having it—she knew her routines and wasn't about to let it slide, even if Quincy was hungover and heartbroken.

"Okay, girl, I'm getting up. Hold your horses." Quincy pulled herself from the couch and got ready to walk her pup. She felt guilty for not spending more time with Jada, especially since she was taking her to her friend's for boarding today. She wanted her to get acclimated before Quincy left on her trip in case there were any issues, and today was the day. While she'd love nothing more than to keep her close for support, she couldn't change the schedule, even for her meltdown. A good walk was one way to lessen her guilt over the past few days and her upcoming trip.

One long walk, breakfast, a shower, and some Tylenol later,

she felt more human. She decided it was time to check her phone for any messages and see what the trolls were saying about her, but she couldn't do it. "Screw it. Just go pack." Vivid memories of Jordan ran through her mind as soon as she stepped into her bedroom. She looked at Jada. "I need to stop this obsession." She opened the suitcase on the bed and went to the closet to pull out outfits.

She put on some music to drown out her thoughts while she sorted through her clothes. The suitcase in front of her was half-packed, but her hands were frozen above it. She was supposed to be excited. This trip was supposed to be her escape, her adventure. But now, every item she folded or tossed in felt like a weight. The photos of Jordan and Juliette kept flashing in her mind, each one a gut punch. The excitement she had from working the LAGP, her trip, and the possibility of a career change was overshadowed by the uncertainty of what was happening with her and Jordan. She'd been hopeful and confident, but now...she didn't know what she felt. Excitement? Fear? Heartbreak?

She shoved a pair of shoes into the suitcase with more force than necessary, then sat back and rubbed her temples. She shouldn't care. They weren't even a thing. *So why does it hurt so much?* It didn't help that the logical part of her brain—her ever-constant need for reason—was completely failing her. She'd always been able to make sense of things, compartmentalize them into neat little boxes. But this? This didn't fit anywhere. Her phone buzzed on the nightstand, and she grabbed it without hesitation.

"Hello, Lar," Quincy said softly.

"Girl," Lauren said. "What's going on? You sound like you're about to implode."

Quincy laughed bitterly, slumping against the wall. "I'm trying to figure out how to pack for a trip, while my brain keeps playing the same damn slideshow of Jordan and Juliette. I don't even know why I care. It's ridiculous. I don't even know what *we* are."

Lauren sighed dramatically. "Look, Q, I'm going to be real with you. You need to get laid."

Quincy blinked. "What?"

"I said what I said. You need to go on this trip, clear your head, and find someone to distract you. Doesn't have to be anything serious. Just get out there, have fun, and let someone else take your mind off—" she cleared her throat dramatically, "other people's bullshit."

Quincy rolled her eyes but couldn't help the faint smile tugging at her lips. "I'm not sure that's the best advice, Lar."

"It's the best advice you're going to get," Lauren said. "You've been obsessing over this situation since you met her. And let's be honest, we both know you're not over her. So go get some closure. The kind that doesn't involve Jordan."

The smile faded from Quincy's lips as she stared at the suitcase. Lauren had a point. *Maybe it's not about Jordan anymore. Maybe it's about me.* But she still didn't know how to move past the feeling of being left behind. She almost dropped the phone when Jordan's picture came onto her phone screen.

"Speak of the devil, she's calling me right now. I've got to take this." Quincy's pulse quickened, and her palms got damp.

"Oh, Quincy, good luck. But protect your heart. Who knows what games she's playing, and I want you all in one piece. I love you."

"I love you too. Talk soon." She ended the call with Lauren but couldn't make herself answer Jordan. She didn't want to hear that it was over. She blinked away tears, but they refused to stay put. Her voicemail notification chimed, and she trembled as she hit play.

"Hey, it's me. Um...we need to talk. It'll be a busy day here, but maybe you can come by the garage? Or I could stop by your house. Let me know. Hope to talk soon. Bye."

Quincy let out a disbelieving laugh. She slid to the floor and rested her head against the bed. When would she learn?

***

Quincy loved the sound of her breath through her diving regulator. The slow and steady passage of air calmed her soul. She floated at sixty feet below the surface of the ocean in the Redondo Beach Canyon and watched as the other scuba divers took pictures of the rockfish, juvenile black sea bass, and bat ray that passed by. She kept her buoyancy above the silty bottom while she reflected on the past few days.

Her friend Lisa's weekly twilight shore dive in the Redondo Beach canyon was a balm to her burned heart. Quincy held back from the group but remained close enough that her light could be seen easily. Being sociable even underwater didn't feel right when she was so distracted. Had Quincy really thought that Jordan Marsh would fall for her? That she'd change for her? Jordan didn't care about her; she cared about her team, her sponsors, and winning it all. Quincy understood that Jordan needed her sponsors' money to race at this level and that not many would fund a woman's team. She respected how hard Jordan had fought to get where she was, but it still hurt to be tossed aside, and in such a public way. Why was she surprised Jordan chose her dream and her passion over Quincy when they'd only just met? She just needed to get through the next few days and then leave for her trip. This was why she should stay rooted in reality and not deal in hope.

Steady breaths helped to calm her anger, but it did nothing to keep the slideshow of images and memories from filtering through her mind: Jordan's bikini-clad body under the outdoor shower. The bliss on her face while she laid in Quincy's arms. Jordan and Juliette together in every type of media.

She was startled out of her reverie when Lisa tapped her tank. She should be present and focused on diving, not daydreaming. She followed Lisa's dive light as a visual guide and saw squid of all sizes around them. She could make out the squid eggs lining the bottom of the ocean as far as her light could shine. There were bigger predators when she looked up to the surface. A dark shadowy figure set against the surface light came closer. The harbor seal dove down for dinner, passing by close enough for her to see its markings, a reminder that her worries were small in comparison to the big, beautiful world around her. It helped…a little.

She checked her dive computer and was surprised that it was time to head in. Lisa led the dive group back to shore, where they stopped to decompress. She timed the surf break and cleanly exited the ocean, placed her gear in a dry spot, and returned to help the other divers from the inky black water.

Quincy peeled her wetsuit down to her waist and wrapped herself in a towel as Lisa came over to her SUV. She leaned against it with her wetsuit halfway down her body and gave Quincy a naughty smile. They'd flirted here and there for more than five years, but nothing ever came of it.

"You never join me last-minute unless you're working through a problem," Lisa said. "What's up? I saw the pictures online. I also saw your face when you arrived tonight. You looked heartbroken. So what happened?"

Quincy leaned against the truck and considered what she wanted to share. She felt too raw to discuss Jordan, but Lisa had always been a good friend, and it'c probably help to talk to someone. "It was my own stupidity. We met while surfing in Hermosa, and she actually saved my life. We had amazing talks and shared our pasts and our current hang-ups. It seemed like we had a real connection. I got to meet her wonderful family and her racing team. We had spectacular sex." Quincy sighed at the memory. "But it was just that: sex. I might have been more emotionally invested in our relationship, but she made it clear that her responsibility was to her team and her racing future. Her priority isn't me. So yeah, I'm a little heartbroken. You can't fly that close to the sun without getting burned." Quincy wiped at her eyes as warm tears fell. Lisa hugged her. "I'm fine. Just emotional."

Lisa stepped back and held Quincy's hand. "It sounds like you're really into her. I'm sorry she couldn't see how great you are. I've learned my lesson with celebrities; they only break your heart."

Quincy chuckled and sniffled. "That's so LA, but you're right."

Lisa blew out a breath and shook her head. "I know firsthand what this feels like. I was with Sara, the Channel 7 lead anchor, for six months, and everything was wonderful until it wasn't. She was offered a national network correspondent position, and suddenly our dreams of buying a home and starting a family were gone. Her career became her priority. She became someone I didn't recognize overnight, and I was tossed aside. There was no discussion. She just said that I didn't factor into her new life, and then she was gone. She wasn't a celebrity on the scale of Jordan Marsh, but it certainly stings to be cast aside for the spotlight."

"Why didn't you tell me about her?" Quincy asked, surprised how closely Lisa's story reflected her own.

"It was before we met, and honestly, who wants to bring up old pain?"

Quincy squeezed Lisa's hand. "Thank you for sharing; it really helps. I hate to cry on your shoulder then leave, but I'm working the race tomorrow as part of the medical crew, and I still need to rinse my gear," Quincy said and walked around to the driver's side.

"You know I'm here for you. I just wish I could've made you feel better."

The change in Lisa's tone suggested she had an idea of how she'd like to do that, and the moment grew taut between them as she touched Quincy's hand.

"You did. Letting me dive with you helped. Thanks for that, and for listening. I feel a little lighter."

Lisa dropped Quincy's hand and stepped back. "Anytime, you know that. Q, anyone who doesn't see what you have to offer is blind. You deserve better." Her smile held a tinge of sadness.

"You leaving too?" Quincy asked, desperate to change the subject so she could hold back the flood of tears that threatened. If only taking Lisa up on her offer was that easy. If only she could get the feel of Jordan's lips out of her mind. If only...

"Nah, I think I'll join the other divers at Duffy's for a drink or two.

Take care of yourself."

"Will do, thanks again." Quincy drove away from the beach, and her tears flowed. She knew she deserved better, but her heart wanted Jordan. And she couldn't change that. She couldn't escape thoughts of her, and that left no space to process the pain, especially with her part in the LAGP. Maybe her South Pacific adventure would be exactly what she needed to heal her heart and regain her control. But would that be enough?

Chapter Twenty-Five

Jordan awoke the next morning, alone, and tired, and thinking about yesterday. The unfortunate events with Tina and Juliette notwithstanding, yesterday had been fabulous. She was pumped about the race car setup, beating Carver, and winning the LAGP's pole position. While she was anxious about the race tomorrow, she knew that Joe and the crew had done fantastic work over the past few weeks getting everything ready. She just had to show up and drive to win. She had the morning off before she needed to head back up to the track to start the celebrity race, so she checked her text and voice messages. Congratulations had come in from her family, along with Dave, Elliott, and a few of her close friends.

Florence had left a message asking if they could meet later today. But there was nothing from Quincy. She should be glad because then she wouldn't have to explain why they couldn't be together, and why money superseded love. Jordan jumped out of bed and paced in front of her view of the Pacific, trying to work through her emotions.

Fifteen minutes later, she decided her emotions might be better examined through a workout. She headed to her home gym to put in the work, but her head and heart weren't any clearer on what to do when she'd finished. She made coffee and went out on the balcony. The salty sea air brought back the memories of the first day she met Quincy and all their moments together since. There was no question; she had to be honest and not string her along, no matter how she felt.

Her hand shook as she scrolled to find Quincy's number. She hadn't felt this connection to someone in so long, and the thought of ending it made her feel sick.

Quincy picked up on the third ring. "Hello?" She sounded out of breath.

"Hey, how are you?" she asked. It sounded inane, stupid. She groaned silently.

"I'm confused. I think we need to talk," Quincy said softly.

Jordan closed her eyes and her stomach did somersaults. "I agree. Could you meet this morning? Name the place, and I'll meet you there."

"I don't think a public place would be a good idea. Where are you?"

"I'm at my place in Hermosa. Do you want to come here? We can walk on the beach and have the privacy to talk." Although a public place would mean less drama, and privacy could mean going to a level she wasn't prepared for.

"Sure, I need to drop off Jada first. I'll be there within the hour."

"Okay. Thanks for making the time," Jordan said, overwhelmed with joy and heartache in equal measure.

"I'll see you soon. Bye."

Jordan showered and made a quick breakfast as she anxiously awaited Quincy's arrival. What was she going to say that made sense? *I want to be with you, but I need to keep my job. I want to be with you, but my sponsors don't think you're good for my image.* It sounded so...blasé. So cold. And that wasn't at all how she felt. She worried over the conversation but continued to prepare her gear for the day. The doorbell rang sooner than she'd expected. Her pulse increased when she saw the video image of Quincy standing at her door. She looked stunning, and Jordan's heart felt like it might shatter.

The look of hurt and pain in Quincy's eyes was devastating. She stepped back and waved Quincy into the foyer. "Thanks for coming over."

"Thanks. Congratulations on your win. I bet you're excited about starting at the front of the pack."

Jordan nodded and shoved her hands in her pockets, so she didn't reach for Quincy. "The team is ecstatic. We're hopeful for a win. Do you want something to drink or eat? Or do you want to head out to the beach?" She could tell by Quincy's erect stance, her hands behind her back, and the fact that she wasn't making eye contact that she was equal parts angry and nervous. Jordan wasn't certain how to proceed.

Quincy took a deep breath and exhaled. "Let's head out to the beach if you don't mind."

Jordan wanted nothing more than to hug her, to kiss her beautiful lips and tell her she was the one Jordan wanted by her side. But she couldn't hurt her any more than she apparently already had. "Okay, let me grab a hat and sunglasses and then we can go."

They headed out through the mud room, where they left their shoes, and walked across the hot concrete strand to the cool soft sand. Jordan couldn't force words from her mouth. Once they reached the shoreline, they walked parallel on the flat, packed sand. Eventually, Quincy stopped walking and faced Jordan, her hands on her hips. Jordan watched the storm build in Quincy's eyes as her hair flew around her face, and she'd never looked more beautiful.

"Jordan, I realize we haven't known each other very long, but I need to know, what am I to you? A one-night stand? A groupie? Someone new you can talk shop with? We both know I don't fit into your celebrity world, and now the world knows you've found someone who does." She swallowed hard and wrapped her arms around herself. "I don't know what's going on."

Jordan gently pushed Quincy's hair back behind her ear. The touch ignited the fire for her even more, but she had to control her emotions. "You've been an unexpected surprise since the day I met you. You're so special, and the time we've had together has been remarkable. I'm sorry if I hurt you; that was never my intent. Juliette is a photo op, nothing more. Quincy, it's not you. It's me. Trust me on that." Jordan heard the words come out of her mouth and wished she could take them back.

Quincy wiped at a tear that streaked down her cheek. "Seriously, Jordan? What a fucking cliché. You don't understand. I never let anyone in or give the control of my heart to someone else. I saw what that did in my parents' marriage, and my dad has never wanted to love again. I opened my world to you. My family, my friends, my home, my future, but most importantly, my heart. I tried to stop it when I thought about the risks in your job, when I thought about your celebrity status and my unease with it, but nothing could stop me from falling for you," Quincy whispered.

Quincy's confession was like a knife in her chest. Jordan hugged her from behind as they faced the ocean. She closed her eyes and took a deep breath, inhaling Quincy's intoxicating jasmine scent mixed with the salt air. "I wish I could be free to love you and live the life I've always wanted, but I just can't. I've got a responsibility to the team. They'll pull my sponsorship if I get into a relationship or play any role they don't think is right for their image. Too many people are depending on me, and I've had to choose."

Quincy turned, her eyes full of anger and heartbreak. "You're a coward, Jordan Marsh, plain and simple. Everyone thinks you're this strong, fearless racer, a woman in control of her own life, but if they only knew the truth. You're a puppet for your sponsors or anyone who can give you the fame you so passionately crave. We're done. Just leave me alone. Good luck with Juliette and your team. I hope they make you very happy."

Jordan watched as Quincy jogged across the beach to her house and then she was gone. She couldn't move from the spot even if she wanted to. The truth reverberated through her. *I am a coward. I've let others make my life decisions for me. First my mom, then Tina, and now the sponsors. So much for living in my truth.* She sank down onto the sand and stared out at the ocean, her mind racing through the different options that allowed her true happiness. She choked back a sob when she realized there were none, not really. She could love Quincy and lose her racing future or have a secure racing future and lose the woman she loved. No matter how she thought about it, she couldn't see a way forward. Her watch alarm went off, telling her it was time to head to the track for the celebrity race. The last thing she wanted was to be in the public eye with a broken heart, but she had a job to do. On autopilot, she headed back to the house, grabbed her gear, and drove to the track. Images of Quincy crying made her want to vomit.

***

Jordan was swamped by IndyCar racing officials as soon as she parked. Flanked with security, she gave her fans a wave and a wan smile as she was led to the starter's stand. She simply couldn't play the game right now. She climbed up and announced on the track PA system, "Drivers, start your engines."

The celebrity drivers started their cars and were led away from the pits by a pace car for the two-lap warm-up. Once the group was in formation and the IndyCar official gave her the signal, Jordan waved the green flag to start the race. She smiled and waved as she climbed down from the stand, then headed to her garage with track security assisting her through the throng of fans. She loved the attention and their support, but her usual exhilaration was diminished tonight. A young woman with a rainbow flag tattoo on her bicep and a cut off T-shirt that said *Dykes on Bikes, Ride with Pride* stepped into Jordan's path.

"Good luck tomorrow. Show them what a woman can do! Live your truth! We're riding with you." She high-fived Jordan then moved to the side.

Live your truth. Words she'd often said in interviews and on social media platforms. What a hypocrite. Jordan waved and smiled to the group gathered outside the garage perimeter. The security guards kept them back, thankfully, because she just couldn't do the full shtick today. "Thank you for your support. I can't wait to tear up the streets of LA and win the Grand Prix tomorrow."

The crowd erupted with screams and waved rainbow checkered flags that danced in the sky. Jordan smiled and thought about all the LGBTQ+ people that she'd promised to represent. She kept her smile plastered to her face and acted like she had it all together on the way to the garage, even though she felt like a fraud. If she lost her sponsorship though, she'd be letting them down too. Joe waved and came over to join her in the RV.

Joe frowned. "How'd the starting call go?"

She sat at the kitchen table in the RV with her head in her hands. "Fine."

"Are you in the right mindset for tomorrow?"

They both knew she couldn't get behind the wheel if she wasn't a hundred percent. "Yes." No? She wasn't sure.

"Jordie, you need to get in the right headspace to drive and win tomorrow, so let's talk it out. This is your confessional. Whatever you tell me, it stays between us."

"I told Quincy I couldn't be with her and why. She didn't take it well." Jordan shook her head and pounded her fist on the table. "Joe, you know the opportunities that would grow out of the kind of money our sponsors are offering. I can't let the team down. I can't let the community down. I just need to suck it up. I'm sure I'll find someone that amazing again when my racing days are done." Jordan's voice broke, and she stood up. "I'll be okay, I promise. I'm headed to my house tonight, but I'll be up here first thing in the morning. Is there anything I need to know? Any issues with anything?"

Joe shook his head slowly. "Quincy's a keeper. I'm sorry you're being pinched like this. Maybe you should talk to them. Or maybe Florence can do something?"

Jordan raised her eyebrow. "Doubtful."

"Well, you need to get your mind cleared. The car is set, the team is ready, and the track hasn't changed since you flew down the streets yesterday. I love you, kid. Take care of yourself tonight, and I'll see you in the morning. Plan to be here and ready for showtime by eight."

"Thanks for being an amazing friend." She hugged him before he left.

She headed into her bathroom to splash water on her face. Her phone pinged, and her heart surged with hope at the possibility it could be Quincy.

Jordie, we saw the cute picture of you and Juliette. So glad to see you're back together. You make a beautiful couple. Better than that blond from earlier in the week. Tina said you had a big sponsorship deal come through. We can't wait to hear about it.

Jordan's rage toward her mom and her never-ending attempt to control her life escalated. *When did you talk to Tina? And why'd you discuss my business? Juliette and I aren't back together. Thanks so much for wishing me well tomorrow. Don't worry, Tito John, Ate Theresa, and some other cousins will be at the race.*

Don't bother with John and Theresa. They're distractions. Focus on your career. We have an event at the club, so we won't be able to watch. Jordie, Tina just wants the best for your career, & yes, she keeps us informed. You just need to listen to her, and you'll stay relevant.

Jordan decided she'd had enough of her mom and her suggestions for one day. No one was ever good enough for Mama Vic, especially her own daughter. She tossed her phone onto the table and ran her fingers through her hair. What was Tina doing talking with her parents, especially about her sponsor deals? *There are no fucking boundaries in my life.* Her phone rang, and she looked down to see that it was Tito John. "Hi, Tito, how are you?"

"I'm good. Congrats on your pole position. That was quite a lap."

"Thanks. Should make the race more fun tomorrow. What's up?"

"Are we on for your LAGP pre-race tradition tonight?"

Jordan didn't respond. She'd forgotten all about it, but he was just the balm she needed. "Absolutely. I should be home in an hour."

"Okay, I'll pick up the food from La Cantina, same as always? You need beer or do you have a stash?"

"Yes, same as always, and I've got the cerveza. See you soon."

Jordan felt lighter as she drove home, but recognized she really was off her game to have forgotten her pre-race traditions when in LA. She always spent time with Tito John. She'd hydrate now while she waited for him to arrive with her carb-loaded meal from La Cantina. She'd wait to have her one and only Modelo with dinner.

The house was too quiet when she got there. No friends were waiting in her kitchen, and there was no promise of time with Quincy later. She put on music, sat at the computer, and watched race footage to distract her from the mess that was her life.

"Jordie, are you here?" Tito John called out from downstairs.

Jordan came down and took the two bags of food from him. "That smells delicious. I'm starving."

"You always get more than you eat, but let's get it on plates and crack open your lucky beer." He grabbed a bottle opener while Jordan loaded up their plates.

She breathed in the simple comfort his company provided. It eased the heartache, just a little.

Tito John picked up his beer. "To my niece, Jordan. May she be safe in God's hands tomorrow. Cheers."

"Cheers. Thank you, Tito." Jordan stared down at her food in a daze. She thought about Quincy, what she might be doing, or who she might be with, and it short-circuited her brain.

"Are you going to eat? What's wrong?" he asked then took a big bite of his burrito.

She traced the condensation down her beer bottle with her finger. "Do you remember Quincy, the woman I brought to the family dinner?"

"Of course. She's a lovely woman."

"She really is." Jordan said. "I think I've fallen for her. You *can't* share this, but my sponsors are offering to invest $20 million in our team, but only if I remain the single, lesbian harlot in the media to bring in more business for them. They want me to cut all ties with Quincy, because she isn't a celebrity. And even a long-term celebrity relationship would be a deal-breaker."

Tito John sat back in his chair and scowled. "Jordie, that's the stupidest thing I've ever heard. Love is more important than a pole position, winning this race, or all the money in the world. It's precious and not easy to come by. I know your parents did a poor job of showing you unconditional love but learn from me. Don't squander this opportunity. You're an amazing driver, and there will be other sponsors."

Jordan set the bottle down and rubbed her temples. "This money doesn't just affect me. The team could grow. We could add a second driver and really be a force within IndyCar."

"Do you seriously think Lex or anyone on the team would tell you to turn away from love so they can improve their standings? I don't think so. Have you talked to Florence? Won't she have the final say?"

Jordan felt a glimmer of hope. Florence had always been supportive of her from the very beginning. Maybe she could talk some sense into the sponsors, since Tina clearly wasn't going to. "We were supposed to meet today, but I never heard from her. I'll reach out after the race tomorrow."

"That's my girl. Come on, we need to get you fed, hydrated, and to bed. You've got a race to win tomorrow," Tito John said and dug into his meal.

"Thank you for being my sounding board. This is the best pre-race tradition ever. Okay, so how much do you and Tito Jack have bet on me?"

Tito John reached over and squeezed Jordan's hand. "I love you, and I'm glad to be here for you. As for the bet, it's better that you don't know," he said and chuckled.

Jordan laughed and her shoulders relaxed a little. Life's giant decisions didn't have to be answered today. Right here, right now, she could simply enjoy the food and company. There'd be time to deal with all the other stuff after she won the race.

Chapter Twenty-Six

AFTER THE STRATEGY MEETING, it was the calm before the storm. Jordan sat alone in her RV for her pre-race meditation. She exhaled and looked at her watch. *One hour.* She gathered her gloves and walked into the garage. She watched Joe as he pulled at his left ear lobe, his pre-race tic, and that simple motion calmed her nerves. "Let's review our first fifteen lap strategy, the weather forecast, and my first pit stop," Jordan said to Joe and Nate. They also discussed the top five cars that would be chasing her and how to drive the straightaways and turns with the most precision. They looked up as an IndyCar official informed them that they'd be rolling out to the pit lane.

Her stomach came alive with energetic herons. She clinked a wrench on a bottle and got everyone's attention. "I just wanted to say, great work on getting us in the top spot. We're going to win this today and show them we're a team to reckon with. Let's race hard, race safe, and let's win!" The team roared with claps and shouts.

Jordan stared at her car, covered with her sponsors' logos. The rainbow graphic that started on the nose cone fanned out across the chassis to the rear wing to connect the pink triangles. She'd been so proud to drive this car under a rainbow flag. Now, it felt like it could smother her. She shook away the feeling. *Focus.*

The car shone in the California sun as the IndyCar official led them out to the number one spot on pit row. The team walked behind the car, and race teams from other garages came out to high-five them. Their acknowledgment and congratulations boosted Jordan's pride. Carver's crew just glared at them, but she kept moving, feeling too good for their nonsense. Fans swarmed the garages and the pit areas, and they were allowed to get close to the cars as they were lined up at the start-finish line. While her car drew hordes of race fans to pose next to it for selfies, her crew monitored them to ensure no damage was done to the car.

Jordan leaned against the pit wall and waited for the introduction of the teams and drivers. Her mind was focused on the race ahead, and she mentally traced the route repeatedly in her mind's eye. She'd completed her pre-race routines and felt calm, even with the increased energy all around her. She wore her mirrored Ray-Ban sunglasses, and her earbuds played her pre-race playlist to keep her in the zone as well as helping to block out thoughts of anything not race-related.

The IndyCar driver introductions started from the back row to the front. The Paramount blue wall and the jumbotron outside Paramount's Melrose gate projected each driver's image, stats, and grid placement for today's race to the crowd in the grandstands. As the pole-sitter, Jordan would be the last to be introduced, and since she had time, she looked around to see if she could spot Quincy. She knew she was here somewhere with the medical team, which settled her despite all that had happened between them. Jordan looked at the infield across from the start line where an ambulance sat, its crew of three ready to assist. Jordan recognized Quincy and waved. Her heart raced when Quincy waved back. Somehow, some way, things had to be okay between them. The two guys that flanked Quincy looked puzzled, but she didn't care.

Joe nudged her. "Jordie, pay attention."

She pulled her earbuds out as the announcer began her introduction. This was it. Her moment to shine. Her moment to show that women, especially gay women, could race. Her moment to show the younger race fans that they could do it too. She was overwhelmed with a sensation of pride, and some fear.

"In the front row of today's LA Grand Prix, we've got Kent Carver in the number two spot and our own hometown favorite,

Jordan Marsh. She's your pole sitter for today. Let's give it up for all our IndyCar drivers."

The crowd erupted with excitement, and the pits were cleared of all fans. Jordan's team completed their final preparations ensuring the team's timing stand and pit lane were set up, and the car was ready for the race. Her team gathered around Jordan and the car for the national anthem and the presentation of colors. Once the song and the B-52 flyover completed, the pit crew helped Jordan with her fire-retardant hood and helmet and then assisted her into her car. She looked over at Joe and got a thumbs up as they went over radio checks. The steering wheel was placed, and her safety harness secured. She looked up to the open straightaway down Melrose Avenue. The adrenaline of racing, especially from the number one spot, had Jordan pumped to get the race started. She wanted to win today; she *believed* she was going to win today. The fact that Quincy was watching made it even sweeter.

LA Mayor, Sharon Glass, was the celebrity starter for today's race, and she called the start to the LA Grand Prix. "Drivers, start your engines."

The high-pitched whine of the powerful engines drowned out any other thoughts. She repeated her safety checks and waited for an update.

"The pace car is coming around... Get ready to start," her spotter said in her ear.

Jordan led the field of cars out behind a Ford Mustang Mach E to begin the first of two warmup laps around the track. The car felt powerful in the straightaways, and the steering was spot-on in the turns.

"How's she feeling?" Joe asked.

"Like she's a perfect extension of my body," she said.

The pace car left the track at the end of the second lap, and Jordan led the pack of twenty-two IndyCars to the start line for the green flag. Jordan sprinted ahead of Carver and led by a half-second margin for the first lap and continued to lead through the first fifteen laps. The world outside the car was a blur of color. The world inside the car was one she controlled, and it made her feel so powerful, it was hard not to grip the steering wheel too tightly. Her prior practice runs helped her anticipate the course, and the car ran superbly. On lap sixteen, Joe told her to pit under the caution. She passed the accident that required a yellow flag and maneuvered her car and the pack behind her through a safe zone around the wreckage. She blocked it out, knowing full well how that kind of thing could be disastrous if she focused on it. She pulled up to her pit box, and her pit crew knocked out her tire change, filled her tank with fuel, and pulled off her soiled aeroscreen shield in record time, quick enough to have her back on the track to keep the lead before the end of the yellow flag.

"Great job," Jordan said. She remained in the lead as the race went back to green. In the zone, she hummed a song to stay focused.

Joe radioed Jordan on lap thirty. "You okay out there?" he asked.

Jordan smiled. "Yep, the car is still running great, and I'm feeling good." Laps thirty through forty-eight were uneventful, although there were two more accidents that brought out caution flags. She maneuvered past those accidents, had successful pit stops, and remained in the lead. Excitement began to flood through her as she held her track position with two laps to go. She passed the start/finish line and received the white flag, which indicated the final lap. One lap to go, and she'd be the first female winner of the LA Grand Prix.

Carver was behind her and tried at every turn to get past, but Jordan was able to anticipate his every move and stop his advances. On one of the final turns, he carelessly tried to pass and almost put them both in the wall. *Damn idiot.* She caught sight of the checkered flag as she drove down the final straightaway to the finish line. Jordan heard the fans in the stands and Joe hooting in the headset when she crossed the finish line and captured the win.

She thrust her hand up out of the cockpit and pumped her arm. She'd done it. She'd won.

"You won the LA Grand Prix!" Joe screamed.

"Damn, this feels amazing," Jordan yelled back. She looked in her mirrors and noticed Carver was gaining on her instead of slowing down. "Joe, what's Carver doing? Why's he still racing?"

"What do you mean?"

"Oh, fuck!" Jordan's head snapped forward from the impact. The racing harness and the HANS device kept her body secured and her neck restrained in the car, but her muscles pulled with the jolt. Jordan's heart raced as she and the car went airborne, helplessly propelled into the chain link fence and the SAFER barrier. The screeching of metal and the crunch of the carbon fiber breaking apart was deafening. Her right arm slammed against the cockpit on impact, and bile rose in her throat from the pain. She bit her tongue as the car fell back onto the track, and the metallic taste of blood filled her mouth. She heard what sounded like raindrops on a tin roof and realized it was debris striking her helmet. The visor cracked, and her right eye burned as her helmet crashed back against the seat. Her back and leg hurt as the car rolled back into the middle of the track. "I'm alive," Jordan said, unsure if her headset worked and the team would hear it. She thanked God her helmet was in place, and she was still securely ensconced in the relative safety of the cockpit.

Oh, God, is that smoke? No, please, God, no. I don't want to burn.

Fear overtook her as the squeal of brakes and the smell of rubber from other drivers braking to go around her invaded her senses. She struggled to remain conscious, willing herself to not pass out. She saw a neon orange car heading directly for her before her vision blurred into blackness.

Chapter Twenty-Seven

QUINCY WATCHED IN HORROR as Jordan's car crashed head-on into the fence and the SAFER barrier, causing debris to rain down onto the track. Just as her car stopped spinning, it was struck by a neon orange car. She was jolted into reality when Tim grabbed her arm.

"Let's go," Tim said, and they all ran to the ambulance and climbed in. He hit the lights and sirens, and they headed to the accident.

Quincy couldn't conceive the possibility that Jordan could be dead or seriously hurt. The crackling of the radio by the IndyCar Safety team and other paramedics filled the inside of the ambulance, but Quincy wasn't paying attention and almost fell off her seat when the rig jerked to a stop. She mentally shook herself into action. *Get your shit together. Jordan needs you. This is what you've trained for.* Mentally, she ran through protocol. Make sure there's no fire. Check drivers for signs of life and mobility. Remove drivers from car. Evaluate. Transport.

The large number of safety staff on the track when she stepped out of the rig was disconcerting. Crushed metal and debris was everywhere. Smoke came from both cars. She watched as IndyCar's Safety team worked to ensure the cars weren't on fire. They then set to extract the drivers from their cars. In the orange car, the driver and assisted the crew with removal of his safety gear. He could move everything, and he climbed out of the car with minimal assistance of the paramedic. The IndyCar Safety team directed another Medical Safety Support team to take that driver, and they walked with him to their rig for transport.

Quincy watched them evaluate Jordan. She remained slumped

to her left side, her helmet covering her face, and she hadn't responded to them as they called to her. Quincy was desperate to run over and help, but they'd been told to only join when needed.

The track safety supervisor ran over. "Stay with your rig. We're going to need immediate transport when we get her out."

They stood at the back of their ambulance, with the trauma bag and gurney prepped and ready for action. Quincy had to be professional, but how could she not *do* something? She put her hands on her hips and pinched her sides as she covertly worked to release the fear that threatened to overwhelm her.

The track crew lifted the visor on Jordan's helmet, and blood covered Jordan's face. Her seemingly lifeless body remained in the wreckage while the safety crew doused the front of the car with retardant and the smoke turned white. Once the safety crew felt the car was secure, Quincy darted forward with her team. Her knees grew weak at the sight of Jordan, covered in blood and her arm at a nasty angle, being lifted from the car. Quincy swallowed the bile in her throat and continued to do the necessary checks. Jordan had a pulse, and that was a miracle.

The crowds gathered at the fence line with their phones raised to capture every detail. *Vultures.* They moved Jordan's limp body onto the waiting backboard and gurney. Quincy assessed her, stabilized her spine, and carefully removed her helmet. Jordan remained unconscious, but when the team attempted to stabilize her right arm, she let out a blood-curdling scream and her face contorted in pain. Her eyes fluttered open for a moment, and then she was out again.

"Fuck, that startled me," Tim said.

"Let's get her in the rig." Quincy tried to project outward calm while her insides quivered. Jordan's arm was undoubtedly dislocated or fractured, and it would have to be better stabilized for the trip to LAMC. That injury didn't worry Quincy as much as Jordan's prolonged loss of consciousness. The signs of a traumatic brain injury due to the force of her impacts with the wall and the other car made it a real possibility. It was the unknown injuries, the ones Quincy couldn't see, that could be life-threatening and worried her the most. They wheeled Jordan over to their waiting ambulance, and Quincy climbed in to guide the gurney into place before securing it. Out of sight of the cameras, she held back a sob as she leaned over Jordan's body and gently caressed her face.

"I need you to fight," she whispered. While she hadn't expected a response, she'd hoped for one. She used her scissors to cut off Jordan's racing suit and then placed ECG leads on her chest. The cardiac monitor showed stable vital signs. Paul joined her in the back just as Quincy pulled herself together. "Okay, Paul, her vitals look stable. Can you record them for me? A heart rate of fifty-six, pulse oxygenation of ninety-nine percent, respiratory rate of fourteen, and a blood pressure of one hundred and eight over fifty-five." Everything looked okay. *But time is brain.* They needed to get moving.

"Vitals are stable," Quincy said. "I'll set this to recheck every minute until we arrive at LAMC. Paul, can you place three large bore IVs and hang a liter of lactated ringers wide open. I'll complete a full assessment on her."

"Roger that." Paul grabbed the IV kits and set to work.

Quincy completed a brief physical assessment of Jordan that included her neurological evaluation, noted injuries, and a summary of cuts, bruises, and bleeding. She did everything she could to separate herself emotionally, but her heart was breaking, and she shook inside. Jordan's eyes fluttered open, and she pulled back her arm. She moaned, but she didn't wake up. She needed a full-body trauma assessment and CT scan as soon as possible.

"Tim, we need to go." Quincy yelled to the front of the rig, overcome with adrenaline to do something more.

"I need an update for the base station," Tim yelled back from the driver's seat.

Quincy didn't look away from Jordan's face. "Just put me on speaker."

"Okay, LAMC base station: ready for an update by Quincy Fitzgerald, NP?"

"Go for LAMC base station," the woman on the other end of the radio said.

Quincy continued to look at Jordan's face, trying to memorize every shadow, every freckle. "Patient is a helmeted, twenty-seven-year-old female, status post-high-speed race car accident, with positive loss of consciousness at scene. Pupils are equal, round, reactive to light at three millimeters, with brisk accommodation. Glasgow coma scale is a nine. E2V2M5. She remains unconscious but maintaining airway. Concern for traumatic brain injury. Right arm with orthopedic anomaly to elbow. Abdominal hematoma noted over left abdomen, positive restraint injuries across chest, laceration over right eye will need sutures. Three large bore IV lines in place with lactated ringers wide open. On one hundred percent oxygen via facemask, vital signs stable, heart rate sixty, respiratory rate sixteen, pulse ox one hundred percent, blood pressure one ten over sixty."

"Copy Rig three-two-three, trauma bay three is ready for your arrival," the LAMC base said.

"Roger that, LAMC. Updates will be provided for status change," Quincy said. "Let's go code three."

Tim opened the side door, and a familiar face filled the doorway. "Paul and Quincy, this is Joe Driscoll. He's Jordan's crew chief, and he'll be riding with us to the hospital."

Quincy saw the fear in his eyes matched her own. He grew pale when he'd gotten a good look at Jordan. "Hey, Joe, have a seat and buckle in." She grabbed his hand and squeezed it. "Jordan's still unconscious, but she's stable." She wanted to hug him and cry on his shoulder, but she had to keep her professional persona and do what was needed for Jordan. "Tim, we're ready to go," Quincy said and was relieved when they finally pulled away from the track with lights and sirens on. She grabbed Jordan's left hand and squeezed it before she leaned closer. "Jordan, you keep fighting. We're almost to the hospital. You had an accident, but I'll take care of you. Joe's here with you too."

When they arrived at the LAMC ER Quincy pulled on her NP persona and hid her emotions. Relief flooded through her when she saw Rochelle and Peter at the ambulance bay, ready to care for Jordan. She'd be in good hands. Tim went behind the rig, released the gurney, and pulled Jordan down. Quincy paused and tried to clear her emotions before she climbed out. Rochelle met her outside the ambulance and gave her a side hug. She cleared her throat and shrugged off Rochelle's gesture as they walked behind Jordan's gurney; it was too much kindness, and it would break her if she gave in to the comfort right now. She had to remain emotionally removed from Jordan to ensure nothing was missed.

Rochelle nodded, her expression searching. "Any updates on the patient?"

"There haven't been changes in her neurological status since she was extricated from the race car. Her coma score remains a nine, eyes open to pain, incomprehensible responses, and localized to pain. She has protected her airway so far no respiratory distress. The left abdominal hematoma hasn't changed or grown. I outlined it with a Sharpie, no abdominal tension roted. Her right arm is immobilized as the elbow is either fractured or dislocated. She screamec when it was moved on scene, but no apparent pain now that we've had it secured. Heart rate has been low in the fifties, but she's an athlete. Otherwise, all vitals have been stable," Quincy said as she helped Tim and Paul wheel Jordan into the trauma bay.

The ER nursing staff took over Jordan's care and gently moved Quincy out of the way. They cut off the remainder of her racing suit and connected her to the ER's monitors and oxygen while Quincy watched. She'd been on the other side of the bedrails many times in her nursing role, but today she was a bystander as she watched them care for the woman she loved.

Rochelle grabbed her arm. "I've alertec neurosurgery, trauma ortho, and plastics, and they'll all be here soon. You know the drill.

We'll get her pan scanned ASAP to see what we can't see on the outside. In the meantime, maybe you could take Joe over to Ruby and get Ms. Marsh admitted?" Rochelle looked at Quincy and then Joe, who stood outside the trauma bay, looking lost.

She understood Rochelle needed to do a full assessment, and it'd be better if she and Joe weren't there for it. "Joe, are you doing okay? Let's go get her admitted while they care for her."

"I'm fine. I just don't like hospitals."

"I understand. Not many people do." She took his hand, and they walked toward Ruby at the front desk.

Joe stopped and looked at Quincy. "Jordan's a fighter. She'll get through this. She's probably done a bad job of showing you, but you should know that she really cares for you. I've never seen her as taken with anyone as she is with you. I know she doesn't make it easy, but she's worth it. Please stick around for her." He squeezed her hands.

Quincy gave Joe a hug, finally allowing the professional demeanor to slide, if only for a moment. "Thank you, Joe. Things are complicated, but I care for her deeply. I'll do everything in my power to make sure she gets the best care. Let me introduce you to Ruby; she'll want Jordan's information to admit her. Hey, Ruby. This is Joe. He's Jordan Marsh's DPOA for healthcare, and he'll provide you with everything you need to get her admitted."

Ruby looked up past the monitor with a small smile. "Hi, Joe. I'm so sorry about Jordan's accident. Let's get down to business so you can get back to her bedside."

"I'm her crew chief, friend, and I have power of attorney in case of emergencies." Joe pulled out paperwork and insurance cards and began to answer Ruby's questions.

Quincy blocked out their discussion and leaned against the counter to steady herself. The adrenaline that had coursed through her veins after the accident dissipated and left her drained. She needed something to eat to help regulate the low. "Joe, I'll be right back. I'm going to get something from my locker."

Her hands shook as she entered the code on her locker, and she could barely hold the energy bar. The lounge was empty, so she sat on the bench and let the tears fall. The images of Jordan's accident and her lifeless body played on repeat in her mind. And that set off earthquakes of grief and fear that erupted within her. She took deep breaths to help her focus as she reined in her emotions. Now wasn't the time to fall apart. First, she needed to know the extent of Jordan's injuries and what the plan of care would be. She had to be strong for Jordan. She devoured the bar and headed back.

Rochelle stood outside Jordan's room with the rolling computer. She appeared to be reviewing the CT scans. "Hey, Q, how're you holding up?"

"I'm fine. How's Jordan? What did the scans show?" Quincy tried to look at the monitor.

Rochelle frowned. "You know I can't say anything to you about her."

Of course. Once again, Quincy was reminded of her place in Jordan's life. She was no one, and she certainly wasn't going to be given patient information, at least, not when she wasn't officially on shift.

"Thanks for your help, Ruby," Joe said.

"Joe, this is Dr. Rochelle Dixon, Jordan's trauma doctor."

"I'm Joe Driscoll, her crew chief, and in emergencies, I'm Jordan's power of attorney for health care. You can speak freely with Quincy here. What've you learned?"

"Let me show you what we've found. I'll start from the top down if you don't mind. First, let's discuss her brain. If you look at this CT image, you can see there's no skull fracture or any intracranial bleeding. While we can't see the concussion on here because of her prolonged loss of consciousness, that's our diagnosis. We'll rescan her brain if she doesn't wake up in the next few hours to ensure she doesn't have any brain-bleeding not seen on the first scan. She doesn't have any spinal injuries in her neck, but we'll keep the neck collar on until she wakes up. That will allow her to tell us if she has pain with movement before we remove the protection of the collar. Unfortunately, she does have two thoracic vertebral burst fractures, but her spinal canal is open, and there's no nerve damage. She won't need surgery, but those fractures can be painful. She'll need a brace to help with that. Plastic surgery has sutured the laceration above her right eye. She also has a posterolateral simple dislocated right elbow, and that's been reduced by our orthopedic trauma team. They said Quincy's decision to immobilize her arm in the field ensured that Jordan didn't develop any neurovascular damage in that arm. For now, she's in an elbow cast and will stay in it for one to two weeks. The hematoma on her abdomen is just a bruise. Thankfully, there isn't any evidence of internal bleeding, nor a fractured pelvis. No other orthopedic injuries were found, but given the severity of the crash, she'll be admitted to our ICU for further observation. All the treating teams will follow her while she's in house. What questions do you have?"

Joe looked between Rochelle and Quincy. "I'm not too sure I understood all of that, but I take it she's going to be okay?"

"It's still early, but all signs seem to point to her having a good recovery. Overall, she has a concussion, two fractured vertebrae, a dislocated right elbow, a cut over her right eye that will need some stitches, and generalized bruising." Rochelle's smile was warm and kind.

Joe blew out a long breath and bent forward, resting his hands on his knees. "Thank you. I'll relay that information to her family. Can we go in and see her?" Joe pulled Quincy forward.

They heard shouting and looked outside to see news trucks lined up across the street and reporters shouting questions to anyone who entered or left the building. Quincy knew from experience that they were thirty minutes away from an ER lockdown to ensure Jordan's privacy.

"Go right in," Rochelle said and followed them in.

Quincy couldn't swallow past the lump in her throat at the sight of Jordan lying still under the unnaturally bright lights. Her right eye was swollen closed, and the laceration above it was covered with a small white dressing. Superficial cuts were dotted around her face like a child had taken a marker to it. Quincy caressed Jordan's left hand and felt reassured by the slow steady pulse under her fingertips matching the echoing heartbeat from the monitor.

She's alive. She's not in danger. Quincy repeated the words in her head. How did people cope with this kind of worry, this kind of pain and fear? In all the years she'd been doing this job, it was the first time she *really* understood what people were feeling.

Rochelle pulled out her penlight from her lab coat. "Jordan? Jordan, can you open your eyes?" There was a fluttering of her left eye, and then she opened it fully. "Great. I'm going to shine a light in your left eye. It's going to be bright. Now, can you show me two fingers on your left hand? Fantastic. Can you wiggle your thumb on your right hand? Okay. Can you wiggle your toes on both feet? Great job, Jordan. Can you tell me your full name?"

Jordan closed her eyes and grimaced. "Jordan Cavite Marsh," she said with a gravelly voice and closed her left eye again.

"What year is it?" Rochelle asked.

"March third, 2025," Jordan said.

"What's the last thing you remember?"

"Everything going sideways. I've got a headache, and my throat's dry. Can I get something for pain?"

Rochelle nodded. "Absolutely. According to your file from IndyCar, you don't have any allergies. Is that correct?"

"No allergies."

"Okay, we'll give you some pain medication through your IV, and that should help. Just so you know, you have two visitors."

Jordan opened her left eye and looked at Joe and Quincy as they stood together by her bedside.

"Hi," Quincy said.

Joe stepped up with tears in his eyes and squeezed Jordan's left hand. "Jordie, you just rest and do what they tell you. They're your crew chiefs now, we'll be here with you as you recover," he said, his voice faltering.

Jordan gave a small, wry grin. "Ouch. My right eye hurts." She reached up with her left hand to touch the dressing.

Quincy gently stopped her. "You had a cut above your right eye, but it's been sutured closed, and your eye is still swollen shut. You'll probably have a sexy scar to brag about. I'm so glad you're okay." Her voice cracked, and she had to look away.

"Don't leave me," Jordan murmured as she closed her eye again and faded back to sleep.

"I'm so glad she's okay. I need to go give everyone updates. You okay to stay?" Joe asked Quincy.

She nodded, relieved that she'd be able to stay by Jordan's side. "There's nowhere I'd rather be. Go ahead and make the calls; I'll stay with her."

Joe headed out, while Quincy held Jordan's hand as the pain medication did its job, and she relaxed. Quincy's thoughts were strangely silent, filled only with Jordan's rhythmic heartbeat beeping on the machines around them and the feel of Jordan's hand in hers. At a noise in the doorway, she looked up to see Jordan's Uncle John. Terrible Tina was behind him.

He pulled her into a hug. "Why am I not surprised you're here?"

She allowed herself to sink into his warm embrace. "I wouldn't be anywhere else."

He pulled back and looked over her shoulder. "How bad is it?"

"Amazingly, not nearly as bad as it could've been. She'll come out with some scars, and she's got a concussion, some fractured vertebra, a dislocated elbow, and some bruising but otherwise, it's a miracle."

He crossed himself and kissed her cheek, then seemed to remember Tina, who eyed Quincy with a hard, impenetrable look. "You two have met?"

"Unfortunately."

Tina barely acknowledged her, but she moved her head as

though telling Quincy to get out.

"You're not in charge here." Quincy crossed her arms and glared at her. Then she turned away, dismissing Tina, and sat beside Jordan again.

"No, I'm not in charge, but neither are you. I'm here on behalf of her parents until they arrive. They wanted me to stay close to handle the press and ensure she's provided the best care."

Quincy rolled her eyes and then looked over at John. "Jordie woke up for a little bit, but she was in a lot of pain. They gave her some medication to help with that, so she'll probably be out for a while. I can run and get her doctor if you want an update. Her name is Dr. Rochelle Dixon, and she's excellent."

"Yeah, we saw Joe on our way in. He said he couldn't remember the details but that she was going to be okay."

"That's the most important part. Let me go get her." She squeezed Jordan's hand and whispered, 'I'll be back." Her heart ached at leaving her side.

Tito John caught her hand as she headed for the door. "Thanks, Quincy. Come back with the doctor. Jordan would want you here."

Tina scoffed and glared at Quincy. Tito John looked over at her, and Quincy ignored her.

She headed to the nurse's station, where Rochelle was at a computer. "Hey. Jordan's Uncle John and her PR-slash-family representative, Tina, are now at the bedside I know Joe went to talk to her parents, but they'd also like to speak with you when you've got time."

"Okay, I'll head over there in a minute. Just let me finish entering these orders."

When she turned the corner on her way back to Jordan's room, she ran into Tim and Paul.

"How are you holding up?" Tim asked.

"How's Jordan doing?" Paul asked, before she could answer the first question.

"Jordan's in critical but stable condition." She looked over as

Rochelle entered Jordan's room.

"We hate to be the bearers of bad news, but we just heard from the IndyCar race officials. We're being recalled to the track for a debrief. They want to go over our memory of the accident before we watch the videos of the wreck or talk to the press. They also mentioned a review of our medical protocols to ensure we did everything by the book." Tim shrugged.

Quincy's stomach dropped. "You've got to be kidding me. There were a zillion cameras at the finish line and around the course, why can't they rewatch those? I mean, there were at least one hundred fans live-streaming our every move, shouldn't that be enough?" Quincy clenched her jaw and tried to breathe. "What the hell, can't we call it in? I really don't want to leave Jordan."

"We asked if it could wait," Tim said, "and they were quick to remind us of the contract we signed about accident reviews and the legal ramifications of our actions or inactions. I won't say they're threatening us, but they did mention *their* lawyer and *our* licenses more than once during the call. I think they're freaked out because it was Carver that caused all of this."

Quincy blew out a heavy sigh and looked up at the ceiling, shaking her head. "Dammit, okay. I'll meet you out at the rig in five minutes. I've got something I need to do first," she said and headed for Jordan's room.

Rochelle came out and shut the door behind her. "Jordan's dad was on the line with her uncle. I think they all feel better now that they received an update. They were concerned she wasn't going to make it."

"Honestly, when I saw the crash..." Quincy shuddered. "I wasn't sure she would either."

Rochelle gave Quincy a quick hug as her pager went off. "Well, she will. I've got to go, but we'll catch up soon."

Jordan's door opened again, and Tina stepped out. "Can you make yourself useful and get Jordan's nurse? She needs more pain medication." She turned to go back into the room, but Quincy touched her arm lightly.

"Tina, just use the call button in her room for the nurse. You know you don't control this environment, so you can stuff your boss-bitch attitude. Jordan can only have so much pain medication. It'll be on her chart to give her more when the time is right." God, she couldn't stand this woman. "Look, I have to go back to Paramount for a debrief. Can you tell Jordan I'll see her later?" She fully doubted Tina would relay her message, but she had to try.

"Oh, I surely will." Tina's smile didn't reach her eyes. "But you should know something." She stepped closer, her eyes narrowed. "If you really care for her, you'll get out of her way. Being with you would cost her millions, her reputation, and maybe even her career. She's worth more than anything she could have with you."

Tina's words hit Quincy like a slap, but she wasn't about to back down, even though every moment of self-doubt assailed her. "You mean you'll lose your meal ticket, so you don't care whether or not she's happy?" She put her hands on her hips so Tina wouldn't see them shake. "But some of us care about her as a person and not because of what she can do for us. You're a leech."

Tina's face twisted into a scowl, but Quincy walked away before she could reply. She headed to the rig with her tattered heart unsettled. Jordan had picked her career over her, so why was Quincy still there, still fighting for her?

Chapter Twenty-Eight

The motion-activated light turned on as Lauren entered the room and woke Quincy. "I'm here, what's happening?" Quincy asked, confused as she sat up from the recliner that doubled as her makeshift bed in the ICU conference room. It was late when the IndyCar briefing, which had turned into more of an interrogation, ended. She'd returned to LAMC and been told Jordan was now in ICU with a restricted visitor list that didn't include her. She wanted to stay close overnight so she could check in on Jordan's progress, and her heart wouldn't let her leave. Fortunately for her, Lauren was the overnight ICU charge nurse, so she allowed her to stay nearby in the conference room. She bedded down there after a shower and a change of clothes from the racing suit to scrubs.

"Hey, sleepyhead. I wanted to let you know it's six thirty a.m. and almost time for morning rounds. Jordan's holding her own, her pain is better, and her cognitive status has improved. They'll re-image her today to check for any missed fractures or intracranial bleeds, but you didn't hear that from me." Lauren looked Quincy over. "You look exhausted. Why don't you go home? The visitor list is on lockdown, and you won't be allowed in there. Jordan's parents will be here this morning." Her phone rang. "Hi, Regina. Okay, I'll head over there now." She pocketed the phone and headed for the door. "They're here. Please promise me you'll go home. I'm worried about you. Your trip that starts in two days. Are you still going?"

Quincy blinked against the gritty sandpaper of her eyelids, her mind slow to comprehend. "I don't know about the trip. I'll let you know when I've decided. I'll go home later today. Don't worry, I won't hang around the unit. Go be the boss." Quincy laughed, and Lauren shook her head and left.

Quincy stepped out of the conference room and watched Lauren approach a sophisticated-looking couple outside Jordan's room. She recognized Victoria Valentine-Marsh and assumed the man was Jordan's father, Rodrigo. It was clear that she took after him in the looks department. The couple followed Lauren into Jordan's room and when the door closed behind them, Quincy felt that old familiar feeling of being shut out.

She was wrinkled and sleep-deprived, so she headed down to the first-floor food cart for a quick jolt of caffeine. She joined the end of the line just as she saw Tito John in his CHP uniform heading toward the couple she'd only just seen upstairs. She stared at them as her thoughts tumbled around her head. She longed to be part of the group who cared for Jordan. Before she could look away, he turned around and saw her. He said something to Jordan's parents, then came over.

"Morning, Quincy. I didn't know you were still in the hospital. How're you doing?"

Jordan's parents came up behind him, and Quincy wanted to run. She didn't need more of Tina's vibe.

"Let me introduce you to Jordan's parents," John said. "This is her mom, Victoria, and my brother, Rod. This is Quincy Fitzgerald, Jordan's close friend. She works here as an NP in the emergency room. She also happened to be on the Medical Safety Support team yesterday and was at Jordan's side right after the accident. It's because of her that Jordan won't have lasting nerve damage in her arm."

In their clearly expensive wardrobes, they both looked like they'd just stepped out of a magazine and weren't a bit travelworn. Quincy felt the rumpled mess she was as Victoria looked her up and down, taking in the wrinkled scrubs, worn clogs, and disheveled hair. She was the antithesis of the Marshes.

Victoria nodded as though she'd made a decision. "Nice to

meet you. Thank you for being there for Jordan," she said and then turned away to talk to her husband.

Jordan obviously hadn't exaggerated her story about her mom. Quincy would never measure up to what Victoria Marsh thought was good for her daughter. She didn't have the patience for her power trip this morning though, and all she wanted was her coffee. "You're welcome."

Tito John caught her eye and gave her an apologetic smile as she headed back up to the ICU to check on Jordan.

Tina stood outside Jordan's room with her arms crossed, blocking the door to Jordan's hospital room like a pit bull guarding a house. She scowled. "What do you want?"

Quincy was ready to fight Tina to have access to Jordan, even if for just a minute. "I want to see Jordan and check on her recovery."

"That's not happening. While her parents are away from the room, I've been asked to ensure only family and Joe enters. She doesn't want to see you. She hasn't even mentioned you, so why don't you just walk away and take your infatuation along with you."

Quincy had had enough. First Mrs. Marsh and now Tina. She was too exhausted to fight this battle. "Please just tell her I was here. I'll check in on her a little later." She turned to leave.

"It's about time you figured out that Jordan Marsh is way out of your league, beach trash."

Quincy slipped into the fire escape and cried. Tina was only telling her what she already thought, but now... God, how it hurt to hear it spat out so cruelly from someone else. Once she gathered the shattered pieces of herself, she made her way down the stairs. She wasn't wanted here. Just as she crossed the courtyard toward the parking lot, she heard her name called out.

"Quincy. Quincy, wait." Tito John gave her a big hug. "Hey, don't cry." He led her over to a wooden bench, away from prying eyes. "Victoria is worried about Jordan, and she can come off as a bitch. You're such a strong woman; surely she hasn't upset you that much."

Quincy hiccupped as she tried to stop the tears flowing down her cheeks. "I *am* a strong woman. I guess it's a combination of exhaustion from being here since the accident, a coffee diet, Victoria, and *Terrible Tina*, who blocked me from Jordan's room. I guess they finally wore me down." She wiped at her eyes and looked up at him.

John frowned. "Wait, if you've been here since the accident, why haven't you been at her side? I don't want to sound mean, but the last time I saw you was in the ER when she was first admitted. You left and never returned. I assumed you'd done your job and gone home."

She relayed her night from hell at Paramount. "I told Tina I had to leave, but it's not surprising that she didn't relay that to anyone."

John shook his head. "No, she didn't mention that to anyone, especially not Jordan."

Quincy looked down at her wrinkled scrubs and worked her fingers over the creased fabric to release some of her tension. "I returned as soon as I could to check Jordan was okay. I wanted to be there so I could help to facilitate whatever she needed. I pulled some strings, and I've been down the hall in the ICU conference room since I wasn't on the visitors list. I wouldn't have left her side if I had a choice in the matter, but my hands were tied." She swallowed hard, not wanting to give in to another bout of crying in public. "I guess it isn't my place."

John grabbed her hand. "Quincy, don't go. I'm sorry about the visitor list; I didn't know you weren't on it. I'm sure Jordan wants you here. Come up with me, and we can sort this out."

Quincy shook her head and stood up. "Tina said Jordan hadn't asked about me. It may seem like it's too soon, but I love her, and my heart couldn't leave here without knowing she'd be okay." It was the first time she'd said the words out loud, and the truth of them was a blow to her soul. She blew out a deep breath and looked down at her wringing hands. "I know that this is all one-sided. Jordan told me as much. Tito John, I'm a realist, and there's no way I can compete with her team, her image, and her family. I know where I'm not wanted or needed. She'll have all the support needed to recover. It's time for me let it go. Last night, I wasn't sure if I'd go on the three-week trip I've planned, but I am now. Please take care of her for me. It's been a pleasure getting to know you, even briefly." She went up on her tiptoes to kiss his cheek, and he engulfed her in a warm embrace.

"I'll take care of her, and I'll make sure she knows you've been here this whole time. I think you should come back up, but she's clearly not able to talk things out yet, and between Tina and her parents, you're probably safer on an island. Maybe, when you get back..." He stepped back from the hug and shrugged. "Safe travels, Quincy."

She watched as Tito John disappeared behind the sliding doors of the hospital lobby. Once he was gone, Quincy sank back onto the bench and buried her face in her hands, suffocated by the embarrassment of confessing her love for Jordan to Tito John. Wiping her tears, she steadied herself and headed to her car. *I love Jordan Marsh* echoed in her mind like a broken record.

Inside the sanctuary of her car, she sighed loudly. "I love Jordan Marsh. God, I really do. I love her so much." A wave of loss washed over her, the initial joy of her realization overshadowed by the weight of reality. "But there's nothing I can do about it." Tears streamed down her face, and Quincy drove away from the woman she loved.

Chapter Twenty-Nine

THERE WASN'T AN INCH of Jordan's body that didn't hurt. Her head felt like it was caught in a vise, and the rest of her body felt pummeled like someone had used her for a piñata. She didn't want to open her eyes; the last time she did, the lights were like shards of glass in her skull. *What day is it? Where am I?* She took stock of what she remembered and realized it was all very fuzzy except for images of her race car flipping over, the ground flying past, the sound of metal crumpling...and pain. What the hell had happened? She'd have to ask Joe. She kept her eyes closed to delay reality for a while longer and immediately recognized the voices whispering in her room. She was surprised to hear her mom's voice so close.

"Tina, you failed us. What a waste of $50,000. All we asked was for you to direct Jordan's career and image the way I told you to. Instead, you allowed our good name to be dragged through all sorts of scandals. And now she's become the patron saint of *lesbians*. You were supposed to stop that sponsor deal, and now it's going forward. Do you know how this affects our image? We're done paying you."

"Screw you, Vic. Fifty thousand wasn't nearly enough to deal with your slut daughter. It's not my fault you were terrible parents and have no control over your only child. I think it's hilarious that your name is being dragged all over social media. That fifty thousand was peanuts compared to what I built into Jordan's new sponsors' deal. I'll be financially secure, and I won't have to do your bidding."

Jordan lay there, stunned but not surprised. She had never imagined her parents would resort to paying Tina to control her, but there it was. It struck her how her entire life had revolved around their need for control—how they always tried to shape her into a version of themselves, a version that made them look good. Even now, as she lay there battered and bruised, it was still all about them and what they could gain. Jordan couldn't stop the tears as they trickled down her face and onto the pillowcase. She felt around for the call button, certain it was within reach. She hit the button and opened her eyes to see Tina and her mom glaring at one another across the foot of her bed, while her father sat in a chair by the door looking at his phone.

"Yes, Ms. Marsh, can I help you?" the voice asked over the speaker.

"Can my nurse please come in here and remove all my visitors? Thank you," Jordan said with a raspy voice.

Her mother frowned. "Oh, Jordie, you're awake. Finally. We're so relieved. Are you in pain? Is that why you want us to leave?"

"Stop the act, Mom. I heard everything you just said. You can all go fuck yourselves. I don't want to hear any excuses; I know they'll all be lies. I don't want to see or hear from you ever again. Get out of my fucking room." Jordan barely controlled her rage and pointed to the door with her left arm. Her head, back, and arm vibrated with pain that made her even more angry. "Tina, you're a conniving bitch. I always knew they had something on you, but I never would've expected it was a bribe. I shouldn't be surprised since you have no moral compass. You're fired, in case that isn't obvious, and I'll make sure you're finished in PR. Good luck getting a new job when I'm done with you. Now get out of my sight before I have you thrown out."

Tina scoffed. "You don't have the power you think you do. I made you who you are. I made you a household name. So what if I made some money on the side? I'll see you in court. You're not taking me down without a fight." She picked up her purse, yanked the door open, and left.

Jordan blew out a breath, the blinding pain in her head and

around her chest throbbing with her movements. She had to close her eyes and take a deep breath to stop the room from spinning before she threw up. She felt her mom's hand on her arm.

"Jordan, are you okay? What can we do?"

Jordan pulled her hand away. "I told you. Get out." She'd had enough of this charade. She didn't have much energy left, but it was time to deal with her parents. She opened her eyes and saw that her dad had joined the act, hovering over her like he was concerned. "Don't for one second act like you care about me. You've only ever wanted the version of me that you could control. It has and always will be about the two of you and how I can make you look better. Well, fuck that and fuck you. That's not how love works." Jordan choked on a sob. "You've never loved me for me and because of that, I always thought I was lacking, that I somehow didn't measure up. I agree with Tina on one thing: you are shitty parents. This ends today. I'm no longer your puppet that you can bring out to impress your friends. We are *done*. Get out of my room, and my life. Now!" Jordan yelled.

Jordan's mom looked like she'd been slapped. "Watch your language. You can't speak to us like that; we're your parents. You don't know what you heard under all that medication. We've only ever had your best interest at heart."

"Yeah, Jordie, we care about you," her father said.

Jordan wanted to laugh, but her head felt like it was being split open with an axe. "Sure you do, Dad. You care about how I make you look. It's too late; I'm done. You can reach me through my lawyer. I want nothing more to do with you," she said softly as each word was a new dagger in her skull. She hit the call light again and a nurse walked into the room.

"Hello, Ms. Marsh. I'm Kara. How can I help you?"

"Kara, get them the fuck out of my room now, and they're barred from ever visiting again. Do you hear me, *Mama Vic*? You're barred from ever contacting me again. Get out!" she yelled.

Kara went to work removing them from the room and then

followed them outside. Jordan sank back in her bed, shaking and exhausted. She'd like to think it was a pain response from her yelling and moving, but she knew better. The anguish she felt at being used, lied to, and manipulated overtook her. Where was Quincy? She'd said she cared, but where was she? Did she leave me like everyone else? Jordan's thoughts started to spiral as she sobbed harder.

"Ms. Marsh, are you okay?" Kara asked when she came back in. "How can I help?" She pulled some tissues from a box and placed them in Jordan's hand. She then patted Jordan's hand. "It's okay. They've been removed from the hospital and placed on a restricted visitation list. I've got you. Do you need something for pain?"

Jordan was blubbering like a child, and she knew it. She blew her nose, took a deep breath, and looked at the Kara, who was being so kind. "Yes, please. I hurt everywhere, but my headache is the worst. Can you turn the lights down?" Jordan asked, feeling helpless. She wanted to ask about Quincy but couldn't bring herself to say the words and add to the disappointment of the day.

"I'll be right back with something for pain. Is there anything else I can do for you?" Kara looked back at her from the door.

Jordan shook her head. "No, thanks, Kara." God, did she wish there was something the nurse could do to fix her damaged soul, but only she could fix that broken piece.

Chapter Thirty

Quincy's hope that Jordan would contact her and tell her not to leave ended when the flight crew closed the airplane door. It wouldn't be long before she taxied down the runway and left Los Angeles *and* Jordan behind. She shut off her phone. Lauren had told her that Jordan was still in the ICU and recovering well, but that was it. A quagmire of emotions continued to assail her, making it hard to function. It was good that Jordan was healing so well. Quincy was overwhelmed with guilt for not staying by her side and sadness for not hearing from her. And, honestly, she was a little angry that Jordan hadn't reached out just to let her know she was okay, if nothing else. The combination of feelings made her tear up, but she was so very tired of crying. She dabbed at her eyes as she situated herself in her first-class seat for the long flight to the Cook Islands. *Now's not the time to cry. I'm going on an adventure.*

The flight attendant breezed by Quincy's seat with a tray. "Champagne before we depart?"

"Yes, thank you."

"Is your trip for business or pleasure?" She handed Quincy a chilled glass.

"Pure pleasure."

"Lucky you." She smiled and walked down the aisle.

Here's to a fantastic vacation. Quincy toasted herself, lifted the champagne flute, and took a large gulp as the bubbles tickled her nose. She'd planned this underwater archaeological adventure for two years. She was excited about getting to dive with underwater archaeologists to uncover possible artifacts. *So what if I'm going alone? That's how I'd planned it from the start.* So why did the feeling of loneliness persist? Jordan. It would keep coming back to Jordan until she could really let go and accept that being in love didn't mean her happy ending. She knew this was going to be a great trip; she just needed to leave everything in LA behind, including thoughts of Jordan and the piece of her heart she'd taken with her onto that racetrack. Quincy finished off the glass of champagne and sank into the comfortable faux-leather seat. As the plane left LAX and soared out over the Pacific Ocean, Quincy felt the pull from the alcohol and the recent sleepless nights. Her exhaustion began to take hold, and she drifted off to sleep.

***

Quincy's excitement built as she looked out the plane window at the large expanse of cerulean water that gave way to the verdant green mountain at the center of Rarotonga. The sky was peppered with painted clouds in the vibrant orange and pink colors of the sunrise. The plane circled the island, providing her with a stunning view of the sandy beaches that blended into the turquoise water of the lagoons. It was simply paradise. She couldn't stop smiling as she deplaned and headed into the warm tropical air. She cleared customs and headed out to the transportation area of the airport for her ride to the bungalow. She looked around and saw a white-haired, solid-looking man holding a sign with her name on it. Quincy smiled and waved at him before she walked over.

"Kia orana," Quincy said. She wasn't certain she got the words out correctly, but his smile indicated otherwise.

"Kia orana, Ms. Fitzgerald. Welcome to Rarotonga. I'm Ramona's brother, Earl. Ready to go? I'll drive you to the Ocean Oasis bungalows." He grabbed her bags and headed to a white Toyota pickup truck.

"Thanks for picking me up, Earl. I can't wait to see more of the island, and please, just call me Quincy."

"Okay, let's go then." Earl flung the luggage into the bed of the truck and opened the door for her.

"Thank you."

They began their journey toward the bungalow where Quincy would stay for the three weeks. She'd enjoyed emailing with Ramona and looked forward to meeting her in person. Earl provided commentary as they made their way on Ara Tapu, the one road around the island. They left Avarua, the largest town, as it started to bustle with morning traffic. Then Earl headed west past the Marae Moana mural and Black Rock, things she'd read about in the travel guide and couldn't quite believe she was seeing in person. The warm tropical sun sparkled like diamonds on the clear blue lagoon, and the warm salty air greeted her as she hung out the window and took in the island life. Earl turned in toward the ocean off the main road and parked near a large yellow home with plantation shutters painted dark green. Four bungalows were dotted down the beach from the main house, all painted white with green trim, and all had a wooden porch on the front facing the ocean. An older woman stepped out of the main house. She wore a colorful flowing dress that highlighted her dark hair, which was streaked with white.

As she got closer, her brown eyes reflected her happiness, and she smiled broadly, highlighting her white teeth in contrast to her brown skin. She raised her arms. "Kia orana, Quincy. Welcome to Ocean Oasis. I'm Ramona. It's so nice to finally meet you. I hope Earl picked you up on time at the airport. He can be lazy." She pulled back from the hug and gave her brother a pointed look.

"Don't start with me, sister," Earl said before he carried Quincy's luggage to her bungalow.

Quincy's heart lifted at their sibling banter. "Earl was right on time, and he gave me a wonderful tour of the island from the airport to here."

Earl sucked his teeth. "See, sis. Cut me some slack."

Ramona shook her head and motioned for Quincy to walk with her. "Okay, let's get you settled. We'll follow him down this wooden walkway to your bungalow. You'll be in number four, closest to the water and furthest from the main house. Earl and I live in the main house, so if you have any issues, just let us know. We have a plunge pool and laundry facilities by the main house, otherwise all amenities are in your bungalow. There are electric bikes, motorcycles, and car rentals across the road if you need them. We've also got two regular bicycles you can borrow. The three other bungalows will be rented the first two weeks you're here, but you'll be alone the third week. The floating dock is ours, and the lagoon is full of beauty. The beach is safe, but there are some over-friendly dogs that may visit you. Just shoo them away, and they'll leave you alone. Okay, here we are. Bungalow number four."

Quincy sighed happily at her accommodation. The simple bungalow had an L-shaped kitchen, which included an eat-in counter and two stools. The small living room held a wicker couch and chair with papaya-colored cushions that faced the ocean. A separate bedroom with a small bathroom made up the back of the building. The place itself was gorgeous, but what was truly amazing was the tri-fold wall of glass that looked out over the powder-white sand beach and the crystal azure water, which was less than twenty feet away. The wraparound porch opened to the soft sand and two palm trees framed the view. One of the trees secured and shaded a hammock that was connected to her bungalow. "Ramona, this is so beautiful." This was really happening. For the next three weeks, this paradise was hers.

"Thank you. I'll let you get unpacked, but we're just over there if you need anything. All the instructions on the bungalow and local information are inside in the binder. The Wi-Fi coverage is a bit spotty. It isn't as reliable as you're used to in the States, but I know you're really here to explore that." Ramona pointed to the lagoon, drawing Quincy's eye out to the translucent water. "Welcome to Rarotonga and the Cook Islands," Ramona said then turned up the walkway back to the main house.

Quincy kicked off her sandals and headed to the water's edge, where she could see beautiful tropical fish that swam along within the brightly colored coral reef. *This will be three weeks in heaven.* For just a moment, she was reminded of the time she'd been out in the water and had met Jordan, the beginning of the journey that had led to heartbreak. She shook it off, angrily dashing away the tears. No. She wouldn't spend her time grieving. The hammock that hung outside her bungalow was shaded by the palms above and would be used frequently, she'd make sure of that. She walked back to her bungalow, where fresh fruit and champagne awaited her as a welcome gift, but her head still buzzed from the few glasses she'd had on the plane. The heat of the day was upon her, and while a nap in the hammock may just help her get on island time, she needed to unpack.

She rolled her bag into the back bedroom and began to organize her belongings. She removed her watch and placed it on the nightstand. "It's official, I'm on island time," she said to the empty bungalow as she stretched to shake off her jet lag. She slipped into her swimsuit and grabbed a towel to go explore the warm tropical waters of the lagoon. She'd have time for a nap later.

Quincy woke in the hammock with sweat dripping down her temple and a feeling of dread in her chest. The images of Jordan's car flying through the air and crash-landing had played in her dreams in slow motion, her screams silent, her feet too heavy to move as she tried to get to Jordan's side as the car was engulfed in flames. The nightmare had everything to do with the call she'd made earlier to the ICU. *You just couldn't leave it alone.* She should've just walked away like she said she would, but nope, she had to call. Thankfully, Jordan's nurse was James, a good friend of hers from way back. She was relieved to hear that Jordan was recovering well enough to likely go home tomorrow. Quincy sat on the edge of the hammock and buried her feet in the cool sand. She tried to make sense of the restlessness that lingered from her dream and the reality of what she meant to Jordan. *She's recovering well without me. I was being silly to think she'd need me to help her heal. I have to let her go.* It felt like a lie, like a platitude that was said but had no real meaning. It wasn't that easy. A part of her that she was desperately trying to ignore couldn't help but wish Jordan was there with her in paradise instead of surrounded by people who demanded she be what they wanted her to be. But ultimately, Jordan made the choice to stay in that world. All Quincy could do now was try to get over her and hope that Jordan could find her way to being happy one day.

Chapter Thirty-One

JORDAN RELISHED THE HEAT of the morning sunlight as it streamed through the window. She rubbed her arms, chasing away the chill from being up most of the night digesting her parents' and Tina's betrayal. How could she have been so stupid not to see how she was being manipulated? Sure, she'd hired Tina because her parents had asked her to, but she'd never thought Tina was actually doing their bidding instead of what was best for Jordan's career. She shook her head and fought off the tears. Action, not tears, would solve this. She picked up her phone and texted Tito John and Joe to come immediately.

Seventy-two hours had passed in a painful blur since her accident, but she was alive and recovering. She now wore a torso brace and a cast on her right arm, and she felt like Frankenstein's monster. Her headaches still lingered but had improved. She'd had physical therapy this morning and couldn't believe how weak she was. She had more work ahead to rehabilitate and regain her physical strength for racing. She hoped her medical team would be by soon to discharge her. She wanted to get back to life outside these pale, sterile walls. The sooner she got out of here, the sooner she could have her privacy and some peace. She looked up at the quick knock. The door to her room opened and a larger-than-life man entered.

"Hi, Ms. Marsh. My name's James, and I'll be your fabulous nurse for the day. How are you this morning? Having any pain? Headache? Are you hungry? Do you want breakfast?"

She felt some whiplash as she watched him move around the room before he opened the blinds. "Morning, James. I'm hurting from the PT, so some Tylenol would be good."

"Let me get you your medication and then contact your medical team and find out when they'll be up to see you. If it'll be a bit, we'll take a walk. Does that sound good?"

"Sounds perfect," Jordan said before he left the room like a Tasmanian devil.

"Good morning, Ms. Marsh. We're here to evaluate you."

Jordan looked up and counted twelve white-coated pros enter, led by Dr. Rochelle Dixon. She was amazed so many people could fit in her room. "I see you have a full dozen today."

Rochelle smiled. "We wanted to perform our rounds together to address any of your issues collectively. We've heard you'd like to go home?"

Jordan nodded emphatically and tried not to show that it made her head hurt a little. "I'm stable enough to go home to continue recovering."

"Okay, our teams will work on our recommendations for follow-up visits and milestones for your concussion, arm, and spine recovery. These will be shared with IndyCar, so you'll need to meet them before you'll be allowed to race again. I think it's best if we keep you until tomorrow, so you can get more therapy before discharge."

Jordan nodded. "Whatever it takes."

"What questions do you have for us?" Rochelle asked.

"What's the earliest I can get out of here?" Jordan asked and gave her a broad smile.

***

Jordan walked slowly around her room, overcome by the massive bouquets of flowers, cards, balloons, and well-wishes on her recovery. After an uncomfortable walk with James, she sat up in the chair to read the cards from her friends, family, and fans just as her nurse came back into the room.

"Good job on walking. You doing okay, hon? Having any pain after the Tylenol?"

Jordan shook her head. "The meds and getting out of bed worked. I'm pain-free right now."

James moved the call light closer to her and made sure she could reach her water glass. "All right then, I'll get out of your way. Just call me if you need anything," he said and left.

Fifteen minutes later, Jordan's world righted itself just a little as Joe and Tito John barreled through the door. The tight band of anxiety wrapped around her chest finally lessened. "Hi," she said, struggling to hold back the flood of tears.

"Jesus, Jordie, what the fuck happened?" Tito John came to her side and ineffectually tried to hug her around the casted right arm and spinal brace.

Joe looked concerned as he held her hand. "You okay?"

It was time to reclaim control of her life. She gave them both a weak smile. "I'm okay. Can you hand me some tissues and take a seat, because we've got a lot to cover."

Tito John pulled up his chair but shook his head as he looked her over. "What do we need to address? You look better now, but your eyes tell a different story. It's clear you, who never cries, have been crying."

Jordan looked away from his compassionate eyes and tried to keep her composure. She took a deep breath and slowly released it before she could start, then she brought them up to speed with Tina, her parents, and the sponsorships. "So yeah, a lot has happened." She sniffled and wiped her eyes.

"I'm shocked." Tito John shook his head.

"I'm not. None of them have ever had Jordie's best interest in mind. Good riddance! Sorry, Jordie. I don't mean to be insensitive, but they really are crap people," Joe said, looking uncertain about his outburst.

Jordan burst out laughing, causing a shock of pain through her brain. "Ouch. Joe, you know I love you, and you're right: they were shit. They were never proud of me. They never supported me. They never loved me for me, and I always embarrassed them. It feels good to be rid of them all, honestly. I'll need to call my lawyer to bring up charges against Tina and to officially fire her. As for my parents, they'll just no longer be part of my life. Tito, if you want to talk to them, that's fine, but I won't be."

"I understand, Jordie. I'm sorry they're so selfish. You know you've got family, lots of it. Don't ever be afraid to reach out. We'll always be there for you," he said and kissed her cheek.

She picked up her cell. "I don't have a lot of energy left, so let me call Leighton, and we can move on. "Hey, Leighton, how's it going?"

"Forget me, Jordan," Leighton said. "How are you? That was one hell of an accident you had the other day. It's so good to hear your voice and know you're okay. We're all so worried and everyone sends their love."

How many times would she need to answer this question in the months ahead? At least she was alive to answer it at all. "I'm banged up but doing okay."

"I'm so glad to hear it. Don't you worry about the wreck. I'm working on your behalf to ensure justice is served. IndyCar has an ongoing investigation into what happened, and while Carver maintains it was an accident, his crew have come forward and told IndyCar and media sources that he panned to harm you. They said he was bragging about sabotaging your car and garage. We have specific details of when it happened and what he did. He'll likely be brought up on felony charges of vehicular assault and battery since it took place on the streets of LA."

Jordan blinked away a fresh wave of tears. "Thanks, Lei. I appreciate all you've done."

"I got you, don't you worry! Just focus on your battle to recover, and I'll take care of the legal battles. Was there something else you wanted to discuss?"

"There sure is. I've got some more work for you. I want to fire

Tina immediately for breach of contract. Can you take care of that for me? I don't want to deal with her ever again."

Leighton laughed. "With pleasure. I didn't think this day would ever come. What happened?"

Jordan told her all she knew. "I don't know the full extent of it, but I imagine you can handle it. I also want to place a restraining order against my parents." She felt deflated at the words she'd never imagined saying.

"Jordie, consider it done. I'm sorry but not surprised. I'd heard some things about their attempts at controlling your assets and buying stories from the *New York Post* so they wouldn't run. It's the best thing you can do, but it must hurt. When you're ready, I'll send you information on other PR and management firms that might fit you better, ones that work with LGBTQ+ athletes."

"Thanks, Lei, I appreciate you. I'll be in touch." She hung up and looked at Joe and Tito John, who were watching her intently. "I'm exhausted, in pain, and this damn crying has worn me out. Tito, can you go get James, my nurse? I want a minute with Joe."

"You bet, Jordie. I'll be right back," he said as he opened the door and headed out of the room.

"What's up?" Joe pulled at his ear.

"You okay, Joe? How's the team? Have you heard from Florence? Any of the sponsors? What's the word on the track?" Jordan asked rapid-fire as her anxiety grew. She'd always been in control at the track and now she felt anything but.

Joe squeezed her hand. "Calm down Everything's fine. I've been worried sick about you and so has the team. We all miss you. All the IndyCar teams have united in their support for you. Trust me when I tell you that Carver will be blacklisted by the team owners from ever driving in IndyCar again, and that's if he doesn't go to jail. I briefly spoke with Florence, and she wanted to give you space to recover, but I've been giving her updates on how you're doing. She planned to text you tomorrow. As far as the sponsors, she's fielded all their questions and is handling them, as you know she does well.

Jordie, you don't need to worry about any of that. Just get better." He smiled softly.

Jordan leaned her head back on the chair, relieved but immediately overcome with exhaustion. She looked up as the door opened, and Tito John and James walked through. It was evident something was wrong. "What is it?"

"Are you going to tell her about giving out Jordan's health update, or am I?" Tito John looked at James with hard eyes.

James wouldn't make eye contact with Jordan. He rearranged the water pitcher five times before his actions started to piss her off. She reached out and stilled his hand. "What did you do?"

"Well, I know I shouldn't have, but she called and wanted an update. We go way back, and she was with the team who brought you in, so I didn't think anything about it, but I realize now that wasn't the right thing to do."

Jordan's stomach dropped as she thought of all the media outlets who'd be dying to get an update on her injuries and family issues. "James, who did you talk to?" she asked as she rubbed her temple.

"I'm sorry, Jordan, but she called from her vacation to check on you, and we've known each other for—"

"Dammit, James, who was it?"

"Quincy Fitzgerald. I spoke to Quincy."

Jordan's heart rate doubled. "Quincy?" she asked in disbelief.

"Yes, I told her you were recovering well and that maybe you'd go home soon. Please don't tell anyone, or we'll both lose our jobs. Q and I go way back to many Pride celebrations and BBQs together. Jordan, you have to believe me that I wouldn't tell anyone else. Q told me about being at the race and that she was concerned about you. She hadn't had an update since the day after the crash, and she was going batty not knowing how you were doing. She may have also mentioned that she still had feelings for you, which sealed the deal," James said, wringing his hands.

"She does?" Jordan softly asked and then closed her eyes

to fight the tears that gathered. *Quincy's trip, of course. She still cares.* After everything Jordan had said and done? How was that possible? The last image she had of Quincy was wearing her racing suit. Her hands and words were so strong, her voice so sweet as she'd told Jordan to fight, to hang on. She hadn't been able to respond, but those words filtered through her dreams each night. *What was I thinking? She was brave enough to offer me her heart, and I swatted it away. And for what? Sponsors who want to buy my whole life?* Things had to change. If this accident had taught her anything, it was that life wasn't guaranteed. It could be over in an instant, and the time for living was now. It was also the time to stop being a coward by hiding behind others. She'd let money, fame, and her desire to win at all costs control her life's direction. It was time she stood in her truth and took responsibility for her actions. Quincy made her want to be a better version of herself. Jordan wanted to be at her side and share all the little things. *I love her!* The pure joy of that truth filled Jordan's soul and spilled out in a broad smile.

"What are we missing?" Tito John asked, looking puzzled.

"I miss Quincy. I need to see her. When can I leave the hospital?" Jordan asked James, who had retreated to the door, seemingly ready to run for cover.

The relief in his expression was clear. "Not tonight. Quincy said she had spotty cell service where she is, so I'm not sure if you can get a hold of her. As far as being discharged, you're set to leave tomorrow, but you look exhausted. Why don't we get you into bed?"

Jordan yawned. "You're right, I am." She gingerly moved back into the bed with James' help and sucked in a sharp breath from the pain in her back.

"Let me get your pain meds. I'll be right back," James said then left the room.

"Thanks so much for being with me on my emotional roller coaster today. Joe, can you set up a call with Florence for tomorrow, and Tito John, I know I've asked you before, but do you think you can help me locate Quincy?" Jordan asked. "I need to figure out how to win her back, but I just can't think right now."

"You rest and focus on recovering," Tito John said, "and we'll help you get the girl, but you need to heal some first."

Joe nodded, and James returned.

"Here's your pain meds." James handed her the pills and grabbed her water.

"Thanks. James. And don't worry about talking to Quincy; your secret is safe with me. I just need a little nap before I work on getting the girl. My sweet Quincy," Jordan slurred as her exhaustion overtook her.

***

Jordan sat in the wheelchair for the ceremonious discharge from the hospital and the slow ride out to her car. She was thankful for the care the LAMC team had provided during her stay. The hospital graciously allowed her to leave via the service exit, so the paparazzi and news crews camped out across the street couldn't capture her picture. She didn't need to see her black eye and casted arm on the front pages of the tabloids for weeks to come. Nor did she want to risk Juliette waiting outside like some lovelorn girlfriend.

Dave opened his arms wide as soon as the elevator door opened. "Hey, Jordie, ready to get out of here?"

Jordan thanked the hospital attendant and stood up. "I'm so ready. Take me home, please." She maneuvered herself into the back seat behind the dark-tinted windows and relaxed for the ride back to her beach house.

"Your wish is my command." Dave smiled at her through the rearview mirror.

Dave lauded her with tales of his latest real estate adventures, Elliott's attempt at cooking, and the supportive response from the sports world regarding the crash. She couldn't focus on him, and she felt terrible because he was such a good friend. In truth, her head hurt a little and her arm ached, and she deeply wished it was Quincy about to go into the house with her. They pulled into her drive, and Dave walked around to help her out, but she was already out of the truck and headed for her front door.

"Go, speedy," Dave said as he caught up to her and unlocked the door.

"Just excited to finally be home." Jordan couldn't believe how good it felt. She took off her awkward spinal brace and sat down on the couch, propped her casted arm up on a pillow and looked out at the glistening Pacific Ocean. Thoughts of Quincy and the first day they'd met made her smile.

Dave stood there awkwardly for a moment, then sighed. "It's good to see you smile. I know you want some space. What can I get you before I head out?"

Jordan looked up, so thankful he could read her needs. "A bottle of water and my phone charger, please," she said.

"You bet. Text me if you need anything, I'm just down the road, and you know I'll come running if you call. 'Il be back in a few hours to make dinner. Just call me, okay?" He kissed Jordan's cheek.

"Yep. I'll be okay. You don't have to come back." She pulled her gaze from the ocean and looked at Dave.

He stopped at the end of the couch. "We'll see. I love you, sweetie, and I'm glad you're okay and finally home. I'll call later, but you need to pick up when I do or else 'Il beat down your door. Bye, boo." He gave her a gentle hug, mindful of her injuries.

Jordan gave him a quick smile and wave as he walked out of the room, and she heard her alarm activate. She was finally alone. She smiled as she reflected on the never-ending support and love that her small circle of chosen family and friends provided. *Love.* She couldn't say the word or even think it without images of Quincy playing on repeat in her mind. She felt electrified by the thought of being with her again. She knew the day they met that she was special.

Jordan was nervous as she thought of the work she'd have to put in to win Quincy back, especially after the terrible way she'd treated her. The quiet and calm of the house surrounded her, and she lost the battle to sleep as the sun set in the western sky.

Jordan awoke to the ringing of her phone. She was slumped over on her couch, and the house was dark. "Hello?" Jordan asked, her voice raspy. She wasn't awake enough to see who was calling.

"Are you okay?"

"Yes." She smiled at the comforting sound of Tito John's voice, which allowed her to be vulnerable.

"Have you eaten? Forget it, I know you haven't. What do you want to eat? I'm coming over, and I'm almost there."

"In-N-Out," Jordan said without hesitation.

"Okay, I'll be there shortly."

Jordan hung up then texted Dave that she was okay and dinner was taken care of. She had an instant response, reminding her that he was just a text away. She got up off the couch and made her way into the bathroom to splash water on her face. Doing it one-handed made a mess and brought on a bout of frustration. She knew Tito John wouldn't care, but she didn't want him worrying about her, so she wiped up the mess as best she could. *I guess I have some things to work on.* The doorbell rang, and she opened it to the heavenly scent of cheeseburgers. "Yum."

"Let's eat outside." John pulled open the slider and set the bag down on the deck table.

"Do you want a beer?" Jordan asked as she opened the fridge.

"You bet. Are you having one? Can you have one, on your medications?" he asked.

"This is the only medication I need right now. I'm just on Tylenol and ibuprofen for pain." She grabbed the beers and an opener, then handed them to him to open.

The cast on her dominant arm made it difficult to eat the warm double-double cheeseburger, but she wouldn't ask for help.

She needed to figure out her own path forward without being waited on. She saw John watching, but he didn't offer, seeming to understand her need to figure it out. When they finished eating, they watched the moonlight dance on the sand and the ocean.

"How are you doing with everything?" he asked.

Jordan took a long pull off her beer. "I think I'm still figuring that out. Physically, it's going to take some time and work to get back on my feet. Emotionally, I'm gutted and embarrassed, because I kept my head in the sand for so long and trusted the wrong people. I'm a little scared of what the future holds. Will I keep my ride or not? There's just a lot right now, but the one shining star is Quincy. If I can have her by my side, I'll be able to make it through anything life throws at me. On that note, what've you got for me?"

"You're pretty fragile right now, but it's no wonder you feel that way, with everything you've gone through. We can talk about Quincy, but you know you have to rehabilitate before you can offer her anything, right?"

Jordan's insecurities surfaced with his question. "I want to run to her today, but you're right. It's for the best I can't meet her with this cast and spinal brace and have her think I'm attractive."

Tito John scoffed. "Whatever, Jordie. She was right there when you were bleeding and broken. Look, I wanted to tell you this last night, but you were so exhausted I wanted to wait. You need to know the whole story about Quincy."

"Okay, you're freaking me out. What don't I know?" She played with the label on the beer bottle for distraction.

"Quincy was there for you from the moment they extracted you from the car. She made sure you didn't have any neurovascular damage by stabilizing your elbow after the accident. Joe said she took charge of your care in the ambulance and on the way to the hospital. She's the one who made sure they fully understood your injuries to have the right teams ready when you got there. She was with you in the ER and directed the physicians and the nurses on the care you needed. She'd already gotten you scanned, and plans were made for your brain, spine, and arm before I even arrived. I don't know if you remember, but she stayed in the ER with you and only left when the IndyCar race officials wanted her back at the track for her statements on the accident. Once that was done, she came back to the hospital, where she kept tabs on you via the nursing staff. She slept down the hall in a chair and ate out of machines for twenty-four hours after your crash." He shook his head, his jaw working with anger. "I found out that Tina kept Quincy's name off the visitors' list, and she told her to stay away, and that you didn't want her there. I recently found out that Tina paid some of the staff to lie to you about Quincy not being around too, if you asked." He paused, and he was clearly debating whether to continue.

"Go on," Jordan said softly. "I need to hear it all."

"I introduced Quincy to your parents the morning after your accident. I told them how pivotal she was in your recovery, and they dismissed her straight away. That was the final straw for her, and she left the hospital crying. She told me that she cared for you a great deal and made me promise to take care of you. So no, I don't think she'll care how you show up, but it'd be best for you, her, and your career that you rehabilitate now and *then* go to her. James helped me get her itinerary so when the time comes, you can go to her. I'm telling you all this so you understand that she hasn't been around simply because she couldn't get to you, not because she didn't want to be at your side."

Tears streamed down Jordan's cheeks, and she dried them with her sleeve. "I knew she was around me. I could feel her near me. I swear I can still feel her presence even now. But this isn't something I want to talk to her about over the phone. I need to do it in person," Jordan said. "It's not just the physical recovery I'm facing. Things need to change all around. Getting rid of Tina and my parents is one thing, but I need to figure out what's best for me professionally, personally, and emotionally. That's not something I've done before, and it scares the hell out of me. I've got some work to do, but the possibility of a future with Quincy is certainly a good reason. I'd love to be able to lean on Quincy's strength and advice, but this is about my future, my growth." She looked up at Tito John, who nodded at her with a look of pride. The anxiety and fear that had plagued her since the accident melted away with this realization. She now had to put in the work, and she never shied away from work. First things first, she had to talk with Florence and figure out her professional career.

John stood behind Jordan and hugged her. "You're not alone in figuring this out. I'm sorry your mom and dad never showed you the love you deserved. They're a selfish couple who only care about their privileged life back East. They've never understood what driving means to you. They didn't get it when you were a child, and they still don't. I love you, Jordie, and I'll always be here for you, no matter what." He squeezed her gently and let go.

"Thanks, Tito. I love you too. You're right, they never understood my passion. I've always enjoyed the challenges on the track and proving to others that I could do what they said I couldn't. IndyCar racing has been a man's sport, but when the helmet is on, it doesn't matter who you're racing against: the best driver wins. I know there are little girls out there karting and thinking about racing in IndyCar or Formula One, and I want to help erase the bias, so they can have a smoother path to the track than I did. My success is proving to the doubters that a woman can win if she's provided with the same support and opportunities. The joy I found behind the wheel of my kart as a kid is the same joy I feel today. I just need to tap back into that part of me and leave the doubters behind." It felt beyond good to say all that out loud, and to remind herself why she'd started racing in the first place. "Speaking of support, I guess I better contact Florence and figure out what comes next while I recover. I have every intention of racing at Indianapolis in May, but I'll have to see what she thinks." She set the phone down after she sent a text to the team's owner asking to meet. Florence was a very busy woman, and it was a little presumptuous to think she'd be available, so she was surprised when a text came back right away.

Jordan, my dear, Joe's been keeping me updated. I hope you're recovering well. I'm sorry we missed one another. I'm available now if you've got time. How about a video call?

Jordan's stomach flipped. This was where the changes began, and she needed to be ready for whatever the outcome might be. *Sounds good.*

Jordan sat down on the couch, opened her laptop, and propped her arm on some pillows while she waited for Florence's call. She fidgeted with the pillows, unable to get comfortable and trying to think of just the right words to say, but it was now or never. The chime that announced the incoming call made her heart rate spike.

Florence's face filled the screen. "Jordan, it's good to see you. I'm sorry I missed you during the LA Grand Prix. Congratulations on the win! How are you? That was quite the accident. Do you remember much of it? I want you to know I've got my foot on the neck of IndyCar and the racing league. Carver won't be allowed to race in this country again if I have anything to say about it, and he should damn well do time for it. Have you seen the footage? Has anyone been around to speak to you about the crash? How can I help?" Florence didn't stop to breathe as she dropped all the questions.

Jordan blinked, trying to determine which questions to answer first. "Thank you for advocating for me. I'm still beaten up a bit and sore. The spinal fractures will heal within the next few weeks. I just need to wear this brace. The cast on my arm should come off in a week, and then I can start PT. My concussion symptoms are lessening, and I'm following the recommendations from the docs at LAMC. I want you to know that I have every intention of racing at the Indianapolis 500."

Florence nodded slowly. "Jordie, we want you at your best and if that means next season, then it's okay if it's next season. We could always bring Lex up in your ride for Indy, since we'll be bringing her up next season for her own team." She gave a broad, knowing smile.

Jordan's nerves made her own smile falter. She bounced her knee out of sight of the camera to offload her energy. "I like your idea about Lex for next year, and I'm glad you see her potential for the team. I do too, but not in my spot for the 500. I promise I'll be ready." She took a deep breath. "There's one more thing to discuss, and it's more personal in nature."

Florence held up her hand. "Jordan, I spoke with Joe, and he told me about the blackmail that Margaret and Amanda tried to pull with you by placing personal demands on their money. I had a chat with them, and let's just say, they've seen the error of their sleazy ways. I've got a newly signed contract with them for the original amount they offered for next season, and there are *no* stipulations on your personal life. You're free to be with the one you love, whoever that may be. I'm sorry that you didn't feel you could immediately come to me. In the future, please call me right away so we can deal with it."

Jordan closed her eyes and fought back the dizziness that came with the tide of relief. "Florence, I can't thank you enough. I'm so happy to hear that. I was afraid that if I said anything, you'd replace me, and I'd lose my ride. Thank you for having my back. I promise you we're going to be unstoppable next season. You need to know that I've fired Tina, and I have a restraining order against my parents as well. I know this is all messy, but it's long overdue, and it'll be for the best. I imagine Joe told you about Quncy?"

"No, he didn't have to say a word. I saw a video of you two together, and the way she looked at you at the track after the crash told me everything I needed to know. But like I said, your personal life is your own. I'm not worried about any fallout from Tina or your parents. They won't want this out in the media considering they're the ones at fault. If it gets messy, I'll help with the clean-up, and if you need help replacing Tina, I'll find you someone." She looked off screen and nodded to someone in the room. "Jordan, please take the time to heal yourself from the inside cut. I won't replace you, but I need you fully healed and hungry to race. You've got until the beginning of May, and I'm certain you can get there."

Jordan was stunned at how easily the conversation had moved in the direction she needed it to. "I'll do that. Thank you, Florence. For everything."

"You bet, Jordie. And congratulations again on your win. Don't forget to celebrate the hell out of it when you feel better."

Jordan hung up full of positivity about her professional future. She'd celebrate when she had Quincy in her arms, and after Jordan had told her how she really felt about her. *But how long will that take?*

Chapter Thirty-Two

QUINCY'S UNDERWATER ARCHAEOLOGY ADVENTURE had been a blast. From the moment she'd discovered out that NUA's underwater find was a scuttled ship that could have been one of Captain Cook's, she'd been buzzing with the prospect of diving here. NUA required non-disclosure agreements, but Quincy couldn't wait to tell her friends and family about her experiences above and below the water.

She'd enjoyed the six a.m. runs to the dock with Earl and the other staff who worked aboard the Good Fortune, but she couldn't believe it was her final day. The vibrant energy of schoolchildren headed to school on the back of mopeds that weaved in and out of traffic invigorated her for the final time. The homes they passed were a punch of color in the thick, lush green foliage and brilliant blues of the ocean as the sun began to rise in the east. For the past couple of weeks, she'd taken the colors, the energy, and the beauty into her soul, and they'd soothed some of the pain, allowing her to live in a world far from the one she'd left behind.

Quincy arrived at the dock with Earl, and they met up with the other underwater adventurers from Sweden whom she'd worked alongside aboard the Good Fortune. Today, they were returning to the 1730 vessel for the final day of exploration with Captain Todd.

"What do you think we'll find today: gold and jewels?" Quincy asked as she boarded.

"Maybe even a mermaid," Marta said and laughed. The boat left the launch and headed out to the site.

The day ended far too quickly. Quincy and the rest of the crew stepped off the boat and unloaded the final haul they'd collected along the seafloor.

She'd miss Marta and Gretchen; they made a good dive team and had helped Quincy settle. The evening sunsets, tropical drinks, and stories of their adventures in the belly of the blue had created great memories, and their friendship distracted Quincy from her heartbreak over Jordan. But when she was alone, her mind returned to what could have been. If only.

Ramona had been right; the Wi-Fi was terrible, and after the first week of not hearing from Jordan, she'd decided to withdraw from the world and focus on reconnecting with herself. She'd given Ramona's number and email to her family in case of an emergency and then shut off her phone. She continued to remind herself that Jordan was doing fine without her, and Quincy didn't need her heart crushed any further with online pictures of Jordan and Juliette, or some other bimbo. But she wasn't sure how another week on the island alone with her thoughts would make her feel.

"I promise I'll stay in touch. I want to come to Sweden and explore it with you," Quincy said.

"We'll let you know when we're planning to be in LA, and for sure, let us know when you want to come over. We love to travel, so we may not be home, but we can plan," Gretchen said, and she and Marta smiled.

"I will." They all hugged, and Quincy waved as they walked toward their rental car. Then she helped Earl load the truck and threw her dive bag in the back of the Toyota. "Earl, do you mind if I walk back to Ramona's today?"

"No problem, I'll put your bag on the deck in the shade," he said.

"Thanks. I'll see you later." Quincy watched as Earl drove off toward her beach bungalow. The festive nature of the last happy hour on the Good Fortune had passed. She was alone on the dock, the only sound being the turquoise water lapping at the wood. She dug her toes in the white powdery sand and headed to her home away from home.

She relaxed into the solitude and sheer beauty that surrounded her. She was looking forward to getting to explore the island, snorkel some reefs, and read some books. She'd have to spend time getting her heart and mind ready for the return to the real world eventually but for now, that could wait. Quincy walked along the water's edge, stopping to uncover shells and beach glass that had washed up.

As she approached her bungalow, she noticed someone lying in her hammock. *I guess the neighbors wanted to use it.* But the beach towel that she'd washed last night hung from the deck... Something wasn't right. It was one thing to use the hammock, but another thing entirely to use her towel. She cautiously approached her bungalow, and her knees went weak when she realized who it was.

"Hi, there." Jordan sat up and swung her legs over the side.

"What are you doing here?" Quincy put her hands on her hips. She didn't know if she should be flattered or angry, or some other emotion she couldn't name just yet. Her heart pounded in her chest, and she was glad her broad-brim hat and dark glasses hid her eyes from Jordan.

Jordan got off the hammock and stuffed her hands in the pockets of her cargo shorts. "Quincy, I'm sorry it took me so long to get here. I'm sorry I was a coward and didn't tell you that I love you. I'm sorry that I let Tina and my sponsors' threats sway me from standing in my truth. I'm sorry for wasting time and not understanding how much you mean to me before you left." She stepped closer and took Quincy's hand. "I love you, Quincy Fitzgerald, for all that you are. You are...so many things. You're so smart, beautiful, kind, funny, and so sexy. I'm here to ask you if you'll give me another chance." Jordan looked like she was going to pass out after she'd delivered her speech, barely taking a breath.

"You...love me?" Quincy slowly pulled off her hat and took off her sunglasses. She looked deep into Jordan's eyes and saw the truth in them, and her legs almost gave way beneath her. "As much as I've tried to fight it, I love you with my whole heart."

Jordan caressed Quincy's cheek. "I've missed you so much. I could *feel* you were there with me when I was injured. Tito John told me about everything you did for me on the track and at the hospital. I even know about the calls you've made from here to check on me. But what I feel for you started the first day I met you while we were surfing. I love you, and I want to make a life with you." She pulled Quincy to her.

The kiss they shared felt like a promise. Quincy caught her breath and traced her fingertips over the healed scar above Jordan's right eye. "Jordan, I want to be with you and share my life with you too. I've never wanted anything more in my life." Their passionate kiss ignited the spark that had laid dormant for the past few weeks.

They didn't break the kiss as they made their way into the bedroom. Jordan slowly stripped off Quincy's bikini top, and Quincy shivered as Jordan slid her fingertips over her sun-warmed skin.

"Your tan lines are so sexy." Jordan traced the thin white lines from her shoulders down to her breasts. She rubbed her thumb across each nipple before she chased the white path across Quincy's ribs to her back. She traced her fingers down Quincy's back and looped her fingers in the stretchy material of her coral bottoms. She then slowly removed the material while drawing Quincy closer to her. "God, you're gorgeous! I've missed you so much. I've thought of you every day since the accident," she said softly. "I want to touch you everywhere and fill you in ways you'll never forget."

Quincy shuddered, Jordan's words setting her on fire. "I want that; I want you. I told myself to stop pining for you, that I'd lost you, but I've thought about you and us together like this so many times."

Jordan grabbed Quincy's hand and led her into the shower. The initial cold splash of water felt good on Quincy's hot skin, but it gradually warmed as did her core. She looked Jordan over while she grabbed the coconut soap and gently washed Jordan's body. "Are you okay? Are you recovered enough to make love?" Quincy ran her fingertips over the faint bruises, abrasions, and pink scars that remained, a reminder of the worst day of her life.

"I am now that I'm with you," Jordan whispered.

Jordan's shimmering eyes drew her in, and she covered Jordan's strong body with her own, the only barrier a ribbon of water from the shower. Quincy felt like she was coming apart as Jordan explored her wet body first with her fingertips then with her soft lips. She placed gentle kisses down the slope of her shoulders and below to her breasts. Quincy's heat coiled within her, and she quivered.

"I want you now," Jordan whispered and shut off the water. Then she led them, soaking wet, to the soft bed where they intertwined in a deep embrace.

Jordan rolled Quincy under her, and she rained kisses down her body. Quincy's breathing came in short bursts as her arousal increased with the tempo of Jordan's loving touch. "Oh, yes. Oh, yes, Jordan." She moaned as Jordan provided the ultimate pleasure. She increased the tempo, taking Quincy over the edge and keeping her there for a beautiful eternity. "I love you, Jordan. I love you so much." Tears escaped her eyes, and she held Jordan's face as she gave her a fierce kiss.

"I love you too, baby. Damn, you're so sexy when you come for me," Jordan said and grinned broadly.

Jordan continued to straddle her, and she found herself in perfect alignment with Jordan's breasts. She used her lips, tongue, and teeth to bring Jordan's nipples to a peak and then sucked each one until Jordan moaned and rocked her hips against Quincy's stomach. She could feel Jordan's arousal and needed to feel all of her. She slipped her fingers deep inside Jordan's wet heat and immediately felt home.

"Fuck," Jordan moaned.

She grabbed the headboard as she rode Quincy's fingers close to her release. Quincy then took control and changed positions, moving down the bed so Jordan's hot sex was above her waiting tongue. She worshipped her until Jordan unraveled.

"Oh, Q." Jordan panted as her orgasm crashed over her. She slowly slumped onto the bed and held Quincy tightly to her. "I've missed you so much. You're so amazing. Thank you for loving me." Jordan choked up as a few tears slid down her cheeks.

Her heart full of joy, Quincy wrapped herself around Jordan and brushed away her tears. She held Jordan while they recovered their sanity. As she lay there, she couldn't escape from her thoughts spinning out of control. She pulled away so she could look into Jordan's beautiful eyes. "I have to ask, because it's running around in my head like a toddler in a candy store. Are you sure about us? I mean, there's Juliette, your sponsors, and a thousand other reasons not to be with me. Jordan, we're talking about *me*, boring Quincy Fitzgerald. I'm not celebrity material. I'll just bring you down, or embarrass you, so maybe we should consider that before we get any further into this." The fear of her heart being crushed all over again overtook her. She needed some protection from her vulnerability, so she grabbed the sheet. It didn't help.

Jordan smiled and rubbed her thumb over Quincy's hand. "I'm sorry I didn't believe in our love. I'm sorry that I ever made you doubt how much you mean to me, how much I love you. The accident was a blessing in some ways. It helped me take a good hard look at myself and what my life had become, and I didn't like it. I've been a pawn in my professional and personal life, but I *allowed* that to happen. After the accident, I realized that my priorities needed to change. I set about making changes professionally, but on a personal note, it all comes back to the beautiful blond I met in the ocean. Quincy, you have my heart, today and always. I love you with my whole being. I don't want anyone but you. Just you." She kissed Quincy passionately.

"Wow." Quincy wiped away the tears as they slid down her cheek. "Okay, I'm in."

Jordan kissed her hand. "I was in a dark place after the accident, but I had an epiphany after talking with Tito John. I realized that you're too important to me to just walk away, no matter the cost. I'd give it all up just for a chance to be with you."

Quincy traced Jordan's dimples with her fingertips and smiled. "That's nice to hear. But I'd never ask you to do that. You love racing; it's in your blood."

"Phew!" Jordan ran her hand across her forehead and sighed dramatically. "My next big hurdle is making sure I can drive the Indy 500 in May. I've been working with my trainer, and I'll need to do those exercises while I'm here with you. I want you beside me as I recover and as I return to racing."

Quincy's heart swelled with joy, but she needed to be honest too. The idea of a future together off this is and made her feel giddy. She wanted to hold on to Jordan forever, and she hoped she'd be able to once they were back in the real world. "I'd love to be by your side at this year's 500 and many more to come. But Jordan... watching that crash, not having control of the situation, and seeing you unconscious behind the wheel..." She swallowed hard and blinked away tears. "It was the worst moment of my life. I really thought I'd lost you. I can still see it in my dreams." When Jordan started to speak, she shook her head. "I'm not asking you to give it up. I told you I'd never do that. I just want you to know how it felt, and that maybe I'll be a little crazy when you're getting ready to go out again. That's the compromise you'll have to make for me." She laughed a little when Jordan rolled her eyes. "I wasn't too sure I should've come on this trip. I hadn't heard from you, and I was being told you didn't want me around, so I left. But I felt so guilty. The people I befriended on the ship had to listen to me go on about you every day. While this had been a great experience, it would've been better if I didn't have a broken heart."

Jordan hugged her. "I'm sorry for everything I put you through. I love you, my sweet Quincy. You're mine today, tomorrow, and forever." She kissed her with pure love.

Quincy cupped her face. "Thank you for coming to find me and for making me whole."

They stayed intertwined, listening to the crashing waves and watching the light change from orange to pink on their naked bodies. Sleep devoured them, and they remained embraced as they slept peacefully. They woke well after dark, and the moon lit up the beach, ocean, and the bungalow. Their hunger for food took over, and they enjoyed easy banter and sexual playfulness with each other as they raided the fridge. Eggs, toast, and juice fed their physical hunger as their sensual appetite continued to grow.

"Maybe we should clean up and find our way back to bed?" Quincy asked.

"Why go to bed when there's a nice sturdy table right here?" Jordan ran her hand up Quincy's inner thigh and lightly brushed her naked mound.

Quincy shivered. She spread her legs wider and leaned into Jordan's hand. Jordan groaned as she removed Quincy's T-shirt. She pressed Quincy back onto the table and slowly grazed her fingers up her body. She moved up her calves, behind her knees, and to her inner thighs. She brushed by Quincy's hot core and gave her clit a deep kiss then moved up her stomach to her breasts. Her nipples were erect and begging for attention, but Jordan continued to her lips. She kissed them until they were as plump and wet as her other lips.

Quincy opened her legs further, exposing her sex to Jordan's hot breath and firm tongue. She writhed with pleasure as she began to ride the wave Jordan was building, bringing her to the brink of abandon. Hot lava ran through her veins, and she was ready to erupt at any minute. Jordan kissed Quincy's hot, swollen lips and teased them with her tongue until Quincy exploded with pleasure. Jordan pressed her body to Quincy's, and they lay on the table, their slick bodies glistening in the moonlight.

"Come with me." Quincy slid off the table and held out her hand. Jordan slowly sat up and followed obediently back to the bedroom. "Are you hurt, baby?" Quincy asked, concerned their lovemaking would set Jordan's recovery back.

"I'm fine. Let's say that some of these positions weren't in my physical therapy sessions. I might be a little stiff, but no pain."

"Good to hear. Lie down on your belly," Quincy whispered and gently pushed Jordan down onto the bed before straddling her. "You've traveled so far for me, and you're injured. The least I can do is give you a massage." Quincy used her erect nipples to softly stroke Jordan from her shoulders to the curve of her butt. "Why don't you spread your legs a little further apart? That's right, baby, open up for me." She continued a light massage with her fingers over Jordan's arms, back, and legs, being careful of her right arm.

Jordan squirmed. "Damn, Q, I can feel how hot and wet you are."

Quincy giggled. "Well, let me check under your hood. I think you should turn over for me so I can feel all your components."

Jordan turned over, fire in her eyes. "My engine is on high throttle. You should check me out," she said with a wicked look.

"Let me run diagnostics." She ran her nipples across Jordan's breasts and belly, then she worked her way down to Jordan's engorged clit and tongued it until she arched off the bed. Quincy met Jordan's arch with her fingers and slid into her warmth. Jordan grabbed the sheets and called out Quincy's name. She matched Jordan's pace and watched as Jordan lost all control in the power of their lovemaking.

Jordan sank further into the bed after her release. "You can check under my hood any day." She gave Quincy a lopsided grin and pulled her close.

Quincy rested in Jordan's arms, enveloped by her strength, and for the first time, the deep peace and comfort of truly being home washed over her. She'd read about it in romance novels and seen it on romcoms, but nothing had prepared her for the overwhelming warmth of *true* love. It was more real, more profound than she'd ever imagined.

Chapter Thirty-Three

The week in paradise was heaven on earth. Jordan enjoyed their uninterrupted talks, amazed at how many similarities there were in their lives. She'd never shared the struggles of her youth with anyone, and the relief she felt at doing that with Quincy was beyond words. The ease with which they lived together and loved together was magical. The many long beach walks, the snorkeling, and the island exploration were always capped by passionate lovemaking. The pressure of the real world inched into their lives as the day to return grew closer, and their last day on the island loomed. Jordan couldn't wait any longer. As they sat in the hammock enjoying a respite from the sun, Jordan knew she had to do it. She glanced up at Quincy and blurted out, "We need to talk."

Quincy frowned. "What do we need to talk about?"

Jordan gave a hesitant smile. "About us," she said as she massaged Quincy's foot. "I'm not sure where to start. You've been a welcome surprise from the moment I met you. You touched my heart, and you made the world around me brighter. I've shared with you my closest friends and family, and I feel like my life is richer and more rewarding because you're in t. The blindfold I've had over my eyes for the past four years is gone, and I now see life in technicolor. That's all because of you. love you with my heart and soul, and this past week has proven that to me time and time again. I want to be the woman *you* need. The woman you want every day the sun rises. I know we have a lot to figure out. My racing schedule is crazy, and I'm on the road six months of the year in a new city or country every week You're still working out your next career move. The thing is, it doesn't matter where I am as long as I have you. I want you by my side, but I know you have an established career and a settled life in LA. I won't ask you to disrupt that. My anxiety about returning to the real world without a plan to be together is overshadowing the joy I have from being with you now. So that's why we need to talk about us. I need to know what you think and feel about our future together." Jordan finally took a breath. It was probably the most honest and forthright she'd ever been with anyone.

Quincy shook her head. "I've never felt for anyone what I feel for you. I'm not letting you walk away again, even if it is for a race weekend. I want to be by your side every day that the sun rises too. Baby, I've got a job that can be mobile if necessary, and you know I've been considering a change with work. I can always rent out my home, and in this housing market, it'll be picked up instantly. The only thing I can't live without is Jada; that's non-negotiable. I'm not a walk in the park either, you know. I like to be in control, and I have issues from my youth like you, but I can't imagine anyone else I want to spend the next fifty years with than you." Quincy wiped the tears from her eyes.

"We'll figure it out together then?" Jordan asked as she slowly rose from the hammock, trying not to flip Quincy.

"Yes, baby," Quincy said. "Together. Now let's enjoy our final day on the island."

When Quincy stood, Jordan kissed her with the promise of her love.

***

Quincy finished her shower and dressed quickly. She pulled on her new blue silk sarong to surprise Jordan, but the little cottage was empty. She could see movement down the beach, so she pulled back the curtains for a better view. Ramona walked by, so she figured it would be a good time to talk to her about her bill. "Hi, Ramona. Do I need to settle my bill tonight or will you be here in the morning before we leave?"

"Good evening, Miss Quincy. No problem. We'll put a bill under your door tonight and email you the final receipt in a week or so if that's okay with you?"

Quincy nodded and hugged her. "Thank you for such a wonderful stay. You're an amazing hostess. This place is incredible, and your bungalows are so wonderful." She looked around and sighed. "I don't want to leave."

"Thank you, my dear," she said, but she was clearly preoccupied with something on the beach as she gazed over Quincy's shoulder.

"Okay, I'll let you get going, but I just wanted to thank you for everything."

Ramona smiled. "It's been my pleasure. We look forward to seeing you and Miss Jordan here again." Ramona gave Quincy another quick hug before she took off for the front of the bungalows.

Jordan had left the bungalow over an hour ago. She'd gone to get a final workout on the beach and in shallow water, but shouldn't she be back by now? Quincy walked into the living room of the bungalow just as Jordan entered from the slider. The jewel tones of the ocean framed her tanned and toned body. "Hey, stranger, where've you been?" The heat in her core increased with Jordan so close.

Jordan smiled. "Just working out. You look beautiful in that sarong. Your eyes are the color of the sea. I'd like to kiss you and more, but I really need a shower. Do you mind waiting for me?"

Quincy felt the heat from Jordan's eyes. "I'd never mind waiting for you. How about I make us a drink? Something strong and cold sound good to you?"

"That sounds perfect." Jordan grabbed a small water bottle from the fridge and planted a light, lingering kiss on Quincy's lips.

Jordan padded off to the bathroom, stripping off her workout clothes as she went, and Quincy was sorely tempted to ditch the new sarong and join her, but she resisted. She went about making the perfect rum cocktail instead. She checked the cupboards for a snack, but they were bare save for water crackers and a block of New Zealand cheddar cheese. She assembled the cheese tray and finished just as the shower stopped. *Time to deliver a refreshing cocktail to my spicy girlfriend.* Quincy's breath caught in her chest as she took in the sight of Jordan, still wet from the shower. Her hair was tousled, and her firm tan body was sculpted like bronze. The jostling of the ice in the glasses brought Quincy out of her voyeuristic trance with a simple thought: *She's mine. And it's me she wants.* "Something cool and refreshing?" She held up the two glasses.

"Yes, you are." Jordan dove in for a deep passionate kiss, pressing Quincy between her towel-wrapped body and the sink. "Mm, tasty," she whispered as she grazed Quincy's lower lip.

Heat filled Quincy's core as Jordan released her and took her drink. "You're going to mess up my hair and makeup."

Jordan laughed and let her go, then she slipped into her white button-down linen shirt and navy shorts.

"What do you think about heading down to the resort for dinner?" Quincy asked.

Jordan shook her head. "Not on our last night. I don't want to share you with anyone. Let's just stay here," she said as she styled her hair.

Quincy met her gaze in the mirror. "I just went through the cupboards, and the crackers and cheese I just put out for a snack are all we have."

Jordan took her hand and led her into the kitchen. "Let's start with this."

They devoured the cheese and crackers along with their drinks.

"We should at least watch the sunset on our final night. Maybe we could go out to the beach and figure out our dinner plans from there," Jordan said.

"Sounds good to me." Quincy opened the slider onto the beach and saw a line of tiki torches leading to the water. "That's odd. I guess someone is having a party tonight."

Jordan circled her waist from behind and placed her chin on her shoulder. "I wouldn't call this a party."

"What do you mean by this?" Quincy inhaled and savored the scent and feel of Jordan's embrace.

"This night is for you. You've given so much of yourself to others, and to me. You saved my life, not just that horrible day on the track, but by loving me and letting me love you. I wanted tonight to be a special memory of our time together. I love you." Jordan kissed Quincy's neck.

She turned in Jordan's arm and stroked her face. "I love you too, Jordan. I couldn't believe the day I came back and found you here. You've stolen my heart, and every day, every moment with you is so special." Quincy kissed her with all the love and emotion she'd kept buried for so long.

"Come with me," Jordan whispered and led her along the pathway toward the water.

The end of the pier had beach chairs and a table set for two, covered with a tropical tablecloth. Two tiki torches were attached to the end of the pier, and two small coolers sat close to the edge, near one of the chairs. Jordan held out her hand, and Quincy took it. They sat down and held hands as they looked out at the horizon. She finally broke the silence. "A workout, huh? I guess I now know what you were up to this afternoon."

"Yep, I wanted to surprise you and make our last night in paradise special." Jordan winked.

"You certainly have surprised me. It's beautiful and so thoughtful, Jordie."

"How about some food?"

"That sounds great."

Jordan tipped back the lid on the cooler and revealed a chilled bottle of champagne and a platter of oysters.

"Wow, that looks wonderful. I guess Ramona had a hand in this as well?"

Jordan chuckled as she poured the champagne into the flutes.

"She had a hand in everything; she was like a mother hen, and I loved it. We've got about thirty minutes until sunset. Maybe tonight we'll finally see the green flash all the locals have been talking about." They watched the small bubbles ignite in the blazing colors of the sunset.

"I think tonight is our night," Quincy said simply. They clinked glasses and slowly sipped the cold champagne. The oysters were clearly fresh from the ocean and tasted briny and sweet with the chilled bubbly. Quincy couldn't tell if it was the small bubbles or the love and happiness bubbling within her that made her feel so good.

After they'd finished the oysters, Jordan stood and walked to the end of the pier. She held out her hand for Quincy. "How about a dip?"

Quincy joined her. They sat on the dock and dipped their feet into the clear water as the sun began its descent into the blue of the Pacific. "This is so perfect," Quincy whispered as a tear slipped from her eyes.

Jordan wiped it away and held her close. They sat on the platform, tangled in each other, and watched as the fiery red sun sank into the sparkling ocean. The sky briefly lit with a green flash and then an artist's palette of orange, purple and pink streaked the clouds above them.

"Amazing. I want to watch many more sunsets in your beautiful eyes. I love you, Quincy!" Jordan kissed her lightly.

"I love you too. And thanks for this special night."

"It isn't over yet. How about some dinner?"

They stood and headed back to the table and chairs. "Sure. Chef Jordan, what're you preparing for us tonight? Or do we need to drop a line and catch our dinner?"

"No fishing for us tonight. We'll be dining on Ramona's fish stew, rice, veggies, and for dessert, her famous guava lime tart."

"That sounds delish. Let's eat."

They did, and they talked about the next day's travel plans as well as what stops they'd be making after they'd gotten home. She'd flown here, alone and broken, and now she was returning, loved and with wonderful changes on the horizon. When they finished dinner, she couldn't ever remember being so at peace inside.

Quincy pushed back from the table. "What a perfect ending to an amazing trip. I'll have to thank Ramona when I see her. I can think of a special way to thank *you* later." She gave Jordan a wicked smile.

Jordan caught her arm and pulled her close. "You're welcome."

Her kiss tasted of the sweetness of her and the tartness of the lime.

Jordan smiled as she pulled away. "Would you like a walk?"

"That'd be great, but what about all this?" She gestured to the table.

"Think of this as a five-star restaurant. Everything will be taken care of. Let's walk." Jordan took Quincy's hand and began the short journey back to the water.

They strolled hand in hand and enjoyed the small waves lapping at the shoreline. The sound of the ocean as it fizzed onto the sand became their soundtrack as they walked at the water's edge. The crashing waves on the outer reef provided a booming background sonata during lulls in their conversation. Quincy leaned into Jordan's embrace as they made their final turn and headed back to the bungalow. The full moon had cleared the mountainous eastern side of the island, and it highlighted the sand and set it aglow. The dark water shone like crystals with the moonbeams dancing on the waves. They passed a small resort and a handful of couples that were out enjoying the night too, and Quincy envied them a little, thinking they probably didn't have to leave in the morning.

Quincy gripped Jordan's hand tighter. "I hope nothing's wrong," she said, looking toward a bright light that shone down into the water from the pier where they'd dined earlier.

"Everything's fine. That's just my last surprise of the night,"

Jordan said and squeezed her hand.

Quincy looked at Jordan and took in her broad smile and twinkling eyes. Her tanned skin made the white linen shirt she wore pop in the moonlight. Her defined abs peeked out from where the shirt was unbuttoned. And Quincy couldn't stop herself from thinking about those long legs wrapped around her later tonight. She hummed with need and squirmed as she thought about kissing Jordan all over. "Another surprise? What have you done now?"

"Let's go take a look," Jordan said, and they headed back to the pier.

Quincy squealed as she looked down into the clear reef water below the pier. "Oh my God, is that a manta ray?" There must have been over fifteen of them within the range of the light. "They look like they're dancing. I read that the light draws the plankton in, and the plankton draws the mantas for their dinner, but I didn't think I'd get to see it." She sighed deeply.

Jordan hugged Quincy from behind. "The light is a bonus for us so we can see them dancing."

"But how did you know this happened here?"

"Ramona mentioned this morning that guests at that other resort were scared there were sharks in the water at night. The locals all knew they were manta rays, not sharks. I asked if there was a way for us to see them. I remembered you saying that you thought they were amazing creatures, and I couldn't wait to see if it would happen."

Quincy let out a soft, happy laugh. "How incredibly thoughtful. Thank you."

"Come on. Let's watch the dancing mantas."

Jordan took Quincy's hand, and they sat on the pier with their feet out of the water so they didn't spook the rays. Hours passed, and along with it, so did secrets and stories of their lives. Everything had moved so fast, but the more Quincy learned about Jordan, her life, and what she'd gone through to make it so far, the more she fell for her. In turn, she talked about her family, and the shame that usually accompanied those stories was blessedly absent. They seemed to have lost their power.

The chill in the night air, along with the moon in the sky, provided the catalyst to leave the water and head back to their bungalow. Once inside, Quincy led Jordan back into the bedroom. The passion they shared, each look, kiss, and intimate touch, sealed their love for each other. The only sounds were the pleasure of their release as they tumbled into each other's arms.

"I love you, Quincy. I want to spend every morning waking up in your arms," Jordan whispered.

She caught Quincy's face in her warm palms and gave her a deep possessive kiss. Quincy's heart raced, not just from the kiss but also from the overwhelming joy that surged through her with every word and gesture Jordan had shared tonight. It was like every moment had been carefully crafted with tenderness and thoughtfulness, making her burst with happiness. "I love you too," she whispered, though even those words felt too small to capture everything she felt. It was more than love—it was a sense of belonging, of finally being seen. As she listened to the steady rise and fall of Jordan's breath, something inside her shifted. The tight grip of control she'd held onto for so long, a defense built over years, began to unravel. In Jordan's embrace, the weight of that control loosened and was replaced by a quiet, exhilarating excitement for the future.

Epilogue

Jordan finished securing her surprise for tomorrow in the pocket of her race suit before she headed outside to where her team, family, and friends gathered for tonight's celebration. Jordan's RV was situated in a prime location on the infield at the Indianapolis Motor Speedway, steps away from the track and Gasoline Alley. She'd been there for the month of May, conditioning, training, and mentally preparing to return to racing. It had been one of the hardest obstacles she'd ever overcome, but the love and support from the racing community, friends, family, and most importantly, Quincy, had made all the difference. Their positive reinforcement pushed Jordan further than even she thought possible, which manifested in her winning the pole position for tomorrow's 120th running of the Indy 500. She'd heard the world of racing's glass ceiling shatter with her unique feat. But the initial joy and excitement of being the first woman had been replaced by a calmness she hadn't expected.

The hamster wheel she'd run on for so long, chasing her future, had finally stopped. The serenity and peace of knowing who she was and what she wanted grounded her in every way. It was true that Quincy had been the catalyst, but the growth came from within, and it had been amazing. She was hopeful that her successes would challenge the next generation of female drivers too. She was ready for tomorrow, but tonight was a celebration for Brian, Quincy's dad, on his seventieth birthday. She stepped out of the RV and into the mayhem.

"Brian, can I get you another beer?" Jordan asked, holding one out. From the first time she'd met Quincy's family, they'd been welcoming and made her feel part of their family, which had been amazing. She appreciated that, while they were there for his birthday celebration, they took every opportunity to show her support as well. The best part was seeing Quincy's happiness around them; it made her heart overflow with love. Jordan hadn't heard from her parents since the hospital drama, and honestly, it felt like a kind of freedom to be out from under their control. She smiled, thinking of her true family, who'd be there tomorrow. Tito John, Ate Theresa, and Tito Jack would be in place with lots of cousins in tow to cheer her to victory.

"You bet, Jordie. Thanks. Anyone seen Quincy?" Brian asked then devoured another taco.

"I'm here, Dad. Sorry I'm late," Quincy said as she leaned down to kiss his cheek. "Happy birthday, Pops."

Jordan's heart raced at the sound of Quincy's voice. She grabbed her around her waist and kissed her. "What can I say? I missed you. How'd it go?"

"Yeah, sweetie, tell us about it. You were so excited about this," Brian said.

"Well, I met with Dr. Mackey, and she gave me a tour of the Infield Care Center as well as their new mobile hospital. It's all very impressive, and I can't wait to learn more when I start as an NP for IndyCar Medical team next month." Quincy grinned broadly.

Everyone whooped, whistled, and clapped for her. Jordan was so proud of her. She knew how nervous Quincy was about the meeting, yet she'd still put herself out there. The joy on her face now warmed Jordan's heart. Over the past month, Quincy had taught Jordan so much about embracing life, and it was exciting to be by her side for this new transition. "Baby, I'm so proud of you. They're lucky to have you." She brushed away the tears gathering in her eyes and kissed Quincy softly.

They fielded congratulations and after everyone had eaten cake, the party dwindled. It was a big day tomorrow, and the pre-race superstitions were beginning.

"Quincy's family are good people, not that I expected anything less. It's just nice to have normal people around, unlike the women you used to date," Joe said as he stood to leave.

Jordan internally winced. "Ouch. Truth hurts. You've been with me long enough to say that and live though." She gave him a menacing look then started laughing. "I can't argue with it. It means a lot that you like Quincy. I mean, you were our matchmaker, really."

"What can I say? I can pick 'em. Just like I'm picking you to win tomorrow. I love you, kid. Get some sleep; you've got a date with history tomorrow." He squeezed Jordan's shoulder then headed to his RV.

Joe was right; it was a big moment. His sentimentality always got to her, and she closed her eyes and envisioned the win, the joy, the excitement of making history. She tried not to give in to the tears. She smelled Quincy's scent before she heard her. When she opened her eyes, her breath caught at Quincy's beauty as she leaned against the RV.

"Penny for your thoughts?" Quincy asked, the love and longing clear in her eyes.

"Hello, stranger." She opened the door, and they went inside. Jordan caressed Quincy's face and kissed her passionately. "I've missed you so much," she whispered, lightly kissing her face and neck. The fire that seared between them was hotter than the candles that had burned on Brian's cake. She brushed her thumb across Quincy's lip. "You're all I've thought about. I hate being away from you, even for a few hours."

Quincy smiled. "I've missed you too. These weeks apart with me in LA and you here have been torture. Watching your TV interviews and knowing I wouldn't get to touch you drove me crazy. I want you, God knows I do. But, baby, you're racing for all the marbles tomorrow. Are you sure we should do this?"

Jordan met her gaze. "You're what I need now, tomorrow, and forever. I love you, and I want to *make* love to you." She stared into Quincy's eyes, immobilized by the passion and love she saw.

She knew that love was mirrored in her own. She hooked Quincy's pinky with her own and walked them back into her bedroom. Jordan wanted her so badly, and tonight, she'd worship Quincy's body and take her to new heights. They enjoyed slow lovemaking through the night, followed by a deep slumber in each other's arms.

The alarm woke Jordan at five a.m. to begin her busy day. Her heart swelled with love, and her throat choked with tears. She watched Quincy's freckle-covered nose twitch and her long silky eyelashes flutter as she slowly woke. When she opened her eyes, she smiled sleepily. "Good morning, my love." Jordan smiled as she lightly placed kisses down Quincy's body from her lips to her thighs before she made it off the bed and headed toward the bathroom. "Shower?" she asked, with her hand held out.

"Yes," Quincy said simply.

They showered together in the tight confines of the RV's bathroom before Quincy left to meet up with her family. She wanted to ensure they found the team's penthouse suite and get them settled in for the race. Jordan needed the time for her pre-race routine to clear her head and ready her body for the five-hundred-mile race ahead. She performed her pre-race hydration, meditation, and visualization before she pulled on her fire suit and racing gear and headed to the garage. Nothing in the world could stop her now.

***

"Hey, Joe, everything all right this morning?" Jordan asked as she entered their garage. She noticed he was pulling on his ear lobe like he did every race day. She hoped that would be a good omen.

"Same as usual, Jordie, except we're going to win the Indy 500 today," he said.

"From your lips to God's ears," Jordan said and chuckled. "I'm heading over to the media room for my interviews. I'll be back as soon as I can."

"Okay, make sure they get your good side." Joe looked beyond her. "Where's our girl?"

Jordan thumbed over her shoulder. "Getting her family set up in the suite. She'll be down soon."

Joe had taken to Quincy like she was family too, and it made for a wonderful dynamic when they were working together. She headed over to the media room to complete the scheduled interviews. With the media frenzy due to the historical nature of today's race and what she'd already accomplished, she needed security to help her maneuver through the fans and press that filled Gasoline Alley. Thankfully, her pole position was a better topic than Carver's sabotage and the crash. His charge of reckless driving stuck even though the more serious charges hadn't, and he'd been banned from racing for life. It was enough for her, and many of his crew had been blacklisted as well. The ones who'd come forward weren't finding it easy to get work either. That was no longer her issue and not a topic she would discuss.

After the interviews, she did the sponsor rounds and posed for pictures with Florence, Eric, Margaret, and Amanda, as well as countless celebrities and VIPs. It was two hours before race time, and the garage was closed to anyone outside her team. She checked her watch and knew they'd have driver introductions soon. Once that started, she'd be out on the pit lane for the rest of the morning before the race. It was time to get focused, to put all the smiles and handshakes aside and focus on what came next.

She retreated to a corner of the garage, placed her mirrored sunglasses on, along with her noise-cancelling headphones, and closed her mind to everything but her racing strategy. Once she'd completed her visual work, she turned on her playlist and opened her eyes to watch her crew make last-minute adjustments to her car. Their slow, calculated movements calmed her nerves until her skin prickled as she felt Quincy's presence before she saw her. When she looked up, Quincy was walking toward her, smiling and nodding to the different members of the race crew. She looked amazing in the team's polo shirt. Jordan jumped down from her chair and met Quincy for a quick kiss that calmed her more than any of her pre-race routines. "Everyone settled in for the day?"

"They are. My family doesn't know what to do with themselves in that fancy suite full of celebrities. I introduced them to Tito John and Ate Theresa. They told me to tell you that they love you, and that they'll meet you in the Victory Circle after the race," Quincy said.

Jordan was delighted that Quincy's family was interested in IndyCar racing since this was her career and now, her second love. She'd give them anything they wanted to share in her passion and make Quincy happy. "They should have a great view of the start/finish line and the pits. They'll also be able to see you at our team's timing stand today, so that'll be fun for them."

Quincy wrapped her arm around Jordan's waist. "It will be, especially when you win. So, you ready to go? I heard the driver introductions are starting soon."

Jordan pulled her into her side, and it felt so right. "We'll wait for the IndyCar official to come get me for the lineup. Since I'm the pole position, I'll be the last to be introduced."

Quincy leaned against her. "Do you want me to leave you alone so you can go through your rituals?"

"No, don't go. If you could just sit here with me and hold my hand." She held out her hand, and Quincy grabbed it and squeezed. She could settle Jordan's nerves more than any routine.

"I'm here, baby. I'll be here. You just visualize crossing that row of bricks in first place and having the crowd go wild." Quincy squeezed her hand again.

As the Zen-like energy flowed between them, they were interrupted by a loud announcement in the garage.

"Jordan Marsh, we're ready for you," said an official dressed in a bright yellow IndyCar shirt.

They held hands and headed out of her garage.

Joe stopped them as they passed and gave them a hug. "We're

going to win this today, Jordie. You ladies smile pretty for the cameras," he said and gave her a playful punch on the arm.

"Thanks, Joe." She and Quincy followed the IndyCar official out of the garage, and excitement surged through her as they walked through the enormous crowd of fans. Their cheers of excitement and clapping showed their support as they made their journey through the masses held back by metal retainers. When they reached the green room of the pagoda, Jordan took a deep breath and squeezed Quincy's hand, ready for her introduction. The IndyCar official directed them forward to the riser.

"And on pole position for today's 120th running of the Indianapolis 500, the first woman to ever hold that title, with the fastest qualifying time at 235.217 mph, the current NTT IndyCar Series point leader from the United States, Jordan Marsh," the PA announcer boomed.

Jordan's heart thudded in her chest as they walked onto the platform. Thankfully, the fans had embraced their relationship. Quincy had quickly learned not to reac the comments sections on any socials—there were always trolls—but mostly people were happy to celebrate that Jordan was in love with a nurse, not some airy celebrity. Even more sponsors had lined up, and a couple had been turned away because their company ethos didn't fit with the Pink Triangle brand. It was a hell of a place to be, and Jordan couldn't be happier. When she wasn't on the track, she was at home with Quincy, and when Quincy had the time, she was at the track with Jordan. Settled life was idyllic, and today's win would seal it all.

After the adrenaline boost from introductions, they walked back to the team's pit lane. Jordan leaned in over the noise and whispered, "Thank you for standing by my side today. I've never loved you more."

"I'm not going anywhere. You've got this, baby, and I'll be here to celebrate with you when you win," Quincy said then kissed her passionately.

Calm washed over her as she pulled back from the embrace. "Well, I guess I better go win this so we can celebrate. I'll see you in a few hours," Jordan said. As Quincy watched, Jordan's team helped her with her hood, helmet, and gloves before she stepped into the cockpit and was secured.

Kennedy Marks was the honorary starter for the Indy 500. She stood at the Victory Podium and gave the instruction through the PA, "Drivers, start your engines."

The loud roar of the engines made Jordan's pulse jump in her chest. She squeezed the wheel to release some nerves as she focused on her racing strategy. Her headset crackled, and she was given the go ahead to pull the car out on the track for a few warmup laps behind the pace car. "I'm doing it, Joe. I'm leading the grid at the Indianapolis 500. This is fucking amazing!" Jordan shouted as the exhilaration of the moment overtook her.

"It is but get to work," Joe said. "The pace car is coming off. Time to race. Go get 'em, Jordie."

"Green, green, green!" her spotter yelled.

The adrenaline surged, and Jordan took a deep breath, her hands steady on the wheel as she rocketed down the straightaway, the engine screaming beneath her. She was going 225 mph—on the edge, focused entirely on the race. She was in the top three the entire race, battling fiercely with the other drivers. Now, in the final lap, she was poised for something bigger than she'd ever dreamed. *It was now or never.* In the final turn, Jordan pushed the car harder, gaining the fraction of a second she needed to pull ahead. She shot toward the finish line, the row of bricks coming fast and the checkered flag waving in the distance.

"We won!" she screamed into her microphone, her voice cracking with the rawness of it. "We did it! Hell, yeah! We won the Indy 500!" Her voice boomed through the coms, and she pumped her arm out of the cockpit, the crowd's roar rising to meet her. "I'm the first woman to win the Indy 500, the greatest race in the world! This is *fucking* amazing!" She didn't try to contain the joy flooding her. Her heart pounded n her chest as she began her slow victory lap, waving to the fans, each moment surreal. The other drivers passed by, acknowledging her with thumbs ups, their respect evident. Tears blurred her vision, but Jordan didn't dare wipe them away. This was the moment she'd dreamed of for so long. The first woman to win the Indy 500. She finished her lap, pulling into Victory Circle as the officials guided her car onto the lift. Her team was there, with Joe first in line, his face lit up with pride.

He wiped at his eyes before leaning in to take off her helmet. "You did it, Jordie. You won the Indy 500. Congratulations," he said, his voice rough with emotion.

"We did it," Jordan said, her voice trembling. "I wouldn't be here without you and our team. This is *our* win." Her breath caught as the full weight of the moment hit her. She'd fought through chaos, pain, and doubt just to get here, and now, standing at the pinnacle of her career, she could hardly believe it. She thought of Quincy, her rock, and how she never would've made it without her love and support. She couldn't wait to hold her in her arms.

Joe stepped aside as an official handed her the red Firestone first place hat. She put it on, then wiped her eyes and nose on the sleeve of her suit. She glanced through the aeroscreen and saw her family, her teammates, her sponsors, Lex, Florence, Amanda, Margaret, and Eric—everyone who had been part of this journey.

"Race fans," the announcer's voice called out, "let's hear it for Jordan Marsh, the first woman to win the Indianapolis 500!"

The crowd exploded into deafening applause. Jordan stood on her seat, pumping her arms in the air as the cheers reverberated through her bones. Her face ached from smiling so big. She stepped from the car onto the chassis. Her pit crew raised her up as the crowd erupted again, and a surge of exhilaration flooded her body. She came back to earth next to her car, drunk with joy as she absorbed the energy. The race oficials placed the victory wreath around her neck and handed her the traditional Indy 500 bottle of milk. She drank it and then showered her team, sponsors, and media in it like it was champagne.

"Jordie, you overcame everything to be here. I'm so proud of you." Florence pulled her into a hug and then raised their arms in victory.

The crowd cheered louder, and Jordan laughed, overwhelmed by the energy.

Amidst all the celebration, her heart ached for one person: Quincy. Where was she? She turned to the outer perimeter of the celebration and scanned the crowd. There she was, standing just outside the throng, looking more radiant than Jordan had ever seen her. Her hair was tousled by the wind and though her face was streaked with tears, it only made her more beautiful. Her eyes locked onto Jordan's, filled with love and pride, and everything else in the world faded away.

Jordan's heart skipped a beat as she left the reporters behind to get through to Quincy. "I won," she said, suddenly tongue-tied, and her voice a little breathless.

"I saw," Quincy said, a teasing glint in her eyes.

Jordan hesitated, suddenly aware of the mess she must be in: sweaty, milk-covered, and disheveled. But when Quincy's smile bloomed, all of her self-consciousness evaporated. It was as if the entire world came into focus in that one moment.

"Congratulations, my love, you were amazing. I'm so proud of you." Quincy draped her arms around Jordan's neck and kissed her, a kiss that seemed to carry all the weight of their shared love and everything they'd overcome to be here.

Jordan's eyes filled with tears. "I love you too, Quincy. I wouldn't be here without you. Without your love, your support...your friendship. You're my everything. I couldn't have won this without you." She took a step back, her heart pounding in her chest. She reached into the breast pocket of her race suit and pulled out a small teal pouch. Quincy's eyes widened as Jordan knelt in front of her, hand trembling as she held out a ring. "I'll always be a winner as long as you're by my side. Quincy Fitzgerald, will you marry me?" The crowd's roar drowned out everything else, but it was Quincy's voice Jordan needed to hear.

"Oh, Jordan! Yes, forever, and always, yes!"

Quincy placed her hand in Jordan's, and she slid the ring onto Quincy's finger slowly. It sparkled in the May sunshine as Jordan lifted her and twirled her around, the crowd's cheers mingling with the sound of their hearts racing in unison

Jordan kissed her then, soft and deep a promise of their future together. Nothing in the world could have felt better than this.

~ THE END ~

Thank you so much for reading my debut novel. I'd really appreciate it if you could pop a review on Amazon for me to help other people find this story too. And if you'd like to keep up with my writings, maybe you'd like to sign up to the Butterworth Books newsletter (bit.ly/ButterBookers). I don't have my own yet, but I'll let you know if that changes!

Thanks again!
Sydney

Other Great Butterworth Books

Driving Me Barking by JP Preston
Sometimes to find yourself, you have to lose your imaginary friends first.
Available on Amazon (ASIN B0DWG1LLXN)

Escape in Time by RJ Nyx
Working in the past is hell on your future.
Available on Amazon (ASIN B0DSJFDZ7R)

Ship of Dreams by Brey Willows
Two rival captains, one deadly mission, and secrets that could set the skies ablaze.
Available on Amazon (ASIN B0DRW1X75N)

Unwritten by Helena Harte
No strings is fun 'til it unravels.
Available from Amazon (ASIN B0DGQFFHYB)

Chucking Putty at the Queen by Simon Smalley
A heartbreaking, humorous, and courageous exploration of what it takes to be ones authentic self.
Available from Amazon (ASIN B0DGGBV22W)

The Promise by Addison M Conley
When the world keeps pulling you under, who do you reach for?
Available on Amazon (ASIN B0DDY9FH6Z)

Back to Back by Jo Fletcher
"When Fred and Ruby's worlds collide, can love rise from the rubble?"
Available on Amazon (ASIN B0D6M49SK2)

Heart of the Storm by Ally McGuire
Sometimes a storm is just what you need to clear the skies ahead.
Available on Amazon (ASIN B0CYTSQXWW)

Sanctuary by Helena Harte
Passions ignite and possibilities unfold. Welcome to the Windy City Romance series.
Available from Amazon (ASIN B0D4B42RRW)

Brave Enough to Love by Valden Bush
In a dance between truth and sacrifice, can they rewrite the rules of love?
Available on Amazon (ASIN B0CQP8PMVB)

Dead Ringer by Robyn Nyx
Three bodies. One killer. No motive?
Available on Amazon (ASIN B0CPQ8HFK7)

Medea by JJ Taylor
Who will Medea become in her battle for freedom?
Available from Amazon (ASIN B0CK2FB7GW)

Virgin Flight by E.V. Bancroft
In the battle between duty and desire, can love win?
Available from Amazon (ASIN B0CKJWQZ45)

Fragments of the Heart by Ally McGuire
Love can be the greatest expedition of all.
Available on Amazon (ASIN B0CHBPHR6M)

Here You Are by Jo Fletcher
.Can they unlock their hearts to find the true happiness they both deserve?
Available on Amazon (ASIN B0CBN935ZB)

Stunted Heart by Helena Harte
A stunt rider who lives in the fast lane. An ER doctor who can't take chances. A passion that could turn their worlds upside down.
Available on Amazon (ASIN B0C78GSWBV)

Dark Haven by Brey Willows
Even vampires get tired of playing with their food...
Available on Amazon (ASIN B0C5P1HJXC)

Green for Love by E.V. Bancroft
All's fair in love and eco-war.
Available from Amazon (ASIN B0C28F7PX5)

Call of Love by Lee Haven
Separated by fear. Reunited by fate. Will they get a second chance at life and love?
Available from Amazon (ASIN B0BYC83HZD)

Where the Heart Leads by Ally McGuire
A writer. A celebrity. And a secret that could break their hearts.
Available on Amazon (ASIN B0BWFX5W9L)

Stolen Ambition by Robyn Nyx
Daughters of two worlds collide in a dangerous game of ambition and love.
Available on Amazon (ASIN B0BS1PRSCN)

Cabin Fever by Addison M Conley
She goes for the money, but will she stay for something deeper?
Available on Amazon (ASIN B0BQWY45GH)

Breakout for Love by Valden Bush
They're both running from their pasts. Together, they might make a new future.
Available from Amazon (ASIN B0CWHZ4SXL)

The Helion Band by AJ Mason
Rose's only crime was to show kindness to her royal mistress...
Available from Amazon (ASIN B09YM6TYFQ)

That Boy of Yours Wants Looking At by Simon Smalley
A riotously colourful and heart-rending journey of what it takes to live authentically.
Available from Amazon (ASIN B09V3CSQQW)

Sapphic Eclectic Volume Five edited by Nyx & Willows
A little something for everyone...
Available free from the Butterworth Books website

Of Light and Love by E.V. Bancroft
The deepest shadows paint the brightest love.
Available from Amazon (ASIN B0B64KJ3NP)

An Art to Love by Helena Harte
Second chances are an art form.
Available on Amazon (ASIN B0B1CD8Y42)

Music City Dreamers by Robyn Nyx
Music brings lovers together. In Music City, it can tear them apart.
Available on Amazon (ASIN B0994XVDGR)

What's Your Story?

Global Wordsmiths, CIC, provides an all-encompassing service for all writers, ranging from basic proofreading and cover design to development editing, typesetting, and eBook services. A major part of our work is charity and community focused, delivering writing projects to under-served and under-represented groups across Nottinghamshire, giving voice to the voiceless and visibility to the unseen.

To learn more about what we offer, visit: www.globalwords.co.uk

A selection of books by Global Words Press:
Desire, Love, Identity: with the National Justice Museum
Aventuras en México: Farmilo Primary School
Times Past: with The Workhouse, National Trust
Young at Heart with AGE UK
In Different Shoes: Stories of Trans Lives

Self-published authors working with Global Wordsmiths:

Max Beeken
Maggie McIntyre
John Parsons
Dani Lovelady Ryan
Kit Stone